TRUST ME

TIFFANY PATTERSON

CHAPTER 1

***K**yle* "I'm about to ruin this motherfucker's birthday," I say to my cousin as I glare across the private room of the exclusive nightclub, The Black Opal.

"Wait for me," I tell Diego.

"I'm not your fucking lackey," he gripes.

Still, I head directly toward my target.

"Kyle, you came," Jayceon Carlson says, grinning.

The crystal chandeliers hanging overhead make the flickering lights from the candles reflect off the blood red velvet walls. The unopened bottles of champagne that come complimentary with the twenty-thousand-dollar price tag for each table remain in their gold coolers surrounded by ice.

Sam Tinnesz' "Play with Fire" booms from the hidden speakers, which seems appropriate.

A smile spreads my lips, but it's not friendly in the least. However, Jayceon doesn't recognize that.

I allow the smile on his face to linger a little longer when I reply, "It's your special day."

I undo the last button of my suit jacket as I look Jayceon over, barely able to hide my contempt for the bastard.

He chuckles and glances to his left and right. He's flanked by several of his employees, and also shrouded in women.

"Guess it only took me turning thirty-five to get this guy out of the office for once, huh?"

My top lip curls.

"He lives like Townsend Industries is his entire life."

The semi-smile I was sporting drops. This douche has no fucking clue. The women and men around him nod in agreement and giggle. The sounds grate on my nerves.

Stepping closer, I extend my hand. "I couldn't let this opportunity pass."

He shakes my hand, but when he goes to pull it back, I tighten my grip. With my free hand, I wrap him up in a hold that, to an outsider, might look semi-friendly.

It's not.

"Especially when tonight will be the end of your career as you know it," I say loud enough for only him to hear.

He blinks in confusion. "What?"

I'm not given time to reply before we're interrupted by a member of The Black Opal staff.

"Sir, we'll bring your cake out shortly," the waitress in skintight, shiny black leggings and a midriff shirt says. It's not the usual outfit for private waitresses at The Black Opal. This leads me to conclude Jayceon put in a special request for the uniform for his party.

Douchebag.

"Kyle, whatever's on your mind, we can discuss it another time," he says, like this isn't the last conversation we'll ever have.

"That won't be possible." I tighten my hold around his shoulders. "As the heir apparent to Carlson Healthcare & Co., you've already ruined the business your father started two decades ago. You did it by fucking with my family." I say the last part with so much venom that Jayceon visibly recoils.

"Everybody who knows me knows I don't mind a little friendly competition. Hell, I almost prefer it if it's a little unfriendly. It keeps everyone on their toes. The heart of what makes a business successful is competition in the market. Yet," I pause and look Jayceon directly in the eye, "you crossed the fucking line when you went after my family."

"I would never do such a thing," he lies.

I know full well he's behind the series of reports that've come out about supposed bribes, blackmail, and violence by my family to secure business deals. Some articles even intimated that the community center my mother, aunts, and grandmother started was nothing more than a front to funnel money into illegal dealings.

Business is business, but insinuating my mother or any of the women in my family is up to illegal activity won't stand. So, I went on the hunt for who was behind these bullshit articles. Aside from the reporters, I came up with Jayceon Carlson, president, and next-in-line at Carlson Healthcare.

One of our company's biggest rivals. Especially for the next acquisition I have my eyes on for Townsend Industries.

"You thought planting the seed of doubt about my company and my family would deter Sam Waterson from selling to us? You didn't plan on your dirt coming to light."

Jayceon's mouth opens and closes a few times. No words come out before there's a uprisal in the surrounding crowd. I lift my gaze to see two of the waitresses entering holding a massive square cake.

"As a special birthday present, I upgraded your cake." I release Jayceon, who looks confused between me and the arriving cake.

Yet, his face pales noticeably when the waitresses lower the cake to the table before us. His mouth falls open as he stands there frozen, staring at the words on the cake.

"Why don't you read the inscription for us?" I say cheerfully.

He doesn't respond.

"Fine, I'll do it. It's a text exchange between Jayceon and a woman," I say while glancing around at the crowd of a hundred or so around us. "Well, not a woman, right, Jay?" I slap him on the back. "No. This girl was only fifteen years old when this text was sent two years ago.

But her sister?" I let out a low whistle. "She was even younger when you approached her, you sick son of a bitch."

I slap his back again, this time harder. "I thought you might want a reminder of the exchanges you had with some of the underage girls you—" I can't even say the final words because of the disgust clogging my throat.

"Don't worry, though, you can still cut into this cake. The proper authorities have already received the necessary evidence to put your scumbag ass away for years to come."

I squeeze Jayceon's neck before letting go. "Happy fucking birthday. Are you going to blow out your candles?"

His face turns from ghostly to a deep crimson, almost matching the color of the walls.

"I'll take that as a no."

With that, I lean over and blow out the thirty-plus candles on the cake.

I swipe a finger through a corner of the cake and taste the icing. I give Jayceon a nod of approval. "Good choice on the cream cheese icing."

After wiping my hand clean, I toss the used napkin onto the cake before striding toward the exit. Onlookers who were partying with Jayceon and kissing his ass, are now snapping photos and, no doubt, sending out social media posts of what just happened.

"Did you have to blow out the man's birthday candles, too?" Diego asks while clapping me on the back as we exit the private room.

I shrug.

"He fucking deserved it, anyway," Diego adds, cracking his knuckles. He looks as disgusted and pissed as I am.

We head to the VIP section of the club, which is on the second floor, overlooking the main dance floor.

"I need a drink," I tell my cousin.

* * *

As soon as we take our seats in the leather lounge chairs across from one another, our waitress sets our drinks in front of us.

"That was fun," I say as I sip the amber liquid in my glass.

Diego snorts. "All it took to get your ass out of the office for once was annihilating a business rival."

"Getting rid of that scum was only one of two reasons for me being here tonight."

My cousin lifts a dark eyebrow.

"The second is convincing you to come with me to Miami for Art Basel."

"I swear to God. Don't waste the fifty grand annual fee we pay … *respectively*, to talk business."

A smirk makes its way to my lips.

Diego downs his drink. "This is about the Waterson deal, isn't it?"

I nod. "This is about Sam Waterson." I pitch forward in my lounge chair. "He's going to be in Miami and has a hard-on for all of that art shit. Same as you."

"Fuck you."

I wave a dismissive hand in the air. "Not tonight. I have to get back to the office."

He huffs and rolls his eyes skyward.

"What do I get out of this?"

"The appreciation of your loving cousin." I sit back and fold my arms across my chest.

"What else?"

"The assurance that coming to Miami will help me land this deal and secure my promotion as Chief Operating Officer."

"I asked what's in this for *me?*"

I hold my hands out wide. "It's not enough that you're helping to ensure our family's legacy."

He deadpans.

"I'll lay off of you for a few weeks about coming over to Townsend Real Estate."

"Months," he counters. "Three months, to be exact. I'm working on landing a huge project at my firm, and I don't need you pestering me about jumping ship right now."

The frown on my face deepens. "You could put that energy to use for Townsend Industries. The company that bears our last name."

Diego is a talented architect. He works for a large architectural firm in the heart of Williamsport. Unfortunately, the firm is not owned by Townsend Real Estate, a division of Townsend Industries. He's wasting his talent.

"We're the oldest out of all of the cousins," I tell him. Between my father and his three brothers—my uncles, there are fifteen of us cousins. I alone have four siblings, including my twin sister, Kennedy. Diego is the oldest, followed by Ken and me.

Diego is not only my cousin, though. He's my best friend considering I'm not a man who keeps friends. Family is all I need.

He rolls his eyes and points at me. "That. That is what you won't do for the next three months if I agree to go with you to Miami."

I grind my teeth. I know my cousin well enough to know something's holding him back from working at Townsend Industries. He's been tightlipped about it, but I intend to figure it out.

I don't go this hard for Townsend Industries for nothing. As one of the oldest of our generation and the son of the CEO, I always knew the weight of our family's legacy would fall on my shoulders. It was never a burden. It's always been meant to be.

As my father's oldest son, I intend to make him and our entire family proud of the man they raised. Becoming COO is the next step to owning my legacy.

"Closing this deal with Sam Waterson in Miami will leave no room for the board to overlook my promotion." Our previous COO retired recently. It wasn't unexpected, but the amount of time that it's taken to fill the role is something I don't like.

"You're twenty-five, and you've risen from intern to become VP of Operations. You work eighty to hundred-hour weeks. You've managed eight-figure deals most people couldn't even dream of. They'll make you COO," he says assuredly.

"Damn straight they will."

Diego says of the board of directors. As a public company, even though the CEO can appoint me directly as the COO, it still requires their approval. Since my father is in Europe on a months-long work trip, he hasn't been in the office to appoint me in the role yet. That'll change after Miami.

"Then remind me why I need to be in Miami again?"

I grunt. "Because I can't stand art and all of the pretentious ass wipes who pretend to be aficionados when they can't tell a Picasso from a Pasteur."

Diego frowns. "Louis Pasteur? Fucking seriously. He was a chemist."

I wave his correction away. "This is why I need you there. I don't give a shit about art. But the brown nosers who'll be there do. You'll help me butter them up, and I can focus on getting Waterson to sign the damn contract. You love those exhibits."

He's holding out, but he's been to Miami multiple times for this event. I know he'll cave.

A muscle in his jaw flexes as he grinds his teeth. He peers at me over the glass in his hands. A smile hits my mouth as I see the moment he makes his decision. His eyes are the giveaway.

"Thanks, cousin. We'll pop a bottle of champagne once Waterson signs the paperwork."

"That will be a huge accomplishment, indeed." A silky voice invades my eardrums, sirening my full attention.

I peer up from the tumbler in my hands to see a woman standing before me. She's not our private waitress.

No.

The woman in front of me is certainly not who's been pouring our drinks for the past thirty minutes. This woman's cinnamon brown skin is glowing underneath the low lighting of the club, full lips painted an unnatural shade of red. On her, the color sets off the red undertones in her skin.

From my seated angle, she's tall, probably around five-nine or five-ten. Her hair cascades over her shoulders, fanning down around her face. Her coffee irises dance with interest as she peers down at me.

Before I open my mouth and demand to know how the hell she got so damn close, a distinct clicking sounds. The woman's eyes widen as she realizes someone has placed a nine-millimeter to her temple.

I sit back in my chair, crossing an ankle over my knee, and study her reaction. She doesn't cower or beg for the gun to be put away.

Interesting.

The usual groupies who invade my space would've had at least one tear fall by now.

I keep my eyes trained on her as I say, "We'll have to discuss why it took almost a full minute for my security to do their damn job." That's when I pin the security guard holding the gun to the woman's head with a glare. I often keep security with me when out in public spaces such as this.

He visibly swallows. This woman should've never gotten this close.

"If you ask me, their reaction time is pretty good," she says as she moves to sit in the chair beside me.

"In case you hadn't noticed, the gun pointed at your temple *isn't* an invitation to stay," I tell her.

Those red-tinted lips spread into a dangerous smile. "That wasn't necessarily an invite to leave, either."

She's bold. I'll give her that. I peer over at my security, who looks completely fucking confused about how to handle this. I wave him off.

He puts the safety on his gun and steps back into the shadows of the VIP section. I'll deal with his ass later.

Movement from across the table catches my eye. Diego, who's been silent throughout this exchange, glances between me and the woman. He stands.

"I'm in," he says, agreeing to Miami. His eyes slide over to the woman next to me. "I'm going to make some rounds." He smirks and saunters off.

"I thought he'd never leave," the woman beside me says.

"Now it's your turn." I don't bother sparing her a look as I down the rest of my drink.

"But we're just getting acquainted. I was interested in the Waterson deal you're working on."

I grit my teeth. That she'd overheard even a part of that conversation pisses me off. I keep tight control over my surroundings for this reason. The VIP section of The Black Opal is supposed to be secure from outside distractions.

I turn to the woman, my eyes scanning her face. "If you were looking to suck my dick, there're better ways to go about it. I don't talk business with strangers."

"But you'll talk about your dick with one?" Her smile grows as she slow blinks at me.

An involuntary sound escapes my mouth.

"Don't worry. It's not your bed I'm interested in, Mr. Townsend."

"Is that so?" A wave of disappointment hits me in the gut. I look her up and down, my gaze wandering over her curves in her tight, black dress. "Could've fooled me."

She lets out a husky laugh. "I doubt you're an easy man to fool. Especially since you've accomplished so much already in your relatively short career."

I scowl at her. She continues to meet my stare, a look I know many men have cowered in the face of. I lean closer.

"What do you think you know about me?"

Her smile doesn't waver. "You work your ass off, carry the family name well, and …" She trails off, glancing away. "You're eyeing a very lucrative deal to acquire Sam Waterson's medical supplies company. I don't doubt that win would solidify you as Townsend's next COO. The position has sat empty for what? Two weeks now?"

A muscle in my jaw ticks. This woman has done her research. Nothing anyone couldn't have gathered from any of the recent news articles about the company with my namesake.

Still, what I said remains true. I don't discuss business with strangers. And no matter how well she's playing, this woman doesn't give a damn about Townsend Industries.

Wordlessly, I toss my hand in the air and wave my security over.

"Please show this woman—"

"Riley Martin," she interrupts, business card in her hand.

"It doesn't matter," I say dismissively. "Show her to the door, and for God's sake, make sure she's not waiting at my car when I leave," I instruct my security. "I've had that happen more times than I care to remember."

Women are pushy when they want to be. Many of them use the guise of business to find their way into my beds. At times I indulge them. Not tonight though. I'm not in the fucking mood. Not even for this woman, who is, admittedly, beautiful.

I keep a tight circle around me. Very few get too close, and I had never trusted a woman enough to lose control over my emotions.

Too bad for Ms. Martin. I watch as my security grips her by the arm, escorting her toward the back exit of the VIP section.

She does have a nice ass, though.

I shake the thought free and check my wristwatch. It's a little after midnight. I need to return to the office to pick up some files on my way home.

CHAPTER 2

Riley

"I'm getting real tired of you holding onto me," I say as I try and fail to tug my arm free from Kyle Townsend's security guard. This guy is holding on for dear life. As if he knows he fucked up and wants to make sure he doesn't do it again.

If I were in a generous mood, I'd tell him that it isn't his fault. Even the best security details in the world have their blind spots. And I was raised to seek out a person's blind spots and use them to my advantage.

That's all scam artists do. Find a person's weakest entry point and poke it until they get in.

All it took for me was to case the club for a few days and accidentally overhear one of the bartenders griping about one of the VIP clients of The Black Opal and how she'd strung him along. I cozied up to that bartender in no time, and before I knew it he got me entry to the VIP section.

Disgruntled employees are often a company's biggest weak spot.

"Where's your car?" The burly man still holding my arm demands to know as he yanks me out to the parking lot behind the exclusive club.

"First of all ..." I wrench my arm free. "get the hell off of me. Secondly, I'll walk myself." I start to stride away with my head held high, but the bastard grabs my arm again.

"Where is it? Mr. Townsend expects me to make sure you leave the premises."

"Do you do everything *Mr. Townsend* asks of you?" I mock.

A deep frown mars his face, but he doesn't respond.

"I'll wait for my Uber out here," I tell him as we reach the front of the nightclub.

As I expect, the security guard waits right alongside me. I'm grateful for not bringing my vehicle. Though I hate waiting outside next to the guard, I'm sure that same guard would've taken note of my license plate.

My self-congratulatory moment ends when my phone rings. My stomach plummets at the unsaved number flashing on the screen. I shift my attention to the security guard, who eyes me warily. The ringing of my phone ends.

I release a breath, but then the ringing starts again. It's the same number.

"Someone really wants to get a hold of you," the guard notes.

I give him the most genuine smile I can muster. "Hey, Dad," I say as I answer the phone.

"Dad? What the fuck?" the man blackmailing me grumbles on the other end of the line. "What the hell have you been up to? It's been two days since I've heard from you."

I lean slightly away from the security guard, hoping he hasn't heard Dean Walsh's voice on the other end of this call.

"Yeah, I've missed you, too." I glance between the guard and the street before us.

Where is that damn Uber?

"Have you made contact with Kyle Townsend yet? It's been two weeks since I came to your office. You need to have something for me soon."

"What?" I ask. "No, I haven't been ignoring you. Work has just been a killer the last few weeks." I do my best to inject my voice with a lightness I don't feel.

"You know what else is a killer?" Dean demands. "Going to jail. That's exactly where the fuck you're going to end up if you keep fucking with me. I've given you six months to get hired at Townsend Industries and get me evidence of that family's illegal activities."

"Right. That's exactly what I'm going to do," I tell him. "How about we do one of those family Sunday dinners you love so much? When things slow down at work."

"Don't you dare hang up on me," Dean threatens.

I pause, my thumb hovering over the end call button.

God, where the fuck is my Uber?

"Dad, I'm sorry you're not feeling well, but right now's not a good time. I'm kind of in the middle of getting kicked out of a nightclub." I peer up at the burly guard whose hard glare remains trained on me.

"What the fuck are you doing at a nightclub?"

I fake laugh. "Yeah, it's kind of a long story."

"Is Kyle there? Why the hell would you go to a club to meet him?"

"Huh? Yeah, no. It's nothing serious. I'll tell you all about it when I see you next week."

"You'll be seeing me sooner than that," Dean says. "Don't mess with me, Riley. I hold your freedom in my hands.

My stomach twists in knots.

"Your niece is depending on you, isn't she? How would she fare with you in jail?"

That's when the phony smile on my face falls away. I tighten my hold on the phone and wish it was Dean Walsh's neck.

"I'll be in touch soon." He disconnects the call.

I look up at the security guard. "Parents, right?" I hold up my phone. "Can't live with 'em, can't get rid of 'em." I shrug. "Or something like that." I try to joke, but the guard snorts and then nods toward the street.

"Uber's here."

I wish I could say I'm relieved, but Dean Walsh's threat continues to pile drive its way through my mind.

***

During the twenty-minute drive from The Black Opal to my condo, I do my best to forget Dean's threats, and focus on my plan. He wants me to get close to Kyle Townsend and unearth the Townsend family's secrets. Dean believes the Townsends have threatened, coerced, and even killed to get their way.

I wouldn't put it past them. Any multibillion-dollar family has enough skeletons in their closet to fill a graveyard. And the last thing I want to do is get near any of those spoiled, trust fund types.

A shudder runs through my body just thinking about having to be near someone like that again. Given my history, I've found they're not all that smart and are pretty easy to manipulate if you know what you're doing.

However, my first encounter with Kyle Townsend hadn't proved as easy as I'd hoped. I run over my short but informative interaction with Kyle Townsend. I had a difficult time finding much information on him. Aside from a few mentions he graduated from university after only two years and immediately went to work for Townsend Industries, there wasn't much.

He no doubt graduated early because of daddy's money, just like most other kids born with silver spoons in their mouths. Unlike many of his spoiled brat contemporaries, he didn't splash his comings and goings all over the society pages. There weren't any mentions of relationships or who he was dating, if anyone.

Even the few articles that mentioned his name didn't go into much detail about him or any of the other Townsend beneficiaries. That told me a lot. Kyle keeps a tight rein on his image. From what I saw tonight, the man is a control freak.

His expression barely changed throughout the duration of our exchange. There was a fleeting moment in which his hazel eye flickered with interest. The comment in which I mentioned his dick. Thinking about that causes my mind to fill with the image of him. He's tall. Probably around six-two or six-three, light, sand-brown skin due to his biracial heritage, and hazel eyes that look right through you.

"We're here, miss." The Uber driver's words jolt me out of my musings.

"Thank you," I tell him as I slide out of the car. I push away the weird direction my mind started to go regarding Kyle Townsend.

He's just another mark, I remind myself as I enter my home. Over the course of my life, I've had dozens of marks. Hard not to when my father had me peddling scams to unsuspecting widows by the time I was three years old.

Kyle Townsend is one last job I have to do in order to get out of this fucking bind with Dean Walsh. I'll have to figure out how to ensure Walsh doesn't return for more once this job is done. That's a bridge I will cross once I get to it. My first objective is to keep my ass out of prison by finding my way into Townsend Industries.

I run my hand across my forehead as a dull pain starts behind my eyes.

"No." I shake my head, knowing I don't have time for one of my migraines. I head straight to the medicine cabinet in my bathroom and pull out my prescription for this occasion.

After downing the pills and an entire bottle of water, I kick off my shoes in my bedroom, strip out of my dress, and toss myself onto the bed. I start to figure out another plan to interact with Kyle outside of Townsend Industries, but my phone rings.

Despite my predicament, I happily answer.

"Hey, Ladybug." I beam, my mood starting to shift already.

"Hi, Aunt Ry."

"It's late for you, isn't it?" It was almost one in the morning in Williamsport. Eve's boarding school was back East, which meant it was even later for her.

"I couldn't sleep, and you said that anytime I can't sleep to call you."

"I meant it, too. Why can't you sleep?"

"I have another test tomorrow, and I don't think I've studied enough."

I open my mouth to remind her that taking a break is okay. She's only in the sixth grade. It scares me to think about what she'll be like in high school or college. The boarding school she attends is very rigorous, but from her grades, she has no problem keeping up.

Instead, I tell her, "You and your big brain worry too much. You've probably studied your entire heart out. You're going to ace that history exam."

"You remembered it was for my history class?"

"How could I forget? You missed my call two times this week because you were studying."

My niece, Eve, is a certified genius. Well, almost. She's in like the top percent for her age in math, science, and all that technical stuff. She does complex equations in her freaking sleep, which is why she attends one of the top boarding schools in the country.

She's not as great with social sciences like history, social studies, etc. Thus, she studies twice as hard in those subjects, even though I always warn her about tiring herself out.

I couldn't be prouder of her. Though I hate that she's so far, my main desire is to give her the best of everything.

She giggles. "Sorry, Aunt Ry. They don't like us to be on our phones in the library."

"You're so studious. Complete opposite of me when I was your age." I wasn't terrible at school. However, keeping up your grades is hard when your father drags you from one state to another.

"Have you talked to my dad?" she asks suddenly.

The dull pain that had started to recede reminds me it's still active. I massage my forehead because the topic of my older brother always gets under my skin.

"No, I haven't."

"I called him last week, but he never called back."

Her sulking tone pulls at my heart, and not for the first time, I want to punch my deadbeat brother in his face.

"Maybe he's just busy, Ladybug. I'll call him to remind him to get in touch with you, okay?"

"Okay," she responds, but the gloominess in her voice remains.

"You're going to pass that test with flying colors tomorrow. And once you're done, there'll be a present waiting for you at the front desk of your dorm."

"My monthly care package?" she asks.

"Mhmm," I answer. "This one has your favorite hot chocolate mix in it, too."

"Thanks, Aunt Ry. I hope I pass my exam tomorrow and make you proud."

The muscle right at the center of my chest tightens almost to the point of pain.

"You know why you're my ladybug, right?"

She grumbles on the other end of the phone. I know she's rolling her eyes.

"Say it," I prod.

"Because I'm your good luck charm."

"That's right. That means even if you get a zero on that exam, I will still love you with my whole being. You know that, don't you?"

"Yes." She draws out the word in a way that reminds me she's on that border of becoming a pre-teen and then, God forbid, a teenager.

"Go get some sleep so you can wake up refreshed and ready to pass that test tomorrow, and then have a cup of your favorite hot cocoa. Call me after your test."

"Thanks, Aunt Ry. I love you."

"Love you more."

As soon as the call disconnects, I dial the number for my brother. Surprisingly, he answers.

"Hello?" Wallace answers. "Ry-Ry?"

I cringe at the nickname.

"Yeah, it's me. Eve said she called you, and you never returned her call."

He sucks his teeth. "Don't start with me. I've got a lot going on."

"Enough going on that you can ignore your daughter?"

"What does she want with me? You're her legal guardian."

I tighten my hold on the phone. Wallace reminds me so much of our father, which is not good.

"Yes, I'm her guardian. But you're still her father. She wants to know that you care about her. Can't you at least call her now and again to check in with her?"

"Look, I gave all that up when I signed those papers, making you her guardian. If her mama hadn't died—"

"Don't you dare blame her mother …" I pinch the bridge of my nose. "Never mind, Wallace. Call your daughter sometime, okay? She doesn't need anything. She's taken care of, but the least you can do is let her hear your voice occasionally."

"Yeah, I'll do that. I have to go."

He hangs up without another word. I stare at my phone, wondering if I'm doing the right thing by encouraging him to reach out to her. Wallace is just like our father, Wallace Sr. All they know how to do is use people for their own gain and toss them aside when they've gotten what they want.

I believe that's the real reason behind Eve's mother's death. She died during birth, but I'm sure it was from a broken heart and embarrassment once she found out my brother used her for the millions of dollars she'd inherited.

My niece is the only family I have. It was rare for me to make friends since I moved so much in my younger years. Also kind of hard to form genuine relationships when you've been taught to lie and withhold yourself from others unless they can do something for you. Hence the reason, I don't have close friends or a family outside of my eleven-year-old niece.

I refuse to let Eve end up like that, which is why I can't go to jail. She has no one but me, and I won't let her go back to my brother so he can use her in whatever schemes he's running.

Eve will never know the life I knew growing up.

CHAPTER 3

Riley

The vibrating phone on my desk jolts my attention away from the email I'm typing. I purse my lips when I see the number that flashes across the screen. I go to press ignore, but I know the son of a bitch will keep calling ... or worse, he'll show up at my office again.

I press the app on my phone to record the call before answering.

"What?" I answer.

"This is the third time I've called you this morning," Dean Walsh responds tersely.

"It's the middle of the week, and I'm busy."

"Too busy to stay out of jail?"

I clamp my jaw tightly, biting back the retort that wants to break free.

"The clock is ticking. I want regular updates. It's been weeks, and you've given me jack shit. You're not even working at Townsend yet. What the hell is going on?"

I press my back against my chair and stare at the ceiling. "These things take time."

"It didn't take time when you scammed Brendan."

Guilt settles in the pit of my stomach. It took me months to work Dean's friend—the same friend who must've told Dean everything. Now Dean not only had evidence from Brendan Chastain, but he also had the incentive to use it against me.

"What have you gotten on them so far?" he demands.

There's a knock on my door. Charlotte, my assistant, pops her head in with an innocent smile. "I'm about to order lunch from Ralph's. Do you want anything?"

"Turkey club."

"Sure thing." She pulls back to shut the door. Right when I release a breath, she sticks her head back in. "Oh, and don't forget you have to finalize that report from that job a few weeks ago. The company's asking for it."

"Right after lunch."

She nods and closes the door.

"Why are you calling me at work?" I demand in a hushed voice.

"Because you've been avoiding my calls and haven't given me shit. I know those fucking Townsends are lowlife criminals, and you'll prove it for me."

"Look, Kyle Townsend is very private and controls whoever gets close to him. He's not like your friend."

Brendan Chastain is the son of a Hollywood director and a famous actress. He'd tried his hand at acting, but even the star power of his parents couldn't overshadow his utter lack of talent for long. He spent most of his time getting paid for nightclub appearances based on his famous last name.

He was an easy mark. Appeal to his ego, convince him I saw talent where there wasn't any, and he was putty in my hands. He believed I was an up-and-coming talent agent who'd help him get his big break. It made it easier for me that his parents refused to have much to do with him due to continuous bouts with the law.

Kyle Townsend is more difficult to get a read on. From the limited media coverage of his comings and goings to our brief interaction at The Black Opal, he plays everything closer to the vest than Chastain.

"I doubt even if I make my way into Townsend Industries I'll be able to get him to give up any real information that'll do his family or his company damage."

"You can and you will," Dean insists.

"Our short talk at The Black Opal proves otherwise."

"The Black— why would you approach him at a nightclub? I want something connected to Townsend Industries. I want to take that family down from the top, starting with the business that made them their fortune."

I hate Dean. He's impatient and petulant, and I doubt he has the wits to pull off this scheme. Unfortunately, he does have the power to put me in jail. After that first meeting in my office, he was more than happy to show me proof of forged checks with my name on them from Chastain.

Though I haven't run a scam in over five years, I used some leftover money from Chastain to move Eve and myself out of L.A. and start my company, Martin Consulting. I consult with businesses in various areas, including employee retention, merger and acquisition transitions, and improving corporate culture.

Until I can figure out Dean's weak spot and get him to back off, I have to play his game. I'll use whatever he gives me in these exchanges to get rid of him. I loathe being used by him or anyone else.

I spent my entire childhood and early adulthood being used and manipulated by my father and brother.

"I went to The Black Opal," I tell Dean, "because I figured it was where Townsend's guard would be down. In the office, he has too much riding on him to be an open book, at least for our first interaction."

While that was the truth, I was wrong on that front.

"Well, what's your next play?"

I roll my eyes. Never tell anyone what your next move is. "I'll figure it out."

"What the fuck does that mean?"

"You know what, Dean? As wonderful as this conversation has been, I have real work to do. I'll let you know when I have something for you." I disconnect the call.

The email I was typing to the Girls on the Move program director stares at me from my computer screen. The longing to be able to focus on this type of work overcomes me. I volunteer and do some pro bono work for the organization that focuses on teen and young adult women with juvenile records who want to turn their lives around. The program helps build the girls' self-esteem, along with educational and business skills in various ways.

It's where my passion lies.

Unfortunately, that type of work doesn't pay the bills.

It also won't pay for Eve's hefty boarding school education. Which I absolutely will not let her go without. As long as she wants to attend the school, I'll ensure it happens.

"Hey, Charlotte," I call right as she's hanging up the phone from ordering lunch. "Could you do me a favor and get me every article you can find on Townsend Industries?"

A wrinkle forms between her eyebrows. "Townsend? Have we been contacted by someone over there?" She starts searching through the notebook on her desk as if looking for information she forgot.

Since most of our clients come by word of mouth, we rarely do outreach to companies to get jobs.

"No," I tell her. "Not directly."

She pauses and then snaps. "Oh, right, you mentioned Kyle Townsend last week. Did you ever get to have that meeting with him?"

Charlotte caught me reading over one of the blog posts about the Townsend family the other week. I'd lied and told her I had a dinner meeting with Kyle Townsend but hadn't gone into further details.

"He ended up canceling." I hate lying to her, but I want to give Charlotte as few details as possible. To keep her out of my mess. Charlotte came to work for me directly from the Girls on the Move program at nineteen. She's working on getting a degree in software engineering, starting at the local community college.

The less she knows, the better.

But my assistant isn't a dummy, as evidenced when she narrows her eyes on me.

"Since when do you want to work with billionaire types?" She half-smirks. "I thought you said they already have a treasure trove of consultants at their disposal, ready to get bent over a desk to work with them."

"Did I say that?" I grin because those were probably my exact words. And precisely how I feel about the likes of Kyle Townsend, Brendan Chastain, and even Dean Walsh.

"Yeah, you did. So, what's up?"

I shrug. "A woman can't change her mind?"

She lifts a skeptical eyebrow at me.

I toss my hands up in the air. "Townsend presents a challenge. Word around town is that he's in line to become the next COO. At only twenty-five."

"Because his dad's the CEO."

I nod. "Probably, but with any major transition like that comes the need for a consultant with my skills. Especially since it's also rumored Townsend's on the edge of acquiring that medical devices company, they'll need a consultant to assist with both of those transitions."

She continues to eye me warily.

"And I like ... no, *love* a challenge, okay?"

"It does sound interesting if I'm being honest. In one of my marketing texts, I read that Townsend's been around for almost seventy-five years. Robert Townsend's credited with steering the company out of a particularly low point by outsourcing and pushing for the company to invest heavily in technology during the 80s."

"Robert Townsend?"

"Yeah, he's the father of the current CEO, Aaron Townsend. Making him—"

"Kyle Townsend's grandfather," I finish for her.

This is good information to know. "Could I get a look at your text?"

"I'll have to bring it tomorrow. Don't have it on me now."

"Cool. Can you get me some articles with this information, too? But, um ..." I hesitate, trying to decide how much I want to reveal to Charlotte. "I gave you access to those private databases, right?"

She nods.

We often use the same databases used by police and private investigators to research a client before taking a job. I'd done preliminary research on Kyle Townsend before approaching him the first time but hadn't found anything interesting. There is always the possibility that I overlooked something.

"Just do a quick scan for Kyle Townsend and his father."

"Am I looking for anything in particular?" she asks.

"The basics. Just making sure they're clean before I decide where to make my next approach."

A frown twists my lips as I figure out how and where to meet up with Kyle again. I'd miscalculated at the club, but I still believe approaching him outside of his office is my best bet. I don't want to use any of my past client connections to put in a good word for me at Townsend Industries. That would be a last resort if necessary.

"Here's an article that says Townsend will be one of the major sponsors at Art Basel."

I perk up. "That's right." I recall back to overhearing Kyle mention going to Miami before I interrupted his conversation with his cousin.

She nods. "They're sponsoring a few showings and hosting a dinner on the second night. Oh, it'll be on Townsend's private yacht."

"Why didn't I think of that?" I mumble to myself.

"Huh?" Charlotte asks.

"Art Basel is one of the year's biggest events in the art world. All of the moneyed elite attend."

My mind starts moving a million miles a minute. Art Basel will be the perfect location to work my way in with Kyle Townsend.

"However, it's this weekend. I'm not sure you'll be able to get tickets this late. Do you want me to make some calls?"

"Huh?" I almost forgot that Charlotte is still here. "No. I'll do that part. I have a friend who DJs at corporate events. She can get me in. Just get me any info you can find on those events or past Art Basel shows they've sponsored."

It looks like I'm headed to Miami for a few days.

CHAPTER 4

*K*yle

"What's the name of the guy hosting this event?" I ask Diego as I button the final button of my double-breasted, tailored suit.

"Mike Deitz. Only one of the most successful art dealers in the world." Impatience and sarcasm drip from every word.

Deitz isn't my concern. Sam Waterson is, and he'll be in attendance at this event. Along with his VP of sales.

"Successful or not, does this event have to be four hours?" I grumble.

"It should be longer," Diego huffs. "This is one of the only events this weekend strictly showcasing art by women of color."

I already know this. I'd committed it to memory over the past few days.

"It's a hell of a showcase. Many artists who wouldn't otherwise have the opportunity to show their work will be featured."

"I'm well aware. Which is also why Townsend Industries is a proud sponsor of this event." However, Townsend's name isn't all over the billboard for this particular event. We were more of a silent partner.

"Sam Waterson is supposed to be there tonight. As long as I make contact with him, my attendance will be well worth it."

Diego doesn't say anything. His expression tells me his mind is a million miles away when I look over.

"Let's go."

As we exit the hotel suite, I nod to the security with us. They know to keep their distance but stay on their toes as we take the short walk from the boutique hotel to the convention center.

When we enter the section where Deitz' event is hosted, I scan the area for Waterson. Naturally, people from business associates to socialites introduce themselves to Diego and me.

"Mr. Townsend," an executive from one of Townsend's direct competitors greets us as if we're old friends.

I grit my teeth before tossing him a smile as we shake hands.

"Looking for Waterson?" he asks.

"I'm here to enjoy the art like everybody else," I say, looking over his shoulder.

He chuckles as he releases my hand. "A chip off the old block."

I snort. He doesn't know the half of it. My father can't stand these types of things, and as soon as I had a year under my belt as a full-time employee at Townsend, I became the face of the company so that he wouldn't have to do as many of these appearances.

"You look fucking constipated," Diego quips. He hands me a drink he manages to snag from a passing waiter. "Club soda."

I take the drink and down it. "Next time, get something with alcohol in it."

"Noted."

"There are some nice pieces in here," Diego says, glancing around. "I'll probably pick up one or two."

"And put them where? Your walls are covered already," I remind him.

"I'll build a new place."

"You're not leaving the condo." He lives two floors above me in a condo in the middle of Williamsport. I live two floors above my twin sister, Kennedy. And yes, Townsend Industries owns the building.

"Isn't that..." He trails off as I look over.

I square my shoulders as I take in the woman about ten feet from us. Same height, same complexion, and when she turns our way, my eyes fall to those same plump lips. They're painted in the same red color as they were the night at The Black Opal.

"Wasn't that the woman who approached you that night?" he asks.

I nod and take another sip of my drink.

"Did you get her name?"

"Riley," I say before I can think better of it.

In my peripheral vision, I see Diego turn to stare at my profile.

"You're shit at remembering names."

I barely manage to keep from flinching. He's right. It's one of the effects of my dyslexia. It takes me a long time to remember small details. My short-term memory is shit, which is why I spent hours going over the names of the events and attendees for this weekend.

"You told me you kicked her out and never saw her again."

"I did," I counter.

"But you remember her name."

I turn away from him without answering. Despite my not wanting to, my attention turns back to the spot where she stands, except Riley's no longer there. It's not like I'm looking for her when I scan the room. I have a deal to close this weekend.

All thoughts about business cease when I spot her again. This time she's talking with the man I came to this showing to see.

"Yeah, I'll see you later," Diego says behind me.

I didn't even realize I had started in their direction.

Riley's light laughter reaches my ears, and my grip involuntarily tightens on the glass in my hands.

"That's exactly what I was thinking," she says to Waterson.

His eyes widen slightly when he sees I've made their duo a trio.

"Mr. Townsend, it's so wonderful you were able to make it.," Sam greets.

"Mr. Townsend is my father, and he's not here," I say. "Kyle is fine."

The older man nods, a smile spreading over his face.

"Besides, we should be on a first name basis, seeing how we will work together soon."

Keen eyes take me in. "The papers haven't been signed yet," he reminds me.

"Sam, you know as well as I do that it's in your best interest."

He chuckles. "Lydia is pestering me to sign the damn papers. I told her that the contract says that even with the merger, I'll remain at the company for at least a year to ensure a smooth transition."

I nod, knowing the paperwork well.

"That's a brilliant clause to include on Townsend's behalf," the woman beside me interjects, obviously not one to be left out. "Mr. Waterson, sixty percent of your employees have been with your company for over a decade. That's an impressive feat, especially in this day and age of job hopping."

Sam Waterson fucking preens under her praise. His smile grows impossibly wide.

"They'll appreciate that even after the merger is completed, you'll still be there," Riley continues. "Transitions take time. People want to feel their leaders are looking out for them."

"Which has been the cornerstone of our business for over three decades," Waterson says, then turns to me. "Kyle, have you met Riley …" He pauses.

"Martin," she finishes for him. "Riley Martin of Martin Consulting & Company." She sticks out her hand for me to shake. "We've met before, but I have to say I don't think I made the best impression."

I glance down at her hand before meeting those coffee eyes of hers again. It's difficult not to let my eyes trail down to her smiling lips, but I manage.

"Ms. Martin," I reluctantly introduce, taking her hand into mine. A feeling I can't explain pushes through my hand at the contact.

"How long ago did you two meet?" Waterson asks.

Before I can respond, she replies, "Kyle not so graciously kicked me out of a nightclub a couple of weekends ago."

Waterson glances at me with bulging eyes.

"Ms. Martin's exaggerating. She was in the wrong section, and I had my security show her where she belonged."

He glances between us, then his eyes drop to our clasped hands. I quickly free her hand, shocked that I still held onto it.

"Well, Riley was just telling me about the work she did for …" He pivots to ask her,

"Who was it?"

"While I don't like to name drop, it was for Chad Reagle's tech firm," she supplies.

Waterson snaps. "That's right. I heard from a few colleagues that he raved about the consulting you did for him."

She nods. "We're proud to work with startups to help get them what they need."

"I'll say," Waterson adds. "The deal you consulted on for him netted his firm an additional eight figures to fund some upcoming projects."

Riley's smile widens, and I can't look away from it.

"That was a merger deal, correct?" Sam asks.

"Yes."

Sam turns to me. "Riley's expertise could be beneficial if this deal between my company and Townsend Industries goes through."

I spare Riley a glance. "I'll consider that," I say, lying. "Since we're discussing the merger, I have the papers in my hotel room if you want to sign tonight."

"I suspected you would. My attorneys are looking over a few more items in the contract. Hey, I see someone I want to talk to. Would you both excuse me?"

"No problem," Riley says.

"Please." I step aside, working overtime to hide my annoyance as he passes between us.

I immediately start in on the woman before me. "What are you doing here?"

Riley blinks, surprised.

It's an act because she quickly recovers and replies, "I'm here as a lover of art just like you, Kyle."

A muscle in my jaw ticks. I want to say it's a result of anger or annoyance at her intrusion, but strangely I suspect it's more related to hearing her say my name.

I look her up and down. In her heels, she's only a few inches shorter than my six-foot-three height. Instead of that form-fitting dress she wore the night at The Black Opal, she has on a pair of loose cream trousers and a silk blouse. I can't help but notice the swell of her hips in those damn pants.

"You are persistent, aren't you?" I say, meeting her eyes. "I've had a few groupies do their best to follow me, but I can't remember the last time one dared to show up at a nightclub and then follow me to Miami."

She lets out a laugh, but it's hollow. "You do flatter yourself, don't you?"

I crook my head sideways.

"Let me get this straight?" She holds up her hand. "You seriously believe that I was so charmed by you the last time we talked that I just had to get on a plane and fly to Miami to see you in person again?"

I step closer, towering over her. "Cut the shit, Riley." My tone is sharp, biting even. I don't have time for distractions. And that's precisely what she is.

Her lips twist sideways, and then her shoulders slump with unease. "Fine. You've figured me out."

Disappointment wells up in me.

"But you've got my motives all wrong."

"Do I?" I ask. "You aren't here as another groupie? I did tell you the other week that if you're looking to get into my bed, there are other ways to go about it."

She rolls her eyes. "I'm sure you don't lack women wanting to screw you."

"You're right about that," I reply before taking the final pull of my drink.

She hesitates as if she isn't expecting that answer. To her credit, she recovers quickly.

"I'm not one of those women."

Another wave of disappointment.

"As you heard from Sam, I'm a business consultant."

"What type of consulting does your firm do?" I ask, half interested.

"Well, I advise companies when they're going through a huge transition. I aid employers who're having difficulties with employee retention. And I can even assist security personnel when tightening up their holes."

"I can assure you none of those problems exist at Townsend. And our security is top rate."

"Really?" she asks in a way that tells me she doesn't believe me.

Still, I answer, "Without a doubt."

Her smile widens, and why do I feel like I'm the one who fell into a trap? That wild, uneasy feeling of losing control starts to rocket within me, and I fight to push down the urge to fight back.

"Aren't you even curious about how I got into your VIP section that night?"

That question almost has me rearing backward on my heels.

"My security got sloppy," I say, finally.

Her dark brown hair brushes across her shoulders as she shakes her head.

"Not quite. It wasn't their fault. And I must say, the security at The Black Opal is also quality. They know their clientele. Still …" She shrugs and looks over before turning to me again. "It's not difficult to get into anywhere if you know what you're doing. Which is how I was able to get a VIP pass to your section that night."

A frown tugs at the side of my lips. "Either way, my security from that night has been fired. He'll never work in the industry again."

She pulls back, a concerned expression hitting her eyes. "You fired him?"

I shrug. "He took too long to respond."

"From what I recall, he quickly put a gun to my temple."

"Took him almost a minute to do it."

"Maybe he didn't see me as a threat."

I look her up and down again. "Which was his fuck up. Either way, he's gone and this conversation between you and me is over. Townsend doesn't now, nor will it ever, need your services."

I leave Riley Martin where she stands. Even as I walk away, I have to force my head not to turn and search the space where I left her. It's a damn shame she isn't interested in being in my bed for the night. That might've gotten her more of my attention.

As it stands, however, I don't have a need or want for her business services.

CHAPTER 5

Riley

I steel myself as I step onto the dock and look at the massive Townsend yacht.

"Do they do anything small?" I murmur as I watch the stream of people heading in the same direction as me. It's the second day of Art Basel, and after making my way through various art venues and showings, it's time for the dinner party hosted by Townsend Industries.

I don't doubt that while at least fifty top business executives, Townsend board members, and some celebrity guests will be in attendance, this event will center around impressing Sam Waterson. Kyle Townsend will be at the heart of it all. If our previous encounters haven't left an impression, this is my opportunity to do so. The third time's a charm. Or so they say.

"Ms. Martin?"

I turn and come face to face with Adam Bachleda. He's one of the more vocal members of Townsend's Board of Directors. It was rumored that his son briefly worked for the company but not for long. I spent about ten minutes talking with him last night about a few art pieces at the gallery.

"Mr. Bachleda, what did I tell you about calling me Ms. Martin?" I say at the same time I wrap my arm around his.

He takes my arm happily as the wrinkles around his eyes increase from his smile.

"Riley," he corrects. "Please, call me Adam. I had no idea you were attending this dinner party."

We start for the yacht.

Laughter and music spill from the boat. The thing feels like it looms over us the closer we get. From my vantage point, I can see that the yacht has three levels. It's easy to differentiate business people from celebrities or socialites by their attire.

I'm dressed somewhere in between with my pair of wide leg red pants and a black silk top. I thought it was best not to wear a ball gown for the event, and I'm glad I went with my gut.

"I don't recall seeing your name on the list," Adam continues, bringing me back to focus on him.

"Yes," I say with a nod. "It was a last minute thing. I have a friend who's here for work. She's DJing one of the after parties and gave me her invitation when she opted not to come tonight."

I glance over to gauge how much of my story he believes.

"She's not feeling well and thought resting before her set tonight would be better."

A deep V appears between his brows. "What's her name?"

"Sharonda Williams." It's not a lie. Shonda—for short—is a friend of mine who's in Miami to work a few corporate parties. She also gave me her Townsend dinner invite because she dislikes Richie Rich types almost as much as I do.

"That's a shame. Hopefully, she feels better soon."

I step onto the yacht, and we're both greeted by a hulking security guard dressed in all black.

"Invitations," he demands, his face and voice unyielding.

"Here we are." Adam hands his over, as do I.

The guard looks over the invites and then at us.

"Pass." He steps aside.

"You'd think they would know one of the most prominent

members of the Townsend Board of Directors," I say to Adam as he escorts me inside of the lower deck.

He chuckles. "I don't take it personally. They're particular about security. I would venture to say, Kyle even more so than his father." He leans in conspiratorially. "And that's saying a lot."

My stomach tightens, but outwardly I grin. "I'll keep that in mind."

I take a quick scan of the surrounding area. The main deck of this yacht is bigger than my first two apartments combined.

"I'm glad I ran into you," Adam says as a waiter stops to offer us glasses of champagne.

I take one of the flutes Adam hands me. "Is that so?"

"You brought up an interesting issue last night that I wanted to ask you to expand on."

"What was that?" I ask, but I'm only half paying attention. While talking with Adam Bachleda is a step in the right direction, I know I'll get a lot further in this endeavor by speaking with Kyle directly. Though Dean Walsh is focused on taking down Townsend Industries, he has a particular disdain for the Townsend family. Until I figure out how to get out from underneath Dean's thumb, I need to get closer to Kyle to at least give the appearance that I'm making headway.

"I did a little research on you after our brief discussion last evening," Adam continues.

I stiffen. For a beat, I think he will reveal that he knows someone from my past. *Why the hell does my past keep coming back to bite me in the ass?*

"Yes, I spoke with Rick Cortese."

A sigh of relief spills from my lips.

"How is Rick?" I ask about my former client. Cortese is the owner of a small financial securities firm. He had been having issues with leaks. Through my consulting services, we were able to track down the source of the leaks—which wasn't a result of malicious intent—and get it sorted out.

"He speaks very highly of you."

"One can only imagine," a deep voice says behind me.

The hairs on the back of my neck stand on end. For a second, I hesitate to turn around. But I shake that fear off and turn to meet penetrating hazel eyes burrowing down on me. At this moment, Kyle's looming over me seems even grander than that of the yacht right before I got onboard.

"Kyle," Adam greets. "Have you met Riley—"

"Martin," Kyle finishes, never taking his gaze off me. "I also know she wasn't on the original invitee list." His face remains neutral as he says that statement, but there's an accusation in his eyes that almost has me flinching away.

I'm not a flincher, so I hold his gaze the same way he's holding mine.

"A friend let me take her place," I explain.

"Friend's name?"

I tell him the name I gave Adam Bachleda earlier.

He doesn't say anything as he lifts his hand and waves one of the security guards over with a flick of his wrist.

"List," Kyle orders, holding out his hand. He takes the clipboard from the security guard, who has to have at least three inches on him. Yet, the guard looks almost nervous about being this close to Kyle. He quickly hands over the list of names.

"Sharonda Williams," Kyle murmurs as he scans the list with his finger. He taps the board twice. "Please have my assistant send a get well basket to Ms. Williams' hotel room." He gives the guard back the list in an obvious dismissal, then looks at me.

I'm confident that's his way of telling his security to go and verify that Sharonda is actually in her room sick.

"We hope she feels better soon."

"I'm sure she will," I say.

"Kyle, I just mentioned to Riley that I've spoken with one of her past clients. He has a lot of wonderful things to say about her work."

"Of course he does," he replies, sounding skeptical. Again the words are spoken to Adam, but his eyes are stuck on me. "Adam, what do you say you leave Riley and me to speak alone." It's not a request.

Adam Bachleda mentions seeing a few other businessmen he needs to speak with before he leaves the two of us. That's when Kyle finally looks away from me and watches Adam's back as he walks away.

"I never pinned you for the type to search for a sugar daddy."

My eyes bulge as I'm completely caught off-guard. "What did you just say?"

He glares down at me. "I think you heard me."

"No." I shake my head. "The words I just heard couldn't have been directed at me."

A smile spreads over his lips, but there's nothing kind, friendly, or gentle about it. A shiver passes through me, and I take a sip of my champagne if only to wet my mouth, which has gone barren from his expression.

"There's no one else that I'm speaking to."

Remembering who I am, I shake off whatever weird reaction my body has to this man and square my shoulders.

"You know, in the three times we've spoken to one another, that's the third time you've referenced sex." I lean in. "If you want to fuck me, Kyle, just say so."

His eyes instantly drop to my lips, and I wonder if I've let myself enter the deep end without a lifejacket. Never in my past had I used sex to get what I was after. Sure, a little flirting here and there, but I wasn't one of those love bombers. I kept business and my love life completely separate. As separated as possible.

So why am I standing face to face with Kyle Townsend as he stares at my mouth, with images of what he would look like without any clothes racing through my brain?

The truth is, I don't even need to ask. From how the button-down white shirt, light blue suit jacket, and white pants perfectly fit Kyle's six-foot-three frame, it's easy to see the man has an insane workout regimen. As ridiculously sexy as he is with clothes on, I bet he would look even more glorious naked.

"That's one way to conduct business," he says, pulling me out of my thoughts.

"What?" I ask as if coming out of a trance. This is not going how I want.

"There has never nor will there ever be a time in which a woman who ended up in my bed also ended up in my boardroom, Riley. Hell will freeze over before I let that happen."

Shit. Why does my name sound smooth as silk coming out of his mouth? I swallow the lump that oddly formed in my throat.

"I assure you, Kyle, my only interest is what my company can do for Townsend Industries."

He lets out a chuff. "As I've already told you, Townsend has all the consultants we need."

"You haven't even given me a chance to tell you what my company can do for you." I decide to make this the moment to pounce with my five-minute elevator pitch. "Martin and Associates is not simply your run of the mill consulting firm. I have worked with small and medium sized companies on everything from employee retention to advanced security breaches that top notch security personnel couldn't fix."

"Small and midsize businesses?" The skepticism drips from every word. "Townsend brings in revenue upward of eighty billion annually and employs thousands of people. Those are our U.S. numbers. That number increases greatly when you add in our international subsidiaries."

"This is why my services would benefit your company."

"Or, all the more reason why your services are lacking when it comes to doing business with us. You don't have the experience."

"Some would say *you* don't have the experience."

He lifts his light brown, almost blond eyebrows.

"You're aiming to become Townsend's next COO, is that not right?" Seeing the anger that instantly covers his expression, I don't give him time to answer. "At your age, I guess there are more than a handful of skeptics who say you're not ready to handle the responsibilities that come with such an important role."

"Not one of them is brave enough to say any of that bullshit to my face," he says so sharply that I hold my breath for a beat. "When I become COO, it'll be because I earned it."

I watch his Adam's apple move up and down.

"Are we clear?"

"If you say so." My reply comes out as skeptical as I want it to. "But I'm sure as capable as you are, every business has its weak spots. It's not shameful to need some help now and again."

His eyes narrow as he scans my face. Somehow, we've managed to move within inches of one another. Kyle doesn't say anything for a long moment. During that time, my heart rate kicks up for no reason.

We're just standing there, not saying anything, but our eyes are searching out one another's.

"Weak spots," he mumbles loud enough for only me to hear. "I don't have any."

"Everyone has them." That time, my voice comes out as a whisper and a hair sultrier than my usual tone.

"Not me. Can't afford them," he says.

Suddenly, I'm wondering if we're still on the topic of business.

Kyle gathers himself first as he shakes his head slightly and steps backward. "Enjoy yourself, Ms. Martin." He looks me up and down. "But not too much."

Yet again, he presents me with his back as he saunters off.

* * *

Kyle

"You're watching her again," Diego leans over and says into my ear.

Even though I hear him clearly, and know I need to, I can't tear my gaze away from her.

Riley fucking Martin.

She's across the room, talking with Adam Bachleda and another board member. When Riley tosses her head back and laughs, I tighten my hand around my glass. I both want to get her off my boat and move closer to her.

"That's when my team was able to build out the systems that grow our reach," Sam Waterson says, bringing my attention back to our conversation. He's going over how his company expanded the distribution of his medical supplies company.

"Yet another reason why your connections will pair perfectly with

Townsend," I tell him as if I was paying attention the entire time. I remind myself that my only objective for the remainder of this weekend is to get Waterson's signature on the dotted line.

That's the only thing that matters.

Yet, as if a damn homing device is attached to her, my eyes land directly on Riley again. This time around, she's speaking with one of the board members' wives. When the older woman pulls out her phone from her clutch, I wonder what she's showing Riley.

Riley's expression softens.

"Townsend is number one in that arena. Isn't that right, Kyle?" Diego nudges me with an elbow.

"Yes, what he said," I say, not knowing what they're talking about now. "Will you two excuse me? Dinner should begin shortly, and I need to make sure we're on schedule."

I hear Diego tell Waterson something about how hands on I am when it comes to events and projects under my charge. What he's saying in not so many words is that I'm a control freak.

I head over to the closest security guard to me.

"How many are onboard?" I ask.

"Fifty-three."

I nod. The dinner is set up for sixty, but a few celebrities exited early as I suspected they would.

"We're right on schedule," Mike, my assistant, comes up and tells me. He's been giving me updates all evening.

I nod and peer down at my Rolex. "In exactly five minutes, gather our guests. I'll make the dinner announcement over the microphone. Are you certain the caterers are prepared?"

He nods quickly. "Everything is aligned to your specifications. The tables are already set."

I nod, knowing as much since I went down and double checked on the dining area myself. We'll be dining on the lower deck of the yacht. It's the perfect space for quieter and more intimate conversation. I'm seated at the head table, of course, with Sam Waterson, a few of his team, and the board members from Townsend. My interest isn't in anyone else at the moment.

At least, that was what I told myself. Yet, after giving Mike a few more instructions, I head in the opposite direction instead of heading to where the live band is playing to grab the microphone.

Without much thought behind my actions, I find myself standing before Riley. She's speaking with another board member and an artist whose work was featured at last evening's show.

"Dinner will begin shortly," I tell the two men without a preamble.

"Time to head down. Riley can continue telling me about her business," the board member says. "She can sit at my ta—"

"She's sitting by me," I cut him off to say.

"I am?" she asks with lifted brows.

"You two can head on down." I nod their way before turning to her. I see them move toward the stairs out of the corner of my eye.

"This is unexpected," she says when I round on her.

"As the saying goes, keep your enemies close."

She lifts a perfectly arched eyebrow. "I believe it's to keep your friends close and enemies closer."

"I don't have friends."

She smirks. "Everybody has friends." She nods over my shoulder. "What about him?"

I glance behind me to see she's referring to Diego. "He's family." I turn to her. "There's an empty chair at my table. You'll take that one."

"What if I wanted to have dinner next to Doug Keen? We were having a riveting conversation on his contemporary art technique."

A muscle in my jaw ticks. "Your plans changed," I say bluntly. "And he's not that riveting." I had a ten-minute conversation with the man the night before. I only remained for that long because Sam Waterson likes the bastard.

"Kyle," someone calls behind me.

Reluctantly, I turn from Riley to see someone I vaguely remember approach.

"It's me, Jake?" he says, patting his chest as if I'm supposed to remember him.

"Jake Albert," I say, knowing the name from the guest list.

"That's right. Man, it's been a long time." He grins wide like we're old friends. But that's not the case because I don't have friends, like I told Riley. There isn't anyone, outside of my family, that I would ever get close enough to call a friend.

"How've you been? I was just in L.A., where I saw your brother."

"Great." My reply is clipped. "Dinner is about to start, and as you can see, I was speaking with—" I break off when I return to where Riley stands to see she's no longer there.

The fuck?

I glance around to see she's disappeared.

"That woman who was just standing here?" Jake asks.

I pierce him with a stern look.

"She looked familiar," he says. "Who is she?"

None of his damn business. "As I said, dinner is about to begin." I step aside and nod in the direction of the stairs. "I have an announcement to make."

"Yeah, okay," he says. "We'll have to catch up soon."

I don't reply as I head to the microphone to announce the dinner.

Ten minutes later, all of the guests sit around nine different tables that have been set out. Only the people I genuinely care about are at my table … and Riley. She'd disappeared for a minute, only to materialize soon after. The original invite had placed her at a table at the opposite end of the room.

Now, she's seated directly next to me. Every time she moves, I get a whiff of her scent. It's disturbingly alluring. A light, floral scent mixed with something that smells, for lack of a better term, exotic. I can't put my finger on it.

Right on time, the caterers serve the watercress and goat cheese salad. I do my best to pry my attention away from Riley's scent and listen to the conversation between Diego and Sam Waterson. While focusing on certain things can be a problem for me, I rarely ever have to fight this fucking hard to focus when it comes to business.

Yet, when I hear soft laughter spill from Riley's lips, I twist my entire body in her direction.

What the hell is so funny? I can barely hold the demand back. Emotions that I'm not familiar with force me to glare around Riley at

Adam Bachleda. The bastard is talking with Riley about something that's making her smile.

I know Bachleda's wife passed away two years ago. He's single. The earlier comment about Riley seeking a sugar daddy comes to mind.

Could she?

Then I recall the offended look in her eyes when I said it. She quickly schooled her features, but I'd caught it. She isn't in the market for a sugar daddy.

At least, that isn't what she's looking for in Bachleda.

"Isn't that right, Kyle?"

I blink and look up to see Bachleda and a handful of other Townsend board members staring at me. While I'm not looking at her, I can also feel Riley's eyes on me.

"What was that?" I loathe admitting that I wasn't paying attention.

"That Merkle data breach that occurred last year." Bachleda shakes his head. "Terrible. It cost them tens of millions, and their market share is down twenty-five percent since it happened."

"Yeah, a shame," I say. "Could've been avoided with better security measures."

Bachleda and a few others nod.

"Not necessarily," Riley contradicts, garnering the attention of everyone at the table.

Something in my chest tightens at the sound of her voice. My first instinct is to silence her unexpected interruption. Yet, she continues before I'm able to.

"It's my understanding that part of the breach came about due to employee failure to secure their data."

"Incompetence," I grumble loud enough for all to hear.

"That's not necessarily the case either," she retorts.

"How is an employee's failure to secure their data not due to incompetence or maliciousness?" I ask. "And if it was of the latter, they should've been arrested and charged with a crime."

Riley tilts her head and looks at me as if searching for something. I stare back.

"Not every employee is out to get their employer," she says.

I know she's speaking directly to me, but she then looks over at Adam. I refuse to allow that.

"Whether they mean to or not isn't the point," I say, bringing her attention back to me like I want.

"It's true that sometimes, employees can be a business' weak spot. But they are also its strength. In Merkle's case, one of the reports I read identified the entry point of the data breach as a company-issued laptop."

"I still don't see how this proves your point," I tell her. The entire table stops their side conversations to watch this exchange. However, right now I don't give a damn about anyone else at the table. Not even Sam Waterson, whom this whole dinner is for.

"Follow me for a moment," Riley says, fully turning toward me. "On any company laptop, there's sensitive data on it, correct?"

I nod.

"Right, and as such, there's encrypted security passwords and whatnot. Many companies don't even allow employees to remove their laptops from the office."

"With good reason," I say.

"Agreed," she concedes. "While a trained hacker could take the time to break into one of the systems, they could spend months trying to get the right access. And any business with decent security is constantly changing its security systems on the back end to keep up with the times. Even something as minor as updating your passwords every thirty days can throw a hacker off for a while."

"Yeah, but it's such a pain," a woman from across the table says.

Riley laughs and nods. "It is, but trust me, you should do it when prompted to update your passwords. Anyway," she turns back to me, "it's not always the most skilled hacker that can breach a company like Merkle. Sometimes all it takes is someone with good social engineering skills to do the job."

"Social engineering?" Adam Bachleda asks.

Riley nods his way before looking out around the rest of the table. "How many of you have received one of those car warranty calls?"

I glance around to see that almost every hand at the table has gone up.

"I'm betting most of you hang up as soon as you've gotten the call," Riley continues. "But you're the lucky ones. Hundreds, thousands, maybe even millions of customers probably were lapsed on a warranty when they received that call. Without even thinking about it, they fed their information to the caller on the other side, and bam, they're taken for thousands of dollars."

"What does this have to do with Merkle?" I ask directly.

Instead of being thrown off, she looks at me with an effervescent smile. Something funny happens in my chest that I don't like.

"It has everything to do with Merkle," she says without missing a beat. "A truly determined individual or group won't need to hack a password when they can hack an individual at the company. If you catch the right employee on a bad day, they'll quickly give up classified information without realizing it."

She nods and looks around the table as if waiting for everyone to absorb everything she says.

"At Merkle, the employee who was identified as the entry point of the breach just so happened to be going through a divorce. As most of you can assume, that's an emotional period for anyone. Said employee took some time to work from home. At which time, she received a call from a man who she believed had just taken over her director role. He pretended to need some vital information in a short amount of time.

"Without thinking too deeply about it, this Merkle employee forked over private information and resources for the company. That was the beginning of the data breach. The caller didn't need the employee's passcode. They got in with a few condolences about the woman's divorce and the guise of being her new director who needed something."

"Huh," Adam Bachleda huffs. "So, social engineering is using someone's vulnerabilities to gain access to secret information?"

"In a roundabout way. Everyone ... you, me, even Kyle here," she says, looking over at me, "have our weaknesses or blind spots, I'll call them. Now, when you multiply that by what?" She pauses. "How many people did you say Townsend Industries employs?"

I frown because I don't doubt she remembers what I told her earlier.

"Thousands," someone from the table supplies.

"Right," she continues. "That's over a thousand entry points for someone with malicious intent. While I'm certain Townsend's security is top notch." She stops and looks me right in the eye. "One of them already held a gun to my temple."

One of the wives of the board members gasps.

"And he was fired," I say, still eyeing Riley, "for reacting too slowly."

Riley clears her throat. "Not everyone who wants their way into Townsend Industries or any other company, for that matter, will do so with a gun or have the skills of a professional hacker. Sometimes they'll use your greatest resource without them even knowing."

There's a long silence. I've lost track of how often I find myself staring at this woman like she's a puzzle I need to figure out.

Because she is.

I don't trust her.

I don't want to be intrigued by her.

But I am.

This is why I feel left wanting when she tears her eyes away from me to face the rest of the table.

"Thank you all for coming to my Ted Talk," she says, holding her hands out.

Unsurprisingly, the rest of the table erupts into applause and laughter as if she did give a Ted Talk.

I'm not one who's easily impressed.

I damn sure do not want a relationship or even a woman to warm my bed. There are at least twenty women on this boat and hundreds of others at the events I'll be attending this weekend that I could use as bed warmers if I wanted.

So, the fact that I can't take my eyes off of or stop thinking about Riley Martin baffles the fuck out of me.

CHAPTER 6

Riley

I press the ignore button on my phone for the third time today. It's Dean Walsh calling for another update. I wish it were his face I was punching instead of my phone.

It's the final full day of Art Basel, and I've made very little headway with Kyle Townsend. After last night's dinner, I barely saw him. I would've sworn I had his attention if someone had asked me. I felt his eyes burrow into the side of my face during my little talk last night at the dinner table.

After serving the main course, more than ten business executives approached me with their business cards. I may drum up some legitimate business for my company, but that's not what this weekend is about, not in the short-term.

"What're you looking so down about?" Sharonda asks as she bumps me with her hip.

We're walking along the beach as the sun starts to set. Shonda has a set to DJ in half an hour.

"Work," I tell her, sparing the details. I met Sharonda over six years ago. We both were nineteen and living in a homeless shelter in Los Angeles. Soon after we met, Sharonda scored her first DJing gig, and

I'd decided that after Brendan Chastain, I wouldn't scam anyone ever again.

I badly needed the money at that time.

Sharonda thought I was another young girl who moved to L.A. with dreams of making it big. After it didn't work out, I moved to Williamsport to start my consulting firm. Neither of us would've found our way out of our pasts if it weren't for Ms. Edith, the woman who ran the homeless shelter. She was like a beacon of hope in the days after I left my father's home once I turned eighteen. She made me want to become better than the life I was raised in.

Two years later, after determining I was done with that life and with my niece in tow, I moved to Williamsport. It was one of the few big cities I'd never lived in with my father. I went to school and started my company there, far from my past. It worked for the past five years, too.

Until Dean Walsh walked into my office.

Bastard.

"I thought you had more work than you knew what to do with," Shonda says, misunderstanding my comment.

"I do," I tell her. "That's part of the problem. Those clients take up so much of my time I haven't been able to take on as many volunteer hours with Girls on the Move. I hate not being able to help out like I want to."

Sharonda nods, a small smile creeping onto her face. "Hey, look on the bright side," she says, using one of Ms. Edith's favorite lines. "It's those big bucks you make with those clients that let you send Eve to that fancy boarding school," she comments.

I nod and smile, grateful that that's the truth.

"First world problems," she says with a roll of her eyes. "Remember your L.A. days when you dreamt of getting that big break? Now, you have your own company and more clients than you know what to do with. I'm guessing that means last night went well?"

That question brings back the impromptu speech I gave over dinner and how I almost ran into trouble before our meal was served.

When Jake Albert called Kyle's name, I recognized his voice immediately. Albert is a close friend of Brendan Chastain's. I've met him a few times, but that was years ago. I'm also pretty sure he was high as hell on cocaine a number of those times. With any luck, he didn't recognize me.

However, I couldn't take that chance, so I exited the conversation when Kyle looked away. Thankfully, Jake hadn't sat at the same table as Kyle and me.

"Yeah, I haven't done so bad for myself," I say in response to Shonda's comment. "Neither have you, party girl. Have an awesome set tonight," I tell her with a wave as we approach the DJ booth where she's about to set up.

"Make sure your ass is on the dance floor. It's your last night in Miami. Live it up!" she orders while putting on her oversized headphones.

I watch her for a beat before I pull out my phone. Part of me wonders if I should head back to my hotel room for the night to give Eve a call. We usually speak daily, but since I've been in Miami, we've only talked once.

"Hi, Aunt Ry," Eve answers, sounding sleepy.

"Were you sleeping, Ladybug?" I check my watch to see it's only a little after eight.

"I fell asleep studying at the library, and the librarian told me to return to my dorm room."

"After that ninety you got on your history exam, you shouldn't have to study for another few weeks."

She snorts. "It should've been a hundred."

My little perfectionist.

"You did your best, which is all I ever ask of you," I tell her. "You probably tuckered yourself out with all of that studying."

She makes a noise like she's stretching. "I should get up to clean my room. The headmistress of the dorm says I need to take better care of my space."

Eve has always been a ball of energy and a little messy. She applies so much energy to studying that it's like she's in another world when focused on something. Then there are other moments when she seems all over the place, focus wise. Kid stuff, I'm sure.

"Put it off for the night. Go rest if you need to, Ladybug."

"Okay," she murmurs with a yawn. "Love you." The two words come out mumbled as if she's already falling back asleep, but they fill my heart with joy.

"I love you, too, Ladybug. I'll call you tomorrow after you get out of class."

After I hang up, I contemplate my next move. Sharonda's words come back to mind. At that moment, I make a decision. She's right. It's my final night in Miami. I'm going to enjoy myself, even for a little while.

"Fuck it," I mutter.

Though Shonda hasn't started DJing yet, a club mix of a Lady Gaga song begins to play. As I sway my hips, the white dress that falls just above my knees starts to swing against my thighs.

The corporation Shonda's DJing has spared no expense for this evening beach event. I snatch one of the mojitos from a passing waiter and down half of the glass in one swallow.

"Another interesting business approach."

I almost stumble over my two feet from the deep, rumbly voice behind me. I turn to face Kyle. He stands there in another button-up top, this time with a dark blue jacket and dark pants with suede loafers.

His eyes are at half mast, and there's a tiny smile creeping across his mouth. He looks ... relaxed. Almost.

I suspect he's had a few drinks already.

"Do you always aim to look like a GQ model?" I ask out of nowhere. As much as I would like, I can't blame the alcohol. I've barely had any.

As I would've expected, his expression doesn't budge. He is the true epitome of poker face. Except, I do know he's intrigued by me. Otherwise, he wouldn't have come up to me out of nowhere.

"GQ models wished they looked this damn good."

"And he's humble, to boot."

He grunts. "What's the point of humility?" he asks and looks as if he truly wants an answer.

"Spoken like someone born with the proverbial spoon in his mouth."

His eyes ignite with intensity as he steps forward. "I'm not humble because I don't need to be. I work my ass off," he says through clenched teeth.

I hold up my hands. "I would never dare to contradict that statement." I infuse my voice with innocence.

"Townsend Industries is the success—" He breaks off when I suck my teeth and look heavenward.

"This isn't a Townsend event, is it?" I already know the answer.

"No."

"Great. Then how about we leave business talk for a different day?"

"There won't be another day for you and me," he insists.

"Fine." I swipe another mojito and hand it to him. "Then why don't we enjoy the night for what it is? No talk of mergers, acquisitions, or anything else business related."

He hesitates before taking the drink from my hand. His fingers brush against mine, and my pulse kicks up. When our gazes clash, I know he feels it, too. Considering our past interactions, I expect him to tell me to get lost before he walks away from me again.

Yet, Kyle is full of surprises, I suppose. Instead of leaving me standing there, he gets closer.

"Business talk is off the table for the night."

It has to be me, but his voice sounds huskier than usual.

He shocks me again when he downs the mojito I just handed him, takes mine out of my hand, and places both glasses on the tray of a waitress who passes. There's no time to ask what he's doing before he takes my hand and pulls me toward the growing dance crowd.

"It's probably better if we don't talk at all," he says, low by my ear. "Show me how you move," he commands at the same time, his hands moving to my hips.

An upbeat Cardi B song starts playing. People around us are dancing and laughing as they sing along to the music. My hands find their way around Kyle's neck, and in the blink of an eye, we're both moving against one another to the music.

I thought this man was stiff and unyielding in our previous engagements, which doesn't typically make for a great dance partner. I don't know if it's the mojito he just swallowed or something else, but Kyle Townsend is anything but stiff as we grind against one another on this beach.

"You're not bad," I say, unable to keep the surprise out of my voice.

"Shshsh," he shushes, his lips brushing against my ear. "No talking." His hand moves up to cup my cheek, and his thumb covers my lips, silencing any retort I might have.

On instinct, I part my lips and brush my tongue against his thumb. Kyle's eyelids lower, and his other hand tightens on my hip, pulling me into his body.

Without losing the beat of the music, he holds me against him.

Oh my god! I scream in my head as I feel a very big, very hard presence in his pants.

There's no way that thing can be real.

Kyle's lips twist into a sideways grin as if he can read my thoughts. And if I said he lacked humility before, I take that back. I highly doubt Kyle Townsend has ever been in the same vicinity as humility a day in his life.

He leans down again, his lips so close to my ear that I can feel his warm breath as it brushes against my skin. My core temperature rises by five degrees.

"Don't worry. He doesn't bite. Unless I tell him to."

Yup, that huskiness I was questioning earlier is now undeniable.

"Keep him to yourself," I reply, my voice thick with emotions I can't even name.

He chuckles. "We both know you're full of shit."

"Excuse you?" I pull back and glare at him. I have to fight hard to hold on to my little bit of anger when I see how he grins at me. There's a sparkle in his eyes. That's the moment I know Kyle had a few drinks before that mojito. I don't know if I'm more disappointed to see that the alcohol has caused him to let his guard down even slightly around me or if I'm happy about it.

"If I—" He starts but stops when someone approaches us. His hand presses into the small of my back, bringing our bodies to flush against one another.

"I see you took my advice," Diego Townsend says as he looks curiously between Kyle and me.

"Maybe," Kyle replies.

Diego pulls back slightly, and a grin splits his lips.

Damn. What the hell is in the water in the Townsend household? Diego's only an inch shorter than Kyle, his skin a shade or two darker, a rich copper tone, and he has dark, curly hair. His eyes are a shade of brown, but there are gold flecks in them. He's as gorgeous as his cousin, although the two look nothing alike.

"Riley Martin, nice to see you again," Diego says as he folds his arms across his chest. The muscles in his arms bulge as he does so. "This is interesting." He draws out the words as his eyes drop to where Kyle still holds me against his body.

"Did you want something, cousin?" Kyle demands.

Diego runs a hand over the back of his head and chuffs. "Yeah." He pauses when something in the distance catches his eye. The affable nature drops as his face takes on a scowl. "Is that ..." He trails off.

"What?" Kyle asks as Diego continues to glare. "Oh shit," Kyle murmurs when his gaze follows his cousin.

I try to turn to look at what they're both seeing, but Kyle's hold prevents me from turning around.

"That motherfucker," Diego growls. He starts off toward whoever he's glaring at, but Kyle throws up an arm, stopping him.

"Move," Diego growls.

"You need to calm down," Kyle says.

During their exchange, I squirm out of Kyle's hold and peer over at the scene behind me. All I see are people dancing and enjoying themselves. In the midst of it all, there is one particularly close couple. I follow where Diego's still staring and see he's focused on that couple.

A man and a woman. I recognize the guy as one of the artists whose work was featured by a gallery earlier today. A tall, lanky, bald, Black man with a woman who appears to be Latina. He whispers in her ear, making her giggle and lean into him. A beat later, the pair are kissing.

"The fuck is he doing?" Diego grits out. Less than a second later, he breaks away from Kyle's hold on him and storms over to the guy.

"Oh shit." I gasp and cover my mouth when Diego hauls off and punches the guy in his face.

The artist collapses to the sand like a house of cards that's had one of its foundations pulled from underneath it.

"Goddammit," Kyle grumbles. He starts toward his cousin.

Before I know what's happening, I get pulled in the same direction. Kyle has taken hold of one of my wrists and drags me to where Diego continues to make a scene.

"What are you doing?" the woman with the tall, Black guy squeals as she leans over him. "Are you okay?"

"Fuck him," Diego barks. "Get the fuck up." With his fists balled at his sides, everyone knows what Diego's intent is once this guy rises to his feet again. If he knows what's good for him, he'll keep his ass on the ground.

"Somebody call the police," the woman shrieks.

"Yeah, that's not happening," Kyle says, sounding almost bored despite the rage emanating from his cousin. "Are you going to hit him again?" Kyle asks.

My eyes bulge.

"He has a fucking fiancée," Diego rages. "Get up."

"What?" the man on the ground asks.

He sits up, but he's smart because he doesn't try to stand despite the semi-circle that's formed around us. He likely realizes that he's outmatched, and I doubt even the onlookers could stop Diego from charging him again. I peek over at Kyle, who's watching the scene play out.

Kyle's not about to intervene on the artist's behalf.

"The fuck are you doing kissing another woman when you're engaged?" Kyle's cousin yells.

"You're engaged?" the woman by the artist's side questions, looking surprised.

"What?" He shakes his head. "No, no."

"Liar!"

"Honestly." He holds his hands out in front of him. "She didn't tell you?"

"The hell are you talking about?" Diego wonders, his eyes still blazing with anger.

"We broke up ... Actually, she dumped me. I-I'm single," he declares, looking at the woman beside him.

She sighs in relief, but Diego is another story.

"You're fucking cheating on her and lying about it to my damn face." He pulls the artist to his feet by the collar of his shirt.

"No. No ... seriously," he pleads. "Monique dumped me. She said she's moving back to Williamsport. I-I thought she would've told you by now. It's been like two months."

"Diego, calm down. I think he's telling the truth," Kyle says, finally trying to reason with his cousin. He places a hand on Diego's shoulder, pushing him away from the guy.

"Honestly, I'm surprised she hasn't told you," the artist says. "But she did say you hadn't been taking her calls. You should talk to her."

"Don't fucking tell me what to do," Diego growls, taking a step forward.

The guy steps back with his hands up. "O-Okay."

"Diego—" Kyle calls.

"Fuck!" Diego curses before pushing past a few onlookers who remain watching all of this.

"Should you go after him?" I stare at Diego as he gets smaller and smaller, heading away from us.

"He needs to be alone when he gets like this." Despite his words, Kyle watches his cousin as well.

"Do you know what that was about?" The question is born out of true concern. Diego was grinning at the both of us one minute and in a rage the next.

"Your guess is as good as mine," Kyle replies. But I can see it for the lie it is. All he's told me is that he's not about to reveal his cousin's business to me.

I get it.

"If you need to go …" I trail off because in all honesty I don't want the night between Kyle and me to end. He was slightly letting his guard down around me. While the purpose of why I'm really in Miami lingers at the back of my mind, the truth is, I want to spend more time with Kyle, the man, not Kyle Townsend, the guy I'm supposedly running a con on.

"Wait." Unthinking, I grab his hand. "Forget what I said about leaving. How about we play a game instead?"

CHAPTER 7

Kyle

I had plans to work from my hotel suite this evening. Sam Waterson has a series of private family engagements that he's attending tonight. Besides, I had a shitload of other work I need to get my hands on. I'd already spent ninety minutes on a call with the VP of marketing to help develop a new brand strategy for one of our products.

But Diego bitched about me working too hard again. He also mentioned I might miss an opportunity to talk with one of Waterson's lawyers or his team. That got me out of the suite, finally. This is my second party of the night, and I still haven't contacted any of Waterson's people.

I have, however, managed to down at least three drinks so far. I suppose that's why Riley's invitation intrigues me as much as it does. I'm attributing my interest in her over business to the alcohol running through my veins, and that's it.

Still, I have to keep her on her toes somehow.

"I don't play games," I reply to her request.

"C'mon, don't be a chicken," she prods. When a waiter passes, she lifts two shot glasses and hands me one. "A friendly game of truth or dare."

Her lips spread into a seductive smile. She's wearing a different shade of red than she wore the first night at The Black Opal. But red is her color. She must know it.

That's when an image of those red, pouty lips wrapped around my cock races through my mind.

Truth or dare.

I've got a fucking dare for that mouth.

There's no way in hell that I'd even consider hiring Riley's consulting firm to work at Townsend but there are other ways I can keep her around.

"No questions about business," I say.

She holds up her free hand. "It's a deal. I'll go first."

"Why do you go first?"

"Ladies always go first. Don't they teach manners over there at Townsend?"

"We learn a whole lot at Townsend." I skim up and down the length of her body, not even bothering to hide the desire in my eyes. This will more likely than not be the last night I ever see this woman. I'm not worried about her knowing I want her. "And we're not talking about business," I remind her.

She rolls her eyes. "Truth or dare?"

"Dare."

"Why am I not surprised?" she asks with a shake of her head. "Okay …" She glances around. I know she's decided on the dare when her smile widens as she peers at the DJ booth.

"I dare you to grab the microphone and do your best impersonation of Britney Spears."

My eyebrows lift. "Are you serious?"

She giggles. "Your drink is right there. Totally understand if you want to back out on your first dare." She looks around us again. "There are a lot of business people around us." She shrugs, and I take it for the challenge it is.

This woman has no idea how competitive I am. If I say I'm going to do something, I fucking do it. No questions.

"Hold this." I hand her my shot glass and head straight to the DJ booth. I whisper in her ear to play my favorite Britney Spears song. The extra C-note I slip her has the song playing almost immediately.

When the opening chords for Britney's "Toxic" start playing, a round of shouts go up around the party. A few more cheers sound on the beach as I grab the microphone.

From the moment the first words start, I'm on it, singing word for word. For good measure I throw in some of my dance moves. I scan the crowd for one woman. I make eye contact with Riley whose smile takes up her entire face. She's clapping and singing along.

Underneath the lights from the party, I can see there's a hint of misbelief in her eyes. As if she didn't believe I'd get my ass up on this microphone and perform.

Hell, I might not be the best performer in my family—that's my younger brother, Andreas—but I can hold my own, and I damn sure am not about to lose a game of truth or dare.

I wind my way over to Riley and sing the chorus directly to her while taking her chin in my free hand. Her dancing is thrown off beat slightly and a thrill buzzes through me. I know I affect her and there's something powerful about that knowledge. That feeling propels me to grind my hips against her while still singing.

"Oh my god." She laughs and covers her face.

I remove her hand and intertwine her fingers with mine as the song finishes. A chorus of applause sounds off around us. I keep my eyes trained on her as I hand someone behind me the microphone.

At the perfect time, a waiter approaches us, and I hand her a shot since I don't know where she placed the other two. She downs the brown liquid without question. My gaze trails down the long line of her neck when she tips her head back—my mouth waters.

"My turn," I say, my voice husky. "Truth or dare?"

"Truth." She slams the empty glass on a nearby table.

Out of nowhere, two new shots appear in her hands.

"What's your biggest fear?"

She stumbles, and I have to hold out my arm to keep her from falling.

"You're just going right in there, huh?"

"You're the one who opted for truth." My words aren't apologetic at all. I'll personally choose dare all day every day.

"Biggest fear," I prod.

"I heard the question the first time," she replies. Riley eyes the drink in her hand, contemplatively. After a beat, her lips twist defiantly, and an almost overwhelming urge to call her a *good girl* comes over me because I know she's going to answer.

"Being used by someone I love." Her answer comes out in almost a whisper. I'm barely able to make out what she says. But I do hear it. Riley's expression is reticent, which tells me she's recalling a time in which something like that happened to her.

The fingers of my free hand curl on their own accord. I want to demand to know who the fuck it was that used her. I want to know who it was, and I want their head on a fucking platter.

"I answered. Drink up," she tells me, pulling me out of those dangerous thoughts.

I remind myself I have absolutely no business having this type of reaction over a woman I won't ever see again after tonight. With that reminder, I down the shot in one gulp. I'm grateful for the burn as the whiskey goes down. It makes me almost completely forget about making her tell me who hurt her in the past.

"Truth or dare?" she asks.

I frown.

"Dare," she says with a laugh. "Of course." She narrows her eyes. "I dare you to call the last person you talked to on your phone and declare your undying love to them." She folds her arms and cocks her head to the side. Like she's finally got me.

I pull out my call and swipe to the call log. The last person I called was my assistant, Mike. He left for home earlier this morning.

I look her in the eyes as I press redial. Per usual, he answers before the third ring.

"Kyle, what's up?" he asks, eager to please.

"Mike, did you get home safely?" I inquire, still watching Riley.

"Got in a couple of hours ago. Did you need something? Is it the Waterson deal? I didn't think you had another meeting with him until tomorrow morning."

"Everything's fine. Hey, Mike?"

"Yeah?"

"I love you."

Riley bursts out into laughter but quickly covers her mouth.

"Oh-okay," he draws out.

"No. I mean, I really love you and everything you do as my assistant. Your work doesn't go overlooked."

"Umm, that's nice."

"That's all I wanted you to know. Talk to you when I'm headed home."

He clears his throat and doesn't say anything.

"Done," I tell Riley as I disconnect the call. "Come harder next time, please."

She waves her hand in the air. "It's not fair when probably everyone in your phone is eating out of your hand." There's skepticism in her voice.

"Excuse me?"

"Please, how many people can you call right now who would fawn all over you? It's what you types—" She breaks off. "Forget it." She takes a shot, and I hate not knowing her complete thoughts.

While I shouldn't want to, I do want to know more about this woman. I step closer.

"Truth or dare?"

She taps her chin.

"Dare."

"Truth then."

"What?" She shakes her head. "I said dare."

"Fine, I dare you to tell me what the hell you were just about to say."

"That's not fair."

"Neither is life," I retort. "Out with it."

"This is a sneaky way to get to the truth."

I lift and lower a shoulder. "Tell me." Somehow, her hand has ended up in mine. Even when she tries to tug it free, I don't let it go. She's like a damn magnet. "What did you mean by you types?"

She glares at me, and this is the first time I've ever thought a woman's glare is cute. No, fuck cute. It's sexy as hell. My hand finds its way to her neck, and I begin stroking my thumb over the vein that bulges slightly.

Riley sucks her bottom lip in between her teeth, and I watch the move with rapt attention.

"Your type," she answers.

"Which is?" My mouth hovers over hers.

"Born wealthy as hell, powerful family, and good looking. You're all spoiled." She snorts. "I bet the day you were born your family made a huge announcement in the papers and all of that mess."

"You think so?"

"I don't doubt it at all."

It must be the alcohol in my system because I find myself shaking my head and telling her, "My father didn't know about us the day we were born."

"We?"

"My twin sister and me. We didn't even meet him until we were six years old."

Her forehead wrinkles. "Why?"

"Long story."

Her eyes move to look at something over my shoulder. When she meets my stare again, she says, "I bet he hates that he missed those first six years. I know the fe— must've been a surprise."

"It worked out."

"I answered your dare. Drink up." She pushes a drink into my hand.

I take the shot like a pro.

"Truth or dare?" I ask after tossing the glass onto the tray of a nearby waiter.

"It's my turn," she insists.

"So? Truth or dare?"

"See?" She slams a hand on her hip, drawing my eyes to the curvy shape of her body. Not for the first time, I admire her long legs and my hands twitch with the desire to trail my fingertips along every inch.

"Pick one," I order cupping her face.

"Dare."

My lips curl into a devious smile. I run the tip of my thumb over her mouth, pulling her bottom lip so low that it makes a popping sound when I let go.

"I dare you not to run," I say on a low growl right before I lean in and take her lips with mine.

A slight inhale notifies me of her surprise, but I don't pull away from her or the kiss. At first, the taste of whiskey is prominent. When I swipe my tongue along the roof of her mouth, she groans. A carnal need to possess her overtakes me. My hand makes its way to the curve of her hip, and I drag our bodies together, allowing her to feel my hard-on.

Riley wraps her arms around my neck. I get lost in the kiss, consumed whole. In fact, when she pulls back, I chase her, seeking more. Usually, such a move would've been unconscionable. I don't chase women, in any regard.

"Truth or dare?" she whispers against my lips.

"What do you think?"

She grins. "I dare you to show me the inside of your hotel room."

"Suite," I correct.

"Of course it is. Show me."

I pause, taking a minute to drink in the look in her eyes. She looks drunk but not from the alcohol. From our kiss. I can only imagine how she'll feel underneath me, our bodies tangled in sheets in my plush bed.

"Let's go."

CHAPTER 8

Riley

I wake up with a start. My heart starts beating rapidly from the realization that I'm not in my hotel room. There's expensive art on the walls, a clothing chest that I bet costs thousands, and the bed I'm laying in feels like a cloud sent from heaven.

My hotel room isn't a dump by any stretch of the imagination, but it isn't anything compared to this.

I attempt to sit up, and both my head and stomach tell me to keep my ass right where I am.

"What the hell?" I croak out while palming my forehead.

As if in response to my question a deep groan sounds beside me. Now is the moment I realize that I'm not alone. Reminders from the night before.

Kyle.

I'm in his hotel room. No, not room. Suite. His hotel suite.

"What the fuck?" he grumpily asks, sitting up. The irritable expression on his face tells me his body is also reminding him of the many, many shots we took last night.

I glance down, relieved to see I'm still wearing the dress I wore to the beach party. Kyle is also dressed in the pants and shirt he wore. A look past him to the armchair in the corner of the room reveals the suit jacket haphazardly swung over it.

"What are you doing in my room?" he demands, anger shooting from his eyes.

I jut my head back in offense but instantly regret the movement when a wave of nausea ensues. I'm not much of a drinker. Alcohol could sometimes be a trigger for my migraines. In addition, alcohol tends to make people loose lipped. For years, I worked on getting other people drunk to get them talking. Not the other way around.

Last night was different. I wanted to forget about the true reason I was in Miami. Let go of the fact that I'm being blackmailed to get whatever dirt I could on Kyle and his family's company.

"Why are you in my room?" Kyle grits out again, moving as far from me as he can.

"You invited me," I tersely reply. "Don't act like a bitch now," I snap because I don't like his attitude and I feel like crap.

"The only bitch..." He trails off with a grumble.

I had my right hand ready to slap the hell out of him if he even dared. He gets up from the bed, and I don't miss his stumble. Kyle quickly recovers and glares down at me.

Most people would wilt beneath the weight of that look. However, I push down the nausea and growing headache, square my shoulders, and stare at him right back.

"Don't bother twisting yourself in knots. It's not like we slept together or anything." I scoff and shudder as if the thought fills me with disgust. I rise from the bed.

After that kiss, we both were drunk with lust. I'd dared him to show me the inside of his hotel room, and he practically dragged me back here. Once we arrived, though, instead of ripping one another's clothes off, Kyle cracked open the very expensive bottle of whiskey from the bar. We continued our game of truth or dare, going shot for shot. Kyle always went with dare.

A memory from the night before surfaces. I dared him to tell me the craziest thing about his childhood. His answer caught me off-guard. He'd said that as a kid, he'd had visions—more like seeing a ghostly woman. Only he could see her. When he got older, his father told him that it was a great-great-grandmother of his that showed up when she was needed.

He'd said he hadn't seen her in years.

Emma. That was her name, according to Kyle.

I had to imagine that confession. A piece of me wants to ask about it, but the way he's looking at me keeps my mouth shut.

A muscle in Kyle's jaw jumps as he searches for something. I realize he's looking for his cell phone when he finds it on the floor. He places a call.

A beat later, he barks into the phone, "Get up here. Now," before hanging up and tossing it onto the bed.

Then he storms over to my side of the bed and takes me by the arm.

"It's time for you to leave," he demands, pulling me to stand.

"I can walk on my own." I rip my arm out of his hold, not liking the way my body warms from even his unfriendly touch. It's as if the Kyle from last night—the one who laughed and sang Britney Spears, and kissed like he couldn't get enough of me—never even existed.

That Kyle has been replaced by this grumpy ogre who wants nothing more than to get me out of his sight. I stuff down the bite of rejection that wells up in my stomach. I should've expected this.

"I need to get my shoes," I insist. A few moments of scanning the bedroom for the sandals I wore last night reveals my shoes are on the floor at the end of the bed.

"Let's go," he demands once my sandals are on. His words are punctuated by a banging on the suite's door.

Kyle yanks it open to reveal a massive guy dressed in all black—another one of his security guards.

"She needs to go back to her hotel room." Kyle takes my arm as if he's handing me off to the security guard.

"Screw you." I can't help the anger that wells up in me. It's my fault. I should've expected this reaction.

Kyle is the type who doesn't like getting close, he's untrusting and guarded. Last night he let his walls slip, as evidenced by the fact that I woke up in his bed with my clothes on.

He doesn't do intimacy beyond sex. And while we may not have shared our deepest, darkest thoughts last night, I recognize enough to see that he's regretting even that tiny amount of leeway he gave.

"Take her," he growls at the guard. He looks at his watch. "Shit. Make sure she's out of this hotel by the time I get out of the shower."

He turns his back on the guard and me, slamming the bedroom door behind him.

"Come with me, miss."

I don't bother protesting my indignation with the guard. He's simply doing his job. It's his spoiled brat of a boss that has me seeing red.

I grab the small clutch I carried last night and hold my head high as I exit the hotel suite. Unfortunately, my final thought as I leave is, *How in the hell am I supposed to get close to Kyle Townsend after this?*

CHAPTER 9

Riley

Three days after returning from Miami, I still haven't found a suitable way to approach Kyle or Townsend Industries. I've ignored calls from Dean Walsh for the past five days. Not the smartest move on my part since the bastard holds my freedom in his hands.

As I enter my office, the weight of the world feels like it sits on my shoulders.

"Good morning," Charlotte greets with a big smile on her face.

"Morning," I mumble before taking a sip of the coffee in my hand. I pass her the caramel latte I picked up for her on my way in.

"Thank you." She holds up the cup, wiggling it a little. "This is my second one of the day. I stayed up late studying." She chuffs. "To be honest, I thought I was going to be the one running late."

I give her a half smile. "I woke up late, and then Ladybug called first thing in the morning. She's freaking out over another exam she has next week. We talked for almost an hour."

Despite my dour mood, the memory of speaking with Eve fills me with joy.

"Hey, did you see this?" Charlotte turns her computer screen so that I can see it. On the screen is a business article. The headline reads "Townsend Pulls it Off."

I mouth the words as I read the article announcing Townsend's successful acquisition of Sam Waterson's medical supplies company.

"He did it," I mumble. Despite the cold way he turned his back on me and practically had me thrown out of this hotel room, a sense of pride comes over me for Kyle.

"The article says Kyle Townsend is going to oversee this merger." Charlotte whistles in admiration.

Clearing my throat, I straighten my back.

"How did your meeting with him go in Miami?" Charlotte asks. "You haven't mentioned it since you've been back."

My reply is cut off when the main office door opens. Dean Walsh enters with the broadest, phoniest smile on his face. My heart plummets.

"Can I help you?" Charlotte asks.

"I believe Riley is expecting me," he says, staring at me.

"Charlotte, hold my calls," I tell her. "Please follow me." I pivot on my heels and make a beeline to my office. A small sigh of relief escapes me when Dean doesn't say anything as he trails me.

"What the hell are you doing here?" I demand after shutting the door behind him.

He snarls in my direction. "Since you're ignoring my calls, you needed a reminder of whom you work for."

"Fuck you," I whisper-yell. "I *don't* work for you. Blackmail doesn't count as work."

"You would know. Maybe I should call Brendan to see how he feels about it. You know he was in Miami this past weekend, right?"

Panic briefly overcomes me as I wrack my mind, trying to recall seeing Brendan. But that's ridiculous. I would've remembered running into him.

"Don't worry. He didn't see you. He was too busy with his friends to go to most exhibits."

"That doesn't answer why you're in my office."

"This." He turns his phone screen to face me. It's the same article

Charlotte and I were reading about the Townsend and Waterson acquisition.

"They fucking acquired yet another multi-million-dollar company, and I had to learn about it from a fucking article!" Dean seethes, a small amount of spit flying out of his mouth. "I should've been informed the minute the dotted line was signed. I could've used it to—"

"To what?" I ask, having enough of his bullshit. "We both know you don't have the resources or power to make a real dent in the Townsend armor. And you damn sure don't have the clout you seem to think you do to avenge your father."

Dean's eyes widen as if surprised. His face turns beet red with anger. "What the hell did you say?"

"Yeah, you didn't think you were the only one who could do research, did you? Your father was sentenced to ten years in jail for corporate espionage. The fines alone crippled your family financially."

"Shut up!" he seethes, his eyes bulging to the point that he looks crazed. "They set my father up."

I did background research on Dean Walsh and his family ever since the moment he approached me. His father's healthcare company went under after he was exposed for corporate espionage. It occurred while the senior Walsh attempted to garner a merger with Townsend Industries. He didn't play his cards right and ended up in jail instead of on the winning side of that deal.

I let out a derisive laugh. "The evidence was pretty evident. Your father pled guilty and gave a heavily detailed confession to his crimes."

"He was bullied into that confession!" Dean insists. "And they still killed him."

I remain silent because Dean seems to believe what he's saying. The reports I came across attribute Dean's father's death to heart failure.

"And you're going to prove it." Dean sticks his finger in my face. "I want some evidence and fucking soon!"

"You gave me six months. These things take time."

"And you've wasted a month on bullshit. Get me the evidence to prove they're engaging in illegal business practices and they're murderers." He gets in my face, but I don't back down. "I don't give a shit what you have to do. I don't care if you need to suck off Kyle in his office. You fucking do it."

"Fuck you."

An ugly snarl breaks out on his face. "I won't wait forever, Riley. Your freedom and your niece depend on your next move."

My fists tighten at my sides at the mention of my niece. I hate Dean Walsh more than anyone in this world.

"Get out."

He steps back and glares at me before exiting my office. I don't realize my hand is shaking until I swipe my palm across my forehead.

"Are you all right?" Charlotte asks. "Are you getting one of your migraines?"

"No." I shake my head, trying to be reassuring even as I need to hold onto my office door for support. "I'm fine."

"Who was—" Charlotte's question breaks off when the door opens again.

I brace myself for another round with Dean Walsh, but it isn't him. My mind scrambles when Adam Bachleda walks into my office.

"Riley," he says, grinning. "I realize this is sudden, but I just discovered your office is actually on my way into the Townsend building." He turns to the man standing behind him. "This is my assistant, Anthony Rogers."

When Anthony extends his hand, I shake it.

"Pleasure to meet you," he says.

"Mine as well." I'm confused but do my best to shake off my emotions from my encounter with Dean Walsh.

"Adam, how are you? What are you doing here?" I ask the member of the Townsend Board of Directors.

"Well, my colleagues and I were intrigued by the talk you gave over dinner in Miami. We have a proposition for you."

"A proposition?" I repeat to make sure I hear him correctly.

He nods. "Yes, can we speak in your office?"

CHAPTER 10

Kyle

Today's the day, I think to myself as I fix my tie in the mirror of my office's private bathroom. Two weeks since returning from Miami, getting the acquisition papers signed by Sam Waterson, and in twenty minutes, I have a meeting with the board of directors.

Today I become appointed as the chief operating officer of Townsend Industries.

There's no doubt who that title belongs to. No one in this company can deny me, not after the Waterson deal.

I smooth my hand over the tailored suit jacket and get ready to grab a few files from my desk to bring with me to the twenty-fifth-floor boardroom.

The phone on my desk buzzes.

"Yes, Mike," I answer my assistant.

"Adam has finally arrived, and your father should be calling in five minutes. We're all set."

I nod even though he can't see me. "I'll be there in two minutes."

All of the board members will be in attendance for this meeting. Though my father is still away in Europe handling our foreign interests, he'll be on a video call on the large screen in the boardroom.

I opt to take the three flights of stairs up to the twenty-fifth floor to go over my Waterson strategy in my head. I know the board will have questions on how I plan to handle this merger. It's bullshit. They know as well as I do I know what the hell I'm doing.

But they need to prove to themselves they're doing their job.

I enter the boardroom and nod and shake hands with the nine board members. There are also a number of the VPs from various divisions of the company. I'm sure Uncle Joshua would be in attendance as well if he weren't also out of town on business. As COO of Townsend, I'll also have a great deal to oversee when it comes to the real estate operations of the company.

It's a huge undertaking but one I was born and bred for. I'm ready.

"Kyle," Adam Bachleda begins once we're all seated. "Thank you for joining us."

I steel my face because why the fuck is he thanking me? This is my job.

"Aaron should be with us any moment."

As soon as the sentence is out of his mouth, the huge screen mounted on the wall draws all of our attention. A beat later, my father's usual scowl fills the screen.

"Aaron," Adam says, his disposition seemingly the opposite of my father's.

You have to know my father to decipher there's actually pride shining in his hazel eyes that mirror my own.

"Adam." My father nods, then greets all of the board members. "Someone's missing," he says.

I look around the room. All of the board members are accounted for, the VPs are all in attendance and even their assistants. *No one is missing.*

That thought ends up punctuated by a knock on the door.

"Here she is now," Adam says as he strides to the door. "Thank you, Linda." He nods at the twenty-fifth-floor receptionist.

A second later in walks Riley Martin.

"Our guest has just arrived," Adam says cheerily.

I glare at Mike, my assistant, giving him the *what the hell is she doing here?* look. He shakes his head as if saying he has no idea either.

"What is this?" My voice comes out louder and more demanding than intended but fuck manners. What the hell is she doing in my boardroom?

"Kyle," Adam starts, "you're already acquainted with Riley Martin." He gestures toward her.

I don't even look her way. "Adam," I say through gritted teeth, "what is going on?"

"Kyle," Walt, another board member, calls. "We'll get there. Why don't we get started with the meeting? We have a great deal to cover."

I look at the screen at my father who watches everything like a hawk but doesn't say anything. He knew this was going to happen. He knew she would be here. Nothing gets past him.

I can barely contain my anger. Even as Adam, Walt, and the other members of the board all congratulate me on a job well done getting the Waterson deal done.

"I don't need your congratulations," I say bluntly. "What I need—what Townsend needs," I correct, "is a COO who is going to have the best interest of this company in mind. The role has sat unfilled for over a month now."

"Yes, that's why we're all here," Tim, another board member, says. He looks around the room. "I think I speak for all of us—"

"No one speaks for me," my father interrupts. But he nods at Tim for him to continue.

Tim clears his throat and sits up straighter. "We have all agreed," he briefly peers up at the screen at my father then back to me, "... that it is in the best interest of Townsend Industries to appoint you as the interim chief operating officer."

"What did you say?" My voice is stern, unbendable.

"You've been appointed COO, Kyle," Adam says and places a hand on my shoulder.

I glare at his hand, and he quickly removes it. "That's not what he said," I say. "You used the word *interim* COO." I stare at Tim as well as the other board members.

Finally, my hard gaze comes to land on my father.

"Yes," he finally says. "The board and I agreed that your great work in closing the Waterson deal proved you're deserving of the role of COO—"

"On an interim basis," I interrupt my father.

All eyes around the room fall on me because no one interrupts my father while he's speaking.

Fuck that though.

What the hell is going on? Interim is the same thing as provisional.

"Are you still interviewing for the position? Is that what the title of interim COO is about?"

A few throats around the room clear.

"We, the board, believe that this is the best way to transition you into the role long-term," Adam says. "The interim role will last for the next three to six months. At which time, you'll also have to agree to work with Riley Martin here to assist you with the onboarding of Sam Waterson's employees during the acquisition."

"Excuse me?" I demand, rising to my feet. I barely control my anger as I glare around the room. Lastly, my eyes land on Riley. She meets my stare head on—coffee irises meeting my hazel ones.

"Is this what you two were talking about in Miami?" I ask both Adam and Riley, but my attention remains on her. I think back to all of those moments in Miami when she looked too fucking chummy with Adam Bachleda and a few other members of the board.

Were they all plotting this shit behind my back?

Another wave of anger and guilt assault my gut as I remember back to waking up next to Riley that final morning in Miami. I disliked how warm and pleasant it felt as my eyes popped open. Her vanilla scent filled my room for hours after she left. I hated how my body longed for it.

"Kyle," Riley is the only one seemingly brave enough to speak into the silence of my outrage. "I know you were worried about my inexperience. However, I can assure you that Martin Consulting is more than capable of handling this transition with the care it deserves."

A muscle in my jaw ticks. Despite my ire, my body reacts to her level of confidence.

I don't acknowledge her. "I don't need a consultant."

Heads look from one to the other.

"The decision is final," my father says. "You are Townsend's new COO on an interim basis for the duration of the first stage of this merger. During that time, you will work with Ms. Martin to carry out the transition. At the end of that period of time, your performance will be evaluated, and a final decision will be made on your role as COO."

"What the—"

"If that is all," my father cuts me off. "Gentleman," he calls the attention of the board to a separate issue, leaving me reeling.

My head spins throughout the remainder of the meeting. I barely notice when my father's image disappears from the screen and people start filing out. Mike says something to me before making his exit, leaving Riley and me alone in the boardroom.

I don't say anything as I glare at her across the table. She remains silent as well.

I cock my head to the side.

"You finally got what you wanted," I say, my top lip curling.

She shakes her head. For a brief moment, there's something akin to sadness, shame, maybe, in her eyes.

"I never wanted this." Her voice is resigned, slightly solemn even.

"Did you screw Bachleda to get them to hire you?"

She pulls back as if my question offended her. I'm not buying it. Her offense turns to anger.

"I didn't need to screw with you to get this job. What makes you think I needed to sleep with Adam?"

I grit my teeth. I don't like her mentioning another man's name. I tell myself it's because I'm pissed that I'm forced to work with her as the fucking *interim* COO. But I can hear my subconscious mind calling me a fucking liar.

"Look, while this may be unexpected on your part," Riley continues, "you're just going to have to trust me."

"Trust you?"

She nods sharply. "Yes, trust that I know how to do my job because I do. My record speaks for itself."

I stand abruptly, almost knocking my chair over. I storm over to her side of the table and get directly in her face. My position is simply an intimidation tactic but her vanilla scent punches me in the gut. A completely involuntary movement on my part, draws me an inch closer. So fucking close that a strand of her hair grazes the tip of my nose. I inhale deeply.

She's so fucking beautiful without even trying.

Riley's breathing becomes noticeably heavier. I drop my eyes to that vein in her neck that beats faster.

"Do not play with me, Riley. You will not like the consequences." My voice is low and harsh, but an undertone of huskiness accompanies it as well.

Riley peers down at her hands on the table for a moment before looking back up at me.

"Maybe it's you who shouldn't play with me," she boldly counters before standing.

I stand to my full height as she gathers her belongings and saunters to the door. My eyes fall to the sway of her hips.

She pauses and turns to me. "You know, in Miami you told me there was never, nor will there ever be, a time a woman ended up in your bed and your boardroom." She smiles from ear to ear. "Looks like hell just froze over," she finishes before exiting the room.

* * *

"Get my father on a call. Now!" I seethe as I brush past Mike's desk.

A second after I slam the door closed, there's a knock on it.

"What?" I yell as I yank it open.

Mike startles, looking nervous. "Um, phone call or video call?"

"Video."

"What if he's busy?"

"Then tell whatever assistant answers on his behalf they no longer have a fucking job if my father isn't on my line in the next five minutes."

Do I have the authority to fire my father's assistant? Probably not. Do I give a fuck?

No.

If he's not on my line in five minutes, I will follow through on that threat.

Three minutes later, my computer screen alerts me that I have a video call coming through. I answer to see my father's stern face staring back at me.

"I was expecting this call," he says calmly.

"You know what I wasn't expecting?" I demand. "To be blindsided like that. What was that?"

"You were appointed as Townsend's new COO."

"On an *interim* basis." I spit out the word interim as if it burns my tongue. "Not to mention that my permanent placement is contingent upon working with Riley." I stop when I see my father's eyes narrow on the word Riley.

"Adam, as well as the other board members who were present in Miami, all spoke highly of Ms. Martin." He sits forward, his hands clasped on the desk in front of him.

"Sam Waterson mentioned her as well. They all say the two of you appeared as if you had some interesting conversations. So …" he draws out that word, "how come you never mentioned her?"

Hell no. I'm not getting caught in that trap.

"She was irrelevant." The lie burns as it comes out, but I manage to not choke on it.

He lifts an eyebrow.

"This isn't about her." I start to pace in front of my desk. "Do you not trust me? Is that what this is about?"

"Son," he starts, but I stop him with a shake of my head.

"You could've stopped all of that. Your word is final. You know it, and I know it. You could've appointed me COO weeks ago. The board would've gone along with it."

As the third generation Townsend to run this company, my father's say goes a long way.

"They might have," he admits. "Maybe not. Either way, I made my decision."

"Then it's true. You don't trust me." Guilt fills the hole in the pit of my stomach. I remember when I almost cost my father this company.

I worked my ass off over the years to redeem myself, but it appears my father, of all people, still lacks faith in my ability to make the right decisions.

I turn away from the screen because I don't want him to see the hurt I know I can't hide from my face.

"Don't you ever say that again," he insists, drawing my attention back to the screen. "There is no one on this Earth who believes in you more than me."

"There is one more," my mother's voice cuts in, and my fists tighten. She's off screen, but my father's eyes move to stare at something behind the camera, and I know she's in his office. She's never far from his side.

"Sorry, sweetness," he mumbles. My mother is the only person my father apologizes to. "After your mother, there is no one who believes in you more."

"Then why do I need a consultant to oversee this merger?" I ask.

"We all have weaknesses. Areas of growth where having a second pair of eyes can help."

"I have enough help. I don't need anyone overseeing me."

My father frowns. "Is this about the interim position or the fact that you have to work with Ms. Martin?"

I look out of the window of my office, avoiding my father's stare before answering. "I can do my job."

"Then prove it."

I turn back to face him.

"Listen, son. Times change. The industry is going through another shift. You're poised to be at the forefront of the market shift and you can lead Townsend into the next era. But you will need the right guidance."

"I get that from you," I insist.

He nods. "You'll also need more assistance to become truly attuned to your blind spots."

"You didn't have any consultants. Why the hell do I need any?"

His lips purse as he looks off screen again. "Because I want you to be better than me."

That feels like a punch to the gut. My father is the epitome of success for me. There is no way to be better than him, in my eyes.

"You'll work with Ms. Martin and ensure the success of this merger."

I continue to pace in front of my desk, knowing the hard edge of his voice means that he won't budge on this. I don't even have a real fucking reason why I don't want to work with Riley. I damn sure can't tell my dad that for just a split second when I awoke with her in my bed, I didn't want her to leave.

And I hadn't even fucked her.

"That's enough talk of work for now," My mother's voice pierces my thoughts. She appears on screen, taking a seat in my father's lap. "How's my baby doing? Are you eating enough?"

I swallow down my previous thoughts and shift my focus. "Hey, Ma."

"Ma," she mocks, making me smile despite myself. "Who is this woman that has you so upset?"

I glance at my father as he strokes his hands up and down the length of her arms. His attention is on her, not me.

"Don't look at your father. What's her name?" She leans in.

"No one."

"That's an interesting name."

"She's just ... someone who they hired. Anyway, are you enjoying Paris?"

"Don't try to change the subject. Is she pretty?"

Too damn pretty for my own good.

Thankfully, I keep the words from spilling out. Though, my mom cocks her head to the side as if I did answer out loud.

"Is Stasi enjoying her cooking classes?" My sixteen-year-old sister, Anastasia, is the baby of the family. She's taking some special class in Paris for the next few months. Initially, she and my mother were supposed to go, but there was no way in hell my father would be separated from my mother for that long, hence why he opted to oversee the annual European trip himself this year. Last year, I was the one who went on said work trip.

My mother frowns. "You're so damn tightlipped. You get that from him." She waves her head in my father's direction.

My father mumbles something in her ear. She swats his hand and turns back to me. These two's intimacy would disgust me if I weren't used to it by now.

"Just tell me, is she pretty?" She smiles conspiratorially.

"Yes, very," I admit.

My mother's smile widens. "That's nice. Maybe you should ask her out. I can't remember the last time you brought a woman home."

I snort. "Never."

"That's right. You've never brought a woman home. Are you a virgin?"

I choke on my spit. "Mom?"

A wrinkle appears on her forehead. "What? It's nothing to be ashamed of. Are you waiting for marriage?"

"Definitely not. Because I'm not getting fuc— married," I insist. "And now since the board went behind my back to hire Riley, there's definitely nothing happening between the two of us. Lest I expose myself to a possible sexual harassment lawsuit." I grind my teeth together in anger but I don't know what it stems from.

"How is Stasi doing?" I ask, attempting to divert my mother's attention again.

"I'm right here!" my youngest sister's voice chirps. A second later, she appears on the screen, taking up the space beside my father. "Hi, Kyle," she gushes animatedly. "Ralph says hi, too!" she says of the bulldog she's had since she was a kid.

In her usual way, Stasi takes over the conversation. It takes me close to fifteen minutes, and many promises to call her over the weekend, to get Stasi to let me hang up. Though, I am happy her interruption ceased the weird questioning from my mother.

My mother's constantly hinting that she wants me to date more and have more of a life outside of work.

Whatever.

I don't have time for that. Not when the legacy of our family rests on my shoulders. And especially not when the last person outside of our family circle I trusted almost led to the destruction of our family's company.

I refuse to let that ever happen again.

All I have to do is what I know how to do. Steer this acquisition the way it needs to go and earn my title as the official COO. I can do that and ignore Riley Martin in the process.

CHAPTER 11

Riley

A week after that almost disastrous board meeting, I've barely seen Kyle. The man spends hours at the office, arriving before everyone and leaving hours after the official workday ends. However, most of that time, he's either locked away in his office or in a series of closed-door meetings that I'm not invited to sit in on.

That all changes today. Which is why I'm carrying two bags of takeout from the Japanese restaurant across the street from Townsend. Mike, Kyle's assistant, let it slip that Kyle frequents said restaurant when he has to remain close to the office for lunch.

"Whatever's in the bag smells delicious," Barry, one of the marketing directors, says as I step off the elevator.

"Are you a fan of sushi?" I hold up one of the bags.

Though Barry is relatively skinny, he does have a bit of a pot belly. One he pats in response to my inquiry. "There's not much I don't like."

I laugh and offer him one of the extra California rolls I picked up. Barry ends up mentioning the Waterson acquisition from a marketing angle. That leads to a conversation with three other colleagues as I discuss a few ways to approach the topic.

"I know Waterson's people are nervous," Barry mentions. "I've gotten a few emails about overlapping positions already. Some are thinking their roles will become obsolete."

"That's typical thinking when it comes to these types of things. But we all know you could never become obsolete, Barry."

That garners a few laughs from everyone. Among the serious back and forth, there are jokes here and there.

"What the hell is going on?" Kyle's deep voice breaks up the rhythm of the conversation.

Barry clears his throat and looks like a school kid who's been thoroughly scolded by his teacher instead of a man twice Kyle's age. The atmosphere turns frigid upon Kyle's approach. More than one of the employees I was joking with makes up a lame reason to excuse themselves.

Kyle's unwavering gaze remains on me until we're the final two in the hallway.

"This is a place of business, not a nightclub, Ms. Martin."

I blink. "Ms. Martin?"

"Is there a problem?" His voice is devoid of any real emotion. I wouldn't say I like this version of Kyle. It's the attitudinal equivalent of the stiff arm. No matter how inappropriate these feelings are, a piece of me yearns for the Kyle I got to enjoy on the beach in Miami. The one that showed me a glimpse of his lighter side.

I shrug casually. "I mean, you sleep in a guy's bed one night and suddenly become *Ms. Martin.*"

His lips form a thin line, and he moves directly in front of me, getting within an inch of my face. "Blame that night on the alcohol. Nothing more." His words are betrayed by the way he eyes my lips.

My skin warms from the way he lets his gaze meander my body.

"If you say so ..." I trail off and step back to hold up the bags of food. "I thought today might be a great time for you and me to have lunch together. I've gone over the poll I took of your previous department—"

His scowl deepens. "What poll?"

"The poll you would know about if you responded to my meeting requests."

"I'm busy and don't have time for your meetings."

"Not even if I think I've figured out a way you could cut costs by twenty percent?"

He wants to call bullshit. I can see it. But Kyle is a businessman at heart. And that number I spat out is too tempting for anyone to turn down.

"Let's do lunch." I wave the bag in the air. "I've already booked boardroom three," I say as I saunter toward the boardroom.

Kyle follows.

I take time to unpack dishes of sushi rolls, seaweed salad, and bottles of water that I purchased for our meal. Kyle sits on the opposite side of the table from me, facing the door.

"You must be busy," I say as I hand Kyle a plate with a salmon roll. Mike told me it was one of his go-to's. "It's been a week, and I have barely seen you."

He peers up at me, his expression muted. "Did you think the COO has time to laugh around the water cooler all day?"

"Ouch," I mock, sounding unbothered. I place my plate down in front of me and fold my arms. "Kyle, I'm not your enemy here."

"You're not my friend either."

"Fine. I'm not that either. But I am your colleague. For now. You could at least try to make this work."

He uses the wooden chopsticks to feed himself a portion of the salmon roll. I watch the movement of his jaw as he chews, noting how the sunlight hitting the hairs of his beard shows their blond coloring. From this angle, the freckles that dot the ridge of this nose and upper cheeks also stand out.

"Tell me about this twenty percent expense decrease," he says.

I sit up and remove my tablet out of my bag. Then, I pull up the spreadsheets and the poll data I took over the past week.

"Before you were promoted to director of operations, you were head of finance and accounting."

He nods.

I explain how those departments performed well under his leadership, but their turnover grew yearly.

"Trimming the fat," he says before popping another portion of his roll into his mouth.

"Could be," I state flippantly. "Or there's a bigger issue."

He narrows his eyes on me.

I cock my head to the side. "Are you always so cold to your employees?"

He doesn't even pretend to be offended. "I'm not here to make friends."

"Right." I nod. "But you are here to make money. Or at least, to ensure the success of Townsend Industries, correct?"

When he nods in the affirmative, I go in for the kill.

"Do you know why Sam Waterson's staff is so loyal to him?"

He doesn't ask, but he looks at me expectantly.

"Because he's shown that he cares about them. As people. I interviewed employees from assistants to VPs. They all say the same thing; Sam cares about them, and they're afraid they won't get that same level of care at Townsend."

"We're not in the business of babysitting."

"No one is asking you to be." I shake my head, feeling flustered. Rubbing my fingers across my forehead, I try to push out the tightness forming behind my eyes. Between Dean Walsh hounding me almost daily for answers and Kyle's bullheadedness, I'm surprised I haven't had a full-blown migraine attack yet.

"We pay our employees above market rate."

"That's a start," I concede. "That works toward Townsend's favor, but people need more than just money."

"You're implying that an increased benefits package would boost employee morale and reduce turnover? That's your bright plan, Ms. Consultant?"

"I'm going to ignore the mocking censure in that question and get directly to my point."

"Please do."

"You suck as a manager."

That garners his full attention. The chopsticks in his hand stop halfway to his mouth.

"The employees at Townsend are nervous about keeping their jobs. They want to hear from the new COO, and you've been locked in your office for days. If you want this merger to go smoothly, you'll take your head out of your ass and get down to a level your employees can relate to. Not as the son of the CEO, but as their colleague."

Kyle's eyes narrow on me. "I did not get this job because I'm my father's son."

"Could've fooled me," I goad. Kyle keeps a brick wall up around him and anyone else. But his façade slips slightly whenever the mere mention that he got to where he is because of his last name is brought up.

"You're skating on thin ice, Riley."

My thighs clench.

"What fun is skating if you only remain in the safe part of the rink?"

Something sparks in his eyes. An electric bolt shoots through my body, startling me. I look down to find Kyle's fingers gently caressing my hand. I doubt he even realizes he's doing it since his eyes remain locked on my face.

"What is it, Kyle, that made you so tightly wound?" I don't mean to ask the question out loud.

"Do you want to know?" he asks.

I nod, unable to form words.

He leans in. "Someone I trusted fucked me over." His hold tightens on my hand. It's not painful, but I take it for the warning it is. "Don't make the same mistake he did, Riley."

I don't have time to respond before Kyle gets up, packs up his lunch, and exits.

A part of me wants to feel rejected yet again. But the spot on my hand where his thumb was making tiny circles still buzzes from his touch. The unguarded look in his eyes that lasted half a second as he watched me chew my lunch is burned into my memory.

Kyle wants me almost as badly as I want him.

That's a complication I cannot afford to get entangled with.

CHAPTER 12

*K*yle

"Goddammit," I grunt as the point of my pencil snaps, causing another smudge on my notepad. I toss the damn thing across my office.

"Yes," I answer the phone on my desk.

"Kyle, there's a Brendan Chastain on the line for you."

I pause, trying to recall who the hell Brendan Chastain is. The name sounds familiar.

"He says you two went to college together?" Mike sounds uncertain. "You're old friends."

I snort. Mike knows I don't have any friends.

But the name rings a bell. "The wannabe actor?"

"I believe so. He says he worked with Andreas a few years ago on a pilot."

With a roll of my eyes. "Tell him I'm busy." Motherfuckers always think they can use a family member's name to get me on the phone or in a meeting. I remember Brendan from college, but barely. He was a few years ahead of me. We most certainly weren't friends.

I hang up with Mike, still feeling agitated.

As if to add insult to injury, another round of Riley's laughter spills from the hallway. I know it's coming from her. In the two weeks she's been consulting for Townsend, I've involuntarily come to memorize her sounds.

Even as I've worked tirelessly to keep my distance.

My anger urges me to storm out into the hallway and demand that everyone gets back to their damn offices and do some work. Yet, I remain in my chair.

I know any outburst I have will directly result from Riley's effect on me. I've already had more than one of the VPs asking me about Riley. When Gregg, VP of finance, asked, I almost took his fucking head off. That was the last time anyone asked me a direct question about her that wasn't solely work related.

That doesn't mean they aren't asking her directly, my subconscious reminds me.

More sounds of laughter from the hallway. My entire body tenses.

I should've fucked her in Miami when I had the chance. I would've worked her out of my system, and these bouts of jealousy wouldn't be occurring now.

Are you sure?

I shrug off the doubtful tone of my subconscious and stand to roll my shoulders. My entire body is tight with unexplainable tension. Yes, I've worked twelve hours, three out of the last four days, but that isn't ordinary for me. My morning workouts remain on par with every other morning workout. So why the fuck am I so tense?

I ponder going back to writing the notes I wanted to follow up on from an earlier meeting. Yet, the words on the paper have been swimming in front of my eyes for the past hour.

I need to go for a walk. I'm sure when I get back, I'll be able to focus more clearly.

By the time I exit my office, the hallway has cleared out. A quick check of my watch tells me it's five after five. Regular closing hours for a business, but I'll be in the office for at least a few more hours.

"Leaving so early?"

I spin on my heels at the sound of Riley's voice. I quickly scan her in the light brown, wide-leg pants and black top. Her makeup is light, her lips slightly tinted. She's not wearing red lipstick, and part of me wants to ask her why not, while the other is happy that she doesn't wear that color at work.

I can only imagine whom I'll have to fucking fire if they see her in that shade of lipstick.

The thought pisses me off.

"Going for a walk," I reply and turn away to head to the elevator. Not even a beat later, I hear the sound of high heels behind me. I stop abruptly, and Riley almost walks right into me.

"Where are you going?" I ask, narrowing my eyes at her as she stands next to me in front of the elevator.

"We're going on a walk," she says cheerily.

"*I'm* going for a walk … to clear my head." I don't know why I give her the added explanation.

Her smile increases. "Is that something you do often? Take breaks throughout the day? It's a good habit to have. You know, I read a recent study …" She continues going even as I step onto the elevator, following me.

I should tell her to stop talking, but I can't help but enjoy the melodic sound of her voice.

"It's a coping strategy," I admit. "For my dyslexia." I punch the button for the ground floor.

That gets her to stop talking. *Why did I say that out loud?*

"I didn't know," she says.

I shrug. "It's not a secret." As we step off the elevator, I turn to her. "And I'm not ashamed of it."

"Why would you be?" Her question sounds sincere enough.

My shoulders relax a little as Riley falls in step with me. As soon as we're out on the sidewalk, I move to the outside so that I'm closest to the street.

"Where are we going?" she asks.

"There's a park a few blocks from here."

"Oh, that pretty one with the duck pond," she gushes.

I give her a sideways glance.

"I've gone out there a few times with a few Townsend employees during our lunch breaks."

"With who?" My voice comes out sharper than intended.

She doesn't notice or read much into it as she shrugs. "Uh." She taps her chin. "Sandy from accounting, Gene from marketing, Sherri from real estate, and Bethanny from Sam Waterson's finance department."

I sigh in relief, not hearing any men in that mix. Unless she left their names out on purpose. If I find out Barry from marketing has been sniffing around her during lunch breaks, he will have a problem.

"Do you like pretzels?" she asks as we approach the park.

I raise an eyebrow, and she nods at the pretzel stand far from us.

"I only ate half of my lunch, and I'm starving. Indulge me."

I find myself following her to the pretzel stand. Yet, when she pulls her wallet out of her bag, I cover her hand with my own. My fingertips burn from the skin-to-skin contact. For the briefest moment, Riley's eyes meet mine. When her eyelids widen, I wonder if she can see how much I want her in the depths of my eyes.

"I got it." I hand the guy money for our pretzels and don't bother to wait for the change.

"This is early for you to leave the office, huh?" Riley says in between bites. "It's not even six o'clock, and you're out of the office. Must feel like a vacation day for you," she comments.

"You notice how long I stay in the office?"

She glances away. "It's part of my job to notice everything happening in the office. Well, not everything. But part of my role is to acknowledge company culture and whatnot. That includes dedication from employees. Things like that."

"And?"

"What?" she asks with a lifted eyebrow.

"What've you noticed so far?" I watch her as I chew my pretzel, suddenly realizing how hungry I am. And it's not only for the pretzel.

"Now you want to know?"

"Tell me," I order.

"Employees at Townsend take pride in their work. For many, it's an honor to be hired at Townsend Industries. But ..." she side-eyes me, "burnout is a factor. Particularly in the executive suite. With hours like yours, I would say it's inevitable."

I grunt. "I'm fine."

"Yeah, but for how long?"

I shake my head. "That social engineering shit you mentioned in Miami is bullshit. All employees need to do is show up, do their job, and get paid."

"That's all you think they do?" She comes to a stop in front of me.

"I know it is."

Her eyes narrow. "You're too young to be so cynical."

"You're too old to be so naïve."

She props her hand on her hip. "Did you just call me *old?*" She honestly sounds offended. "We're the same damn age."

A grin spreads across my face. "You're not old, Riley," I reply. "But it's time to take the rose-colored glasses off. Employees are a valuable resource for Townsend, but they're just that. They'll never take pride in Townsend like I do because they don't have to."

She throws up her hands. "You might be right about that. However, it doesn't mean they're out to get you. It's okay to let your walls down a little around them. Make them believe they're a part of something special. Sometimes people are put in bad situations, and they make mistakes."

I frown. "You learned all of that from your psych degree?"

Her eyebrows pop. "You know my degree is in psychology?"

I nod. "Bachelor's in psychology from Williamsport U, with a double minor in sociology and business administration. Started Martin and Associates three years ago doing consulting work for small and mid-size corporations, mainly in tech and healthcare." I look pointedly at her. "Did I get that right?"

"What else have you learned about me?" There's something in her voice I can't identify.

"You come highly recommended based on your ability to read people and situations clearly for executives interested in securing a deal. So, you learned to read people from your psych degree?"

She looks away. "Partially. I'm a people watcher. I always have been interested in what makes them tick. We like to think people always make the most logical choice, but we fail to consider various factors."

"Such as?"

"Hundreds of things. Past trauma, emotional upheaval. Heck, a bad hair day can have someone making an irrational choice."

I snort. "A fucking bad hair day?"

"You mock, but it's true. Humans aren't machines. Our emotions effect our decision-making. This is why it's important to consider some of those factors when working with others. And, in your case, running a company."

"I'm not running the company."

"Yet," she quickly adds. "That is your end goal, right?"

I eye her warily. She makes me want to share more than I ought to. No, it's not a secret that I aim to be at the helm of Townsend Industries. Yet, she has me wanting to reveal that my reasoning is to make my family proud and prove that every privilege they've given me over the years has been worth it.

And to show them that I can be trusted not to fuck it up. Not after I trusted the wrong person, and it blew up in my face.

"What's it to you?" I ask Riley instead of telling her all of that.

"It's my job as a consultant to further your company's goals. Besides..." She hesitates and looks away. "No one, even if they receive a nice paycheck, likes to feel like they're being used." There's that tone in her voice again. The one I remember from Miami when she told me her deepest fear.

Riley dips her head, but I catch her by the chin, lifting her face so that I can see her eyes. She blinks, and the sadness in those depths is gone. But the tightness in my chest remains.

"Tell me more about this social engineering bullshit," I say suddenly.

She takes a step back, breaking our contact. I do my best to ignore the sense of loss that floods my senses.

"Uh." She glances around and smiles when she spots something behind me. "It's not bullshit, and I will show you."

With that, she moves around me and makes a beeline for one of the most expensive hotels in Williamsport.

"Follow me."

Like a sailor guided by the luminescence of a lighthouse, I follow.

* * *

RILEY

We stop on the sidewalk directly across the street from the main entrance of the Renaissance Hotel. I watch for a few beats, noting the stream of people who walk past the hotel since it's still rush hour.

I turn to Kyle and almost slip off the sidewalk when I realize how close he stands behind me. His hands on my waist stop me from falling.

Quickly, I re-gather myself and ask, "Truth or dare?"

"I have a shit ton of work to do. I don't have time for games." Even as he says this, his hands tighten around my waist.

"This is work related. Truth or dare?"

He frowns.

"Dare," I say for him. He would never choose truth. "I dare you to watch me break into one of those hotel suites."

His eyebrows quirk, but then a glint of interest enters those hazel pupils. All of a sudden, I find myself wondering how long it would take for me to get tired of staring into his eyes.

Never.

"Dare," he says.

"What? Right." I shake myself out of silly thoughts.

I turn to face the hotel and contemplate how to approach.

"Let's go," he says, starting for the hotel.

"Wait." I press my palm to his hard chest and instantly regret that move. My mind scrambles. "You can't come with me."

"Why not?" he asks while scowling.

"Because you're Kyle freaking Townsend," I remind him. "You've probably had countless work lunches and dinners in this hotel."

He looks between me and the hotel. "So?"

"So? They'll know you and will roll out the red carpet. I'm trying to prove to you that even a lowly consultant like myself can get past this hotel's intense security."

"Then you want me to stay here? How the hell do I know you won't lie, sit in the lobby for a while, and then come out and tell me you made it to one of the exclusive suites."

Of course he doesn't trust me. He shouldn't, but that's not the point.

"Give me your phone." I hand out my hand.

"No."

I suck my teeth. "You're so damn difficult. Fine." I pull a pen out of my bag and take his hand. I write my cell phone number on his palm. "Call me in five minutes."

He parts his mouth, but I put my finger to his lips to shush him. "Just follow along. Call me in five minutes."

I wait until he nods to remove my finger.

As I head into the hotel lobby, I search out the different employees behind the counter. I decide to approach the employee who looks the youngest and least confident.

"Oh my god," I say as soon as I get to the counter. My outburst startles her. I drop my eyes to read the name tag on her vest. "Callie.

"You have to help me," I insist, looking at her nervously. "I just started as the executive assistant for Mr. Caldron. Do you know him?"

She shakes her head.

"How could you ..." I trail off. "He's only the CEO of WineCorp. We're in Williamsport for the big wine festival that's this weekend. You know about it, right?" I gesture to the huge sign in the middle of the lobby welcoming visitors to the Williamsport Wine Festival.

"You have to help me." I take Callie's arm to increase the desperate look I'm going for. "Mr. Caldron left an important file in his suite. He *needs* this file for his meeting today. I told him I would come back and get it for him. But of course, I forgot to get the keycard from him. He's waiting at our meeting spot, thirty minutes away. I know you don't normally do this, but is there any way ..."

I trail off to let her figure out what I'm asking.

Callie bites her bottom lip and looks to her left at her other colleague. Thankfully, the other employee is busy with another huge group of patrons.

"Please, it's the Luxe Room. I just got this job and cannot afford to lose it. Mr. Caldron is very demanding."

She starts typing something on her computer. "W-We don't have a reservation under that name."

While she's glancing at the computer screen, I hang my hand with my phone in it over the desk. From this angle, I can read the reflection of her screen.

"He never books under his name. Can you try Emerson? It's his wife's maiden name. A little trick he uses for privacy," I say, able to read the name from the reflection in my phone.

She nods but then straightens. "Um, well."

"Please, I'm—" I hold up a finger when my phone rings. "Hello? Mr. Caldron?" I look at Callie as I answer Kyle on the other end.

"Who the fuck—"

"Yes, sir. I'm at the hotel. The problem is, I-I ..." I turn desperate, seeking eyes to Callie and mouth. *'Please.'*

She nods, and I know I'm in. She quickly writes down the hotel suite's elevator code and opens a lock drawer handing me a keycard.

'Thank you,' I mouth and wave. "Yes, sir. I'm on my way up to your suite now," I say as I walk away just for good measure.

When I reach the elevators that lead up to the suites, I tell Kyle, "Meet me in the Luxe Room," before hanging up.

The elevator ride is short. Less than ten minutes after entering the hotel, I walk into one of the most fascinating suites I've ever been in. By the bathrobe strewn over the back of the couch, I guess the actual guests of this room are out for the day.

Still, I should spend as little time here as possible.

"Shit," I startle when a knock on the door. My phone buzzes with a text from Kyle.

210-900-0000: **Open up.**

"Welcome," I say as I pull the suite door open.

Kyle's expression remains unimpressed, but there's a spark in his eyes.

"Not bad, considering I got in for free, huh?" Grinning, I hold my arms out wide. "That's one hell of a view." It looks down onto the park where we just were.

"The suite two floors up is even better," he comments.

"I assume you've stayed in the Grande Suite then," I say with a roll of my eyes.

"Once or twice." He's so casual about it. One night in one of these suites is more than most people make in an entire month.

"You've made it into the suite. Congratulations. What were you trying to prove?" He follows me as I move around the suite, being nosy.

"It proves that social engineering works. This hotel probably spends millions on security, but in less than ten minutes, I was able to get into one of their most exclusive rooms."

"The hotel employee that let you up here should be fired."

My sharp intake of air pierces the quiet of the room. "No, she shouldn't," I say, guilt peppering my words. "She looked young. If I were to guess, I might even say she's new to the job. She was doing what she thought was the right thing. Do you know how many clients probably come in here making outrageous demands?

"I wanted to show you that social engineering can work anywhere. This is why the new COO needs to make more of an effort to get to know his employees. Not just the VPs and executives."

"How will getting to know them better prevent someone from social engineering their way into my company?"

"It might not," I admit. "But it could help decrease fallout. Employees who fear management or don't have a relationship with them also keep secrets. Imagine if someone makes a mistake like that Renaissance employee downstairs? What do you think will happen if management were to find out?"

"They'd be fired," he says without hesitation. "We don't deal with incompetence."

"Exactly. This incentivizes them to cover it up instead of being honest from the beginning. The worst damage is often done in the cover up, not from initial error."

He eyes me suspiciously. Kyle goes to say something, but out of nowhere, there are voices outside of the door.

I gasp and then take Kyle's hand. He doesn't budge.

"What are you doing? We have to hide," I whisper.

"I don't hide. They can't do shit to me."

I suck my teeth and pull on his arm harder. "Let's go."

He drags his feet.

"If they find us here, the employee who let me in here will be fired."

"So?"

"Kyle, please," I plead.

"Fine," he grumbles while the alarm disengaging on the door sounds.

He pulls me into the bedroom and then into the spacious walk-in closet. Kyle presses my back against the closet wall and stands against me. We're face to face. Our bodies flush against one another's.

A giggle from the bedroom startles me, and Kyle places a palm over my mouth.

"Shshsh." A slight smirk plays on his lips, and a glint in his eyes. It's not a humorous look, however. There's deviance behind it.

He moves forward, pressing his body even farther into mine.

"Don't be too long, darling. Our dinner reservation is in thirty minutes," a male voice calls from somewhere in the suite.

Kyle's free hand trails up the length of my thigh. The skin beneath my pants scorches from his touch. Our eyes clash as he lets the hand still covering my mouth fall away. His thumb traces my bottom lip.

"I thought I left my heels in the closet," a woman calls.

I stiffen as her steps grow closer. Kyle doesn't stop feeling me up.

"What are you doing?" I whisper.

That deviant smile grows, and my nipples harden.

"No, they're in here, hun," the man says.

Footsteps move away from the door.

"Do you remember that kiss in Miami?" he murmurs, his thumb still moving along the ridge of my lip.

"Yes."

"I've craved the taste of your mouth every day since that night."

That's all the warning he gives me before he slams his mouth against mine. I'm barely able to hold back my moan. Kyle devours my mouth. The kiss isn't hurried or rushed despite our current predicament.

No matter how bad of an idea this is, I give into the kiss, surrendering to wherever he's leading me.

"Hun, do you want your coat? It's chilly outside," the woman on the other side of the door calls.

I pull away, but Kyle isn't deterred. His lips trail down my neck, pressing butterfly kisses down my vein. I squeeze my eyelids, attempting to hold myself together. I can't make any noise.

One false move, and those people will know we're in here.

I pull back and press a finger to my lips to remind Kyle that we have to be quiet.

Does he listen to me?

If the way his hand moves from my hip to the button of my pants is any indicator ... no.

He doesn't give a damn.

My breath hitches when he pops open the button of my pants. His massive hand easily finds its way into my panties. Kyle looks like a sexy devil incarnate when his fingers find that sweet spot between my legs.

"You're so wet," he murmurs against my lips.

"Did you say something, sweetie?" the man on the other side of the closet door asks.

I glance worriedly toward the only thing separating us from being found out.

"Truth or dare, Riley?" Kyle's hand moves lower, finding my swollen clit.

My heartbeat pounds in my ears. I know Kyle isn't going to let up at whatever game he's playing.

"Truth." I peek at the door again as a second pair of footsteps enter the bedroom.

"Tell me," his lips curl into a devilish smile, "are you a screamer, Riley?" He plunges one of his long fingers inside of me.

I part my lips on a silent scream and slap my hand over my mouth because I don't trust myself not to yell out. Kyle's hand proves devastating for my composure. He uses my bodily fluids to swirl delicious circles around my clit.

I let out a whimper before burying my face into the crook of my neck. This is absolute madness.

"Look at me," Kyle demands, tilting my chin up so I can't hide my face from him. "Show me the faces you make when you come," he growls.

"Paul, we'll be late if you look for anything else in that closet."

I'm half out of my mind and want to scream at the woman in the bedroom to shut up. At the same time, I'm too enraptured by Kyle's fiery gaze on mine. His entire being is demanding that I come.

And I do.

Right when I'm about to let out the scream that I know will get us exposed, Kyle slams his mouth over mine. I roll my hips into his hand, seeking every bit of pleasure. Not until my release ends does he break the kiss.

There's a door slam, and as I come to, I realize the couple must've exited the suite.

Kyle never takes his eyes off me when he lifts his finger to his mouth and licks it clean. A muffled whimper escapes my mouth.

His eyes burn into mine, and the large bulge in his pants tells how badly he wants me.

But he takes a step back.

"I won't fuck you in a closet. Not for our first time."

It sounds like a threat and a warning. My nipples ache.

"I have to get back to the office." He starts for the closet door but stops. "I'll be out of town for a few days for business. But there's a meeting next Friday afternoon. Between Waterson's execs and Townsend's. You should be there."

Standing straight, I try to get myself together. This is the first time he's invited me to sit in on any meeting of his.

Guilt swirls in my belly. "I-I'll be there."

He doesn't say anything else as he slips out of the door.

CHAPTER 13

Riley

Days after that hotel incident with Kyle, I stand at the end of the hallway on the fifteenth floor of Townsend Industries. This is the accounting department. All of Townsend Industries' books are kept on this floor.

Heaviness weighs down my stomach, making it challenging to make my next move. Dean Walsh called me a couple of days ago and all but demanded I find out about some abandoned houses that Townsend Industries supposedly owns. It's in those abandoned homes where family members conduct illegal business.

If they own the buildings, as Dean said, there's a chance they can be traced through the numbers on accounting. Or the real estate department.

"Riley, right?"

I turn to find a tall woman with a smile on her face.

"Rachel?"

She nods. "Yes, I've been expecting you." She waves a hand for me to follow her. "Tom had me put together a few files for you." Rachel turns to me. "You needed the numbers for Townsend's past few quarters, right?"

"Yes," I lie. I already received those numbers a week ago.

Rachel enters her office. She pauses with a hand on her hip. "Tell me, you're a social engineering consultant?"

I nod and glance around. "Yes, something like that. I do a bit of everything."

"Then you mostly work with people. What do you need accounting numbers for?" Her smile is pleasant enough, and I understand she's asking out of genuine curiosity.

I give her my usual spiel about numbers being a reflection of what's happening on the human level. She accepts that answer and gives me the files.

"Where's the bathroom?" I ask.

She points me across the hall. I go in and then leaf through the papers in my hand, biding my time. I check my watch and pace the floor. As soon as five-fifteen hits, I peek out of the bathroom. A few voices can be heard, but they're at the far end of the hallway.

I know that while Townsend security monitors the main hallways of the offices, they're shut off after five-fifteen.

Carefully, I make my way back to Rachel's office. Her door isn't locked. Also, lucky for me, she's left her computer on for the evening. A quick click of the monitor and the screen asking for password entry pops up.

I hesitate, hating that I have to do this. I let the moment pass before I type in the password I memorized from watching Rachel in our previous meetings. Within seconds, I'm logged into her computer and able to pull up Townsend's secure databases, including their accounting files.

I thumb through some of the unimportant files before coming to the real estate portion of the books. This company is truly worth billions. Their real estate division alone brings in about ten billion in annual revenue. I'm not a specialist in accounting or numbers, so it all looks on the up and up to me.

Right before I close out, I see an asterisk on the spreadsheet that directs me to a locked page. When it asks for a password, I again type in Rachel's code, but it's incorrect. I try a second time with the same result.

I know that trying a third time with the wrong password would then require a password reset. That would alert Rachel that someone was in here. I don't try again. Instead of trying to guess the password, I navigate out of that file and download a few other files. I send them to my work email.

As I'm leaving the office, the ringing of my phone startles me.

"Hey, Ladybug," I answer, hating the uncertainty I hear in my voice.

Eve doesn't pick up on it. "Hi, Aunt Ry. Did you finish work for the day?"

"Um, almost." I glance around the empty hallway before planting my back against the door. The knots in my stomach continue to twist as Eve tells me about her day. Usually, a call from my favorite girl helps with any stress I may be feeling. However, right now, I can only think that if I don't get Dean the information he wants, I'll leave Eve with no one.

Yet, providing Walsh with whatever he's looking for leaves me with tremendous guilt and unease. All I can see is Kyle's intense, untrusting stare looking at me. I like him more than I should. Also, the people who work for Townsend Industries are good people.

I've gotten to know many of them in the few weeks I've consulted for this company.

What will happen to them if it's proven Townsend Industries is behind some illegal dealings?

"Did you hear me?" Eve asks, calling me back to the conversation.

"Yes, you scored another one hundred on your math exam," I tell her. "I can't believe you're taking trigonometry. When I was your age, I couldn't even spell it."

She giggles. "It's not *that* hard."

"For you it isn't," I reply. "Ladybug, I was on my way out of the office. Can I call you back when I get home?"

"Um, wait. I want to ask you something first."

"What's up?"

"When can I come to visit?"

The softness in her voice tugs at my heartstrings. I flew east a month ago to have a long weekend with Eve. We spent it in New York City.

"You can come anytime you want. Or I can come to you. Is everything all right?" I hadn't received any calls from Eve's teachers, dorm coordinator, or the headmistress alerting me of any problems.

Every weekly report I get says that she's doing great in all of her classes, and aside from being a little messy, her behavior is good.

"I miss you. That's all."

"I miss you every day, Ladybug." I pause and try to rework my schedule in my head. "I should be free to take a week off in a few weeks. How about I fly up there to stay with you?"

"Or, I can come to Williamsport," she offers, sounding more excited.

"That too, but I'd prefer to come to meet you to fly back with you. I don't want you on a plane by yourself."

"I'll be twelve soon," she reminds me. "That's the young adult status on most airlines."

I grumble. "You are not an adult. Please stop trying to give me grey hair before my time. I'm not even out of my mid-twenties yet."

She laughs.

"I have to make a stop after work, but I'll call you as soon as I get home, okay?"

"Love you."

I disconnect the call with Eve and square my shoulders. I don't like what I have to do, but it's my only option now.

"Kyle." I stop short right as I round the corner. He went out of town the day after we ended up in that closet at the Renaissance. I hadn't seen him since. "I thought you were coming back tomorrow."

A sly smile spreads across his face. "Is that your way of saying you missed me?"

He's so damn cocky.

"No comment."

"What are you doing down here?" He looks past me down the hall.

I hold up the files Rachel gave me. "Going over a few numbers for this Friday's meeting."

"Thorough."

"I have to be."

"Are you ready for the meeting? We're going over strategy for the next six months. I thought you could pitch a few ways to handle the complexities of merging our labor departments."

I nod. "I have a few ideas."

"Good—" He stops short from the ringing of his phone. He pulls it out and frowns down at the screen. "I need to take this."

"I need to head out anyway." I pivot before he can say anything and head for the stairs. I take them to the ground level. All the while, I keep wondering how my next move will blow up in my face.

* * *

THIRTY MINUTES after leaving Townsend's offices, I pound on the door of the Inn Hotel, located just outside of Williamsport. As I hear rustling on the other side of the door, I glance around, taking in the leather loveseat at the far end of the hallway and the original paintings that hang on the wall.

How the hell is Dean Walsh affording this?

"What the hell are you doing here?" he asks, swinging the door open.

"Here." I thrust the files into his chest and start to walk away.

"Where are you going?" He grabs my arm too tight, and I stumble, bumping my head against the wall.

"Motherfucker," I grit out at the same time I shove him off of me.

"Get in here." He pushes me inside of the room before slamming the door. "How did you find out where I'm staying?"

I let out a derisive laugh. "Do you think you're some special criminal mastermind? All it took was a little poking around on the databases I have access to find you."

I glance down at the file in his hands. "Those are the accounting records you wanted. And I'm sure I could go to jail for giving you those."

He thumbs through the papers. "This doesn't give me shit. It's basic numbers."

"Well ..." I turn and head for the door.

He grabs me by the shoulder, spinning me around.

"What the fuck do you think you're doing? This is not what I asked for!" That half-deranged look takes over his face.

"That's all I could find."

"Bullshit. There's more. There has to be. He said—" He stops.

"Who? Who said what?" I ask, feeling like this is part of something bigger than I initially thought.

"I told you about the abandoned houses. Are those on these records?" He holds up the files.

We both know the answer.

"There was a file I couldn't get into," I admit, hating myself for doing so. "It's password protected."

"That's it." He claps the file in his hand. "I fucking knew it. You're going to get into that file."

My eyes bulge. "I just told you it's password protected. They won't give me access to it."

"Kyle knows. You'll get the password from him."

"Oh yeah, I'll just stop by his office tomorrow morning and casually ask him to give me the code to the super secure accounting files that probably point to abandoned houses where his family has allegedly committed crimes."

"Don't fucking get sarcastic with me, bitch," Dean yells.

"Don't ever call me a bitch again. You bastard. Since you seem to know so much about Townsend's crimes, why don't you go to the police yourself?"

"This is bigger than the cops. Besides, that family has paid all of them off, anyway. My father knew it, and he was going to expose them. That's why they had him killed!" he declares.

Dean sounds so sure of himself that I don't even try to convince him otherwise.

He points a finger at me. "You're going to get access to those files, and that is what I'm going to use to take that entire family down."

"I'm not doing shit," I state. I'm sick of Dean Walsh and this entire fucking scheme. "Whatever you think is happening at Townsend Industries isn't. So what, I couldn't get into one encrypted file? There are probably hundreds of files only certain people can access for security purposes."

"No!" he seethes, pounding his fist into his hand. "They've been up to no good for years. I know it. My father knew it. That's why he did what he did. He was going to make them pay him millions to keep quiet."

A chuckle spills from my lips. "So your father wasn't Robin Hood after all, huh? Of course he wasn't. He only wanted to profit from what he believed were illegal activities happening."

"I'll make them pay and more! Me and—" He breaks off. Dean blinks a few times and then steps threateningly close. "You're going to get into that file to get me the information I need. I don't give a fuck if you have to suck Kyle Townsend's dick every day in the office for the next two and a half months. You will prove that they pay money and keep secret houses where they threaten, coerce, and even kill to get their way!"

"Fuck. You," I say through gritted teeth. A searing rage almost overtakes me. My hands squeeze into fists, and I have to fight the urge not to punch him.

After leaving my father's house, I swore that I would never let someone use me as a pawn in their screwed-up life ever again. Yet, here I am, back at square one.

This is for your Ladybug, that calm, rational voice inside of my head reminds me. I'm not doing any of this to help Dean or even myself. Yes, staying out of jail sounds nice, but I need to be out for Eve. She's my only concern.

"You don't know who the hell you're messing with," Dean threatens.

I take a step back, inching my way toward the door.

"One phone call, and your life is over. No more running that consulting business or kissing Kyle Townsend on the beach in Miami."

I blink in surprise.

Dean lets out a hollow chuckle. "Yeah, I know about that. Tell me? What do you think Townsend will do to you if he finds out what you've really been up to?" He looks me up and down, and disgust rolls through my belly. "Jail will be a fucking cakewalk."

Memories of almost every interaction with Kyle Townsend flood my mind. He remained so calm and collected while his bodyguard cavalierly held a gun to my head. His multiple reminders not to betray him because I wouldn't like the outcome.

Hell, even the way he remained so controlled when he made me come inside of a hotel room closet when its occupants were mere feet away from finding us.

A chill runs down my spine.

It's a reminder that prison might not be the only thing I have to fear if Kyle ever discovers the truth.

"I-I'll get more information. I need a few days," I tell Dean, my voice shaky.

Without waiting for a response, I turn and make a beeline for the door. I ignore the quivering of my belly and the unsteady way my hand turns the doorknob. I need to get out of here before I scream.

"Don't try to run, Riley," Dean threatens behind me. However, his warning doesn't hold the same weight as the cold look in Kyle's eyes. While I don't doubt Dean would follow through on making a call to the police, I know Kyle would be the type to leave the police out altogether. He would take revenge himself.

That thought has me swallowing hard.

CHAPTER 14

Kyle

"What is it, Mike?" I ask into the phone while simultaneously checking my watch. I have a meeting in ten minutes. It's with all of the department VPs. It'll be my first official meeting as COO.

While I'm not nervous because I know my shit, I am anxious to get it started. There are several projects I'm overseeing and need to implement. None of which is more critical than ensuring this merger goes smoothly.

"I just got word from our contact at The Daily Report," Mike says.

"And?"

"Supposedly, they're running an article on Townsend Industries soon."

"About the merger?" I ask.

"No." He sighs. "One of the reporters got an anonymous tip that Townsend is involved in bribing and paying off political officials to get permits approved. They say he has evidence that out of the number of permits Townsend real estate applied for, they all went through ten times faster than other companies' applications."

I pinch the bridge of my nose. "Another fucking article," I grunt. I thought I was done with the negative articles when I got rid of Jayceon Carlson. "Call Uncle Joshua's people." My uncle has been the head of Townsend real estate for more than two decades. He'll be the first line of defense against any bad press concerning our real estate division.

"They're on it," Mike tells me. "I spoke with his PR rep."

"Good," I say. "Then schedule a meeting with him for tomorrow morning. Tomorrow is Saturday, but if this is an issue, it must be handled immediately. My uncle will understand."

"One more thing," Mike says.

I push out a frustrated breath but hold my tongue.

"Brendan Chastain has left another message. He wants you to get in touch with him."

"What the hell?" I sigh. "Listen, the next time he calls, tell him I don't have time to waste with him. I'm not a fucking Hollywood exec. And despite my brother's connections, I wouldn't give his ass the time of day."

"Do you want me to tell him that?"

"In those exact words," I grit out. Brendan Chastain was the type who liked to be seen more than he wanted to work. And he wondered why no one took him seriously.

"He's been insistent. He called twice yesterday and at least once this morning."

"Is this an issue you can't handle, Mike?" My voice sounds borderline lethal to my ears. I didn't deal with incompetence. Mike has been my assistant for three years, and he does a hell of a job, but if he can't handle Brendan Chastain, who's nothing more than a minor nuisance, we'll have a problem.

"If he calls again, I'll take care of it."

"Good. Make sure there aren't any more interruptions for the next ninety minutes." I exit my office a minute later to head to the conference room.

On the way, I find myself uncannily anticipating the sight of the one person I have no business wanting to see. Riley Martin.

Throughout my business trip, my mind kept going back to the expression on her face when I made her come.

Fuck. What I wouldn't give to hear her scream my name as I slide my cock deep inside of her. And her taste?

Holy shit.

When I licked her juices from my finger, I wanted more.

Never have I mixed business with pleasure before. There have been many opportunities to do so. But Townsend Industries had always been my priority. Mixing business with emotions gets messy. And I damn sure am not about to let something as ridiculous as *feelings* get in the way of seeing to the company's success that bears my family name.

I run my hand through the short curls on top of my head and force myself to push down thoughts of Riley. I know well enough by now that they won't go away completely. But I can think of her naked, writhing beneath me, later. Not when I'm standing in the middle of all of the VPs for Townsend Industries.

"Gentleman and ladies," I greet as I stand at the head of the table. Six men and five women compose our company VPs, and three more VPs from Sam Waterson's medical supplies firm.

I scan the room only to notice a noticeably absent face. Where Riley should be seated is another woman.

"Who the hell are you?" I demand to know.

Her eyes widen into saucers.

"I-I—"

"How did you get in here?" My finger itches to call security.

"This is Charlotte Greenwald. Riley's assistant," Mary, the VP of technology, says.

"Her assistant," I repeat as if not hearing her correctly. Everyone in the room tenses, especially the woman named Charlotte.

She briefly circles the room with her gaze. "Yes. Riley asked me to sit in on the meeting because ..." She hesitates.

"Why?" The one-word question causes her to jump. Obviously, my voice came out louder than intended. Strangely, I don't know if my irritation is due to the fact that I missed seeing Riley's face or if it's because there's someone in this very important meeting who I don't know.

"S-She couldn't make it, but don't worry. She gave me all of her notes and the reports she wrote up. I've already handed them out and I have my voice recorder here," she holds up her phone, "to record everything for her."

"Get out," I say, the words coming out before I even have a chance to process them.

Charlotte's shoulders slump. She looks defeated, and that makes me even angrier because she's not the woman I want to see.

Someone across from me clears their throat. "Kyle," Barry from marketing says. "Ms. Greenwald has given us the report that Riley so diligently wrote up. We've had a few minutes to look it over and I do believe it's worth getting into. I believe we've come to know Riley well enough to know that if she's not present, it's for a good reason."

Barry recoils suddenly, and that's when I realize that I'm snarling in his direction.

He thinks he *knows Riley well enough*? What the hell does he know about her that I don't? I'm half tempted to ask if he knows what the inside of her pussy feels like when it tightens around his fingers as she comes.

I know for damn sure he doesn't.

But I do.

The thought alone, however, sends burning anger through my stomach. I have to think about something else. I'll find out what the hell is going on with Riley as soon as this meeting is over.

"You'll stay," I tell Charlotte as calmly as I can manage. "However, if one word of this meeting is shared with anyone that it isn't supposed to be, I'll know who to go looking for first."

Charlotte visibly swallows. A part of me should feel bad for threatening her, but the real reason I'm angered isn't here, so she takes the brunt.

I'm determined to go find out where the fuck Riley is as soon as this meeting ends.

*　*　*

BEING A MAN OF MY WORD, as soon as the meeting ends and I finalize a few words with some of the VPs, I head down to the fifteenth floor. That's the floor where Riley's been assigned an office.

Her assistant, Charlotte, remained silent throughout the meeting, diligently taking notes. I'd admire her work ethic if it weren't for the fact that I'm still so damn annoyed. Charlotte left directly after the meeting to return to Riley's real office.

"Mr. Townsend," Darius, the receptionist on the fifteenth floor, stands and greets.

"Have you seen Riley Martin?"

His eyebrows lift. "No. Not since this morning. I thought she had that big meeting with you and the VPs."

I grind my teeth. "Thanks," I murmur as I move past his desk and head down the hall to her office.

From the office windows, I can see the lights are out and there's no one at her desk. "She better not be wasting company time," I mumble while twisting the knob.

"Riley," I call out as I barge into the office.

There's no answer.

But she's in here. Call it crazy or intuition. I can *feel* her presence.

I charge inside of the office. "Riley, what f—" I stop short when I find her crumpled in a ball behind her desk.

"Riley, what's wrong?" I crouch down.

"Shshsh, please," she mutters, the words coming out on a croak. "Not so loud."

"Why are you down here?"

Her face tightens into a grimace with every word I say. Though she covers her ears to keep from hearing me, she responds, "I-Is the meeting over? I sent Charlotte to take notes on what I missed."

Instead of answering, I reach down and place the back of my palm to her forehead. "Are you sick? Is it the flu? Do you need a doctor?"

"Please lower your voice."

I know I hadn't been yelling or speaking above a normal conversational tone. I stand and move to turn on the light in her office. As soon as the light comes on, Riley groans out in agony.

"No, please. Turn it off," she hisses.

I turn it off, shrouding us in semi-darkness again. Yet even with the blinds drawn in her office, we're not in complete darkness.

"It's j-just a m-migraine. It'll go away s-soon," she stammers out.

"Just?"

She looks like she's in so much anguish, and I can't *not* do something. I have never experienced migraines, but I've heard they can be extremely painful and debilitating.

"Do you have any medication?"

"Mmm," she moans and shakes her head a little. That slight movement causes her to hiss and squeeze her eyes even tighter. "Ran out."

I glance up at her desk to see an empty prescription bottle with a white lid sitting next to it. I grab the bottle, and sure enough, it's empty.

I crouch down, afraid to touch her because I don't want to create more pain for her.

"It'll be fine. I can get up and drive home soon. I'm sorry about missing the meeting." Her voice gets lower with each word.

"Fuck the meeting," I say without thinking. "There's no way you should be driving anywhere."

I don't know how long her migraine usually lasts, but considering she missed a ninety-minute meeting, I'm betting it'll be at least a few more hours before she's any better.

It's a little after three in the afternoon. I have a shit ton of other work to do, but I make a split decision.

Pulling out my phone, I call Mike's desk.

"Have a driver waiting for me by the private elevator in five minutes."

I disconnect the call and kneel by Riley. "Riley?" I make my voice as low as possible.

"Huh?"

"I need your address."

She mumbles the address, and I plug it into my phone.

"Can you stand?" I stroke her arm lightly.

"Why?"

"We're going to take you home."

My chest tightens as I help her up. Her face is a mask of anguish, and I'm certain she keeps her eyelids almost closed to keep tears from spilling out.

"Lean on me," I encourage, wrapping my arm around her waist and lifting her from the floor.

"I can walk," she insists, even as she rests almost all her weight on me.

"I've got you." Somehow my lips find their way to the top of her head. She lets out a moan and presses her body into mine. I force myself to ignore thinking about how good she feels like this as we make our way out of her office.

Even as she willingly lets me escort her toward the elevator, she continues to insist that she'll be fine soon. On the way down, she apologizes a total of three times for missing the meeting, all while she rattles off stats and figures that were mentioned in her report.

"I'm not a slacker," she says at the same time we make it to the awaiting car.

"I know," I tell her because she doesn't need to tell me that. Yet, I won't argue with her. Not while she's in such pain.

"I think I'm going to be sick," she blurts out a few seconds before she falls to her knees behind the car and spills out the entire contents of her stomach.

I immediately hold back strands of her hair that fall into her face. I order the driver to retrieve some towels and hand wipes from the car. My free hand moves up and down Riley's spine soothingly.

"I-I'm so sorry," she says, embarrassed.

"Don't." I wipe her face with the towel and hand her the hand wipes right before putting her in the backseat of the car. I put her seatbelt around her and give the driver the address before going around and sliding in next to Riley.

As we exit the underground garage, I roll up the divider to minimize the amount of sunlight that streams through the windows.

During the twenty-minute drive, I remind the driver to slow the fuck down. Every minor bump we hit causes Riley to hiss in pain.

Her pain causes a ripping feeling in my chest.

"Here."

I help Riley up to her condo once we arrive at her place. I root around in her purse for her key, and as soon as I open her door, the scent of vanilla fills my nose. It's her, all her.

Riley doesn't fight me as I help her remove her shoes by the door and then lead her down the hall to where I presume her bedroom is. While still latched onto my side, she pauses at the first door on the left and heads in. I help her onto the king size bed and then cover her with the blanket.

"Blinds," she murmurs.

I glance around and realize she's asking me to close the blinds. The bedroom is at a perfect angle for the midday sun to enter the room. Which, today, is not a good thing.

I press the lever next to the floor-to-ceiling window, and the blackout curtains shroud the room in darkness.

Pausing for a beat, I note the absolute silence. Riley's bedroom is … interesting. Among what must be thirty or so pillows, there is a cornucopia of colors. Above the bed are three separate paintings. One is of a sunset, the other of a woman and a young girl, and the other is a scene of ladybugs. The paintings are filled with bright colors that match her bedding and pillows.

There are four different plants on either of her nightstands that sit in painted, colorful clay pots. There's a framed picture on one of the nightstands. I lift it to read the words "Look on the bright side" on the small postcard.

I only take a moment to take in her room before I focus back on Riley. She's so still except for the small up and down movements of her body, indicating her breathing. I don't want to disturb her. But I need to be near her.

I move to the side of the bed and feel her forehead again. I realize a migraine doesn't come with a temperature but it's the only excuse I have to touch her. Her face flinches slightly but then she relaxes again.

"Riley, do you have any more medicine for your migraine?" I whisper.

"M-Medicine cabinet."

I go searching for her bathroom where I hope to find the medicine cabinet. When I do, I'm out of luck. Aside from some over the counter cold medications, there isn't shit there labeled to take for a migraine.

That's when I pull out my phone and call the specialty healthcare service I use when I'm under the weather. It only takes a few minutes before I'm having Riley's prescription refilled, a nurse practitioner on the way, and food delivered.

After that, I call Mike to have him deliver my work laptop along with a few files I need from the office. I don't know how long Riley will be like this, but until she's better, I'm not leaving her side.

CHAPTER 15

Riley

I wake up slow. As my eyes peel open, one at a time, I come to the realization that I'm having one of my migraines. My first thought is to get to my medication, wherever that may be.

"Whoa, where are you going?" A deep voice startles me.

"Kyle?" *What is he doing here? Wait, where is here?*

I slow blink and look around, realizing I'm in my bedroom. On an inhale I try to remember how I got here. The last thing I recall vividly is starting to feel the dull pain at the base of my skull. I went to my purse to pop one of my migraine pills. They usually do the trick, reasonably quickly. But the damn bottle was empty.

That was when the pain grew worse, and I knew I had to call Charlotte to have her sit in for me at the meeting with Kyle and all of the VPs.

How long ago was that?

"What are you doing here?"

He takes a seat on the edge of my bed, coming into my full view. The only light on in the room is a small lamp I have on top of my vanity. Even with the dull pain still throbbing in my head and the low lighting, I drink Kyle in.

The top button of his white shirt is undone, exposing a small amount of his chest. His suit jacket is off, and he's rolled the sleeves up to his elbows. My eyes trace the veins that run along his forearm. When I raise my gaze to meet his, something I never thought I'd see meets me.

Concern.

There is genuine concern plastered all over his handsome face. It's in the way his eyes scan over my face and body, the pinched skin in between his eyebrows, and the way his fingers trace along my forehead, pushing a strand of hair behind my ear.

"How're you feeling?" His voice is low but firm.

"Better." For my part, my voice sounds weak to my own ears.

Kyle's lips pinch, and I know I've done something to irritate him.

Is it because I missed the meeting?

"Don't lie to me, Riley," he says sternly. His hand drops to my shoulder and then to my arm. "How are you feeling?"

I swallow. "My head still hurts," I admit.

He nods, satisfied with the truth. "The nurse said you might still be in pain for a while."

I squint. "Nurse?"

Kyle cocks his head to the side. "You don't remember?"

Shifting my gaze down toward my arm, I notice there's a bandage with tape over it on my forearm.

"I had a nurse practitioner come. She gave you an IV of fluids since you ran out of your prescription." He holds up my empty pill bottle. "They said the electrolytes and stuff could help. I also had—" He pauses when there's a knock on the door.

It causes me to wince in pain.

Kyle lets out a low growl. "Sons of bitches. I told them to call me... hang on."

He gets up and walks out of the room.

Leaning back against my pillows, I take in deep breaths. My mind is swirling as I try to remember the events of the past few hours. Unfortunately, the pain still raging in my head and sleepiness make it difficult. All I can focus on is Kyle's voice telling me everything's going to be okay, and to lean on him for strength.

That's when the memory of him finding me in my office, helping me out of the building, and getting me back home, come back. I even vaguely recall the voice of the nurse practitioner. I believe I had signed some sort of consent form for her to give me the IV.

The pain is still present but the throbbing and nausea have decreased significantly.

"Here we are," Kyle says as he enters the room, holding a tray of food.

I struggle to sit up higher in bed.

"No," Kyle commands in that low but insistent voice of his. "Don't move too much." He sets the tray directly over my lap.

"What's this?" I look down, trying to make sense of the multiple plates and bowls of food that cover the tray.

"For one," he holds up a prescription bag, "your newly filled prescription."

I blink. "How did you get a new prescription so quickly?" I usually have to wait at least a day or so before my prescription is filled. And I hadn't even had a chance to contact my physician.

Kyle simply blinks at me. Then I remember.

Right. His family likely has an entire staff of healthcare professionals on call around the clock.

"But it's not as effective if it's not taken within the first thirty minutes of the signs of a migraine," he continues, placing the medicine on my nightstand. "It's well after six o'clock and you haven't eaten since this morning. Plus ..." He doesn't continue.

"Plus, what?" But before he can answer, I remember. "Oh my god," I groan as I recall throwing up all over the underground garage. "That's so humiliating." I cover my face in shame.

Kyle takes a firm grip of my wrist, pulling my hand away from my face. "You have nothing to be embarrassed about." He looks me directly in the eyes as he says this. As he continues to hold onto my wrist, his thumb starts to make little circles, stroking the vein there.

The air in the room shifts and the pain in my skull, while still active, subsides a bit more. Out of nowhere, my stomach growls.

"Shit." Kyle lets go of my hand and adjusts the tray of food. He lifts the lid off of one of the bowls. "Tomato soup." Then he moves to lift the lid covering one of the plates. "And grilled cheese."

A smile I can't suppress covers my face.

"This delicacy is one of my grandmother's favorites," he explains. "She would always make a grilled cheese and can of tomato soup whenever we stayed over with them for the night. Or if she heard one of us had a bad day."

A half smile touches his lips, and in this moment, the hard ass, career-driven, workaholic heir diminishes. His face takes on an almost boyish look.

"That's sounds so sweet of her."

"Yeah," he agrees. "She's good like that." He sits again and peers up at me. "Unless you don't like grilled cheese. I also read that sometimes dairy can cause or even make migraines worse. So …" he lifts the lid of the other bowl, "I also got you chicken noodle soup and crackers."

"Both? For me?" I assumed that one meal was for me and the other was for him.

He nods. "You have to eat. The IV fluids will help but I always think real food is better over that other shit."

He rises and hovers over the bed. For a moment, I wonder what he would do if I decided not to eat.

I grin.

"What?" A wrinkle appears in between his brows.

"I'm just picturing you prying my mouth open and shoveling this soup down my throat." I laugh, but then quickly regret it when my head throbs. Groaning, I lay my head against the headboard.

"Dammit, Riley," he whispers.

In no time, he's leaning over me, gently placing a pillow behind my head. It's comforting in a way I haven't been taken care of in a long time, if ever.

"Thank you."

"Eat," he insists. "Which one? Chicken or tomato. I can get rid of the dairy." He doesn't even wait before he's lifting the grilled cheese and bowl of tomato soup.

"No." I wrap my hand around his arm, stopping him. "I'm okay with dairy, and that looks delicious."

Thank God the nausea has gone away. I take my first bite of the grilled cheese and sigh in relief. The sourdough bread is buttered and crisped to perfection. The cheddar cheese melts as soon as it hits my tongue.

"So good," I groan.

When I open my eyes, which I hadn't realized I closed, Kyle is standing over me, those hazel eyes not missing anything.

"Thank you for this."

He nods in the direction of the soup bowl. "It's even better if you dip the sandwich into the soup." He looks at me expectantly, as if he just gave an order to follow.

An involuntary laugh spills from my lips.

"What?"

I shake my head but quickly stop when the movement reminds me that I'm not out of the woods yet with this migraine.

"Of course, you even try to control the way I would eat the food you ordered for me."

His eyelids narrow. "I'm not controlling. Just letting you know what tastes better."

I smirk but don't say anything. Instead, I dip the edge of the sandwich into the soup. Yes, he's right, using the grilled cheese as its own conduit to get the soup into my mouth makes it even better.

"Told you," he mutters even though I didn't say anything. Kyle reaches over me and takes the other plate and bowl. "I'll put these in the refrigerator in case you want them later or for tomorrow," he explains.

"Are you leaving?" I quickly ask.

He stops and turns to me. "No. You're still in pain. I can see it in the lines on your forehead."

My heart swells with gratitude.

"I had Mike bring over my laptop. I'm going to get some work done in the kitchen, though."

"Bring it in here," I blurt out. "I won't ask you about it." I glance at the other side of my bed. "And my bed's big enough."

I almost cover my mouth because the meaning of what I just said could be construed a number of ways. Kyle doesn't answer with words, though. He nods and then leaves my bedroom. I don't know if that response is a yes or a no to my invitation to stay. In my bed, no less.

A breath escapes my lungs when, a few minutes later, Kyle comes sauntering into my bedroom, laptop and a few files in hand. I hadn't realized how much I wanted his company until right now.

I watch his fluid movements as he adjusts the comforter, pillows, and bedsheets to make room for his lengthy body. Due to my own five-foot-ten height, and the fact that I never had my own bed as a kid or young adult, I made sure to buy the bed of my dreams when I got this place. It's long enough for me, but it feels almost like a twin when Kyle gets in.

Though our bodies aren't touching, his warmth envelopes me.

"I take it you like it." He juts his head at my almost empty soup bowl.

I grin. "I can't remember ever having grilled cheese and tomato soup together." I lift and lower one shoulder. "One of the elementary schools I went to served grilled cheese every Wednesday. But they kept them in these foil sandwich bags, and by the time my grade had lunch, condensation had gotten into the bags and the sandwiches were soggy."

"That sounds terrible." He grunts and turns up his nose.

I roll my eyes even though that causes the pain in my head to worsen a little. "We can't all eat caviar off of gold-framed plates every night."

"Is that what you think my life was like growing up?" He sounds almost offended.

I look away.

"My grandmother loves grilled cheese and tomato soup so much because that's what her parents made for her ... but theirs came out of a can. She wasn't born with a silver spoon. In fact, she probably never even saw *real* silver until she went away to college. It's hard to find in the backwoods of Appalachia."

"Appalachia?" I ask.

He nods. "That's where she's from. Barely had running water growing up."

His words sound earnest. Kyle isn't the type to make things up to get anyone's approval. So, it must be the truth.

I probably should apologize for my assumptions but I don't. Instead, I go with the truth.

"We had running water, but we moved around so much when I was a kid, it was hard even remembering my address most of the time."

"We?" he questions.

"My father, older brother, and me. Well, Wallace Jr, my brother, is ten years older than me. So, when I was about nine he left home and went out on his own."

"Your father raised you?"

I notice Kyle hasn't even opened his laptop. His long legs are stretched out on the bed, crossed at the ankles. He looks perfectly comfortable as he leans back against the headboard. And his presence feels ... right.

My heart squeezes in my chest, and I become aware that it aches for things it shouldn't want.

"If you can call it that," I scoff. "He was my guardian. My mother split before I turned one."

"You two aren't close?" he asks.

"Weren't ..." I give Kyle a look out of the corner of my eye. "He's dead."

He pinches his lips. "I'm sorry. Even the death of a shitty parent can be painful."

I swallow the sudden lump that occurs in my throat.

"No big deal," I say, my voice sounding thin. "I've made due on my own. I left his household the day I turned eighteen and never looked back." Well, not really.

"That must've been tough," he says.

Is that admiration I hear in his voice?

"I lived at a homeless shelter for eighteen months." Why am I telling him all of this? "It wasn't a big deal, and it all worked out," I quickly say, injecting my voice with a cheeriness I don't feel.

"I told you once today not to lie to me."

The dark tone his voice takes on, pulls my gaze to meet his.

"You don't ever have to sugarcoat shit. If your life then was fucked up just say that."

My vision suddenly becomes blurry, forcing me to look away from Kyle's penetrating stare. I don't like thinking about the memories of that time. It was painful realizing that I had no one to depend on but myself. That my family of origin was just one fucked-up group of people with similar DNA.

"I'm not lying," I reply. "I'm looking on the brighter side of the situation."

He frowns and then his eyes move to the picture frame on my desk. He nods toward it.

A genuine smile tips the corners of my mouth. I pick up the framed postcard.

"Ms. Edith. She was the director of the homeless shelter. She used to always say, 'look on the bright side.'" My smile widens at the memory. "You have your grandmother's grilled cheese and tomato soup, and I had Ms. Edith's reminder on the really bad days." I hold up the frame. "She sent this to me when I moved here to Williamsport from LA."

"That's why you keep it close."

I nod. "She passed away two years ago."

Cue the blurred vision again.

Kyle lifts the tray from my lap and places it on the floor on his side of the bed.

I go to wipe away the tears, but Kyle takes my hand, intertwining his long fingers with mine. I hold my breath as he brings my hand to his lips, kissing my knuckles. With his other hand, he wipes away one of my tears. And then another.

I lay my head against his shoulder, feeling safe and comforted. The rational voice at the back of my mind screams out for me to remember that Kyle is not someone I can afford to fall for. But my heart isn't listening at the moment.

"You're an enigma, Riley Martin," Kyle murmurs, his lips brushing against my forehead.

"How so?" I whisper. My eyelids fall closed.

"I can't figure you out," he admits. "Part of me doesn't want to because then I'm afraid I won't be able to trust you." He sighs and leans back, making himself even more comfortable in the bed.

I take that as an opportunity to lay my head against his chest. His heartbeat is so strong and its rhythm is like a lullaby, drawing me deeper into sleep.

"You have to trust somebody ... sometime," I mumble, not even sure it's loud enough for him to hear.

He grunts. "The last person I trusted betrayed me, and it almost cost my family too much."

I'm not sure I hear him correctly but I'm too tired to ask him to repeat himself. It's like a dream when his hand begins stroking my hair.

The last thing I remember hearing is Kyle saying, "And I think I like you too fucking much to be unaffected if you betrayed me."

I like you, too, is my last coherent thought before sleep pulls me under.

CHAPTER 16

Kyle

When I awaken, the next morning, it's with the full knowledge that I did not sleep in my bed the night before. My second thought is to wonder why the hell I'm surrounded by about ten pillows.

Soon after, though, the scent of vanilla hits my nose and memories from yesterday before come flooding back. I become well aware that I'm laying in Riley's bed, my arm draped over her waist. Almost, protectively.

She's still sleeping, peacefully, and I take the opportunity to study every part of her. Riley's so fucking beautiful. From her smooth, even brown skin, her pert nose, and full kissable lips. The amount of time I've pictured kissing or sticking my cock between those fucking lips is, honestly, obsessive at this point.

I trace my thumb over the side of her cheek, noting the pillow marks that reside there. I hope that means she had a goodnight's rest. I hated seeing her in pain yesterday. Even though the pain seemed to have subsided by the evening, I caught her flinching whenever she would move her head too quickly or laugh.

"Where the hell did you come from?" I whisper, still running my thumb along the ridge of her jawline.

"Los Angeles," she mumbles, her eyes still closed.

A chuckle spills from my mouth.

"Did I wake you?"

Her eyes slowly open and it's like a punch in the gut. All of the air escapes my lungs. This is the second time I've woken up in a bed with this woman beside me, and we both have all of our clothes on.

Not the next time.

That promise comes out of nowhere, but I don't even try to refute it. I'm damn sure the only reason Riley isn't naked right now is because she was too ill for me to do anything with her yesterday.

"No, not really." She goes to sit up and squeezes her eyes shut.

"You're still hurting." I'm up in a flash, taking her head between my hands, looking her over.

"No. It's a lot better. Just the residual dizziness and light throbbing."

My frown deepens. "I'll have the nurse practitioner come back. I have her on standby for the weekend." I move to grab my cell, but Riley's hand stops me.

"It's not a big deal. Seriously. The worst of it is over. Besides …" She picks up her cell on the nightstand, checking the time. "It's almost eight, and I have somewhere I need to be at nine."

"Where?" Did my question come out sounding possessive as fuck? Yes.

Do I give a shit?

No.

She presses a palm to her forehead, taking her time to answer. She's in obvious distress. There's no way I'm about to let her go anywhere. Not like this.

"A breakfast for an organization I volunteer with. I have to give a speech." She moves gingerly as if trying to get up from the bed.

I'm on my feet in a flash and round to her side of the bed. "Stay your ass right there," I tell her at the same time I push her legs back onto the bed.

"What the hell are you doing?" she insists.

"You're in pain," I say as if it should be obvious.

"I'm fine."

"You're lying."

"Get out of my way." She moves to get up, only to be stopped again.

"Don't you dare get up from this bed." When the fuck did I start sounding like my mother?

Her eyes bulge and then narrow. "Kyle, I told you I have a very important event to attend. It's for the organization 'Girls on the Move'. They're expecting me."

"You're sick."

"I'm not."

"You were too sick to attend a very important meeting at work yesterday."

"That was yesterday," she balks.

"Is this organization paying for your time?"

She blinks at me in confusion. "No, I volunteer with them and take on pro bono work for them when I can afford to."

"So, the consulting work you're doing at Townsend for a seriously hefty fee, you couldn't attend because you were too ill. But you're healed enough to *freely* give your time to another organization. Is that what you're saying?"

I fold my arms across my chest and glare down at her.

"What? No. You're making it seem like—"

"Because," I cut her off, "Townsend doesn't take lightly the money we pay to our consultants. And I would hate to have to sue you for our money back since you obviously are well enough to volunteer but not well enough to work."

Her eyes narrow to slits as she scowls.

Fuck, she's hot when she's pissed.

"You controlling motherfu—"

"Thank you. And don't test me, Riley. I will sue your ass from here to kingdom come if you try to get out of this bed one minute before you're ready."

Her shoulders slump. "I don't put it past you either."

"You're smart."

"And I'm going to kick your ass as soon as this migraine and dizziness are completely gone."

"I look forward to you trying."

She looks away. "I can't leave them hanging though. These women are counting on me to show up. Angie, the director, helped me out a lot when I first moved to Williamsport. She's a friend of Ms. Edith's."

"I'll go," I say before even thinking.

She swerves her head around to look at me and then grimaces in pain. It's a good thing she's sitting in bed because her entire upper body sways from the dizziness.

"H-How are you going to go?"

"It's a speech about business, right? You think they wouldn't want me?" I stand there with a smirk on my face, feeling confident.

"Kyle, you're Townsend's COO. Organizations would pay five figures for you to give a speech."

"Six figures," I reply. "Which is why I know those women won't be disappointed to see me coming through the door instead of you. What's the topic of your speech?"

She hesitates.

"Let's go, Riley. It starts at nine." I hold up my phone, showing her it's ten after eight. "I already had one of my assistants drop off a change of clothes for me yesterday."

"Mike was here?" she asks.

I shake my head. "I keep him for high-level stuff. I have a personal assistant for this type of thing. Speech topic," I divert her back to my question.

"Right. Uh …" she pauses, "it's on the importance of networking and finding mentors. I can email you what I have written."

"Do so. I'm going to take a shower."

"You really don't need to do this. I'm fine to go."

"Move one inch from that bed and I'll have my team of lawyers draw up paperwork and deliver it by this afternoon. You'll be sued not only for what we've paid so far but also for any and all possible financial damages that my lawyers can tack on."

"I don't doubt it," she gripes.

I grin and turn toward the bathroom, even as she chucks a pillow at my head. It hits the back of my shoulder. When I turn to face her, she's glaring at me with her arms folded. I let my gaze drop to those perfect lips of hers. She's still wearing the button-up top that she wore to the office.

For a beat, I regret not helping her change into something else. But that would've been too much of a perverted move on my part, considering how much pain she was in yesterday.

"Nice aim." I laugh as I close the door only to hear a thud against it when she throws a second pillow.

CHAPTER 17

Kyle

Hours after waking up that morning, I step off of the small stage in a conference room of a local hotel.

"Mr. Townsend, thank you so much," Angie, the director of the Girls on the Move organization, thanks me not for the first time today. "Your speech was wonderful. I think our girls got a lot out of it. And you were so gracious to stay to answer questions."

I nod as we shake hands. "Not a problem at all. I know Riley would've stayed." I'm confident of that. Considering the woman has texted me three times and called once to ask how it was going.

"Riley is wonderful. We missed her today." A look of panic passes over Angie's face. "Not that you weren't spectacular. Because you were, it's just that many of these young women look up to Riley. Her assistant, Charlotte, is a member of our group. That's how she met Riley. When Riley needed to hire an assistant, she didn't hesitate to give Charlotte a chance, even though she had a criminal record."

Angie's lips pinch, as if she knows she probably said too much.

"I'm sorry. I tend to gush a lot when we find someone special, who takes the time to work with our young women. Even when some of them can be a little rough around the edges."

Her smile is genuine, and it doesn't take a genius to see how fond she is of Riley.

"Please tell her we hope she feels better soon."

"I will," I promise. "She'll be back to volunteer with you all in no time."

"Damn migraines," Angie continues. "I know all about them. Used to get them often. Not so much anymore." She looks around the room and claps her hands together. "Well, I'm sure you have to get going. Thank you again for taking Riley's place today. And for handing out your business cards."

I give her a half smile. "You never know where our company's next VP will come from."

It's a little after noon when I leave the event. Riley must be hungry by now. I had my personal assistant put in an order at my favorite restaurant. I stop by and pick it up on my way back to her place.

"Mr. Townsend," the nurse practitioner greets me as I enter.

"How is she?"

I place the food on the kitchen island, as the nurse runs down how Riley's doing.

"She's feeling much better. Still a little tired, so I made sure she's resting. She showered and changed. I didn't give her an IV since she's been drinking enough and she had breakfast before I got in this morning."

"Anything else?"

"Aside from her being slightly miffed that you required me to stay here the entire time you were gone ..." She trails off.

A wry chuckle escapes my lips. "I bet she is."

Oh well, she'll get over it. I wasn't about to leave her alone when she wasn't a hundred percent yet.

"Thanks," I tell the nurse as I see her out.

I go down the hall to check on Riley. She's laying down with her back to the door.

"You didn't have to make her stay," she says, her voice low.

"She was compensated well for her time," I retort.

Riley sucks her teeth and rolls over to face me. "How many times do I have to remind you that it's not *only* about money?"

"How many times do I have to tell you that she, like my employees, are paid to do a service and paid well? Which allows them the freedom in other areas of their lives."

She sucks her teeth again and gives me her back.

"What if she has a family that needed her home today? A son or daughter who had a soccer game or something?"

"Now you're being ridiculous." I sit on the edge of the bed, next to her. "How are you feeling?"

"I'm not being ridiculous," she says, ignoring my question. "Money is great, necessary even, but if people are expected to be at your beck and call to make good money how are they able to enjoy it? Or take care of life outside of work? Take Colin James, for example."

"Who the hell is that?"

Her eyes roll toward the ceiling. "A junior accountant. Over the past few weeks, he's put in at least four or five twelve-hour days."

"And?"

"*And,*" she mocks, "his wife just had a baby three weeks ago. A sick baby who's still in the NICU."

I jut my head back. "How do you know that?"

"Because I talk to your employees. How do you think I came up with the preliminary report for yesterday's meeting?" She sits up and folds her arms. "Or did you not read it?"

I press her shoulder, making her lay down again. "Calm down. I read it. Let's not talk about work for now. You're still on the mend."

"I'm fine."

"The nurse said you're still a little dizzy and really tired."

Her lips part, and I think she's going to protest, but instead, she lets out the biggest yawn I've seen her take.

I lift an eyebrow.

"Shut up," she mumbles and rolls over.

"Lunch is here when you wake up."

She doesn't say anything as she wiggles into a comfortable position on her side and rests her head against her mountain of pillows. I don't realize how long I stand here, watching her sleep. Her breathing grows even, and something pulls at the inside of my chest.

I should leave at this point. She's obviously feeling better. I have a shit ton of work I need to get back to. Hell, I even have a meeting scheduled to make up for a dinner meeting that I missed last night. Yet, my feet remain where they are. Watching her.

I brush a few strands of hair that've fallen over her face, and tuck them behind her ear. Riley stirs a little, making the cutest murmuring sound before going quiet again.

That's when I realize that I don't want to leave. I'm not just there to watch over one of Townsend's assets or whatever bullshit line I fed her to keep her in bed. At this moment, I have no desire to do anything that would pull me away from her side.

"Dangerous," I mutter before running a hand through my hair.

I start to reach for her again, to touch her and make sure she's real, but her cell phone buzzes.

I lift it from the nightstand and read the name across the screen.

Ladybug.

I frown. *What the hell kind of name is that?*

As the phone continues to ring in my hand, I look from it to Riley. I can't bear to wake her up, not when I know she's not fully recovered.

A sane man would recognize they have no business answering Riley's phone.

He's not me.

"Hello?" I answer as I step out of her bedroom, closing the door behind me. "Hello?" I say more insistent when I don't get a response the first time around.

"You're not Aunt Riley. Who is this?" A young girl's voice pushes through the phone line. "Oh my god, is she okay? What happened? Who is this?"

"My name's Kyle," I answer.

"Where's my aunt? Is she hurt?"

"Your aunt's fine," I reassure. "She's resting, so I answered the phone."

"A-Are you sure?" The quiver in her voice unnerves me slightly.

"Positive. She wasn't feeling well yesterday and earlier this morning. But she's better now, just sleeping."

"Did she have one of those headaches she gets?"

Obviously, this girl knows about her aunt's condition. I wonder how frequently Riley gets these migraines.

"Yes."

"Did her medication not work? She always tells me not to worry."

"Because she's right. Your aunt's tough. She ran out of medication, which was why this one was a little bit worse, but she's better now and has her meds."

There's a pause on the other end, and I suspect she's taking in what I just said.

"What's your name again?" the girl asks.

"Kyle. And yours is Ladybug?" I take a seat on one of the stools in Riley's kitchen.

She lets out a small giggle. "Only Aunt Ry calls me that. My name is Eve."

"Nice to meet you, Eve."

"How do you know my aunt?"

"We work together." That's the truth but Riley is a hell of a lot more than a colleague. She's quite literally the only woman I've shared a bed with on more than one occasion and hadn't fucked yet. But I doubt her niece needs to know that.

"Thank you for taking care of her."

I adjust my position on the stool, feeling something warm move through my body at Eve's words.

"I-I got scared when she didn't call me yesterday night or this morning. Aunt Riley always calls me on Friday nights."

The fear in her voice twists my damn stomach in a knot.

"That's probably my fault," I confess. "I made her stay in bed longer than she wanted because she was still in a little bit of pain."

"Oh," she says, sounding innocent. "She likes gummy bears after one of her headaches."

My eyebrows lift.

"Not any brand, though. She only eats Haribo gummy bears. She says anything else is a cheap knockoff."

A deep chuckle spills from me. I grab a pen from the counter and a piece of paper from a notepad Riley has on the refrigerator and write 'Haribo gummy bears' on it.

"Anything else?"

"Um …" She thinks for a moment. "She likes the blue flavor sports drink. The really popular one. She drinks a lot of those after one of her headaches."

I write down the brand I think she's talking about.

"And she doesn't like hot chocolate."

I frown because I found a couple of boxes of gourmet hot chocolate mix in one of Riley's cabinets.

"She keeps them at home for me," Eve explains as if she knows about the boxes in the cabinet. "She says hot chocolate is nothing more than warmed chocolate milk. But she's wrong. They have very different flavors," she says in such a serious tone, I don't refute.

"And her fuzzy slippers are her favorite. Her feet get cold like mine."

I honestly can't even believe I'm writing all of this shit down. But I do.

"Kyle, have you seen my—" Riley appears from the hallway.

I stare at her in the long T-shirt she's wearing that stops at her mid-thigh. Riley has long, shapely legs. I can't pull my eyes away from them anymore than I could pull myself away from her bedside, not too long ago.

What the hell is going on with me?

"Is that her?"

Eve's question pulls me out of my musings.

"Yes."

Riley approaches the kitchen.

"It's your niece." I hand her the phone.

My heart kicks up a beat when Riley's smile expands over her entire face. "Hi, Ladybug."

I can't hear Eve's response, but it makes Riley laugh. My body responds to the deep, sultry sound, even when I know she's not intending to be sexy.

"Yes, but I'm much better now." She pauses. "No, I'm not lying. I promise, I am."

She gives me an exasperated look as if to say *can you believe she doesn't believe me?*

Yes, I can believe it. Riley's the type to push through, even when she's in pain. Something I've learned about her in the past twenty-four hours. She's also someone who makes people care about her.

The women at the Girls on the Move event gushed about her. While Angie, the director, thanked me for staying and taking questions, about half of the questions weren't about networking or making an entryway into corporate America. They were about Riley; how she was doing, when she would be back, if she needed anything.

And hearing the love and concern her niece had for her further proves my point.

Then there's me.

I know my ass should've been out of here hours ago. Riley obviously knows how to take care of herself.

Yet, I'm still here, watching her talk with and reassure her niece not to worry about her.

"I'm your guardian, remember?" I hear Riley say, in a tone that reminds me of my mother when she used to tell me not to worry about things.

That's when it dawns on me that Riley isn't simply Eve's aunt. She's her caretaker, her mother, in a way. The loving tone Riley used with Eve, the affectionate nickname, all point to a deeper bond than an aunt and niece just catching up.

"Why not?"

Riley's question pulls at my attention.

"That doesn't seem fair. Do you want me to call the headmistress and ask her what's going on? You should be allowed to go to the movie, too."

I sit up, a protective instinct overcoming me.

"Are you sure?" There's a concerned note in Riley's voice. "Okay,

Ladybug. It's your call. Clean up your room as your floor leader says and maybe next time you can go."

Another pause.

I should mind my damn business. But it feels like Riley, and by extension Eve, *are* my business.

I run a hand through my hair. This is insane.

"All right, I'll give you a call tomorrow. I promise. I love you."

My stomach clenches at those final three words. Because I want her to say them to—

Fuck no.

"Thanks for taking that."

Riley startles me out of that mental spiral.

"I think she might've hopped on a plane if you hadn't answered." She laughs and takes a seat on the stool across from me.

The T-shirt slips down her shoulder, leaving it bare. My mouth waters.

"Why do you call her Ladybug?" I ask to get my attention off of the many ways I want to fuck her.

She's probably still not a hundred percent.

"She's my good luck." Her smile is wide. "My brighter side," she adds.

I quirk an eyebrow.

Riley glances down at the dark grey and black swirls in the granite countertop before looking back up at me.

"When I decided to take custody of her from my brother, I knew I had to make some big changes in my life. And I did. It was all for the better. If it weren't for her, I don't know who I would be."

I snort as a memory resurfaces.

"What?" Riley asks.

"You sound like my dad."

"I sound like *the* Aaron Townsend? How?"

I chuckle at the impressed tone of voice. "He once said something like that to me about my sister and I, and my mom, of course. He told me he doesn't know where he'd be in life if he hadn't found out about us and made my mother marry him."

Riley blinks. "Excuse me, did you just say your dad *made* your mother marry him?"

"More like blackmailed her into it." I shrug.

She continues to gawk at me.

"It worked out. They happily went on to have three more kids."

"You're one of five, right?" She asks.

I nod. "And a shitload of cousins from my uncles and aunts. My point is, my father says that one decision ended up making him a better man. Because it forced him to grow into a more selfless person."

She shakes her head. "I don't see how that's possible. How could your mother even forgive him after that?"

"Love is strange," I grunt. "Or so I hear." Not that I've ever felt that shit. A silence falls between us, and I find myself staring into Riley's eyes. Her eyelids grow heavy, and for a moment I think it's because she's still tired from recovering from her migraine.

However, when my gaze drops to the counter, I realize that my hand is covering her wrist. My thumb makes tiny circles, stroking the vein there. I can feel her heartbeat speed up from my touch.

When our eyes collide again, I recognize the altered breathing, increased heart rate, and the slight flush in her cheeks for what they are.

"Are you hungry?" I ask as my attention drops to her lips.

A small groan escapes my throat when Riley licks her bottom lip. I'm not even sure she's aware of what she's doing. I don't move my hand from her arm because it feels unconscionable to break our physical connection.

"Yes." Her voice is a whisper.

"For food?"

The slight shake of her head is all I need to rise so fast from my stool that the damn thing falls over. Not even the crashing sound as it hits the stone tiles of the floor stops me. One second I was sitting across the kitchen island from Riley, and the next, I have my hands cupping her face, my body barreling in between her legs, forcing her thighs to make room for me, and her back pressed against the counter.

"How does your head feel?" My voice is brusque.

Her forehead wrinkles in confusion.

"Are you still in pain?"

She swallows, and then a deceptive smile crosses her lips. My dick bulges, pressing against the zipper of my pants.

"My head is fine. The dizziness is gone. But if you don't fuck me soon, I will be in a different kind of pain."

Fuck.

My lips crash down on hers, claiming what is mine. This kiss is even better than the one in Miami and the kisses we shared in that closet in the hotel room. Instincts take over and I do my level best to taste every part of her mouth, to devour her.

Too soon, though, kissing is not enough. I pull back as I entwine my fingers in her hair, gripping it tightly. I tilt her head at an angle that leaves her nowhere to look but in my eyes.

"Riley, know this. Once I fuck you, that's it. You're mine. I don't share, and I don't let anyone touch what belongs to me."

"I belong to me," she insists.

My hand tightens in her hair.

"Once my dick makes you scream my name, that statement is no longer true." I don't even know where these words are coming from. I've never claimed a woman in my life. This one, however, is mine. I can feel it down to my soul.

"Kyle, I'm not—"

I cut that bullshit off with another kiss, once again possessing her. Showing her without words that, yeah, she might be her own person, but she's mine.

"Don't let that pretty mouth of yours get you into trouble, Riley," I say against her lips.

She lets out a moan, and I can tell she's on the edge.

"Do you want me to fuck you, Riley?"

"Yes," she whimpers.

"Then say it," I command.

Her hands clutch at my shoulders almost desperately. "Say what?"

"That you're mine."

She swallows, hesitating.

"Say it."

"Kyle."

My name on her tongue with that sexy, desperate tone causes all of the blood in my body to rush to my cock. It painfully presses again my pants, begging for me to fuck her right then and there.

But I'm a man of control, if nothing else.

I can wait until she gives me the words. I want her surrender.

"Tell me, Riley." My hand fists in her hair even tighter.

"Yours," she whimpers. "I'm yours, Kyle."

CHAPTER 18

Riley

I'm yours, Kyle.

I had no idea three simple words could mean so much. As soon as the phrase pushes through my lips, Kyle is everywhere. He's kissing me, his hand in my hair massaging my scalp, while his other hand runs up and down my thigh.

And he steps in closer to the stool, forcing my legs even wider to make room for his bulky frame. A tremor runs through my body at the feel of his very large dick pressing against my core. The seam of my panties becomes soaked with evidence of my need.

I gasp in surprise when Kyle suddenly pulls back and swiftly lifts me off of the stool. All of this is done in one fluid motion. He carries me to the bedroom.

"As much as I want to fuck you on that countertop, I want our first time to be in a bed. I want to see what you look like with your hair spread on the pillows, calling my name as my dick claims you for the first time."

We're really going to have to discuss him *claiming me* and *making me his*. I'm not a damn possession. But that conversation will have to wait because as soon as my back hits the mattress, Kyle is right there again. He strips the baggy T-shirt off of me, leaving me in just a pair of light pink, cotton panties.

Kyle sits back on his knees between my legs and stares down at me. He looks as if he's committing my body to memory. A glint hits his eyes when he pauses at my breasts. His large hands cover them, squeezing my nipples.

I arch my back into the warmth of his hands.

"Tell me what you like, Riley," he orders. His fingers pluck my nipples.

"That. Do more of that," I urge.

I intake a sharp inhale when he pinches them a little harder. My pussy becomes so hot and wet, I wonder if I've melted the fabric of my panties. Kyle moves a hand from my breast down to trail along my thigh, running along the seam of my panty. He inserts one long finger and I moan, my eyelids falling shut.

"You like a little pain with your pleasure, huh?"

I don't respond. But when he squeezes my nipple even tighter than before another moan escapes my throat.

Kyle makes quick work of stripping me out of the underwear. Then he begins adjusting a few pillows behind my head.

"I want you to sit up so you can watch me while I eat you out. I want you to come in my mouth, Riley."

I almost come from his words alone.

Then he dips his head between my legs and—

Oh. My. God.

My back bows off the bed from the first lick of his tongue. He takes that opportunity to hook his arms underneath my thighs, throwing my legs over his broad shoulders.

I drop my head backward and Kyle immediately stops.

"Wh-What?" I can't even form a complete sentence.

"I said watch me make you come."

His voice is like a hand wrapping around my throat, trapping me in place. I can't look anywhere but at him.

He keeps his eyes locked on mine when he lowers his head again.

My mouth falls open but no words come out. A moan sticks in my throat.

Kyle breaks our eye contact, dropping his head to pay full attention to my core, but I don't dare look away or close my eyes. No matter how heavy my eyelids become. I'm afraid that I'll self-combust if he stops again.

Soon, my legs begin quivering, and just like that, I'm exploding in his mouth. The groan that he makes as he laps up my juices has me coming even harder. Not until I come down from my first orgasm, does he pull back.

His eyes have darkened to an almost forest green. He looks more like a predator stalking me as he crawls up the length of my body. I lift my hand to run my fingers through the soaked hairs of his beard. I don't know why I find that sexy as hell but I do.

Kyle brings our lips together again, allowing me to taste myself on him. It's a mix of his strength, power, and my spiciness. It's alluring as hell. A craving I've never felt before takes hold of my lower abdomen.

"I need you inside of me," I beg, shamelessly. I might die if I don't feel his cock soon.

A sly grin spreads over his pink lips, wet from my juices and our kiss. "I knew you would beg eventually."

Cocky bastard.

"Fuck you," I groan as his hand cups my pussy.

"You're about to, baby," he promises against my lips.

Kyle quickly disposes of his clothes. I watch with my bottom lip tucked between my teeth as he rolls the Magnum over his massive rod.

"Is ... that thing real?" I say without thinking.

His eyes land on me, that arrogant smirk of his growing. "Are you scared, Riley?"

Kind of.

I scramble for an answer, but Kyle's faster. He leans in and kisses my forehead, the tip of my nose, and finally my lips. Tension seeps out of me with each press of his lips against my skin.

"It's all real," he says before biting my earlobe. "And all for you." That's the last warning I get before he's pushing inside of me.

I go to wrap my arms around his shoulders, but he takes my wrists in one of his hands and pins them over my head. With his other hand, he tucks my leg high on his waist. This position gives him more room to slip deeper inside of me.

"Breathe, Riley."

I exhale for the first time in I don't know how long.

He doesn't move at first. Instead, his eyes search mine as if he's making sure I'm okay. That same cockiness is there, but it's accompanied by a level of caring and sweetness that I never would've expected from Kyle ... not before this weekend.

I give him a slight nod.

That's when he starts to move. His eyes never leave mine as he pistons his hips. He feels sinfully good inside of me. He drops his head to the crook of my neck and traces the veins there with his tongue. All of the sensations filling my body blur my vision.

I attempt to wiggle my wrists free from his hold. I want to touch him, to pull him closer to me. But Kyle never breaks the grasp he has around my wrists. He does capture my lips in another searing kiss. Our bodies move against one another's, finding a rhythm that matches us perfectly.

He's demanding yet gentle and soft at the same time. Kyle is all consuming as he plunders my body, chasing me higher and higher up the ladder of pleasure. Soon, I feel as if I'll break apart.

And that's when the explosion happens.

The orgasm overtakes every inch of my body. I don't even realize that I'm yelling his name until I come down from my high, my voice hoarse.

Kyle tenses above me, and his hand clenches around my wrists firmly as he empties into the condom.

For a while panting is the only sound in the room.

Then Kyle rolls us over so that I'm laying on top of him. He's still throbbing inside of me.

"That would be a yes," he murmurs, smirking.

"What are you talking about?"

That grin of his grows. "You're a screamer."

CHAPTER 19

Kyle

"I cannot believe how damn competitive you are." Riley glares at me over her shoulder from the kitchen.

I lean back against the arm of the couch and drag my eyes over the black lace panties, garter belt, and skin tone stockings she's wearing. Over the panties she wears a red apron that skims the tops of her thighs.

"You shouldn't have dared me," I reply, my eyes firmly planted on her ass.

Riley is half naked in her kitchen, chopping vegetables because she dared me to a game of bowling. She thought she could beat me. That's when I bet her that if she lost, she'd have to cook me dinner in nothing but a pair of heels and a panty set.

She lost because no fucking way was I about to miss out on this opportunity.

"You could've let me win." She points the knife in her hand in my direction. "I was on my deathbed mere hours ago."

I chuckle and take a long pull from the beer in my hands. It's either keep my hands wrapped around this bottle, or bend Riley over that counter and have her scream down the roof.

But I'm relishing watching her wearing next to nothing while she cooks for me.

"You weren't dying when you were constantly telling me how *fine* you were. Even when I could see you were still in pain." She's a hundred percent recovered from her migraine. I wouldn't have taken her out to bowl, let alone cook for me in the kitchen with heels on, if I thought otherwise.

"What happened to the considerate guy who was ready to hand feed me grilled cheese and soup? He would never have me doing this."

She's complaining but her ass continues to chop those vegetables.

"He," I start as I place the bottle down on the island and move to stand behind her because I can't *not* be close to her any longer; I press my front against her backside and lower my chin to her shoulder, "absolutely would have you half naked in the kitchen, cooking. You're just lucky that I'm hungry enough not to have bent you over a stool yet."

I smile when a tremor runs through her body. She gives me a side-eye before going back to mixing a bowl of eggs.

"What are you making anyway?" She hasn't told me what we're having. There are numerous bowls, dishes, and appliances going.

"Breakfast for dinner," she says cheerily. She can gripe all she wants but Riley is enjoying being the loser of this bet as much as I'm enjoying being the victor. "We're having omelets with spinach, mushrooms, and bacon. And a personal fave of mine, sweet potato waffles."

She points to the waffle maker to her left that's warming up. I glance around, noting the various appliances and how comfortable she is around the kitchen.

"You like cooking," I say.

She smiles at me over her shoulder. My eyes drop to those red lips. Yes, I also insisted as part of the bet that she wear red lipstick while cooking for me. My dick presses against my pants as the image of that lipstick smeared over her mouth while she's sucking me off makes its way to the forefront of my mind.

I take a step back to break our physical contact. Otherwise, she won't get to finish preparing this meal. Over the past day and a half,

I've taken Riley at least four different times. And that's just with my dick. It's not counting the number of times I've had my head between her legs.

Her pussy needs a break.

Which was why she insisted we go out bowling.

"Did you grow up cooking?" I ask, needing to think about something other than screwing her again.

She lets out a hollow laugh. "If learning to boil hotdogs and microwave chicken nuggets counts as cooking, then yeah." There's bitterness in her words. The same tone that was present when she talked a little about her father two nights ago.

"When Ladybug came to live with me, I decided to learn to cook. I didn't want her eating microwavable meals and whatnot every day."

From my position, I can see her profile. Her face lights up when she mentions her niece.

"How long has she been with you?"

"Since she was five. So, almost six years."

"But she goes to school back east?"

She nods. "Bowen Boarding Academy."

I blow out a whistle. "I went to college and grad school with a few people who graduated from there. It's a hell of a school."

Riley beams with pride. "That's because my baby's a genius."

Again, she reminds me of my mom when she's talking about one of us.

"She's in like the top two percent for math and analytics. She's crazy smart when it comes to numbers and formulas, and science and all of that stuff. That comes naturally to her, but she works hard to be as good in the social sciences, too. Too hard, in my opinion. I often have to remind her that it's okay to take a night off from studying."

"She sounds like a hard worker." I move to her side and watch as she ladles a scoop of the sweet potato mix onto the griddle.

"She's only eleven. There's plenty of time for her to work down the road. Her job is to remain a kid for as long as possible."

"She can't be a child forever. I was in the Townsend offices at that age."

Riley frowns up at me. "You can't be serious."

"I am. It was the best training ground for my career."

She rolls her eyes. "You were a child. You should've gotten to have childhood experiences."

"I did. Make no mistake. It was my choice to be there. It's still my choice to make my family proud."

She pauses and looks at me with sincerity. "I don't want her to worry about adult things until she needs to. She's already halfway across the country from me." Her frown deepens. "I miss her."

"How long has she been at Bowen?"

"Two years. Feels like longer, even though she comes home for the summers and school breaks of course." Sadness infiltrates her voice.

I move behind her again and run my hands up and down the length of her arms. Though she's barely wearing any clothing and she looks hot as fuck, my movements are more for comfort than for pleasure.

"What happened to her parents?"

Riley stiffens at my question. I realize right away it's a sensitive topic. But I'm greedy and I want to know more about Riley's life. What makes her tick? She obviously has a deep love for her niece.

"Her mom died soon after she was born. She had a rare heart condition. The pregnancy exacerbated that. That's what my brother told me. And he …" She trails off. "Well, he took after our father. When I saw that, I couldn't sit by and let her be subject to that. I convinced him that she would get a more stable life with me."

She snorts.

"The irony. I had only moved into an apartment from the homeless shelter two months before that. But I knew I could give her more than what my brother was willing to give her."

"Family's important to you?" I ask.

"Ladybug's the only family I really have."

She lowers the lid of the waffle maker before turning to face me. Our fronts brush up against one another. I bracket her in place with my hands on either side of her body against the counter.

"I already know family's important to you. Tell me about your siblings."

A smile crests on my lips. "Kennedy and I are the oldest."

"Twins, right?"

I nod. "Then Andreas and Thiers. Also twins."

"Wait," she spins to me with a spatula in her hand. "Your mother had two sets of twins?" Her eyes bulge when I chuckle and nod.

"That's insane."

"Then there's the baby of the bunch, Stasi."

"What are they like?"

"Kennedy's headstrong."

Riley snorts. "She's not the only one. Ouch!" She yelps when I smack her ass.

"I'm not headstrong."

"Stubborn is more like it. Keep going."

"She's early in her career as an investigative reporter. Because of it, she's out of town a lot. Plus, she likes travel. She got really into it when we went on an around-the-world trip as teenagers."

"Really?" Her eyes go wide. "Your whole family?"

"It was a year after my mother went into remission for breast cancer."

Her eyes sadden.

"She's been in remission for almost a decade now. Andreas is the outgoing, charming type," I continue, changing the subject back to my siblings. "He's always been a performer, which is why he's in L.A."

Riley gasps. "Wait, your brother isn't Andreas Briggs, is it? From that teen sitcom *Over the Bridge?*"

My eyebrows pop. "How'd you put that together?" Andreas goes by a different public last name. It's to keep his professional and personal life as separate as possible. For the past two years, he's had a starring role in a popular teen drama. At nineteen, he's poised to make a big splash in the entertainment industry.

She stares at me. "I see the resemblance. He looks like a younger version of you and your father."

"He's one of us."

"Is his twin also an actor?"

My heart sinks slightly at the thought of my youngest brother. "Thiers is in the Army. He dropped out after only one year in college. He's the most reserved out of all of us." My brother wouldn't be caught dead performing for an audience. He'd just as well shoot them.

"Stasi is still in high school. But she loves cooking and tells anyone in earshot that she's going to open her own restaurant someday."

"That's amazing. You talk about your family with such pride in your voice."

Her smile is tender.

"I'm proud of all of them. And we haven't even gotten to my cousins yet. They're all younger, though. Still in middle and high school. But I know they'll all take on the world one by one."

"Just like they're older cousin leading the way." She looks me in the eye as she says this.

My heart swells with something I want to bottle up and keep close to me forever.

"I'm not the oldest, though."

"That's Diego right? How is he? I don't think I've seen him since that night in Miami. I'm surprised he doesn't work for the family company."

"He left that same night he stormed off the beach. Spent two weeks out of town with Monique—his best friend, and he's been busy with work." I don't mention why he doesn't work at Townsend real estate because, honestly, I still don't know what's holding him back.

She looks me directly in the eyes, searching for something. "That's why you work so hard, huh?"

I lift an eyebrow, wondering what conclusions she's drawing about me. Ordinarily, I don't care for anyone figuring me out, but I don't mind it so much with her.

"Most people would assume it's born out of pure ambition. Or just because you're some crazy workaholic who gets off on sixteen-hour days. But you do it for your family."

"Family is everything."

She cocks her head to the side like my comment surprises her.

"You don't agree?"

"No, I do. It's just ... I haven't really ever had a real family, not in the typical sense. Anyway, dinner's done," she says, turning again to the counter.

She may have lost the bet, but I'm not a total asshole. I help set the table for our breakfast-dinner meal. But when Riley starts to round the glass table to sit on the other side, I wrap my arms around her and pull her onto my lap.

"You'll eat from here."

"First you make me cook while naked for you. Now you're not even going to let me eat in peace." She huffs but I see the smile she's working to suppress.

"Be lucky I'm not feeding you my cock for dinner instead."

She almost chokes on the sip of iced tea she just took.

I pat her back a couple of times before rubbing my hand up and down her spine. "Was it something I said?"

She glares at me, and dammit if she keeps that up, we're not going to make it through dinner.

"I suggest you eat quickly," I growl. "I can only sit with you like this for so long before I have you moaning my name."

***

RILEY

"What?" Eve sounds absolutely outraged. "Aunt Ry, did you hear what he just said?" she screeches.

I shake my head and give Kyle a pitiful look as I hold my phone between the two of us. We're sitting on the couch in my living room. We almost made it through dinner before Kyle started to feel me up. Beneath my butt I felt the swell of his dick, which caused a growing warmth in my core.

However, when Kyle started to lift me onto the counter, my phone rang. Eve was right on time for our usual Sunday evening call. Now, she's chastising Kyle for his poor movie viewing habits.

"How could you not have seen *The Greatest Showman*?" she demands to know.

"I'm not into musicals," he replies, sounding casual and not at all offended.

"How is that ... Have you seen *Hamilton*?" she tries again.

I can see by the expression on his face that the answer is going to be a no.

Eve groans as soon as she hears his answer. "I can't believe it." She sounds truly in awe. "It's the best musical ever!" she exclaims. "It's not exactly historically accurate but you know what they say about creative direction and that stuff."

Kyle plays along and adds, "I do know. My brother does a little bit of acting."

"Really? Is he famous?"

He hesitates. "Probably nothing you would know."

"What about—"

"Eve, isn't it time for you to take a shower and get ready for classes in the morning?" She was only an hour ahead of us but it was still getting late for her.

"Yes, Aunt Ry," she drones.

"Did you clean your room like the dorm leader asked you to?"

There's a pause.

"I tried."

I frown at the inflection in her voice. I take the phone off of the speaker and get up from the couch, leaving Kyle there.

"Is everything okay, Ladybug?"

"Yes." She answers too quickly.

"What about last night? Did you get to go out to the movies?"

"No, that's when I was cleaning. Can we have our visit next weekend in New York again, like you said?"

I look back at Kyle to see he's watching me. A part of me wonders what it would be like if he and I had plans the following weekend. *Is this just a one-off thing for him?*

Then I push those thoughts aside for two reasons ... One, I

should've never slept with him considering the reason I even met him. And two, Eve takes priority over everything. Always.

"Yes, of course," I tell her. It would do us both some good to see one another, I think. "I'll book my flight and make reservations by the end of the day tomorrow, okay?"

"Okay." She sounds happy, which lightens the heaviness weighing on me. "I love you, Ladybug. Now go get ready for bed and for school tomorrow."

Kyle watches me as I make my way back over to the couch.

"Uh, uh," he warns with a shake of his head as he pulls me in between his legs. "You sit over here."

My body eases into his warmth as I lean back against his chest.

"Where were we?" he murmurs in my ear before pressing a kiss to my earlobe.

My body shudders. He quickly undoes the strings of my apron, removing it and tossing it to the floor. Then, he slides a hand over my shoulder to cup my breast, covered only by the lacy fabric of my bra.

"Oh no." I snatch the remote control from next to us and turn the television on.

"The hell are you doing?"

I laugh. "You disappointed my niece. And I cannot hang out with someone who lets her down by not watching one of her favorite movies ever." I navigate to the correct app and pull up *The Greatest Showman*.

"Riley, we're not *hanging out*," he comments. "We're about to fuck."

Before I can respond, he moves his hand lower to cup my sex. My determination wavers briefly before I summon the strength to take hold of his wrist.

"No, you have to watch it."

"Next time." He plants a kiss to the back of my neck.

"What if there isn't a next time?"

He jerks back. "Why wouldn't there be?"

I shrug. "I don't know. I didn't realize this wasn't just a weekend fling for you."

Kyle sits all the way up, somehow keeping his hands on my waist.

He maneuvers my body so that I'm sitting with my legs straddling his as we sit facing one another.

"Riley, I told you once I put my dick inside of you that you're mine, didn't I?"

He's so vulgar. And yet, my nipples harden from his words.

"Y-Yes."

"Do you take me for a man who doesn't mean what he says?"

I shake my head.

"What was that?"

"No," I answer, knowing he wanted to hear me say it out loud.

He lifts his fingers and traces my lips. "I've wanted you ever since the first moment I laid eyes on you."

I blink in shock. "The way I recall it, you couldn't wait to get rid of me. Your security guard threw me out of that club."

He has the audacity to chuckle. "Yet, here we are."

All types of emotions I can't name roll around in my belly. One of which I can identify as guilt.

To avoid thinking about the guilt, I pull back when Kyle moves forward to draw my lips to his.

"You have to watch the movie."

He scowls and tightens his hands on my ass, squeezing it.

"Riley, if you don't—"

"You cannot disappoint my niece like this. What if she quizzes you the next time you talk with her? She'll expect you to have watched it."

He leans back against the couch, and I can't help but think of a king on his throne. His hands are still firmly planted on my ass.

"You want me to watch the movie?"

I nod, thinking I'm making progress.

"Fine." He runs his pointer finger along the seam of my panty. "I'll watch it," he says, seductively. I know there's going to be a catch. "While you ride me."

There's a ripping sound, and I gasp upon realizing he's torn my underwear.

"You son of a ... those were new."

He gives me a half smile. "I'll buy you more."

He doesn't waste time sparing an ounce of guilt for destroying my panties. Kyle guides my hands to his belt buckle.

"Take me out." He lifts the remote and presses the play button.

"You want me to screw you while we watch a damn musical."

"*I'm* going to watch. You're going to be busy," he corrects.

"You're insane."

That makes him laugh. Yet, I find myself undoing his jeans and pulling his massive rod out of his pants.

"Fuck," he groans as I stroke him a couple of times.

I stare at this part of his anatomy.

"You know," I pause to run my thumb over the tip, "you have a very pretty dick."

"What?" Surprise stretches across his face.

I casually lift and lower a shoulder. "I don't know. Most guy's dicks aren't that attractive. But yours—" I'm cut off by a growling sound emanating from his throat.

"What other guys?"

Is that jealousy in his voice?

"No one in particular. I mean, you do realize I wasn't a virgin before yesterday, right? And I've watched my fair share of porn and whatnot. Cocks aren't particularly pre—"

He kisses the words back down my throat.

"Don't ever talk to me about another fucking man." His hands tighten on my ass and his eyes take on a murderous glint.

"I wasn't talking about anyone specific." I suck my teeth. "Can't you take a compliment?" I stroke him again, and the deadly look in his eyes starts to fade into a look of lust.

"Fuck me, Riley. If you want me to watch this movie."

He hands me a condom that must've come from his wallet. Even as my fingers tremble, I'm able to slide the latex over him. He helps me with his hands on my waist as I lift my body and seat myself onto his shaft.

We both sigh as he enters me.

"So fucking good," he breathes out.

"Watch the movie," I direct.

"Keep fucking me and I will." He smacks my ass, urging me to move.

"So damn pushy."

"I'm about to push you over onto this couch and fuck you senseless if you don't—"

"Okay, okay." I laugh as I lift my waist and slowly lower onto him. I grip him by the shoulders before grinding my hips against his. Pure bliss takes over me as Hugh Jackman's singing takes place behind me.

"Shit, don't stop," Kyle commands. His hold on me is firm.

"Keep watching," I whisper.

"Take this off." Before I can follow instructions, he's pulling and tugging at my apron and bra. All the while, he's keeping his eyes on the television screen.

His hands find my breasts and squeeze. I cover his hands with mine, keeping them right there as I continue the movement of my hips.

"Right there, baby," he murmurs.

Why does it feel so good when he compliments me like that? Like I'm truly his.

"You're so damn beautiful sitting on my dick, Riley."

I moan, and another flood of juice coats his cock.

Words of affirmation must be my love language. No matter how much my subconscious tries to remind me how wrong this is, I can't help but to be drawn deeper into his haze of want, desire, and lust. Kyle's hands are all over me, his dick deep inside of me, and right now, nothing else matters.

"That's it," his deep voice encourages, and I tighten my pussy walls around his shaft. My desire to please him overcomes me, and soon I feel his body stiffen. His fingers dig into the skin of my back, pressing me to him. He holds on as if I'm the only thing in the world.

My hold is just as tight around his broad shoulders.

We're coming together.

I can't remember the last time—if ever—I've experienced something so intimate.

That's the moment I realize that I'm in serious trouble.

CHAPTER 20

Riley

A week after my weekend with Kyle, I'm back east, having spent the past two and a half days with my favorite person in the world.

"I'm going to miss you, Aunt Ry," Eve says with a sadness in her voice that grips my heart.

We're standing outside of her dorm building. This is the part of our weekends together that I loathe the most. But something in Eve's voice makes me dread this good-bye even more.

"Ladybug, is there something you need to tell me?" I grip her shoulders.

She peers up at me with those light brown, honey eyes of hers. At times, her eye colors shift to hazel.

That thought pulls me out of the moment, harkening me back to another pair of hazel eyes that I've missed more than I care to admit. As much as I thought it would be, the past week at Townsend wasn't awkward at all. If anything, I felt as if we'd made headway on the professional front.

Kyle inquired about my opinion more and showed more interest in my suggestions regarding the implementation of certain employee benefits. I hate to think it's what's between my legs that's gotten Kyle to become more amenable to my suggestions.

Though, thinking of the time when he *accidentally* found me in one of the conference rooms alone, locked the door, and made me come with his fingers, it's hard not to think that's the only reason he finds my work helpful.

"I'm just thinking about the big test I have coming up," Eve says, pulling me out of my thoughts.

Her eyes dart away from mine, and that sinking feeling in my stomach deepens.

"Eve, you know you can talk to me about anything. There's nothing you could tell me that would make me love you any less than I already do. It's just not possible." I squeeze her shoulders.

"I know that." Despite her words, she begins fidgeting from one foot to the other. "I'm tired, Aunt Ry. But I should probably study before I get to bed."

"Ladybug, tomorrow's Monday. Worry about school then."

She's shaking her head before I can get the full comment out of my mouth.

"I want to make you proud."

I kiss the top of her head. "You already have. Anything else you do or accomplish is just icing on the cake."

Her face wrinkles as she grins. "I love you, Aunt Ry."

She throws her arms around my waist, and I hold her tight to me.

I don't want to leave her.

"Let me help you carry your bag up."

"No," Eve bursts out. "It's fine. I got it. You know I don't like good-byes either," she adds in a hurried tone.

"But—" My phone beeps. Ordinarily, I wouldn't pay it any mind because I'm with my Ladybug, but the dread that's been nothing more than a nuisance in the pit of my belly for the past six days grows.

"One sec." I hold up my finger and pull out my cell. It's a text from Charlotte.

Charlotte: **Have you seen this?**

In the text she's included a link to an article from the *Williamsport Daily*.

"Are the Townsends What They Seem?" The headline reads.

My stomach bottoms out because I just know this is somehow connected to Dean Walsh, and the information I passed over to him.

I skim the article.

"Sources say that for years, the Townsend family has manipulated, bribed, bullied, and possibly even committed crimes to expand their billion-dollar empire," I mumble as I read.

"I'm going to head to my dorm room. Bye, Aunt Ry."

I peer up to see Eve starting to walk away.

"Hey, wait," I call out, stopping her. I shove my phone into my pocket. I'll have to take care of that later. "Let me help you." I try to take the backpack she brought for our weekend trip, but she holds it firmly.

"No, it's okay."

We're in a brief standoff, and I start to wonder what's going on with her. In my peripheral, I hear the door of the building open up. I keep my attention on my niece.

As I start to demand she tell me what's going on, a woman calls my name.

"Ms. Martin?"

I recognize it as the Eve's dorm leader, Scarlett Winters. When I break eye contact with Eve, she uses it as an opportunity to get away.

"Eve!" I call, but she gives me a short wave and an *I love you* as she looks from me to Scarlett, before making her exit.

"Ms. Winters," I greet. "How are you?"

"I'm so glad I ran into you before you left," she says.

I nod but look over her shoulder to see Eve disappear onto the elevators up to her dorm room. I go to head in that direction, but Ms. Winters steps in front of me, blocking.

"Is there a problem?" I ask, getting irritated.

My phone in my pocket buzzes again. My fingers itch to answer, suspecting it's not going to be good news, but I refrain.

"Well, no, not a problem per say." There's a hesitance in Ms. Winters voice that I don't like.

"Is Eve in some sort of trouble? Because—"

"No, nothing like that," she answers quickly.

My shoulders drop but I'm still on the defense.

"Eve is a great student. You know how smart she is."

"She's brilliant." My voice comes out more defensive than I intend but I don't like the tone this woman is taking.

"Yes, of course. As you know, we have a lot of brilliant, as you say, students here at Bowen."

"But none of them is Eve," I respond.

This school is one of the top schools in the nation. It's hard not to be when the children of senators, former presidents, fortune 500 CEOs all attend. Close to ninety five percent of graduates end up at Ivy league universities.

I want to tell Ms. Winters it's not because most of them are as half as bright as my niece. It's because their parents have the money to afford this school, the best tutors, and extra classes to get them into those schools.

She gives me a plastic smile. "Yes, of course. Eve is wonderful. All of her teachers adore her."

I nod because that's exactly what her last student report said.

"However, there is an issue with Eve's ... tidiness, and with some of the girls on her floor."

I squint at her. "What girls?" My voice grows louder. Eve never told me she's having a problem with anyone.

She glances away and then looks back at me. "Eve's a bit messy. Some of the girls saw her room and mentioned it to me. It was no big deal. But when we try to get her to clean up, she seems to have trouble remaining on task."

"She's eleven," I defend. "Do you know many eleven year olds who put cleanliness at the top of their priority list? And why were those girls in her room in the first place?"

Eve's had a private room since the beginning of this year when her roommate abruptly withdrew from Bowen due to a family member's illness.

"Well, it was during social hour." She scratches the back of her head. "It was nothing, really. However, she seems to have a problem focusing on tasks."

"Eve's the most focused person I know," I counter, feeling defensive. "Is she having any behavioral issues?" The question is preposterous because I know my niece. She's the sweetest, most loving child you could ever meet. Her teachers have always loved her.

"Not quite."

I open my mouth to ask her to explain, but instead of a text my phone starts ringing. On instinct, I pull it out to send the caller to voicemail. I freeze at the sight of the number on the screen.

Dean Walsh.

Fucking bastard.

"You appear to be busy," Ms. Winters says, bringing my attention back to her.

I stuff my phone back into my pocket and shake my head. "No. I'm never too busy when it comes to Eve."

She takes a step back. "Really, it can wait. You will be returning in a few weeks for Parents' Weekend, yes?"

Each quarter the school hosts a Parent Weekend, in which all parents and guardians gather for events and whatnot throughout the school's campus.

"Yes, I will," I promise. "But if there's an issue you need to address with me now—"

My phone rings again. He's been quiet for the past week, but Dean obviously has something to say. I bet it has to do with that article Charlotte sent.

"No, it's not an issue that we can't address during that weekend," Winters says as she heads up the stairs that lead to the front door of the dorm.

With my phone ringing and Ms. Winters getting farther and farther away, I feel stretched thin.

"I'll be back in a few weeks," I promise.

"Yes. We'll see you then."

I press the ignore button on my phone and pull up the text thread between my Ladybug and me.

Me: **I love you. I'll see you in a couple of weeks for Parents' Weekend.**

A few beats later, Eve responds.

Ladybug: **Love you too. Travel safe.**

I receive a notification that the rideshare I scheduled to meet me in front of Eve's dorm is arriving to take me to the airport.

My phone starts ringing again as I reluctantly walk out to meet the driver waiting for me.

"What, Dean?" I seethe as I answer yet another call.

"Where the fuck are you?"

"None of your damn business," I almost shout. I pause and glance around, remembering where I am.

"You need to get back to Williamsport. There's something I need you to do."

"How did you know I wasn't in Williamsport?" I pause right before I open the car door.

"I guessed," he replies.

The hairs on the back of my neck stand up.

I look up and down the almost empty street. I'm on Eve's campus, a few yards from the main entrance that's protected by a large steel gate. The campus is secure, I remind myself.

"Anyway, I know Townsend is in a tailspin from that article."

The car horn honks, making me startle.

The driver rolls down the window to ask, "Riley?"

I nod. "Yes."

He pulls off as soon as I close the door behind me.

"That was you?" I ask Dean.

"Of course. I told you I know people. I have a contact at the Williamsport Daily."

He says it like it's a badge of honor. However, that paper is the smallest one in the city. It has a circulation of fewer than ten thousand subscribers or something like that. It's not a huge imprint and has maybe double that amount of online followers, which is nothing compared to the heavy hitting presses.

Yet, any article that points to illegal dealings is bound to garner some negative attention. Not what Townsend Industries would want.

"Listen," Dean continues, "I'm going to need you to meet someone."

"What? Who? I'm not—" I break off as my eyes meet those of the driver. Lowering my voice I say, "I'm not meeting anyone for you."

"You are. I'll text you the name, time, and location. He's got something he's going to give you to help you gather more information on those sons of bitches."

With that he disconnects the call.

My mind is going a million miles a minute. Between Eve, this bullshit with Dean, and whatever is growing between me and Kyle, I can't keep up with it all.

CHAPTER 21

Kyle

"This is defamation," I growl at the five people on the conference call. One of which is my father, calling in from Paris, and another is my Uncle Joshua.

Earlier this morning that fucking article in *The Williamsport Daily* came out. Even though it's Sunday, the first thing I did was demand that two of my family's top attorneys make time for this call.

I'm at Buona Sera, an Italian restaurant owned by my family, in one of the private dining rooms.

"First we're going to sue those fucking reporters, and second, I'm going to sue the entire paper and put those sons of bitches out of business."

"Calm down, son," my father says.

I blink and glare at the phone. "Did you just tell me to calm down?" I can hardly believe what he's saying.

"He's right, Kyle," Uncle Joshua adds.

I shake my head in disbelief.

"Nothing good will come of this if we make any rash decisions," Dad replies.

"Do you hear yourself?" My father has gotten soft in his old age.

"Jake, I want the defamation paperwork filed for tomorrow," I instruct, ignoring my father's advice. Him being in the City of Love has gotten to him. I can tell. As soon as he's back home he'll be singing a different tune.

Which is why I'm not waiting around to get the ball rolling.

"Kyle, we can do that."

"Then do it," I order, feeling like he's about to stick a 'but' on the end of his sentence.

"But we're not quite certain anything contained in that article constitutes defamation."

A growling sound escapes out of the back of my throat.

"We know that article is not accurate," Amelia, the other attorney on the line, adds. Her voice is firm. "If you want to sue them to hell, I'll get the paperwork done by the end of business tomorrow. But you may also want to think about how this all looks," she continues.

While I want to tell her to go to hell and just get the job done, my uncle instructs her to, "Keep talking."

Reluctantly, I listen.

"*The Williamsport Daily* is a small fish. A few thousand people may have come across that article. And with the latest report I've seen on the paper's demographics, they don't have the pull they had even five years ago."

Amelia is a former PR associate and she's obviously putting that experience to use.

"If you sue, you run the risk of exposing the accusations in that article to even more eyes. However, I know you have connections at *The Times Daily* and others."

I nod even though they can't see me. I can see where she's going. *The Times*, as it's called for short, is a national publication with millions of subscribers in print and online.

"Mr. Townsend, your daughter works for *The Regal*, doesn't she?" Amelia asks.

"Leave her out of this," my father snaps, sounding like the hard ass I know and love.

My twin sister, Kennedy, is an up-and-coming investigative

reporter. My end goal is for our company to purchase the press she works for and eventually have her run it. But that's not what this conversation is about. And Kennedy, like Diego, shies away from working in the family business.

I plan to change that in the future.

"We have multiple contacts we can reach out to at *The Times*," I say to Amelia.

We spend the next twenty minutes coming up with article ideas that highlight the good Townsend Industries has done for the city of Williamsport and beyond. When Amelia suggests that we do an interview about the community center my mother, aunts, and grandmother founded, that's where my father, uncle, and I draw the line.

"Keep their names out of these articles," my father says. I can imagine him gritting his teeth. All of the men in my family are protective over the women in our lives.

"Yes, sir, Mr. Townsend," Amelia replies to my father, sounding a notch less confident than a moment ago.

"I have to go," I say after an hour on this call.

Once I wrap up the call, I head to the car waiting for me.

"Williamsport General," I tell the driver.

Seconds later, we pull off in the direction of the city's largest hospital. The article from the *Daily* continues to linger on my mind. I want to know who's the source of the article. I know it isn't Jayceon Carlson. He's mired in legal battles and public scandal since the night of his birthday party.

Was he working with someone else?

I become lost in my thoughts, so much so, that the fifteen-minute drive to the hospital goes by in the blink of an eye. Before I know it, we're pulling into the hospital's private entrance.

"I'll be a few minutes," I tell the driver and head up the back stairwell to a set of elevators that few people know about.

One of the security guards for this entrance nods at me, giving me the go ahead to enter through the double doors. I enter the neonatal intensive care unit, otherwise known as the NICU of the hospital. I do my best as I pass the large windows that show into the rooms with sick infants in them, without staring too closely. Even the most hardened bastard would have trouble seeing sick babies.

About halfway down the hallway, I look straight ahead and see the room I'm searching for. 3B.

"He's making great progress," a woman in scrubs, a nurse I presume, says cheerfully as she wheels a large incubator out of a room.

"When do you think we'll be able to take him home?" a familiar male voice asks.

I stop a few feet away, clearing my throat. Though it was unintended, I catch both of their attentions. The man's eyes bulge.

"Mr. Townsend," Simon James says. "Are you ... what are you doing here?" He's obviously startled.

"I'm going to get this little guy back to the general room. We'll be back in a few hours for another visit."

Simon nods and gives a small, sad smile at the nurse. His eyes drop to the infant in the incubator.

"See ya soon, bud." He watches the nurse roll away with his son, then looks back up at me. He blinks as if remembering that I'm there.

I watch the incubator roll away also. "How long has he been here?" I ask Simon.

"Uh, he was born exactly forty-three days ago. We've been here ever since."

It's on the tip of my tongue to ask what happened but I hold back. However, Simon supplies the information anyway.

"He was born a little early. That wasn't so bad, but Meghan's labor was long and hard on her body. During the birth, he swallowed some of the meconium and aspirated."

"Meconium?" I have no idea what that is.

"Uh." He rubs the back of his neck. "A baby's first poop."

I nod, as if I have any idea how that would happen. I don't even want to imagine it.

"It was pretty serious for a while but he's getting better." He injects cheer into the last sentence. While he probably is feeling relieved, I can see tiredness in his eyes.

"Are you here about the Waterson merger? I've been working with the marketing team closely, and I think—"

"That's not why I'm here."

He deflates. "Oh, then it's true."

"What's true?"

He clears his throat. "The redundancy issue. You're going to have to let some people go and I'm one of them."

Jesus, does he really think I'd show up to the hospital where his sick kid is to fire him? What type of fucked up—

With a shake of my head, I tell him, "I'm not here to fire you. I wouldn't ... You're an asset to our company. I've looked over your records and saw aside from two days, you haven't taken any personal time. Someone told me that you had a sick baby in the hospital, and I wanted to visit myself."

His eyes bulge and he looks like he can hardly process what I'm saying.

"I-I broke my ankle a few months ago and used up most of my sick days because I had to have surgery. My income is our primary source of income since Meghan went down to part-time once she got pregnant." It sounds like he's defending himself.

"I speak for Townsend Industries when I say we recognize your hard work and are grateful for it." I don't even think about my next statement as I say, "I've spoken with HR and we're able to give you four weeks' worth of parental leave. This won't impact your personal or sick days. You'll receive one hundred percent of your salary for all four weeks. Should you decide to extend your leave, you're eligible for another four weeks, at which time your salary would go down to seventy percent, but your job is guaranteed to be there upon your return to the office."

"Thank you," he gushes. "Wait, are you sure?"

"I am. Riley ..." I pause and clear my throat. "Ms. Martin recommended that Townsend implement a series of improvements to our employee benefits package. Increasing paternity leave was among them."

She told me about Simon's situation last weekend, and I spent the past week asking around, prodding HR on what the numbers look like, as well as consulting with my father. He agreed to the strategy.

"Also ..." I hand Simon the bouquet of flowers. "Congratulations to you and your wife. Please accept my apology on behalf of Townsend Industries for the lateness of this gift. I'm certain your son will heal quickly."

I pull a business card out of the inside pocket of my suit jacket. "If you need anything, medical wise, don't hesitate to contact this number." I tap the card as he holds it.

"CEO," he reads.

"Walter McNielson. He's the CEO of Williamsport General. He's also a personal associate of my family. If you have any trouble, tell him I sent you. He'll take care of it."

"I-I don't know how ..." His voice trails off.

"You don't have to. You've done a great job at Townsend for the past five years. Thank you."

"Thank you."

With that, I turn to exit. Not for the first time, I start to wonder how many of my employees are going through something. Riley's talk from that night on the yacht in Miami comes flooding back. It took me a while to admit it, but she might have a point about considering our employees as a whole, not just as workers.

I wonder how that could improve Townsend's overall operations.

"Kyle," a voice calls from me as I stride toward my awaiting car in the hospital's underground garage.

I turn to find a familiar face. I know him from somewhere, but I don't immediately recall his name.

"It's me," he says as he gets closer, pointing to himself. "Brendan Chastain."

The name rings a bell. The same fucker who can't take a hint. He's been calling my office for a few weeks. The calls stopped over the past week, so I thought that meant he recognized that he was barking up the wrong tree.

"I tried to catch you at Buona Sera," he says, breathlessly.

"Are you following me?" I demand.

He flinches. "N-Not exactly."

I get in his face. "Not exactly? What are you doing here?" My hands ball at my sides. I don't have security with me, since I only use them for major public appearances. Besides, I don't need them to handle Chastain.

I can put him on my ass myself without breaking a sweat.

"What do you want?"

"I need to speak to you."

"You don't know when to take a hint, do you? Did the countless times I had my assistant tell you all but to get lost not clue you in?" Hell, I told Michael to tell Chastain to fuck off. But knowing my assistant, he told him in a much kinder way, which is probably why Chastain is standing in my face now.

"It's important."

"Everyone thinks their bullshit is important."

I turn to make my way to my car.

"Kyle, please." He moves to stand in front of me.

"You've got from now until I reach my car door to make your point." I walk directly past him, taking long strides to get to the car where the driver stands with the door open.

"It's about Carissa."

"I don't know any Carissa." I don't bother looking back at him as I say those words.

"No. Um, her real name is Riley. Riley Martin."

My chest tightens and my legs stop, just as I reach the door to the backseat of the car. Slowly, I turn to face Brendan.

"She's not who you think she is," he says.

I narrow my eyes and glare at him. "You think you know more about Riley than I do?" My voice is a block of ice and dread. The mention of Riley's name pisses me off.

Brendan rocks back on his heels.

"I have proof," he says. "You want to see what I have. She's not what you think she is, and if she's working for Townsend, she can cause you and your family a lot of trouble."

My entire body grows hot with anger. At first, my instinct is to punch Brendan Chastain until he begs for me to let him up for talking shit about Riley. But I restrain myself because, despite my irritation, I can hear the urgency in his voice.

He's serious.

"Get in," I order and step back, making room for him to get in the backseat of my car.

As soon as he's in, I pull out my cell phone to call the person I go to in any significant security situation.

"Who're you calling?" Brendan asks.

I glare at him out of the corner of my eye. "None of your business."

I send a text.

Me: **Can you meet me at Townsend in thirty minutes?**

Uncle Brutus has been my family's head of security for almost two decades now. Though semi-retired, he still takes on cases concerning our family's security. He also trains all incoming security staff, whether they work for family security or business.

Uncle Brutus: **I'll be there.**

With that settled, I direct my driver to take me to Townsend Industries instead of home as I planned.

Then I turn to Brendan.

"Start talking."

CHAPTER 22

Riley

I sit in my car, flipping the computer drive over and over in my hands. This is what Dean Walsh wanted me to speak to his 'guy' about. It's been two days since I returned from my visit with Eve and met up with John, the guy Dean told me about.

We met at some rundown diner where he handed me a thumb drive that I'm to insert into Kyle's work computer. It'll copy and download all of his private files. That way Dean and whoever he's working with can gain access to private data.

For the past two days, I haven't been able to do it. One because of my mounting guilt. But the other reason is that Kyle hasn't been in the office yet this week.

As fucked up as everything is, I went into work Monday morning, looking forward to seeing him. Yet, he never showed. And he hasn't texted or called me since this past Sunday morning. Part of me wonders if that article has something to do with it.

Now, I'm sitting in the parking garage of Townsend Industries, thumb drive in hand, wondering how I can get out of this. Not only have I come to care about Kyle, but a lot of the employees at Townsend Industries. I don't know if everything Dean believes is true but if it is, and it becomes exposed, the Townsend family won't be the only ones who suffer.

They employ thousands of people around the world. That has the potential to get really ugly.

Sighing, I run my hand through my hair. I've taken one of my migraine pills not too long ago. The stress of everything is getting to me. I typically only get migraines a handful of times a year, thankfully. Within the last month and a half, I've had to use my pills more and more to stave off impending migraines.

My phone suddenly rings, jolting me out of my contemplation. I groan at the number on the screen.

I hit the app to record the call right before answering.

"What, Dean?"

"Have you done it yet?" he demands.

I look at the thumb drive. "He's still out of the office."

"That's bullshit," he seethes. "Where is he?"

"I don't know." The truth is, I hate that I don't know. Kyle didn't have any work trips on his schedule. When I asked when he would be back in the office, Michael gave me an evasive answer.

"Are you lying to save your boyfriend?"

"What?" I sit up.

"I know about the weekend you two spent together a few weeks ago. I bet he wasn't just admiring your apartment decor," he mocks.

"I got sick," I defend.

He snorts. "I bet. You'll feel even worse if you don't put that thumb drive to use by the end of this week. I want it by this weekend."

"Fine," I respond. "But that's it."

"What are you talking about?'

"If I do this, if I get the information onto this thumb drive, I'm done. You and I are even. You won't call and demand anything else from me. You'll throw away any evidence you have against me and leave me alone for the rest of my life."

Instead of an answer, a cackling laugh comes from the other end of the phone.

"You think this will end? Do you believe that's your deal to make?"

"I know it is," I reply. "If you can't get whatever you're looking for from that thumb drive, you'll never get it."

"That drive will only have his work files on it. I don't doubt that he's stupid enough to have all of his illegal dealings on his work computer. That drive is only part of the plan," he says.

"No," I say forcefully. "I'm done with this shit. Whatever vendetta you have against that family is yours and yours alone. I want to be left out of it."

"I don't give a shit what you want!" he yells. "You will do as I say."

His words harken back to something similar my father said to me when I told him I wouldn't say I liked lying to people.

"If you want to eat, little girl, you will do as I say!" he said right before he backhanded me across the face for talking back to him.

I flinch at the memory.

I was fifteen years old and growing tired of the constant manipulation and lies my father made me tell. That, probably not coincidentally, was right around when my migraines started.

"I don't know who the fuck you think I am, but I'm not your employee or a fucking lackey of yours," I tell Dean.

"But you are someone who wants to stay out of jail. Am I right?"

I tighten my grip on my phone.

He cackles again. "It's not like you can do anything." He huffs. "You've already provided me enough information that would have Kyle and those boneheads at Townsend suing you and have you arrested for corporate espionage. The same bullshit charges my father was arrested for."

I want to argue, but I knew I had committed a crime when I handed Dean those files I got from the accounting office. Would Kyle overlook something like that?

I recall the cold, hard look in his eyes the first time I met him. The way he talks about Townsend's legacy and how protective he is over his family. It's such a contrast to the man who held my hair when I got sick in the company's garage.

Despite how intimate we'd become, I don't think he could overlook my betrayal.

I swallow the lump in my throat as my vision blurs. I refuse to let the tears fall.

"No," I say adamantly. "I'm done. Find someone else to do your bidding." With that, I disconnect the call, hanging up on Dean. He'll try to call back, so I instantly block his number.

I swipe the unshed tears from my eyes and make a decision.

I dial Kyle's cell number. After a few rings, I get his voicemail. I hesitate, but then say, "K-Kyle, it's Riley. I have something I need to talk to you about. It's urgent. I know you're on a work trip, but please call me back as soon as possible."

I don't feel any less anxious after making the call. I could've just blown up my entire life.

Eve is the first thought that comes to mind. What will happen to my Ladybug if I'm in jail?

I shake my head, pushing that thought aside. Somehow, I'll have to convince Kyle and possibly the board of directors not to press charges against me.

My heart squeezes in my chest because I know that as soon as Kyle finds out, he'll want nothing more to do with me. He's the type to cut someone off without a second thought for lying to him. And I know I'll deserve it.

For the first time in years, I've felt a genuine connection with a man, and now it's all about to end.

"It's fine," I tell myself as I start my car to head home. I'll opt to give Kyle one more call.

* * *

I couldn't even get inside of my condo before I redialed Kyle's number. This one goes to voicemail, also. I sigh and hang up without leaving a message. The longer I put off saying what I need to say to him, the greater my anxiousness grows.

I pause at my door and massage my temples, willing the impending headache to subside. I console myself with the knowledge that I will tell Kyle the whole truth as soon as I can. As I put my key into the lock, I wonder if I shouldn't go directly to the board instead. The longer I sit on this, the worse it'll be.

But something about not telling Kyle directly doesn't sit quite right with me. I need to tell him to his face. It's the least I can do.

With that decision made, I unlock and enter my condo. I go to flick on the light switch right next to the door, but a lamp on the far side of the room turns on instead.

I gasp at the sight of Kyle seated at the end of my sofa, glaring at me. His eyes spit fire in my direction. My entire body stiffens, and I can't bring myself to take another step.

He knows.

It takes a moment, but that's the one coherent thought my mind can process. The coldness in his demeanor, and the rage in his eyes, all point to the fact that he's somehow found out the truth. Before I could tell him.

"Didn't I tell you not to cross me, Riley?"

His voice is low, deep, and dangerous.

"How did you get into my home?"

He slowly blinks as he looks me up and down. Kyle doesn't answer my question as he rises to his full six-foot-three height. While it's not the first time I've noticed how tall and large Kyle is, this is one of the first times I've truly taken in how imposing he can be.

He slowly strides in my direction. I step back until the back of my heel hits the front door.

"Are you certain that's the question you want to ask me right now?"

I swallow. Probably not, but too many questions are racing through my mind to find the right one to ask now.

"Kyle, I—"

"You what?" he asks through gritted teeth. "You're going to tell me you aren't a conniving fucking liar?"

His words almost bowl me over. I avert my gaze because looking at him with that venom in his eyes is too hard, not after seeing him when he looks at me with such tenderness and care.

"I'm sorry," I whisper.

A laugh breaks free from his lips, but there's nothing humorous or lighthearted about it.

"Not yet, but you will be," he promises.

"A-Are you going to call the police?"

His lips tighten as he folds his arms. "Why, Riley? Why would I call the police? I want to hear you say it out loud."

I fist the strap of my handbag and turn my head away from him. "I lied to you."

"A lie is telling someone you're six-foot when you're five ten. What you did was more than a fucking lie!" His voice raises this time.

"I'm sorry," I repeat because I'm at a loss for words.

"Stop saying that. We both know you don't mean it."

"I do," I protest because I hate the look in his eyes. "I never wanted any of this. I had no intention of deceiving you or anyone at Townsend Industries."

He snorts. "Right. You just intended to fuck me so you and my former best friend could sneak your way into my family's company to get what you wanted."

"What?"

"Don't fucking play dumb, Riley. You know damn well what Dean and his family tried to do to me."

I shake my head adamantly. "I don't know. I mean, I do know his father went to jail for corporate espionage, but that's all."

Kyle's frown deepens. "Bullshit. Don't act like Dean and you didn't have a laugh over him sending you in to do the same shit he did to me. He used our friendship to try to get files from my father's office. Isn't that what he sent you to do this time? Except, he told you to fuck me to do it, right?"

"No." I shake my head adamantly. "That's not what any of this was about. That wasn't what *we* were about."

"There is no we!"

I feel my heart breaking. It's absurd because what Kyle and I shared was so short-lived. But it felt so real. My heart started to want more.

Foolish girl.

"You and fucking Dean Walsh set this shit up from the beginning, right?"

"Wait, what?"

"Cut the bullshit, Riley! Don't pretend like he wasn't behind this with you."

"He was ... he is," I insist. "But it's not like that. I was never working *with* him. He-He's blackmailing me."

"This is fucking rich," he laughs. Again, there's no humor. "Do you truly expect me to believe that?"

"Yes, because it's true. I never asked Dean Walsh to walk into my life. He just showed up one day and started making these demands. He ..." I trail off because I don't want to admit the last part.

"Let me guess. He used your past of conning Brendan Chastain against you?" He quirks an eyebrow.

"Yes, that's exactly it. How did you know?"

Kyle's eyes darken considerably. "He's been trying to contact me for weeks now," he explains. "He showed up at the hospital where I was like a fucking stalker to tell me about you."

I shake my head. "The hospital. Are you hurt?" I check him over, wondering what he's talking about.

"Don't fucking act like you give a shit about me," he barks. "Chastain told me about the money you stole from him. What was the name you used? Carissa Carlyle? Of course, I didn't tell him he's an idiot for even believing a name like that."

He takes a step back and looks me up and down.

"Guess he'll believe anything once he's fucked you."

I bulge my eyes and shake my head adamantly. "I never slept with Brendan. I—"

"Don't say his goddamn name!" he barks. "And don't expect me to believe a damn thing that comes out of your mouth from now on."

I clamp my mouth shut because, at this point, I wouldn't expect him to believe me. It's obvious he's not open to hearing my side of things. Kyle believes whatever lies Brendan Chastain made up about me.

But I did lie to the man. I'm guilty of that. I don't have much of a leg to stand on. Despite that reality, I have to try to explain myself.

"Kyle, I know whatever Brendan told you doesn't look good. And yes, I did run a con on him. Just like—"

"Your father?"

His question stops me in my tracks. A lump forms in my throat.

"What? You didn't think I would find out you're the daughter of Wallace Martin?" He chuckles. *"My father's dead,"* he says in a mocking tone. "Isn't that what you told me?"

"He is dead to me," I retort.

"Yeah, well the state of California has him marked as very much alive. Inmate number 12345-068, also known as Wallace Martin Sr. Serving a twenty-year sentence for bank fraud," Kyle says before he walks over to the kitchen aisle and slams a folder down onto it.

"That's just one of the many crimes he's serving time for. Not to mention credit card fraud, impersonating a police officer, and more." He pauses and looks me in the eye. "He taught you well."

"I'm nothing like my father," I argue.

"Aren't you? Sleeping with any and everyone to get what you want."

"I never slept with Brendan Chastain! Or Dean Walsh, or anyone else that—"

"What about me?" he yells so loud that I jump.

"I-I never meant for it to go that far between us."

Another derisive laugh that makes me sick to my stomach. God, how I wish the ground would swallow me whole right now. I can't stand the way he's looking at me.

"Bravo." He slow claps, and the sound reverberates around the room. "My brother could learn a thing or two from you. You deserve a fucking Academy Award." He pauses, a muscle in his jaw ticking. "But I wouldn't let you within a mile of anyone in my fucking family."

His voice is so resolute. He's looking at me like I'm the shit on the bottom of his shoe.

This is what heartbreak feels like.

"Look, I already know you're not going to believe a damn thing I say, but this is the God's honest truth. I never asked for any of this. Dean Walsh appeared in my life one day like the fucking rat he is and demanded I do this or he'd send me to jail.

"I don't know if he and Brendan are working together or what, but I've never slept with either one of them. Yes, I'm guilty of conning Chastain, but that was a long time ago. I regret it. It was the only life I knew back then, and I had ..." I trail off.

"I had to do what I had to do." I won't go into detail about living in a homeless shelter for over a year at that point. Then suddenly discovering I had a five-year-old niece who I desperately needed to get away from her father.

"If I could go back in time and change my actions, I would. But I can't change the past."

He makes a huffing sound and turns away from me. I take a tentative step farther into my condo. The tension in the air is so thick I feel like it's going to suffocate me.

"Were you behind that article?" he asks, his back still to me.

"I don't know," I answer honestly.

He whirls around, with eyes sparking in anger all over again. "Don't fucking play with me, Riley."

My shoulders slump in defeat.

"I'm serious. Dean asked me to find out whatever I could and I ..." I know what I'm about to say next will implicate me in any number of crimes. I confess what I did to access the accounting files and that I passed it along to Dean.

Kyle remains silent as he listens to my confession. Yet, his body remains rigid.

"You never spoke to any reporter yourself?"

"No," I answer adamantly. I move closer with an urgency to make him understand. "I never spoke to anyone at *The Daily* or anywhere else. I would never."

He scoffs but I keep going.

"This is not a con that I wanted or asked to be a part of. Dean has a vendetta against you and your family. He found out about me through Brendan and decided I was his perfect pawn. I never wanted this. I've recorded almost every phone conversation I've had with him. Here, listen."

I pull out my phone and bring up the recordings I saved on it. I play the last conversation I just had with Dean before I arrived home.

Kyle listens intently, hearing me tell Dean that I would do his bidding for the last time. I flinch as I hear the desperation in my voice while Dean laughs.

The only reaction from Kyle is a slight flaring of his nostrils.

I thought I would experience some level of relief once Kyle found out the truth. That's not the case. All I want is to go back to the way he looked at me that weekend. The one weekend we shared together.

"I called you," I say once the recording ends. "Right after this phone call, I called you to tell you the truth."

His eyes narrow but he doesn't say anything.

"I left you a voicemail. Here's the thumb drive he gave me." I pull the thumb drive out of my purse.

He looks from me to the thumb drive and back again.

"So, to save your ass you wanted to tell me the truth."

God, the way he's twisting everything makes me sound like a horrible person. Maybe I am one.

"I wanted to tell the truth because I hate this. Despite what you think of me, given what you know about my history, I'm not this person. I walked away from my father and my brother. I ran my last con on Brendan because I had no choice. I—" I break off on a sigh because what's the use?

Kyle won't believe anything I have to say.

Another long silence falls between us.

"Are you going to call the police?" I ask tentatively. As much as the thought pains me, I have to know what he's thinking. Somehow, I'll have to make preparations for Eve. The only thing coming to me is that I'll have to track down my brother to have him take care of her.

I can hardly bear the thought of that happening.

"I should, shouldn't I?" he says grimly.

"You have to do what you have to." I lift my chin and meet his stare. I'll accept whatever hand fate deals me.

"When did you first meet Dean?"

"About three and a half months ago. He was waiting for me at my office one morning."

Kyle cocks his head to the side as if studying me. I try to will into him that I'm being truthful.

"You never knew him before that?" he asks.

"No."

"I'm not going to call the police," he finally says.

I hold my breath because while that declaration should be a relief, I can feel there's more to it.

"Why?" Everything I know about Kyle up until this point led me to believe that he'd swiftly take revenge once he found out the truth.

"Because there are other ways to make someone pay."

Panic seizes my insides, and my heart rate kicks up. Dean's declarations about the Townsends having abandoned houses where they conduct some very ugly business come back to mind.

"What are you talking about?"

Kyle approaches me, slowly, his hard glare never wavering from mine.

"I'm not going to send you to jail, Riley," he answers. "Because you're going to marry me instead."

My eyes bulge so wide it's possible they may pop out of my head. "Wh-What?"

"Did you not hear me the first time? I'm not going to send my *wife* to prison. Not yet, anyway. Not before I get what I need from you."

"Th-That doesn't make any sense. I'm not marrying you."

He snort laughs. The sound is ugly as I suspect it's intended to be. "You will as you have no choice. I'm not giving you one. If Dean wants you to put on a fucking show, we'll give that son of a bitch one."

I shake my head in confusion. "How does marriage accomplish any of that?"

"Come on, Riley," he mocks. "You're a con artist. You know how important it is to make a story believable. Dean wants you close to me, right? There's nothing closer than marriage."

"Kyle, I'm not marrying you." *That's absolutely absurd.*

He chuckles. "It's so fucking cute you believe you have a choice in the matter."

My first moment of anger rises in my chest. "I do. You can't force me into a marriage."

"I can't?"

I blink because he sounds so cocky and confident that this marriage is a done deal.

"Absolutely not."

He takes a moment to look me up and down. Then he tosses another folder onto the kitchen aisle.

"Open it," he orders.

With trembling fingers, I do as he says and gasp. On top of a stack of photos is a picture of Dean Walsh, outside of Eve's boarding school. I flip through image after image of him in front of the school's large gate, talking with the gate security guard. But it's the last photo that almost buckles my knees.

In the photo, Dean is in front of Eve's dorm, talking with her. The timestamp is from several months ago. Right before he ever approached me.

"What is this?" I ask as vision my blurs.

"That, is what could happen if you don't agree to this marriage."

I whip around, seeing red. "What the fuck are you talking about? My niece has nothing to do with this," I shout.

"Does he know that?" He asks the question so calm that it triggers my anger all over again. He dips his head toward the picture. "You say you two aren't in this together."

"We aren't!" I insist, feeling helpless.

"Then it looks like the bastard is willing to use whatever he can to keep you in line."

He pauses, and I suspect he's doing it to let all of this sink in.

"How do you know all of this?"

"My head of security reached out to a few nearby contacts. They were able to get intel from the security cameras and staff around the campus."

I recall back to the time when Dean all but threatened my niece if I didn't do what he wanted.

"Back to you and me," Kyle says. "I can protect her. She'll never know or see any security around, and Dean will never get near her."

"How can you do that?" I'm still staring at the pictures.

"My security team. But—" He stops.

I turn to face him.

"Only if you marry me." His condition is final.

I look from him to the picture of Dean Walsh standing in front of Eve's dorm, talking with her. My stomach twists painfully. My head starts to throb. I don't know what to do to keep her safe.

"For how long?"

His eyes shift from the drive between us then back to me. "Until I'm appointed as the permanent COO. By then I'll have what I need from you to take down Dean and anyone he's working with. Along with implementing your recommendations to secure the Waterson acquisition goes smoothly."

I'll have what I need from you.

Those words shouldn't hurt the way they do. Kyle wants to marry me because I'm a means to his end goal.

I'm used to being used.

"Okay. I'll do it."

CHAPTER 23

Riley

Three days after what has to be the most absurd proposal, I sit in the backseat of a chauffeured car, next to my new husband. We're attending a business dinner with a business owner who's been holding out on the sale of his company.

I stare at diamond ring and white gold wedding band on my left ring finger. They feel suffocating.

"Proof," Kyle says, looking straight ahead as he hands me something. He's barely spoken more than five sentences to me since we recited marriage vows two days ago. Our marriage took place in a judge's chambers, after hours.

Our witnesses were one very large security guard Kyle referred to as his Uncle Brutus, and another security guard named Ron. Both men barely looked at me.

"What's this?"

He doesn't answer beyond gesturing his head toward the file. I take that as him telling me to open it.

I do to see more pictures of the campus of Eve's school.

"The man on the right in the first picture is one of mine."

I flip to the following picture. This one is from inside of Eve's dorm, on her floor.

"The other one has been given a room directly next to hers. He can easily access her room if he needs. She won't know he's there."

"How?" These guys don't look particularly inconspicuous to me.

That's when Kyle turns his head in my direction. "They know what they're doing." His tone is clipped, as if he doesn't want to expend more breath on me than necessary.

Again, I peer down at the rings on my finger. I twist them around and around. A habit I picked up in the past two days. This is not how I ever dreamt of getting married. Hell, I never dreamed of marriage. I wasn't one of those girls who thought I'd ever meet my Prince Charming and fall in love.

"She'll remain safe as long as you keep up your end of the deal."

"I married you, didn't I?"

"That's just part of our agreement. Did you memorize the name of tonight's guest of honor?" he asks.

"Todd Smith. Owner and President of Righteous Corp. Its major business is the medical services app, Righteous. He developed the app with his best friend who recently died from pancreatic cancer. Acquiring the app would allow Townsend to partner it with Waterson's Medical Supplies company to streamline your healthcare services."

If Todd agrees to a partnership with Townsend, it would grow their market share by double digits before the year is over.

"Did I get all of that right?" I give him a smug smile because I know I did.

"Read his body language or whatever it is you do to figure out why he's holding out. And don't fuck it up," he says before the driver opens his car door and he steps out.

I let myself out of the car, then smooth down the sides of the long, black dress Kyle had delivered to my home today. Admittedly, the dress is beautiful and fits me perfectly. He's nothing if not detail oriented.

Kyle moves beside me and looks me over. His eyes pause, lingering on my lips. They narrow. He appears as if he's truly looking at me for the first time tonight.

"Why are you wearing that color?" he asks. His jaw is rigid.

I touch my bottom lip. "What? Oh, it's my favorite," I say of the Ruby Red lipstick I opted to wear tonight.

"Take it off." He's doing that low growl, rumbly voice thing he does so well.

"Why?"

A muscle in his jaw tightens. "Remove it."

"Is it smudged or something?"

"It's not appropriate. Let's go." He doesn't let me respond before he takes me by the elbow into the restaurant.

"Welcome, Mr. Townsend," the hostess greets with a warm, professional smile.

"Bathroom?" Kyle brusquely questions.

She blinks, but then quickly escorts us to the restaurant's restroom.

"Take it off," he orders, pointing to the bathroom door. "Wear a different color."

"What is this about?"

"It told you it's not appropriate for a business dinner."

"That makes no sense."

Onlookers who pass by throw curious looks our way. Then it dawns on me. That weekend we spent together. Kyle mentioned how much it drives him crazy when I wear this color. He even had me wear it when I lost that bet.

A smile spreads across my lips. "Sure thing, husband," I say in a mock sultry voice. I don't miss the way his nostrils flare and his lips part slightly, before I enter the bathroom.

That controlling bastard thinks I'm going to remove my lipstick just because it sparks a little too much emotion for him. *Fuck that.*

I take the time to carefully reapply my favorite color. Then I add a coat of my sheer lip gloss to give the color an extra pop. It's not an overly done look, but it is slightly sultrier.

I agreed to this marriage to protect Eve from that psycho Dean

Walsh. I'll allow Kyle to use my skills and connection with Dean for his revenge or whatever, but I will not be controlled by him.

My smile widens as I stare in the mirror.

When I exit the bathroom, Kyle isn't there. I start for the front of the restaurant but a voice on the other side of the men's bathroom door stops me.

"He's here tonight with her. Yeah, dinner with Todd Smith."

I perk up because I suspect this person is talking about Kyle and me. The male voice sounds familiar, but I can't put my finger on who it is exactly.

"Mrs. Townsend."

I look over to see the hostess.

"Your husband is waiting for you."

With a nod, I follow her to meet up with Kyle. As soon as he sees me a deep V forms between his brows and his entire face morphs into a scowl.

"Something wrong, honey?" I ask in an overly sweet voice.

I know as well as he does that him asking me to go back and change this lipstick will make us even more late for dinner.

"We should hurry if we don't want to keep Todd Smith waiting."

Kyle doesn't say anything as he takes my elbow. "Let's go."

"Right this way." The hostess steers us toward one of the private dining rooms.

There are three couples already in the room when we arrive.

"Kyle," one of the men greets as he rises from his chair.

"Todd." Kyle stretches his hand out to greet Todd Smith. He must not be aware of what he's doing because his other arm slips from mine, but it falls to the small of my back. He's holding me to him.

"And who is this?" Todd Smith turns to me with a smile.

Kyle hesitates, his gaze falling to my lips again. "This is Riley," he announces. "My wife."

Stunned silence takes ahold of the room. I'm among the surprised ones. I thought he'd introduce me as his date for the night—a contractor working with Townsend Industries for the next few months.

I suppose I can't hide the massive rings on my left hand, however.

"Wife?" Todd looks between the both of us. "I never even realized you were seeing someone seriously."

"Let's sit," Kyle says, making it obvious he doesn't plan to give more details on our relationship.

He almost knocks me over in surprise again when instead of allowing the host to do it, he holds out my chair for me to sit.

It's only an act.

We're putting on a show. I have plenty of experience with this.

I square my shoulders and become the show pony that Kyle expects me to be. I'm not worth anything to Kyle if I'm not useful to him. And I need to be worth something in order to keep my niece safe.

That's what it all comes down to.

"It's a pleasure to meet you, Mr. Smith," I say. "And Mrs. Smith," I include the blonde woman sitting across from me, who I know is Todd's wife.

"Please, Todd and Amber are fine." Her smile is genuine.

The rest of the guests are introduced.

"I'm so stunned to learn of your marriage, Kyle," Amber Smith says.

From his profile, I can see Kyle debate on how to answer her. The stiffness tells me he's vacillating between telling the woman to mind her damn business and blowing her comment off.

"It was kind of a whirlwind thing," I interject.

All eyes turn to me.

I take the opportunity to look toward my new husband. I plaster the biggest, brightest smile I can onto my face as I stare into his hazel eyes.

"When love hits there's no stopping it. Isn't that right, hun?"

"Right," he answers.

"When you know you know," I tell the rest of the table. "We were so ready to spend the rest of our lives together we didn't want to wait to plan out a whole big wedding." I look back at Kyle as one of the women at the table audibly swoons.

Kyle's still staring at me.

"I'm getting butterflies in my stomach remembering you saying your vows," I lie. That was not a happy moment.

I don't know if he realizes it but Kyle leans in slightly. I can feel the eyes of our audience on us. Thus, I do something I probably shouldn't.

Without giving it too much thought, I lift my hands, cup Kyle's face, and pull his head to meet mine.

The kiss is brief, but still, my body warms.

"I bet that'll be a wonderful story to tell your children and grandchildren."

The moment is broken when Kyle starts coughing, presumably from the shock of Amber's comment.

I clear my throat and hand him a glass of water.

While he takes a sip, I decide to get the topic off of this fake relationship.

"Todd, I would like to take the opportunity to tell you how sad we all at Townsend Industries were to hear about the passing of Anderson James," I comment on the passing of Righteous Corps.' co-founder and Todd's best friend.

Todd clears his throat and sits up, obviously emotional. "Thank you, Riley. And that goes double for the lovely flowers Townsend sent over. Donna, Anderson's wife, loved them."

"The least we could do," I add, feeling Kyle's eyes on me.

Dinner progresses over the next hour. The business talk is interspersed with personal discussions on this or that. The conversation flows smoothly until we get to the real reason for this dinner.

By the time we have dessert, only Todd, Amber, and Kyle, and me remain. The other couples had previous engagements. Todd becomes visibly irritated at the numbers Kyle so casually throws out.

"This company is my blood, sweat, and tears," Todd says.

"Townsend has just as much skin in the game as Righteous," Kyle responds, unbending. I can feel the tension growing in the room as the two men attempt to negotiate back and forth.

"Do you even have the authority to make this type of deal?" Todd challenges. He leans against the table, folding his arms. "Aren't you the interim COO? How do I know that once Townsend finally decides on the new COO, they won't renege any deal we've come to?"

Kyle's entire body goes rigid. I know he sees Todd's questioning as an insult.

"I am the COO," he says, his voice unyielding. "There won't be a new COO until I resign from the role to become the CEO."

Todd appears slightly flustered, likely from the hardness in Kyle's tone.

"Todd," I say without thinking, "wasn't Righteous nominated for the Best App awards last year?"

He nods as a wrinkle appears in between his brows. "Yes."

"In my opinion, you should've won the top slot. I mean the way your program connects patients in need with the medical professionals who can give them what they need?" I shake my head. "It's so simple yet so genius. And we all know how navigating today's healthcare system can be taxing on someone with even the best resources at their disposal."

"We wanted to make getting treated as simple and easy as possible," he adds.

"Your app is leading the way in its field. I bet Anderson would be proud." I give him a sympathetic smile.

Todd's eyes drop to the table. Amber covers his hand, squeezing it. She looks at me.

"Anderson grew up poor. He often talked about seeing his mother struggle with multiple health problems." She looks to her husband. They share a look of true understanding. "They wanted to help people like Anderson's mother. I don't think either one of them expected it be the success it's been."

"One that you both should be proud of," I say to Todd. "But everyone needs help at some point. By partnering with Townsend, we can utilize your app with the recently acquired medical supplies company to streamline medical care for help not just thousands, but millions of people. Isn't that yours and Anderson's vision?"

I sit forward, looking at Todd and then his wife.

"Under Townsend's direction, Anderson's legacy will live on. In that, you can rest assured."

Todd meets my eyes, and they soften with gratitude.

While everything has yet to be signed and formal agreements made, it feels like we crossed a bridge.

Thirty minutes later, our driver holds the door open for me. Kyle gets in behind me.

There's silence between us which I expect to remain for the duration of the ride. Kyle, however, breaks the quiet.

"I should've seen it," he says almost to himself. But then he turns to me. "How did you pick up on it?"

I'm confused. "What?"

"What he needed. You saw I wasn't getting through to him."

"Oh." I turn toward the front of the car. "The man just lost his best friend of almost forty years. He's thinking of selling the company they started a decade ago." I look over at Kyle. "He didn't need to hear about numbers or profit margins. He needed empathy."

The Adam's apple in his neck bobs up and down. "Look deeper," he murmurs.

"What was that?"

He looks at me. "It's something my father told me once." He shakes his head. "I should've fucking seen it."

I don't know why but the desire to reach out and touch him overtakes me. I follow my instinct and cover his hand with mine, squeezing it. It's the same move Amber Smith did for her husband when he got emotional at the table.

A part of me expects Kyle to reject my touch, to push me away. Instead, he unfolds his hand and flips it over. Our fingers intertwine, and he stares at our clasped hands. It's the first genuine touch between us since before our wedding vows.

"Todd needed someone to see him. To know that the dream he and his best friend had wouldn't disappear. He's still grieving."

Kyle's hold on my hand tightens. "His legacy will live on. I'll make sure of it."

I nod because I can hear the resoluteness in his voice.

"I don't doubt you can accomplish anything you set your mind to."

Those words come out as naturally as opening my eyes in the morning. They're true. I don't think there's anything Kyle can't do if he wants it bad enough.

Our car stops, and I look out the window to see we've reached my condo.

Kyle suddenly snatches his hand away from mine. The spell is broken.

He doesn't move or even look at me when he asks, "Do you still have the thumb drive?"

I search my memory, having almost forgotten about the damn thing. "Yes."

"Good. Don't do anything with it before I tell you to."

I bristle at the command in his voice. "What are you going to do with it?"

He looks at me, that coldness back in his eyes. "You'll know when I tell you."

I sigh and don't bother asking anything else because I know he's not going to give out any more details.

I go to open the car door but his hands on my wrist stops me.

"Clear out space in your closet."

I give him a confused look.

"I'm moving in tomorrow."

The car door on my side suddenly opens. Our driver stands by the door, waiting for my exit.

"What do you mean?"

"Goodnight, Riley." Again, he says the words without looking my way. He's like a damn brick wall when he's like this. Short of a damn bulldozer I'm not going to make any headway in this conversation. Not until Kyle is ready.

My phone rings. It's Eve.

I climb out of the car and answer her call.

"Hey, Ladybug," I say, switching from fake wife mode to Aunt Riley.

I don't know what Kyle's expecting but we will not be living together.

CHAPTER 24

Kyle

Sean: **ETA - 2 hours, 20 minutes.**

I check the text from the lead guard assigned to Eve.

"Fuck," I grunt. I thought we would've had more time.

"What's all of this?" Riley asks as I follow the team of three who're moving some of my belongings from my penthouse apartment to Riley's place.

"What does it look like?" I say as I enter, scanning her place. Her furniture is decent. It'll do for now.

"Take it all to the bedroom," I instruct.

"Excuse you," Riley says as she blocks the path to her bedroom for the movers. "What do you think you're doing?"

"I told you I was moving in today." My tone is casual, as if we're having a conversation about the weather.

"I thought you were joking."

I stare at her. Bullshit she thought I was joking.

"Would I kid about something as serious as living with my *wife?*"

Her eyes widen for a millisecond. The same look she always makes when I call her that. Truth be told, the words startle me every time I say them. But I like seeing the reaction they elicit from her. I still haven't made mention of the fact of our marriage at work yet. I know Riley hasn't either because no one has said anything to me about it.

Riley has made a habit of not wearing her wedding rings when we're in the office.

She sighs in exasperation when, on my cue, the movers brush past her to head toward her bedroom.

"When you said to make room in my closet, I hadn't anticipated all of … this." She stares at the suitcases and boxes being carried down the hall.

"You should've," I say as I move to the kitchen island to set up my work laptop. "We didn't have time in the office today. Do you still have it?"

She swings her head in my direction. "The …" She looks to the movers. "Yes."

"Bring it to me."

She plants on her hip. "I'm not your fucking gopher."

A muscle in my jaw ticks as I look her up and down. She's changed from the black pants and white silk blouse she wore to the office earlier. Now she's dressed in a pair of loungewear shorts with a matching V-neck top. A pair of fuzzy slippers adorn her feet, and the pastel pink color of her toenails peeks out the top of the slippers.

"The thumb drive, Riley," I say between gritted teeth.

"Say please."

"The fuck?"

Her eyebrows lift. "You're not about to boss me around in my own home."

"*Our* home." A condescending smile crosses my face.

"My name is the one on the mortgage."

"And my last name is on the owner of the entire building," I say casually.

Her mouth falls slack.

I turn away because those fucking thoughts of sliding my cock in between those plump lips continue to assault my mind.

"The thumb drive," I say again.

Her mouth snaps shut. "Say please."

"Fuck no."

She folds her arms across her chest, causing her breasts to stick out more. That's when I realize she's not wearing a bra.

My gaze moves to the men still coming in and out.

"How much longer until you're done?" I snap at them.

"A few more boxes, Mr. Townsend," one of the guys answers. "You also asked us to unpack. That'll probably take us another hour."

"Drop the last box in the bedroom and then get out," I bark at them. My anger is irrational, but Riley standing there half fucking naked with other men in the room doesn't sit well with me.

"That was rude," Riley says as soon as the last man exits.

"They get paid to accept my rudeness."

"Such a bastard," she mutters. "No one gets paid to accept abuse."

I wave her off. "They weren't abused."

"Talking to your employees like they're lower than dirt is a form of abuse. Have you not heard of the Great Resignation?"

I wrinkle my forehead and stare blankly at her.

"The record number of employees who quit their jobs because of shitty working conditions. Pay isn't everything. But of course, for someone like you, that doesn't mean anything, does it?"

I move around the kitchen island to stand over her. "What the hell do you mean somebody like me?" I don't like the tone she uses whenever she says that shit.

"Someone who looks down on everybody else just because you were lucky enough to be born to a family with a nine-figure bank account." She huffs as she shoots daggers my way with her eyes.

"Twelve figures," I correct.

She sucks her teeth. "Cocky son of a bitch."

Anger aside, a smile crests on my face. "And that would make you Mrs. Cocky Son of a Bitch."

She snarls, and I'll be damned if my cock doesn't stir to life.

"I can't wait until this sick game you're playing is over and we can annul this marriage."

"Counting down the days already?"

"Yes," she answers tersely.

"The thumb drive, Riley." I bring the conversation around to our original topic because we're running low on time.

"Say please," she says again.

"Get me the damn thumb drive."

"Use the fucking manners I suspect you were raised with and say please, you pompous, entitled bastard she yells." Her eyes scream out her frustration. Though she continues to glower at me, she moves her fingers to her temples and begins massaging them.

Memories of finding her curled up underneath her desk in pain come to mind. I swallow my pride.

"Please," I say the word but it's clipped.

She curls her top lip but turns away from me and heads down the hall. A half a minute later she charges back up the hall and slaps the thumb drive into the palm of my hand.

"Thank you," I add to be an ass.

She makes a face, and I chuckle.

I move to the dummy laptop I've had set up for this wave of deception.

"You're going to give him your work files?" Riley asks from over my shoulder.

She's so close. My eyes drop to her lips and remain there for longer than I like. It's ridiculous how angry I was a week earlier. Learning the truth about who she was from Brendan Chastain pissed me off beyond anything I could imagine. I literally couldn't see because I was blinded with rage.

I had my Uncle Brutus verify everything Brendan told me. The records line up with Riley's movements, the bank transfers, fake ID she used. They confirmed it all, right down to the homeless shelter where she lived. That night in her condo when I confronted her, she filled in a few of the gaps.

There isn't a record of her visiting her father in jail. Ever since she's moved to Williamsport it looks like she's been legit. Her consulting firm has a stellar reputation.

Still.

She lied to me.

And fucked me to do it.

I can't ever forget that.

"You're going to give him these files," I reply to her question.

She looks at me with raised eyebrows.

Again, my eyes drop. The shirt she's wearing hangs low in the bent over position she's standing in. It allows me a clear view down her shirt.

Riley gasps when she realizes what's caught my attention.

"Have some decency." She clasps her shirt tight to her chest.

I frown. "We both know it isn't anything I haven't seen before."

"Well, it's nothing you're going to see again."

My eyebrows lift. "That sounds like a challenge."

"It's me telling you the reality of what this marriage is about."

I chuckle. "If you say so."

"I do," she says petulantly.

We'll see about that.

The thought takes me by surprise. It's not like I want to fuck Riley again. She lied to me. She's a fucking con woman, and if I hadn't found out the truth, she could've jeopardized everything my family has worked for generations for.

I shake my head and remind myself to get real.

"This," I point at the laptop, "is a dummy computer. I had my security tech guys download a bunch of bullshit onto the computer. I'll download it all onto the drive, and you're going to pass it along to Dean."

"That's it? I give the drive to him after telling him I successfully snuck into your office or something?"

I watch the computer screen tick along the percentage of the files downloaded onto the drive.

"It's a start," I reply.

"What do you think he'll do with these?" she asks.

"He's going to dig his own grave," I say.

Riley grows silent, looking contemplative. After a few beats she turns and exits the kitchen without a word. I watch her walk away, keeping my attention on the sway of her ass.

***

An hour later, I get out of the shower to a text telling me that we're about to have company in ten minutes.

I toss the phone on the nightstand closest to the door.

"What are you doing?" Riley asks as she enters the bedroom.

"Getting ready for bed. I have a five a.m. alarm set, and a breakfast meeting at eight o'clock."

"No." She shakes her head. "I mean, why does it look like you're getting ready to get comfortable in *my* bed."

"Because I am. This is something we'll have to change, by the way. I like my beds bigger than this."

"Then you should go stay at your bed in your own home."

"Is that anyway to make your new husband feel welcome?"

"I have a few ways I can think of to make you feel comfortable," she says, anger in her words.

Yet, I can't help fucking with her.

"Sounds tempting. What did you have in mind?"

"How about a swift kick in the ass?" she seethes.

"Sounds fun but too much trouble. How about you turn around and show me your ass? I have something I can stick up there."

"Grrr!" She growls in frustration at the same time she launches one of her fifty pillows at me.

I catch it with ease. That only angers her more if the way she stomps her foot is an indication.

"Why would you even want to share your bed with someone like me? Don't you think I'm some sort of awful person?"

"Awful person or not, you're still my fucking wife."

"Not by choice," she yells.

"You had a choice."

"Right," she scoffs. "Marry you or go to jail. Oh, and jeopardize the safety of the most important person in my life. Great choice."

"It was a choice nonetheless."

"I'm not sleeping with you."

"You already have, Riley," I remind her.

She narrows her eyes at me. "Not anymore." She gathers an armful of pillows and then snatches the comforter off of the bed.

I barely bite back my laugh when she gets tangled up in the blanket, stumbles, and almost falls.

"Get off of me," she hisses when I reach out to steady her. She snatches away from me.

"Where are you going?" I ask, although I know the answer.

"This is not the only bedroom in here. If you won't leave, I will."

She starts to stomp down the hall. I follow her.

She's mumbling something about me being a pain in the ass when the front door opens.

"Eve!" Riley says in surprise.

"Hi, Aunt Ry," Eve greets as if it's totally normal for her to be here. The girl's eyes move around her aunt and find me. They widen in surprise.

Riley glances over her shoulder. "Oh God," she groans. "Ladybug, what are you doing here?"

"Why do you have your pillows and blankets in your hands? Were you planning on having a living room camp night like we did this summer?"

"What? No. Wait, one thing at a time." Riley moves to the living room and drops her pillows and blanket onto the couch, then turns to Eve.

I stand back and observe as Riley clasps Eve's shoulders.

"How did you even get here? Are you okay?" She checks her niece over.

"I'm fine. I told you I could travel by myself."

"How did you manage this?"

"The airlines will let someone my age travel alone. And I used the emergency credit card you gave me."

"That's for emergencies. Did something happen? Why didn't the school call me?" Riley looks beside herself with worry.

"It was really simple, Aunt Riley. All I had to do was book my flight and then catch a cab from the airport here. I memorized our address three years ago like you taught me to do."

"Baby, that doesn't explain what you're doing here. You should be safe in your dorm room. You have classes tomorrow. I—"

"No, please don't make me go back there," Eve cries out. She wraps her arms around Riley's mid-section and holds tightly.

Riley returns the hug before kissing the top of Eve's head.

"What happened? Tell me what's wrong?" she pleads.

My chest tightens watching the scene in front of me. I hate hearing the desperation in both of their voices.

"Nothing's wrong. I just missed you. Can I stay?" Eve asks on the verge of tears. "Please, I'll be good. I promise. I missed you so much." At this point she's crying.

Riley hugs her tighter. "Of course. I would never kick you out. I want to know what's going on, that's all."

"Nothing." Eve pulls back. "I'm really tired. Can I go to bed?"

Riley cups her face. "Are you hungry?"

"I ate on the plane."

"Okay, come on. I'll tuck you in. But tomorrow you're going to explain everything to me."

Eve nods and then starts to turn for the other hallway that leads to her bedroom. The same one Riley planned on sleeping in.

"Who's he?" Eve suddenly acknowledges me for the first time since she entered.

I should've let them have their moment and gone back to the bedroom. But something holds me in place. A feeling I don't care to explore at the moment.

"He's ... uh," Riley hesitates. "Kyle."

Eve blinks. "Oh, Mr. Kyle. I talked to you on the phone, right? When Aunt Ry had one of her headaches."

I look up at Riley who's avoiding my gaze.

"That's me."

Eve smiles, and something funny happens in my chest. I don't have time to process it before Eve moves over to me and wraps her arms around me. Similar to how she hugged Riley.

"Thank you for helping my aunt." She smiles up at me. "She says

I'm stubborn and don't like to accept help, but I think I get it from her."

Eve untangles herself from me and rushes off down the hall. Riley looks between the two of us before she quickly follows her niece.

Speechless.

That's exactly what I am because all of a sudden, I miss Eve's hug. I don't know how long I remain standing there. I thought I was the one who had this situation under control.

Yet, when Riley emerges from Eve's bedroom the dumbfounded expression on her face matches my mood.

"What happened to your security?" Riley hisses, bringing me out of my stupor.

"They were supposed to be protecting her." She keeps her voice low but there's venom in her words. "You fucking made me marry you under the agreement that she would be safe! What the hell happened to that?"

"She was safe," I say. "My security was with her the entire time."

"Then why didn't I know she was on her way here?"

"Because I knew," I blurt out. It's not until then that I suspect it was an asshole move on my part to keep that knowledge to myself.

"You knew that my eleven-year-old niece was getting on a plane to fly halfway across the country alone? And you didn't think to tell me that?"

"Like I said, she was safe," I defend. "My security detail was with her the entire time, and they were giving me details along the way. She was never in any danger."

"That's not the point!" She throws up her hands, exasperated. Riley brushes past me and heads to the bedroom, leaving me to trail behind her. "No!" She declares as soon as I enter the bedroom.

"You know what, that's even worse." She's pacing in front of the bed, hands balled into fists at her sides. "You knew every step of the way where she was and you never said anything."

"Now you know how it feels," I blurt out.

Her eyes bulge. "So, this was some sort of sick payback?"

"You lied to me since the first moment I laid eyes on you. I withheld some information, but Eve was never in da—"

"Shut up!" she hisses. "This is nothing like what I did to you."

"Your scheming with Dean Walsh potentially endangered my family," I argue back.

"I've barely given him anything. This not the same. Eve is a child!" Her voice grows louder but her eyes quickly dart to the door.

With a lowered voice she says, "She was out in the world alone."

"She was never al—" I try to argue but Riley cuts me off.

"She *believed* she was alone. She didn't know she was being trailed by your fucking security. And what if something did happen? Let's say some crazy stranger tried to do something and your security swooped in. She wouldn't know who they are. Eve would've been terrified."

Her bottom lip trembles. She gives me her back.

The room falls silent as a sinking feeling comes over me.

"I—" My voice croaks and the words stick in my throat. I believed I had thought this through but the distress in her voice is making me rethink my decision.

"Riley."

She doesn't turn around when I call her name.

"I should've told you where she was."

My wife scoffs at the same time she whirls around on her heels. With narrowed eyes, she looks me up and down before saying, "You're sleeping on the couch or the floor."

"What?"

"You've got two options. Eve's room is obviously taken. And you are *not* sleeping in my bed. So, you can take either the couch or the floor. Or," she pauses, "you can take your ass back to your home and sleep as comfortably as you want. I would prefer you take that option."

With that, she storms out of the room. I go to follow her, but she moves so quickly, she's halfway back down the hall with the blanket and pillows that she'd thrown on the couch.

She ignores me as she brushes past and remakes her bed.

"I'm not sleeping on the fucking floor," I gripe as I move to the other side of the bed.

"The couch is that way." She points over her shoulder.

"You're being ridiculous."

"If I was a violent person, I would punch you right now. Just like a man to call a woman ridiculous when she's setting a boundary," she murmurs to herself.

When I attempt to get into the bed, she pushes me out.

"No." Before I know it, she's spread herself over the entire mattress.

"This is childish."

"So is blackmailing someone into marriage. Yet here we are." She reaches over to the nightstand and turns off the light, leaving me standing by the bed like a fool.

She's not sleeping. Riley's trying to make a point, to push me out of the door and out of her life. She won't get off that fucking easily.

That's how I end up sleeping on the floor in my wife's bedroom.

CHAPTER 25

Riley

I wake up early the morning after Eve's arrival. Although it's a Wednesday morning and I have meetings I need to prepare for at the office, finding out what's going on with my niece is my first concern.

Eve's always been a sensitive child, and when the subject of her attending Bowen Academy first came up, I was against it. She begged me for weeks to let her try it out. I rub a fist against my chest, massaging the spot over my heart when the thought that I made a mistake in letting her go reverberates through my mind.

I peek over at the floor on the side of my bed to find the pallet of pillows and the blanket gone. Kyle slept on the floor the entire night. Well, maybe only half of the night. The fact that everything's gone and he's nowhere in the room, tells me he likely got a clue and took his ass to his real home.

Selfish bastard, I think as I climb out of bed and hurry to brush my teeth, wash my face and then head to the kitchen to make some coffee. The moment I step into the hallway, sounds from the kitchen greet me.

It's the sound of Eve's voice. It's barely seven in the morning and she's up.

I come to the open living room to find Eve and Kyle side by side on my kitchen stools at the island. They're both staring at his laptop.

"See, this is why the numbers weren't coming out correctly. It's a simple fix."

It takes a few beats for my brain to register that Eve's explaining to Kyle some sort of mathematical equation.

"I can't believe you were able to catch that from a cursory look," he tells her, grinning down at her.

I give him a once over. He looks perfectly rested, like he had a great night sleep in a nice, warm, comfortable bed.

There isn't one of his short curls that's out of place. The morning sun coming through the kitchen window highlights the various shades in his hair.

The crisp, white button down he's wearing is rolled up to the elbows on both of his arms. I can't help but stare at the veins that run up and down his forearms. No one is supposed to be that tempting after a night of sleeping on the floor.

He probably did go back and sleep in his own bed.

"It's not that hard," Eve says nonchalantly, as if the way her brain works when it comes to numbers isn't a big deal. She's like that though, always playing down her strengths. "Here, let me show you something else."

She starts typing on the laptop. Kyle watches diligently. Neither one has realized it's no longer just the two of them.

Kyle laughs as he peers at the screen. "It took the guys in my accounting department three days to come up with those numbers. You did it in a matter of minutes." He sounds astonished. He places a hand on her shoulder. "You're going to make a lot of money one day. When you're ready, give Townsend Industries a try."

That's when my protective instincts kick in.

"Ladybug," I call out.

Kyle looks my way, but I keep my focus on my niece.

"Morning, Aunt Ry," she murmurs but she keeps her attention on the laptop, typing something.

"Ladybug, why don't you go and brush your teeth and change out of your pajamas? I'll make you breakfast."

"Okay, I will …" She trails off but doesn't make a move to get up from the stool. She's hyper focused on whatever's in front of her.

"Eve," I say more sternly. "Go brush your teeth."

I move into the kitchen, still ignoring Kyle as I start to prepare my morning coffee. However, it's already made. Someone already brewed the coffee. I turn my attention back to Eve, who hasn't moved.

The screen in front of her holds all of her attention.

"This where you can add in the other numbers you were looking over—"

"Eve," I say, cutting her off.

"One sec, Aunt Ry. I'm just explaining how to do this."

"I said go brush your teeth and change out of your pajamas. Now!" I don't mean to scream but my voice comes out loud.

The room grows silent, and Eve looks up at me with wide eyes.

She tucks in her bottom lip and slowly nods. When she scurries off without another word, my heart sinks. I don't ever yell at her. I know how sensitive my niece is and how lost she can get when she's concentrating on something. Especially when it has to do with numbers.

I'll have to apologize to her later.

"She was helping me."

I whirl around on Kyle, pointing at him. "She is not a part of your plan!" I hiss.

His eyes narrow as he looks from the tip of my finger to my stare. "What?"

"Don't *what* me. She is not part of whatever scheme you've blackmailed me into. You want to use me to get back at Dean Walsh, fine. I'll do it. But you will not use my niece to further whatever business you're trying to accomplish. She's not one of your employees."

His eyes narrow to slits but I remain undeterred.

"She's a child. Eleven years old. You leave her out of whatever designs you have to get back at me or anyone else you think has screwed you over."

He doesn't say anything as he unfolds his long body from the stool. He looms over me, but I continue to glare up at him.

"Do you think I would use a child to get back at you? Is that what you think of me?"

I thrust my head back, surprised at the hurt in his tone.

No, it can't be hurt.

He would have to have genuine feelings in order to be hurt. Kyle is too conniving and manipulative to feel anything akin to hurt.

"Yes," I lift my chin in defiance, "since you didn't tell me she was coming as a way to get back at me."

He flinches as if I struck him and takes a step back. That cold, blank look enters his eyes.

"I've apologized for that."

"Those were just words. Sorry doesn't make everything better. You will not use my niece in anyway. I'll die before I let anyone use or manipulate her."

His eyes narrow and his nostrils flare.

"You seem to not know me very well, *wife*," he says through clenched teeth. "I was up working, and she got up early and asked what I was doing. She saw numbers in the spreadsheet I had open and got excited. That's it."

I think over his words. They're probably true. Eve has done the same thing whenever I brought accounting or finance work home from the office. She can't turn down the opportunity to work with numbers.

"I'm working from home today," I say instead of responding to his last comment. I fold my arms across my chest, readying myself for a battle. Since the day of our marriage, Kyle has insisted that I ride into the office with him.

It's one more way he wants to control what I do.

No doubt his moving in with me is another way to do that.

"Of course you will. You can't leave Eve by herself."

His words surprise me, but I school my features to not let it show on my face.

"I've already put a call into Bowen Academy to figure out why the hell no one noticed that she isn't there yet. It's going on nine o'clock back east. They haven't called you yet, I presume?" He raises an eyebrow.

That's when I realize he's asking me a question.

I look around the kitchen for my phone. It's on the island. Grabbing it, I see I have no missed calls.

"No."

"She's been gone for over twelve hours. They should've noticed by now," he says. "They either haven't noticed or they're covering it up. Either of those scenarios is unacceptable. I'll have my attorney call you to start the paperwork for a lawsuit."

He closes and stuffs his laptop into his briefcase before grabbing his suit jacket from the back of the couch.

"Wait, what?" I ask right before he gets to the front door.

He turns to me. "What part do you need clarification on?"

I blink. "All of it. What are you talking about a lawyer? What lawsuit?"

"You're going to sue that damn boarding school for losing Eve. If not for my security team, we wouldn't have known that she was on a trip halfway across the country until she arrived."

I frown. "Something you neglected to tell me on your own."

His frown matches mine and he briefly looks down.

Is that shame?

Bullshit. Kyle Townsend doesn't feel any shame.

"A fact I told you I regret."

I wave his comment off. "I will contact the school," I say, not knowing what else there is to say. I'm too speechless. It's almost like he cares.

I glance down the hall as Eve comes back up from her bedroom. She's dressed in a T-shirt and a pair of jeans. Her dark brown, curly ringlets bounce around her shoulders as she walks.

"Are you leaving?" She looks to Kyle with sadness.

He nods. "I have a breakfast meeting," he explains.

"Um, okay," she says, her voice softening. Then her eyes brighten. "Are you sleeping over again tonight?"

Kyle's eyes meet mine. For a nanosecond he looks as if he's at a loss as to how to answer that. A piece of me revels in his confusion. Yet, another part of me wants to save him.

"Eve, we're—"

"Married," Kyle blurts out. "I married your aunt," he finishes, looking over at me.

Eve gasps and covers her mouth.

My heart sinks for the second time this morning. *What is she thinking? Is she upset?*

"You're married. Like, husband and wife married?" Her gaze shifts between the both of us.

"Yes," Kyle answers firmly. "We are. Your aunt wanted to tell you, but things moved quickly. She was going to tell you on her next visit to school. But you surprised us."

"Oh." She looks around, then says, "Does that mean we can all have dinner together?"

"Excuse me?" I finally say.

"Dinner." She repeats the word like I'm the dummy who doesn't know what it means. "Like a real family."

That last sentence bounces around in my head. I hear her desire for it louder than anything. All of a sudden, thoughts of Wallace Jr. come to mind. My shiftless brother, who still hasn't contacted Eve almost a month after she called him.

I look up at Kyle knowing that he's not going to go for it. I have to intervene before he says something that stomps all over my niece's heart.

"Kyle usually works late hours," I explain. "He won't have time."

"I'll be here. How does six-thirty sound?"

Eve's face lights up at his words. "Okay." She nods giddily. "My aunt cooks really good. She can make almost anything."

"Not anything," I mumble, feeling like this conversation has gotten away from me.

"Whatever she makes, I'm sure it'll be great," he says with such confidence that I almost believe him.

I stand there trying to figure out what's going on while the two of them say their good-byes. When I hear the door close, I look down at my niece.

She's grinning from ear to ear.

"Can you cook burgers and home fries for dinner? I love your home fries, and Kyle just said he loves burgers, too."

I shake my head because I completely missed that part of the conversation.

"Eve, we need to talk."

"Wait, if you two are married does that make him my uncle? Should I call him Uncle Kyle?"

The idea of what she would call him hadn't even occurred to me. "I'm not sure he'll be comfortable with that."

Her shoulders slump, but I think it's for the best if I don't let her get her hopes up. This isn't a real marriage and it'll be over soon enough. The last thing I want is for Eve to get her heart broken when this all ends.

"What about the home fries?" She goes back to talking about dinner.

"Yes, I can make you what you want for dinner. But first, we need to talk about what happened at school and why you're here."

"Are you going to kick me out?" Her voice becomes shaky and her eyes watery.

"No, Eve. Of course not." I squeeze her shoulders. "Why would you even think that?"

"Because I begged you to go to Bowen, but now I don't want to go anymore."

"That's what I want to talk to you about. Why don't you want to go?"

She can't answer before the loud ringing of my phone interrupts our conversation. It's early and I doubt it's work related.

"Hang on."

I run-walk down to the bedroom to answer before it stops ringing. It's the headmistress from Eve's school.

"Ms. Martin ... er, Mrs. Townsend," she corrects. "I want to be the first to apologize for the mishap that occurred with Eve. I'm glad to hear that she's back with you, safe."

I can barely get out my hello before the headmistress at the school is profusely apologizing over and over. I allow her to apologize only half listening because I'm too focused on one question.

What did she just call me?

CHAPTER 26

Kyle

"No." Riley adamantly shakes her head.

"It wasn't a question," I reply while buttoning the cuff of my sleeve. "We're going to be late." We're about to leave Townsend offices to go to an after-work lounge where we're going to meet with Dean Walsh.

Riley is going to pass him phony files via the thumb drive he gave her.

"This wasn't the plan." She plants her hands on her hips. The move distracts me for a moment before I refocus.

"Plans change."

"How are you going to come with me to meet him? That doesn't make any sense. Our cover will be blown."

A muscle in my jaw ticks. She has a point. The original plan was for Riley to meet up with Dean at the location he specified, which is a hotel. Presumably his hotel room.

I'll be damned if I let that happen. The thought alone causes heated anger to course through me. After spending the past few days listening to the recorded conversations Riley had with Dean, I refuse to let her be alone with the bastard.

He's unstable.

The idea of him being with her in a closed room makes me almost blind with rage.

"You're good at lying, aren't you?" I tell her. "Make the story believable."

She tosses her hands up, exasperated from my unbendable nature, I assume.

Tough shit.

"This is because you don't trust me." Her eyes roll toward the ceiling. "God, what do you think I'm going to do? Sit on his dick while you listen in?"

I'm around my desk and grabbing her by the arms before she finishes that sentence. The tiny gasp she lets out causes the jealousy raging through me to burn even more. "What the hell did you just say?"

I keep my voice even, but I allow my glare to burrow into Riley's eyes.

She swallows but shakes free from my hold. "You're the one who wanted this fake marriage to get your revenge on Dean for trying to set you up. If he sees us together, he'll—"

"Believe it's working. Dean isn't smart enough to think I've figured his scheme out. Since you're so good at what you do," her eyes narrow on me when I say this, "then you can make him believe that I'm so in love that I just had to marry you."

She blinks. "You're doing this because you're so damn controlling and manipulative that you can't bear not being in the room. You think I'm going to screw you over somehow. You still don't believe I wasn't working with Dean even after those recordings I let you listen to."

"We don't have time for this," I say, brushing her comment off. "Eve is expecting us at home for dinner."

Sucking her teeth, she snatches her bag off of my office chair. "Let's go."

Riley whips around so fast that her hair nearly smacks me in the face. I have to take extra long strides to keep up with her. It's clear she doesn't want to be anywhere near me. Yet, I don't want to be too far from her.

No, I don't trust Dean Walsh at all.

I shouldn't trust her, either. After all, she's been lying to me for weeks. She had the opportunity to tell me the truth that weekend we spent together.

But she didn't.

That should disqualify her from taking up so much fucking space in my head.

It's not working out that way, however.

***

Riley

"What are you looking for?"

I barely spare Kyle a glance as we pull up in front of the lounge. While I continue to rummage through my purse for my Ruby Red lipstick, I can feel his eyes on me. I don't want to give him the satisfaction of looking his way.

"None of your business," I mumble, still searching.

"It won't be in there," he says before getting out of the backseat our driver holds open for him.

That's when it dawns on me that he's taken my red lipstick.

"What the hell is wrong with you?" I blurt out as I get out of the car, uncaring that we're in the middle of the sidewalk. It's after five-thirty so there are loads of people leaving work around us.

"You actually stole my lipstick?"

He shrugs like it's nothing. "It fell out of your bag, and I picked it up." He smirks like he's proud of himself. "I told you not to wear it."

"And I told you to go fuck yourself. You can't control what the hell I do or don't wear."

His eyes darken slightly. "Or don't wear?" he repeats.

Every time I get into one of these fucking back and forths with him, it's like a head trip. He'll use anything to twist and manipulate to win. Doesn't matter how big or small the win is, he just wants to win.

I give him a glowing smile. "It's not like that's the only tube of that color I have." I bat my eyelashes and turn on him.

Before Kyle can reply, I pull out my phone and text Dean.

Me: **Change of plans. Work event I can't get out of. Meet me at McCullin's Lounge in ten minutes.**

"There," I tell Kyle, waving my phone in his face. "Done. He should be here soon."

His jaw tightens as he eases his hand to the small of my back. I inhale deeply because I should not be as affected as I am by his nearness. It's abnormal. Especially since he doesn't even like me.

"We'll make this shit quick."

"Yeah," I agree. Eve is waiting for us. It's been a couple of days since she arrived in Williamsport. Charlotte is home with her now, doing me a favor since I had meetings all day and I didn't want to leave Eve alone.

I fiddle with the thumb drive in my pocket, wishing all of this were over. I need to focus on my niece. After her headmistress called and apologized repeatedly and said she would do whatever she needed to make up for the oversight, I completely lost it on her. I cursed her out from here to kingdom come.

That was the second tongue lashing she received that morning. Kyle had already made a call to the academy and was the one to alert them that Eve was no longer there. After which he had a team of lawyers start a lawsuit and media exposure that would harm their stellar reputation.

Eve is not going back to Bowen Academy, which means I need to find a school in Williamsport for her.

My phone buzzes, and as I expected, Dean's pissed about the change of location. Kyle's jaw becomes rigid when I show him Dean's irate message.

Me: **It can't be helped. Meet me at McCullin's or you don't get this drive.**

I stuff my phone into my purse, knowing Dean will be here. He wants this too much.

Kyle and I find a seat on the second floor of the lounge. The place is packed from the after-work crowd. Pop-techno music plays loud enough for people to loosen up but not loud enough that you have to yell for the person next to you to hear.

"Kyle," Dan Greene, a member of Sam Waterson's finance team, says as we take our seats.

Dan's joined by a few other colleagues from both companies. Even as Kyle engages with them, his hand remains on my left knee. Part of me wants to push his hand away while the other part enjoys his touch.

A few of our co-workers don't miss his hold on me. They don't say anything about it to either one of us, however.

After a few minutes, I look up to find Dean Walsh entering this part of the lounge. I nudge Kyle with my knee and then stand.

"I'm going to get a drink," I tell the rest of the group.

With a wave of my head, I motion in the direction of the bathrooms. Dean makes his way over there, and I follow.

"Why the fuck would you demand that we meet here?" he seethes. "Especially when Kyle's right there." He points over my shoulder toward the open part of the lounge.

"I told you there was a work meeting and I couldn't get out of it."

He looks like he wants to say more but he just asks, "Do you have it?"

"Here." I thrust the thumb drive in his face.

"What the fuck are you doing?" he demands, glancing around the hall but no one's around.

He lowers my hand, but pauses when he feels the rings on my left finger. His eyes widen as he holds up my hand. "What the hell is this?"

"None of your business," I say, snatching my hand away.

"Why're you wearing wedding rings?"

I part my lips to make up a lie, but a deep voice behind me says, "Because she's married."

I suck in a breath as I turn to see Kyle, eyes blazing, as he glares at Dean.

What the hell is he doing?

He approaches, his strides casual, but I can sense the anger in the way he looks from my hand to Dean. Kyle wraps an arm around my waist, firmly pulling me into his side.

"Kyle," Dean says, sounding like he doesn't know what to say.

Kyle narrows his eyes and then widens them as if in surprise. He snaps his fingers. "Dean? Dean Walsh? Wow, it's been what, almost ten years?"

Dean glances from me to Kyle, at a loss, seemingly. "Y-Yeah, it's me."

Kyle looks him up and down, and for a beat, I almost think he's genuinely surprised to see him.

"It's been a long time. How've you been?"

"G-Great." Dean clears his throat. "Yeah, we haven't seen each other since…" He trails off.

"All of that crap went down between our families," Kyle finishes. He shrugs. "Water under the bridge, right?" He actually sticks out his hand for Dean to shake.

Dean hesitates but then shakes it.

Kyle's hand visibly tightens on Dean's.

"Sorry about earlier," Kyle says. "I thought some random asshole was hitting on my wife."

Dean coughs.

Kyle still hasn't let his hand go. Dean's face starts turning an interesting shade of red.

"You know how some jerks can be. They don't know how to take 'no' for an answer when it comes to a beautiful woman." Kyle looks me right in the eye.

For a second I swear that compliment is genuine. The stupid flutters in my belly make me want to believe he means it.

"I can't leave her alone for too long before the dogs come sniffing around. Isn't that right, babe?"

"Right." I meet his smile with one of my own and wrap my hands around his arm. "But I keep telling my husband I can take care of myself."

"As long as you're married to me, you won't have to," Kyle quickly replies.

Another round of butterflies in my belly.

Dean manages to yank his hand free from Kyle's hold.

"Shit, sorry about that. I get lost looking into her eyes."

Damn. He's good.

"Is your hand okay?" Kyle questions.

Dean shakes his hand a little. "Y-Yeah, fine. It's good to see you again, Kyle. I, uh, I'm glad to hear there're no hard feelings."

Kyle drapes an arm over my shoulder.

"None at all. I was sorry to hear about your father." Kyle stares Dean directly in the eyes.

The way Dean flinches tells me how much of a gut punch that remark is.

"Everything happened the way it should've," Kyle continues. "Well, I have to get the missus home. Take care."

Kyle takes my hand as we head out of the hallway, making our way past the few co-workers from Townsend that remain and down toward the exit.

The car we arrived in is directly in front of the entrance. Kyle stops us at the door of the car and rounds on me.

"Do you think he believed it?" The cockiness in his tone answers his own question.

"Maybe," I say.

"Then let's make sure he does." Final words before he leans in and captures my lips.

My mouth parts, giving in to his kiss. I expect it to be brief, but Kyle has other plans.

The next thing I know, my eyelids are falling closed and I'm falling into the kiss. The feel of his lips, arm, and body against mine are too good to pull away. Even with my mind yelling at me that this isn't a good idea.

Kyle is the first to pull back. Then he surprises me again when he plants a kiss on my forehead. It's tender and endearing. It confuses the hell out of me briefly, but then I remember ...

He's faking it.

As long as I can keep that reality at the forefront of my mind, I'll be all right.

"Let's go home," he says, holding the car door for me.

CHAPTER 27

Riley

"He's texting me," I tell Kyle as we come to the door of my condo.

Dean: **Are you still with him?**

"Tell him no. I went back to the office," Kyle orders.

I grit my teeth, not liking taking orders from anyone, but I reply with that message to Dean.

A beat later my phone starts ringing.

"Speaker," Kyle says before I answer.

I put Dean on speaker.

"You fucking married him!" he cries out before I can even say anything.

"Yes." I meet Kyle's gaze.

His expression remains neutral. I hold my breath, wondering if Dean is going to buy it.

"That's fucking brilliant! I knew he would fall for your lies."

Kyle's glare hardens but he remains silent.

"How did you do it?" He sounds a lot more excited than he should if he knew the truth.

"Do what?"

"Get him to fall for you? Hell, at first, I was skeptical, but then I saw the way he looked at you. It's real. That dummy actually is in love with you."

Kyle's hazel eyes meet mine. A deep shudder moves through my chest from the way his gaze remains locked on me. I swear there's a slight softening in his expression. The way he's looking at me now makes me wonder if there's some validity to Dean's words.

"Don't call him that," is all I manage to tell Dean.

He remains silent for a second. "Did you fall for him, too?" he asks, sounding appalled at the idea.

Kyle's eyes burrow into mine. The 'no' is on the tip of my tongue but it feels heavy. Slowly, I answer, "What's it to you?"

"Because that motherfucker is going down. The fact that he married you is perfect. Gosh." He pauses. "I never would've expected him to actually fall in love with you. Fuck you? Yeah."

"Excuse you?"

He huffs. "Don't get all offended. You're a con artist, sweetie. I know you'll use what's between your legs to get whatever you want. Hey. It worked on Brendan."

"For the life of me," I murmur. "I never slept with that spoiled brat!" I'm getting real tired of people insinuating it. "Anyway, you got what you wanted. I have to go."

"Wait," he insists. "I almost forgot. The thumb drive was a jackpot, too. The stupid idiot put all of the information right there on his work drive." He giggles—actually giggles—like a schoolboy. "I knew he was dumb as shit. There are addresses, and I bet those are the abandoned houses his family owns. It looks like there's evidence of payouts to politicians, too. Fuck! This is a goldmine."

He sounds giddy. "Gotcha motherfucker."

Kyle grabs my wrist. 'Hang up the phone,' he mouths.

"I need to go. Kyle will be back soon."

"Yeah, whatever. Make sure you erase those texts and this call log. I'll be in touch soon."

I disconnect the call.

"I'm going to fucking kill him," Kyle declares. The lethal nature in his voice sends a chill down my spine. He says it like he means it.

I swallow and turn to unlock the door.

"Surprise!" Eve yells as we enter.

* * *

I WALK into the condo to the scent of tomato sauce, oregano, and cheese in the air. "Eve?" I call out, taking a tentative step in her direction.

"Hey," Charlotte says as she stands from the couch. "Uh, she wanted to cook you guys dinner for tonight. She refused to let me help."

A warmth presses against my back, and I realize that Kyle's stepped in behind me. I move away from him, going to Eve.

"Ladybug, what are you making?"

"It's a surprise," she declares.

"I'm going to get going," Charlotte says, tentatively looking between me and Kyle. I have a feeling she's afraid of him.

I walk her to the door. "Thank you for this. I promise, I'm going to find a real sitter soon." I pull out my wallet to pay her, but her hand stops me.

"It's cool it, boss lady. We had a good time. She's fun and even helped me with my finance homework." Charlotte laughs as she holds up her hands defensively. "Don't worry though, I didn't let her do it for me. But she was so interested in it that I let her help me to check that my answers were correct. Then she started making dinner."

I nod and hug Charlotte, discreetly sliding money into her back pocket. Fun or not, I don't like the idea of taking advantage of her kindness.

"See you tomorrow morning at the office."

"You both are late," Eve says accusatory, looking between Kyle and me.

"That's my fault," Kyle jumps in with a quick response. "Work ran over, and your aunt stayed late to help me finish up. Forgive me?"

The tone he uses with her melts my heart. I both love him for it and hate that it has that effect on me.

"How about this ..." he starts before she can answer, "I'll set the table to make up for us being late."

"Okay." Eve slaps the wooden spoon in her hands. "Oh no." She pulls a face as she realizes that she's splashed tomato sauce into her hand.

"It smells good, Ladybug," I tell her as I enter the kitchen. "Do you need me to do anything?"

"Uh, can you grab the pitcher from the fridge?" she shouts over the running water. "I made your famous lemonade-iced tea."

Her voice is so full of pride that I don't allow myself to listen to the voices of doubt in the back of my mind. Eve can be a bit ... scattered.

While she has an incredible mind for numbers, practical things like following a recipe can be problematic. I don't think she's ever made her own meal without help from me.

I grab the pitcher and carry it over to the dining table. Kyle has beautifully set up my good China set. While I rarely used this set in the five years I bought it, it's gotten plenty of use since we've been doing these family dinners, as Eve calls them.

"What made you decide to cook for dinner tonight?" I ask my niece.

"I wanted to do something nice. I made one of our favorites, Aunt Ry. And don't worry, Kyle," she tells him. "It's something you'll like, too." She's so confident, her energy is infectious.

The day after Eve came back, she asked me what she should refer to Kyle as. When she asked him later that day, at our first family dinner, they both settled on just Kyle for the time being.

Whatever you're most comfortable with, he'd told her.

"I'm going to go change and wash my hands before we eat," I tell her.

Minutes later, I return to the dining area to find Eve and Kyle standing by the table. I notice for the first time how messy the apron she's wearing is. There's red sauce splashed all over the front. I don't let myself look over at the kitchen to see how much of a mess that is.

"Ta-da," Eve says as she steps aside and gestures to the table.

In the middle is a large pan of lasagna next to a basket filled with garlic bread.

"It looks amazing, Ladybug." I kiss the top of her head.

"As the man of the house, Kyle should be the one to cut into dinner and serve it," she says.

"I, what?" I screech.

She blinks at me like what she said makes perfect sense.

"You're the chef," Kyle interjects. "It's only right that you make the first cut into the meal you worked so hard to prepare."

Eve nods and then shrugs.

Kyle's gaze locks with mine when we both hear a crunching sound as Eve makes the first cut. My stomach sinks a little but I don't say anything. Minutes later, we're all sitting around the table. Eve eagerly looks between the both of us, anticipating us taking our first bite of the dinner she prepared.

I watch Kyle as he's the first one to taste our dinner. I do my best to ignore his pink lips as they wrap around the tines of the fork. Despite his lips being a distraction, I don't miss the crunching sound as he chews.

He flinches for a moment but quickly covers it. His chewing slows as he brings his fist to cover his mouth. Kyle's poker face is good enough to fool Eve but not me.

I take a bite of the lasagna on my plate. Almost immediately, I know why he responded the way he did. The noodles are hard, almost cutting my tongue as I try to bite through them. Additionally, the taste is ... off.

Our eyes lock and a silent communication occurs between me and my husband.

Neither one of us wants to be the bearer of bad news.

"Ladybug," I say after forcing that first bite down my throat. "Um, did you, by chance, boil the noodles before you put the lasagna in the oven?"

She frowns, her bottom lip poking out. "Was I supposed to do that?"

I take a sip of the lemonade-iced tea she made and almost gag from the amount of sugar in it.

"The recipe didn't say I had to do that." She hands me her phone with the recipe on it.

"This is for the no-boil noodles. But I only had the kind you have to boil first, here."

Eve's shoulder's fall along with my heart.

"It's okay," I console. "It's a mistake anyone could've made."

"No, I screwed up," she says, rising out of her chair.

Despite my assurances and gentle voice, Eve's bottom lip starts trembling. My heart crashes against my ribcage.

"Eve," Kyle says, startling me. He rises from his chair. "Your aunt's right. An honest mistake. It could've happened to anyone. Hell, that's why I keep my ass—" he stops and looks at me, "self out of the kitchen. I mess recipes up all of the time."

I give him a smile of gratitude.

Unfortunately, Eve's already in her downward spiral. I'm not even sure she's hearing what he's said.

"No, it's all my fault. I ruined our family dinner." Big, fat tears start streaming down her cheeks. "This is why no one wants me around. I always screw things up. I'm too much of a mess."

I go to wrap my arms around her, but she pulls away and rushes out of the kitchen.

My feet start moving before I know what I'm going to say or how I'm going to comfort her. All I know is that I can't let her sit alone with whatever thoughts she's having.

"Ladybug," I call out as I knock and push open her bedroom door. She's a pile of tears and misery on her bed.

I kneel by the bed and stroke her back as her body trembles. For a long while I don't say anything. I let her cry her tears and get them out. I run my fingers through her curls and push them behind her ears, doing my best to comfort her.

It feels as if a band tightens around my throat, constricting any words that might come out.

What do I say?

I never had a mother or even a real father figure to help me understand what the hell I was feeling at such a young age. The closest thing I had was Ms. Edith when I went to live at the homeless shelter.

Look on the bright side. I'm sure that's what she would say at some point.

"Ladybug, can you tell me why you're so upset?"

"I ruined dinner. Just like I ruin everything else."

I have to blink away the tears. "You know that's not true."

She slowly sits up. Her face is beet red and blotchy from crying. I grab a couple of tissues from the box at the side of her bed and wipe her face.

"Why would you say something like that?"

"Because I wanted to make a nice dinner. You love lasagna and Kyle said he really likes it, too. He told me his mom makes it for him on special occasions. But I messed it all up." Her face crumbles again.

"Why didn't you let Charlotte help you?" I ask.

"I wanted to do it on my own. Because … because now that we're a family, we should do things like that for each other."

I have to look away from her. I feel like the shittiest person in the world. She's really latched on to this family thing.

Shaking off the shame I feel, I look back up at her. "You know what else families do for one another?"

"What?"

"They forgive when one of them makes a mistake. You haven't ruined anything. It's just a meal. We'll have thousands more together. You'll have more chances to cook for me."

I make sure to say me because I don't want her to continue to focus on Kyle as part of our family. He's a short-term thing. I hope.

"But I get so careless. That's why I messed it up. Even my dorm leader says I'm a mess. That's why my bedroom is always such a disaster and why I can't clean it up like everyone else. I'm just a scatter-brained person."

I blink and then blink some more. I'm doing my best to suppress the hot anger I feel rising in my belly. "Is …" I pause and clear my throat to remove the growl. "Is that what she told you?"

Eve's watery gaze meets mine. She shakes her head slowly. "No, not to me. I heard her laughing about me with some of the other girls in my dorm."

"What?"

She startles as I surge to my feet.

Get ahold of yourself, Riley.

It takes a few attempts, but I gather myself enough to calm down and sit on the bed next to Eve.

"You know that's not a nice thing for an adult to say about a child, don't you? And she was completely in the wrong for doing something like that." I wrap my arm around my niece and hug her to me.

"You know I love how smart you are, right?"

She nods.

"Your brilliant mind is going to take you far, one day. But it's not just your math skills that will be the reason for your success. It's also that big, giant heart of yours."

"I'm too sensitive," she murmurs, her head laying against my shoulder. "Some of the girls at school say that's why I cry all of the time. Because I'm too sensitive." She sniffles.

"You are perfect," I reassure. "You're my Ladybug. There's no such thing as being too sensitive. You just have to find the right people who you can share your true feelings with. Those girls weren't it."

Those pompous bitches. I swear I'm going to find out every single one of their names and sue their asses. Or find some way to bury them.

"But I'm so scatterbrained all of the time." She pulls back and peers up at me. "I lied to you about my history exam. I only got a B- on it because I couldn't focus long enough while studying."

I start to let out a laugh but hold it in. "Ladybug, only you would think a B- is a terrible grade. You should see the grades your aunt used to get in school." Granted, my poor grades were due to the fact that I moved around constantly and I had a father who didn't give a shit about my education.

"You're close to a straight A student at one of the most prestigious schools in the country." I cup her face. "And you don't have to earn another A to ever prove to me that you're worthy of being loved. Okay?"

I hold her face until she slowly nods.

"Okay." Her answer comes out in a whisper but I hear it. "I don't have to go back there, do I?"

"To Bowen?"

"Yeah. I know how much you pay for me to go and you'll lose a lot of money if I don't return. If you want me to, I'll go back ..."

"Hey, you let me worry about the money. That's not your job. We'll find a school here in Williamsport for you to attend."

For the past few days since Eve returned, I've been trying to get her to open up to me about why she came back all by herself. She just kept telling me that she missed me, that was all. I knew it was more than that.

I hold my niece for some time, the both of us silent as we hug. I start to murmur all of the things that I love about her. Eve giggles when I bring up that I love how much she sings off-key when she gets really into one of her favorite musicals.

We're in her bedroom for at least a half an hour before I say, "Come on, we can probably find some leftovers to have for dinner. If not, I'll order something."

It's been quiet up the hall. I've almost forgotten about Kyle. He probably went down to the bedroom, or more likely, back to his own place while I dealt with what I imagine someone like him would deem *the drama.*

People like him wouldn't stick around for anything too emotional. They might say nice things here and there, and get your hopes up, but they aren't the type to be relied on. Not that I should be even thinking of relying on my fake husband for anything.

He'll get what he wants out of this marriage and then leave.

I shake those thoughts off as I follow Eve out of her bedroom.

"Kyle," Eve calls out as we re-enter the living room.

I look over to find him standing over the dishwasher, loading it. Scanning the kitchen, I find that it's immaculate.

Did he clean up?

"Are you feeling better?" he asks Eve.

"Yes," she says shyly. "I'm sorry for ruining dinner."

I start to tell her that she hasn't ruined anything but Kyle cuts me off.

"Ruined?" he scoffs. "Who doesn't enjoy crunchy lasagna?"

Eve actually giggles.

I'm blown away because right now my husband's voice sounds ... playful and comforting.

"We never got to finish dinner," he continues. He takes Eve by the shoulders and guides her to the dining table. There's an entirely new setup. He must've cleared away the plates and dishes of lasagna. In their place are bowls and plates of ...

Grilled cheese and tomato soup.

He tells her about his family's tradition.

"Grilled cheese is one of my favorites!"

He pulls out a chair for her to sit. And then, he does the unthinkable, and pulls out a chair for me. I hesitate because this feels too right. It's wrong though.

"Are you going to sit, Aunt Ry?" Eve's sweet voice invades my thoughts.

I nod. "Thank you," I tell Kyle as I sit.

He resumes the seat directly across from me.

We eat dinners of delicious grilled cheese and tomato soup while Kyle tells Eve about all of the times when he screwed up in the kitchen when his mother tried to teach him to cook.

CHAPTER 28

Kyle

"Set the meeting for tomorrow at ten a.m.," I tell the person on the other end of the phone.

"Absolutely, Mr. Townsend. Will you be in attendance as well?" the Vice Principal of Excelor Academy asks me.

I peer down the hall, deliberating.

"Yes."

"Our staff will be ready."

With his assurance, I hang up the phone. Excelor Academy is the most prestigious private school in the state. Myself, my siblings, and all of my cousins attended the school from elementary level through high school.

Now, so will Eve.

I overheard part of her conversation with Riley before they came back up the hall. There's no way in hell she's going back to that boarding school. I don't give a shit how accomplished it is. Excelor is just as good, and she'll be closer to home. Which is what she needs.

With that settled, I start down to the bedroom where Riley is to tell her about the appointment. I pause in the doorway of the bedroom. She's sitting on the bed, her back facing me, her shoulders curved inwards. Riley looks utterly defeated.

I enter and quietly close the door before making my way over to her. I sit so close that our thighs touch. She doesn't move.

In her hand is a photo of her and Eve. Eve looks no older than four or five years old, and all around her mouth is melted ice cream. She's holding the cone up for the camera. Riley's smile is wide as she takes the selfie of them.

"This was the day I knew she had to come with me," Riley starts talking.

I reach over and take the photo from her hands.

"How old is she here?"

"Five and a half. She was little for her age." Riley laughs a little, but it's strained. "She would proudly announce her age to anyone who asked. I'd only met her two weeks earlier."

"How is that possible?"

Riley snorts. She turns to me, her face a mask of seriousness. "You know what I am. I'm a con artist, the daughter of a con artist, the sister of a con artist. Wallace Jr. learned everything he knows from our father. I left my father the day I turned eighteen. That's how I ended up at a homeless shelter.

"Wallace Jr. is ten years older than me. I only heard from him when he needed something. I met Eve's mom once. She was one of my brother's victims. She was the daughter of a wealthy, Italian businessman. He'd left all of his estate to her. But she didn't exactly fit the L.A. look. Wallace saw her as lonely. He got her to fall for him."

Riley looks away, lowering her eyelids, shielding her gaze from me. I want to cup her face, to make her look at me when she's speaking. I want to see every emotion in those damn eyes. But I keep my hands where they are.

"She had a heart condition Wallace didn't know about. It worsened when she got pregnant. But by then it'd been a few years and Wallace had completely drained her account. She died shortly after Eve was born, too much strain on her heart. Wallace Jr. raised Eve for the first five years of her life.

"I never saw him. He was too busy finding other victims and using Eve to help him. But he eventually made his way back to L.A. He called me out of the blue one day. I had just gotten out of the homeless shelter a month earlier. I had a tiny apartment with a roommate. I met up with him, and that's when he introduced me to my niece."

She laughs and looks upward.

"She was the cutest thing I've ever seen. All plump cheeks and curls everywhere. Anyway, Wallace says he has to go somewhere for a few days and asks if she can stay with me. I knew he was probably up to no good but I didn't question it. I was trying to get my own life together. While he was gone, I would pick up on little things Eve would say or do to get her way.

"It went beyond the normal kid stuff of crying or faking to get what they want. She knew exactly what to say to make someone feel sorry for her. That day ..." she gestures toward the picture in my hand, "we went to get ice cream. There was an older woman there who started gushing all over Eve. My sweet niece instantly started going into a story about how all she wanted for her birthday was two scoops of ice cream. But her aunt couldn't afford it.

"I stood there stunned because it wasn't her birthday and she knew it. And two, I never said anything about not being able to afford to get her what she wanted. I had told her I wouldn't get the two scoops because I didn't want to spoil her dinner.

"The old lady bought it. and before I knew it, my niece had the ice cream she wanted. Right then I knew. Even as I let her eat the ice cream and we took that photo, I knew I had to get her away from her father. He was teaching her to be a little con artist. The same way my father used me.

"People love a victim story. Even more so when there's a cute kid attached to it. My father would have me lie about not having clothes or food or whatever, so he could get money. I didn't want the same life for Eve. She shouldn't have to grow up not knowing what it's like not to be loved by your parent.

"I begged Wallace Jr. to let me raise her. I convinced him that having a kid would cramp his style. You know what he told me?"

She looks at me expectantly.

I shake my head.

"Pay me," she scoffs. "He wanted me to pay him twenty-five-thousand dollars and he'd sign the papers that would give me full guardianship of Eve."

She pauses and looks away.

"It's not right and the irony isn't lost on me, but that's why I did to Brendan Chastain what I did. The money I stole from him I used to pay off my brother, gain custody of Eve, and then move out here to Williamsport."

She shrugs.

"It's probably why I've failed her. Because at the core of it all, I am what I am."

"You haven't failed her," I say, the words coming out in a rush. "She's amazing."

"I obviously can't give her what she needs," Riley argues. "I thought sending her to that damn school was the best thing for her. Look how I fucked that up. She was being bullied and I didn't even notice! How could I not see it?"

She shakes her head. "She thinks she's a big loser."

"That's not your fault," I growl. While I waited for the food I'd ordered to be delivered, I overheard Eve telling what she'd heard the leader of her dorm saying about her. That bitch just had the last day on her job. She won't be able to find work, part-time, at a daycare center once I finish with her.

I pause briefly to rein in my anger. That fucking school will catch my wrath as soon as they open tomorrow.

"Have you ever considered that Eve might need some additional help?" I ask as gingerly as possible.

She wrinkles her forehead and looks at me with curiosity. "What type of help?" There's a defensiveness in her question.

"Have you noticed that Eve can swing in different directions? She can be super focused one moment on something, and then a little ... adrift the next?"

"She's not adrift." She stands from the bed and looks down at me, anger starting to rise.

"Not adrift then. Maybe unfocused is a better word."

"She's eleven." Riley throws her hands out to the side. "There's nothing wrong with her."

"No." I shake my head. "I'm not saying there's something wrong." Sighing, I ready myself to divulge things about my family I never talk about to anyone.

"When I was little, I hated reading."

Squinting at me, she folds her arms across her chest but remains silent. I take that as an opportunity to keep going.

"My mother is a librarian. She reads hundreds of books a year. Reading is like my mother's love language or some shit. My twin, Kennedy, is just like her. For a while, we all thought she'd become a librarian like our mom. But me?"

I scoff. "I would cry when she tried to get me to pick out a book at the library."

"You? Cry? I don't believe it."

"Ha-ha," I say wryly. "I was three. Anyway, it wasn't until we moved in with my father that I learned what was going on."

"Dyslexia?" Riley asks.

"Yeah. It runs in families. My father is also dyslexic. He taught me it's nothing to be ashamed of and that it meant I just needed some extra help. He started with teaching me the fundamentals of reading. I had tutors and special accommodations in class for tests and lectures."

"Eve doesn't have any trouble reading."

"I know," I agree with a nod. "But dyslexia isn't the only type of brain disorder in my family.

"My youngest sister, Stasi. She was diagnosed with ADHD when she was in the third grade. One of my uncles and a few of my cousins are also diagnosed with it. It tends to be diagnosed more in boys over girls."

"Why?"

"Girls mask better than boys."

"Masking? You mean like cover up or hide their true selves?"

"Pretty much. Girls adapt more than boys. But Stasi has always moved to the beat of her own drum. Some of Eve's tendencies remind me of my little sister. She can get hyper-focused on one thing, and talk about it for hours. But then a task as simple as cleaning up after herself will take days because she's constantly finding something else to do."

"Eve can be that way," she concedes. "And she always wants to please others. Do you think that's why she masks?"

I shrug. "I'm not a child psychologist. I don't have the credentials to label her officially with anything. But it feels similar to what I've seen in my family."

"How did I not see this?" Riley's eyes start to water.

When her bottom lip begins trembling, I can't keep my hands to myself any longer. I take her by the shoulders and squeeze. Though the urge to touch her a hell of a lot more intimately than this overcomes me, I restrain myself.

"How would you have known if you had no experience with it?"

"I just thought some of the things were her own little quirks. Yes, her untidiness drove me up a wall sometimes, but I thought it was just her being a kid. I thought it would get better."

"It can get better. Having ADHD doesn't make her defective by any means. *If* it's true that she in fact has ADHD, there are strategies that a psychologist can help you and her put in place. There's medication also, if you want to go that route. More so, there are tens of thousands of people living successful, happy lives who are diagnosed with ADHD."

Riley nods. "I know. I just hate that I didn't realize this could be going on with her. Why didn't I help her sooner?"

"Why couldn't my mother, who's a librarian, help her son to read?"

She meets my stare.

"I don't know a damned thing about being a parent. But it looks to me like being a good one isn't about being perfect. Or always knowing the correct answer at the right time. But more importantly, knowing where and who to go to ask for help. To give your kid what they need. My father was probably the only one who could've gotten through to me when I was that young and hated reading.

"If you love Eve, and there isn't a doubt in my mind how much you do, then it's okay to love her enough to ask for help."

Riley stares into my eyes for a long while. There's total silence in the room for what feels like forever. I start to wonder if I've overstepped. Then I recall the devastation on Eve's face when she realized she'd made a mistake while cooking our dinner.

She went from excited and joyous to self-hatred in a matter of seconds. Seeing that expression on her face, and hearing the words she'd overheard the leader of her dorm say, tore at the inside of my chest.

Riley wipes away her unshed tears. I release the hold I have on her shoulders, surprised at how difficult I find it to do so. I want to touch her.

"I-I don't even know who to contact. I don't know where I'm going to send her to school. I could probably start with the local school district. But I want to look into their rankings to find out—"

"We have an appointment tomorrow morning at ten a.m. with the principal of Excelor Academy."

Her eyebrows lift. "Excelor?"

"It's the school my entire family attended. Including my parents and my uncles. They have a stellar reputation. And they're familiar with the name. My father only had to threaten to buy the whole school and shut it down once before they got their shit together."

Riley gives me one of her *what are you talking about* looks.

A tightening in my chest starts as I admit, "I was being teased by a kid a few years older than me."

Her mouth falls open.

I shake my head. "Don't worry, Diego helped me beat him up. Oh, my twin, Kennedy, jumped in, too. That was the last time another kid tried to tease me about anything."

"I bet."

"Tomorrow. Ten a.m. They'll have Eve's school records by the time we arrive tomorrow morning. We can speak with a school psychologist then, if you want."

"H-How did you arrange all of this?"

"A few phone calls. Not a big deal."

She pushes out a breath, and for the first time since we started this conversation, she looks slightly relieved.

"Thank you."

"Don't thank me," I insist, sounding slightly angry to my own ears. I don't even know why her thanking me irritated me. But it does.

"I'm going to change."

Without a backward glance, I head to the bathroom to shower and change for the night. By the time I return to the bedroom, Riley is laying in bed on her side. She looks at me in surprise.

That first night, I stubbornly slept on the floor, but it was hell on my back. Since then, I've opted to sleep on the couch, making sure to wake up before Eve gets up to take all of my pillows and shit back to the bedroom. She believes Riley and I are in a real marriage.

But that ends tonight.

"I'm not sleeping on the fucking couch anymore," I declare as I move into the bedroom, close the door behind me, and then climb into bed, daring Riley to say anything.

She doesn't.

A few minutes later, she turns out the lamp on the nightstand by her side of the bed. I do the same for the one on my side. It must be exhaustion because less than a handful of minutes later, Riley's steady breathing alerts me that she's asleep.

I sit up in bed, unable to fall asleep.

Instead, I watch her. The rhythmic rise and fall of her chest soothes something inside of me. She's pulled her silk pressed hair up into a headscarf for the evening. It allows me to see her face unobstructed as she sleeps.

I don't know how long I watch her. For what, I don't have a fucking clue. She's not doing anything. And I don't even like this woman.

She lied to me.

She's a con artist.

Though she might have had a good reason for why she did what she did, the fact remains that she entered my life under false pretenses. A zebra can't change their stripes. Or however the fuck the saying goes.

People don't change.

That's not something I can ever forget.

CHAPTER 29

Kyle

"You married her?" Diego asks, holding his arms out wide, a basketball in his left hand.

We're at our gym in downtown Williamsport, playing a pickup game. It used to be a weekly thing of ours. In the last few months, we're lucky if we make it happen once a month.

"How many times are you going to ask me that? I told you we're married."

He shakes his head, then bounces the ball in my direction. I catch it and dribble several times before shooting from the foul line.

"Then let me ask you a better question. Have you lost your damn mind?"

"Don't be dramatic."

He scoffs. "You blackmailed a woman into marrying you, and *I'm* the dramatic one?" He catches the ball as it falls through the net, and chest passes it to me.

"When you put it like that," I say low enough that he can't hear. "It was a business decision."

His frown deepens. "Signing a contract with another company to expand distribution is a business decision. This is a marriage."

His questioning stokes anger in my gut.

"I know what I'm doing."

"Do you?"

I glare at him.

He lifts an eyebrow, unaffected by my anger.

He lets out a wry chuckle. "The man who swore he'd never fall in love or get married–"

"Who said anything about love? This marriage is about–"

"Yeah, yeah. Business," he mocks. "Didn't she lie to you? You, who have trust issues up the wazoo. She lied to you, and instead of tossing her out of your company on her ass and suing her to hell and back, you put a ring on her finger."

A muscle in my jaw ticks. "She did it to protect her niece," I say louder than intended. A few guys playing on the opposite end of the court look in our direction. I ignore them.

"She has an eleven year old to protect. That motherfucker threatened Eve." Fury laces my tone as I think about Dean threatening a child. I hate that Riley lied and manipulated her way into my life, but ultimately, I can respect why she did it, if nothing else.

She's the only family I have.

I know how deeply she loves that little girl.

Diego looks me up and down, then nods. "Family is everything." There's a shift in his tone as if he gets it too.

I swallow. "She did try to tell me the truth," I add. I just found out before she could tell me.

"But do you trust her?"

My heart knocks against my chest from that question.

"What does trust have to do with anything?"

He rolls his eyes and shakes his head. "Only you would ask something like that."

"I'm serious. This marriage is about revenge. Trust doesn't need to factor into that. I'll uphold my end of our agreement, and she'll do her part." The words sound like bullshit even as they come from my mouth.

Trust has never come easy for me. Finding out Riley lied initially made me furious enough that I couldn't see straight. But seeing that photo of Dean on Eve's campus, hearing the desperation in that voicemail she left me, and realizing the lengths she's gone through to give her niece a safe home...

My 'trust is irrelevant to this marriage' feels more like something else. Maybe the opposite of that statement.

"I had a dream," I confess to Diego after a few beats of silence.

He narrows his eyes before his eyebrows pop. "One of those dreams?"

I nod. He knows all about Emma and my weird family history of seeing ghosts. It's apparently from my father's maternal side, so not all of us experience it.

"Emma?" He asks.

I nod. "She told me to go visit my parents. To talk with them."

"That's it?"

I shrug. "You know those dreams come and go; not much is ever revealed." I hadn't had one in years. A part of me wanted to deny it was even real.

I ignored the dream I had a few nights ago because I talk with my parents often enough. Yes, it's mainly to my dad and about business, but I plan on telling them about Riley and Eve at dinner this weekend.

"Still can't believe you got fucking married," Diego gripes before shooting from the three-point line. The ball makes a whooshing sound as it goes directly into the net.

"Jealous you weren't the first one to get married?" I taunt after bouncing the ball to him.

He freezes mid-shot.

I struck a nerve. And since his questioning, my marriage pissed me off, I push even more.

"How is Monique these days? I've barely seen your ass since I heard she was moving back to town."

"Don't test me." His voice hardens, which makes me smile. My cousin has a temper when pushed. Especially when it comes to her.

Hence, why he laid out her fiancé on the beach in Miami when he thought the man was cheating on her.

"Is she back in town?"

"Not yet," he mumbles.

"And once she is?"

He shoots the ball.

"She'll be back home," he says like it's not a big deal. I doubt he hears the relief in his voice. "Look, lay off me and my relationship. You worry about your *marriage*."

A smile crosses my lips.

His forehead wrinkles. "What?"

"You just called it a relationship. Not a friendship."

His Adam's Apple bobs up and down. "Whatever. You need to fucking concentrate on your marriage. If you're having dreams and shit, you're likely going to fuck it up somehow. Try all you want to downplay why you put a ring on her finger. But it's deeper than revenge, and you damn well know it."

I scoff. "Yeah, I'll take that advice. But you can chew on this. Your best friend isn't engaged anymore, and she's moving back home. What's your excuse for not getting off the bench now?"

"Worry about your relationship and I'll worry about mine," he says before taking a shot. The ball bounces off the rim.

CHAPTER 30

Riley

Am I ready for this? I ask myself as we pull into the driveway of Kyle's parents' home.

Two weeks after the lasagna incident—as I now refer to it as—I'm going to meet my in-laws for the first time. Strange since Aaron Townsend is the CEO of the company I've been consulting for, for well over a month. He's been out of the country on business.

Two days earlier Kyle shared over dinner that we were invited over to his parents for Sunday dinner.

"Wow, it's so big," Eve declares as she pops her head in between the driver and passenger seats. This is one of the only times I've seen Kyle drive. And, of course, he owns a Bentley. What a casual car to pull up to dinner with the family in.

"Why is your seatbelt not on?" I chide Eve.

"We're here," she announces like I can't see that. "Kyle, is this where you grew up?"

To be honest, I'm a little surprised that the house isn't much larger. It's not quite mansion size, but massively bigger than anything I lived in as a child. However, I would've thought anything Kyle Townsend grew up in would've been double the size.

I thought all rich types loved to flaunt their wealth with the ridiculous sizes of their homes.

"This is it," he answers. He climbs out and then holds the door open for Eve. My fake husband is an asshole for forcing this marriage, but he is super kind and sweet with Eve. He might even love her.

I startle when my car door opens. Kyle stands there with his hand out for me to take. He must be putting on a show for his parents.

"Do they even know we're married?" I ask out of the side of my mouth so Eve won't overhear.

He looks me up and down. "They will after tonight."

I slump my shoulders and stop walking. Eve is in front of us and doesn't notice. Kyle pauses next to me.

"How could you not tell them? What the hell? How are you going to introduce me?" I whisper yell.

Kyle rolls his eyes.

"Hi!" Eve greets.

I look up to see she's already reached the front door and is talking to whoever's answered. A second later, a woman steps out onto the porch.

"Let's go."

"Kyle," the woman with brown skin and short sister locks greets him. It's the sound of a mother welcoming her adult son home. I recognize Patience Townsend from the photos in Kyle's office and a few news articles.

"Hey, Mom." Kyle greets her with a kiss on the cheek and a huge hug. It's not practiced or phony. It's a warm embrace, one that's taken place between mother and son thousands of times. Kyle shows his family a different side than he shows to outsiders.

My heart squeezes in my chest as I realize I'm one of those outsiders, despite the massive ring on my finger. It shouldn't bother me.

"And who's this?" Kyle's mother's question brings me back to the present moment.

My niece waves her hand as she introduces herself, "I'm Eve."

"Nice to meet you, Eve." Mrs. Townsend gives Kyle a curious look before her eyes meet mine. They widen in surprise.

"Mom, this is Riley." Kyle looks over at me but doesn't move closer as he finishes with, "My wife."

That's when his mother's eyes bulge in blatant surprise.

"Why don't you come inside?" She steps aside, and I awkwardly follow Kyle inside of his parents' home.

I tighten the hold on the strap of my handbag as I glance around the home he grew up in.

The interior is decorated in a classic style of décor. Yet, it feels warm and inviting. Not stuffy and pretentious like I would've assumed.

"Mrs. Townsend—" I start, but am suddenly interrupted by a loud noise barreling down the stairs.

"Kyle, is that you?" a young female voice yells. Her voice reaches us long before she appears in the entryway where we're all standing. "It is you!" the girl screeches as she makes a beeline for Kyle. She's a blur of long, spiral curls, arms, and legs as she barrels down on Kyle.

"Hey, Stasi," Kyle murmurs, hugging his youngest sister. "Ouch!" Kyle barks when Stasi pulls back and punches him in the arm. "What the hell was that for?"

"Watch your mouth," their mother interjects with a calm that tells me this is nothing new for this family.

"That's for not calling me all last week. You said you would."

"I've been busy. I did text you."

"A text is not the same as a phone call. How can you be sure it was me on the other end of the phone responding to those texts?" She throws up her hands in frustration.

Frowning, Kyle looks down at her. "You're the only sixteen year old on the planet who prefers phone calls over texting."

She shrugs and grins from ear to ear. "Thank you."

That's when she turns to me. She has hazel eyes like her brother, but her heart-shaped face belongs to her mother. I'm surprised to realize that one side of her head is completely shaved and has a line of ear piercings running up her entire earlobe.

It was the heavy combat boots on her feet that had made so much noise as she rushed down the stairs.

"I'm Anastasia, but Stasi for short. Only my parents call me Anastasia, and that's when they're pissed at me," she rattles on.

"Stasi, language," their mother interjects again.

"Sorry," she mumbles before sticking her hand out to me. "Who are you?"

"This is Riley," Kyle's mother introduces. "And this is Eve." She nods toward my niece. "Why don't you take Eve into the entertainment room for a minute while we wait for everyone to arrive and for dinner to be served?"

"Cool." Stasi shrugs. "What do you like to do?" she asks Eve.

"I like math," my niece answers.

Stasi gives her a skeptical look. "Not my favorite subject." Then she snaps. "Ohh, maybe you can help me with my latest measurements for this recipe." She takes Eve by the hand and pulls her out of the room.

I watch my niece eagerly trail the older girl.

"Don't even think of turning on one of your true crime podcasts for her to listen to," Kyle calls after his sister. "The last thing we need is for Eve to have nightmares from listening to that shit," he grumbles.

I stare at him as he continues looking after the empty doorway where his sister and my niece exited. From the wrinkle in his forehead, I can see that he looks worried.

"They'll be fine," his mother finally says. "Besides, don't you have more pressing matters to discuss?"

The *like how in the hell you're married with a whole family* goes unsaid.

I look between the two of them because I also wonder how Kyle plans to explain this situation. Is he going to out me to his entire family?

"What's to discuss?" Kyle says so nonchalantly that my mouth falls open.

Mrs. Townsend, however, must be used to this side of her son because she doesn't even look annoyed at his response.

"Maybe the part where you're married all of a sudden? Let's start there. How did this come about? Just a few weeks ago you weren't seeing anyone. You were more married to that damn company than to anyone else. You must really be in love to move this quickly."

A snort falls from my mouth accidentally, causing them both to look my way. "Love, yeah right," I mumble. "He blackmailed me into it."

His mother's eyes widen and then dart over to Kyle. "What? Tell me that's not true."

Kyle looks between me and his mother. "I have my reasons."

When I think his mother is going to demand more of an explanation, she simply stands there. She glances between Kyle and me, as if trying to figure us out. Good luck to her. I can't even figure this situation out.

"The apple doesn't fall too far from the tree," she finally says, surprising me.

I want to ask her what she means by that, but another set of footsteps start coming down the stairs. My heart rate quickens. Not from the knowledge that I'm pretty certain I'm about to meet Kyle's father for the first time face-to-face but because Kyle moves closer and places his hand at the small of my back.

His mother looks me over. "You've married the apple. Now it's time to meet the tree."

I scrunch my face in confusion but I'm not given time to ask what the heck she's talking about.

A few beats later, Aaron Townsend enters the room. The scowl on his face would put me off if it wasn't a well-known fact that this is his regular expression. His eyes, the same color as his son's, move around the room and soften when they land on his wife, who stands in front of Kyle and me.

Then they light up even more at the sight of his son. Finally, his gaze lands on me and his scowl returns.

"Who is this?"

I part my lips to reply, but Kyle beats me to it.

"This is Riley."

"Our new daughter-in-law," Kyle's mother finishes for him.

His father's gaze never wavers from me. It's not difficult to see at all where Kyle gets his imposing nature from.

Mr. Townsend raises an eyebrow at Kyle. That's when I think he's going to drop his hand from my waist and drop his head in shame or wither underneath his father's stare. Hell, I feel my insides start to cave in beneath the weight of his attention myself. My heart races, and I wouldn't blame Kyle if he told his father right this minute what I'd done.

"Mr. Townsend—" I open my mouth to confess myself, but Kyle's voice interrupts me.

"She's my wife," Kyle says, looking his father directly in the eye.

His father looks me over, scowl in place, but doesn't say anything.

"My office," is all he says before he pivots and exits the room.

I start to follow, but Kyle's hand stops me. "Just me."

I watch as he heads in the direction his father left, wanting to follow but stilling myself against doing so. Silence surrounds me for a brief moment before Patience Townsend moves into my line of sight.

The expression on her face isn't as friendly as it was when we were first introduced. While it isn't friendly, she isn't scowling either. There's a pinch between her eyebrows as if she's trying to figure me out.

"You think my son doesn't love you?" she asks with folded arms.

I snort again at the thought. "All due respect, Mrs. Townsend, I'm pretty certain your son hates me."

Her eyebrows lift. "You believe so?"

I nod but can't bring myself to tell her exactly why I know how Kyle feels about me. Sure, he feels some affection toward Eve. She's a child and who wouldn't love her? And yes, there might have been a time where Kyle felt something other than annoyance or even just physical attraction for me, but the truth of why I entered his life destroyed all of that.

Now, I'm just a tool for him to use as payback.

"Yes, ma'am. I do."

It's Mrs. Townsend's turn to snort. "Riley, if my son hated you, there's no way you would've made it within fifty yards of this house." Her eyes meet mine again. "Con artist or not."

I suck in a breath because ...

What the hell did she just say?

* * *

Kyle

"Is this necessary?" I ask my father as he perches his body on the corner of his desk in his home office in the basement.

He doesn't say anything as he folds his arms across his chest and lifts an eyebrow.

"My wife's waiting for me upstairs. And Stasi's probably talking Eve into shaving the side of her head by now, too. Why would you let her cut her hair like that?" I admonish.

"Are you telling me how to raise my daughter now?"

"You would've never let me or Kennedy walk around with our hair like that." I grunt and shake my head. "Parents really do go easy on the youngest."

The ringing of the doorbell sounds from upstairs. A beat later, I hear my sister Kennedy's voice.

"You can give me shit when you become a parent," my dad says, lifting his gaze to the ceiling.

My breath catches in my damn chest.

"Choking?" he inquires casually, without moving, once I start coughing.

"Clearing my throat," I reply.

"Tell me about my new daughter-in-law."

"What's to tell? We're married."

He narrows his eyes. "So fucking stubborn."

"Wonder where I got it from."

He snorts. "Your mother."

At that I laugh because we both know that's not the case.

"Riley Martin. The same Riley Martin we hired to consult with us throughout this merger process?"

"Yes."

"And the same woman who infiltrated my company to sell business secrets to your former best friend."

Of course he knows.

"Uncle Brutus told you."

He gives me a deadpan expression as if to say *what the hell do you think?*

"Yes," I answer, looking him in the eyes.

"You trust her enough to fucking married her." It's not a question.

I fold my arms across my chest. "It's a business decision." My chest tightens from those words. It's true. It was a business decision to marry Riley.

Then why does it feel like more?

"Elaborate."

I hate justifying my plans to anyone, but as my father and CEO he's the one person I should probably open up to.

"She's damn good at what she does," I say, defensive. "On one hand, she got me to believe her."

"Not an easy feat," he snorts.

I grind my teeth because it still pisses me off that she lied to me from the beginning.

"Yet, a number of the strategies she's recommended over the past few months regarding the transition are working out well. It's going smoother than expected and that's thanks to her expertise."

Riley knows people, and that's translated well into the type of consulting she does. I will give her that.

"Then, you blackmailed this woman into marrying you because she's good at her job?" He dips his head toward the doorway.

I shrug without shame. "She's valuable ... for business. We still don't know what Dean is up to or who he's working with. She can help with that."

"Then this marriage is strictly for convenience's sake?"

I tighten my fists at my sides. "Convenience my ass. This is about retribution," I reply, feeling irritated by this line of questioning.

"Was retribution the reason you flew back east and had staff at a certain boarding school fired? Or why you have a team of lawyers suing said school?"

I slide my hands into my pockets. "They deserve it." A muscle in my jaw ticks from the thought of Eve's former school.

"Multiple educators there will likely never work in education again thanks to you."

"And that'll be too soon," I reply without a shred of guilt. *Fuck them.*

A slight grin makes its way across my father's face, but he quickly stifles it. "This is for business, huh? Care to clue me in since I'm the CEO?"

"I'm handling it."

"Is that why your wife thinks you hate her?"

I turn to see my mother leaning against the door, arms folded. Her eyes are shooting daggers my way.

What the hell did I do?

"No, she doesn't."

My mother huffs as she strolls into the room. "That's what she just told me."

My heart clenches in my chest. Hate.

That couldn't be furthest from the truth.

"You must've been mistaken."

"My ears work just fine."

My mother eyes me up and down. As she does so, my father, seemingly unable to keep his hands off of her if they're in the same room, pulls her against his chest.

These two.

I roll my eyes. Their constant displays of affection aren't anything new. But oddly, it makes me think of Riley. Does she honestly believe I hate her?

"Is that all right with you, Kyle?"

I blink and look back at my mother. "What did you say?"

"Eve has taken a liking to Stasi. They both have. And Eve asked Riley if she could spend the night."

I missed that entire conversation. My thoughts were too centered on my wife.

My fucking wife.

The fact that the thought alone doesn't cause the uncomfortable tightening in my chest should send up a red flag. Yet, it does the opposite.

"What did Riley say?"

Instead of answering me, my mother looks back at my father. They share one of those fucking annoying looks that communicates something only they understand.

"She said she didn't want to inconvenience us. But it's no problem. With you and Ken out of the house, Andreas in L.A., and Theirs ..." She trails off, her voice getting slightly heavier at the mention of my younger brother. Thiers in the military, like our Uncle Carter. I know my mother hates it. "I kind of miss having all of you kids in the house at once."

My father snorts. "I don't. Take her and Stasi with you."

My mother elbows him, making him grunt. He mumbles something in her ear. Again, my thoughts go back to Riley.

"I need to get back to Riley." The words tumble out of my mouth without thought. I head back up the stairs.

"You're freaking married?" Kennedy bellows as soon as I enter the dining room.

A slow grin creeps across my face. "Hey, twin."

"Don't hey twin me." She shoves my shoulder. "You didn't even invite me to your wedding."

"That's because we didn't have one," Riley tells her. From the look they exchange, I get the feeling these two have hit it off already.

Kennedy slaps her hands onto her hips and frowns. "All of that money he makes at Townsend and you didn't make this guy," Kennedy thrusts her thumb in my direction, "give you a proper wedding?"

"Hell, it's not like you keep your ass in town long enough to attend a wedding," I say. Kennedy has a job at a paper in the city but it often takes her out of town. Add to that she loves adventure sports and takes trips, and ... well, she's gone a lot.

Kennedy shrugs. "We'll have to plan one then."

Riley looks to me. "That won't be necessary."

"Oh hell no," Kennedy insists. "You have to—"

"Watch your language in this house," my mother interrupts.

"Sorry, Mom," my twin mumbles. "Hey, Daddy."

While my father pulls her into a hug, Stasi and Riley emerge from the entertainment room.

"Aunt Riley, Stasi cut her hair herself. Isn't it cool?" Eve asks Riley. "Can I—"

"No!" Riley and I say at the same time.

She turns and looks at me, surprised.

"You are not cutting your hair like that," I say firmly.

Stasi rolls her eyes. "It's not your fault, Eve. My brother wouldn't know cool if it bit him in the a—"

"In the what?" my mother chides.

Kennedy laughs and high-fives our sister.

"Oh, and Stasi was showing me how she keeps notecards and alarms on her phone to use when she's in the kitchen, so she doesn't mess up what she's making. Isn't that smart?" Eve says enthusiastically.

"Yeah, if you have ADHD like me, we can probably come up with some techniques to help you out, too," Stasi replies. "Come help me in the kitchen. I was only allowed to make tonight's dessert, but I need to do a few things before dinner."

In a flash the two are off.

I turn to tell Riley something, but she's busy talking with my sister and mother. I squint, wondering how they started a conversation so quickly. I watch my wife as her smile widens at something my mother says to her. A small laugh spills from her lips. My heart quickens from the sounds.

This feels right. Like she belongs as part of this family—my family. Unease bristles in my chest.

But can you trust her?

I want to shake it off as indigestion but I know better. Ever since I moved into her place, I've spent weeks in her bed, lying next to her but not touching her. I've told myself it's because I want to make her as uncomfortable as possible, or it's because I need to play the role in front of Eve.

It's all bullshit.

My fucking dreams have been haunted by that weekend we spent together.

I want to touch her.

"It's about time they got here," my father says.

That's when I realize the doorbell is ringing.

"That should be Carter and Michelle." My mother goes to greet my aunt and uncle, leaving Riley and Kennedy talking.

My father moves in front of me.

"You're looking at her like she's on the dinner menu," he says.

"She's my wife." The words spill from my lips without conscious thought.

"Business my ass," I think I hear my father mumble but I'm still too focused on Riley to really hear him.

"Kyle, you son of a bitch, you didn't bother to invite your favorite uncle to the wedding?" my Uncle Carter says, grabbing my attention.

He passes a look over to my father. I ignore the teasing that comes from my uncle, and soon after, my Aunt Michelle. Despite having conversation with my father, uncle, and the rest of the family throughout dinner, I keep finding my gaze going back to Riley even as she sits right beside me.

She, Kennedy, and my mother talk off and on about everything from Riley's work to Eve's school now that she's attending Excelor Academy. I listen more to their conversation than to my father mentioning business. Or Uncle Carter telling the both of us about what's happening at the fire station.

My uncle rose up the ranks to become Battalion Chief.

An hour goes by in a blur as we eat the catered dinner. I don't even know what the hell we've had since I'm so focused on Riley. By the time Stasi's dessert of the cinnamon-honey creme brulee is brought out, I'm ready for the night to be over.

"I got to show Eve how to use a blowtorch," Stasi says a little too excitedly for my liking.

"Be careful with that thing," I admonish, and then turn to my parents. "Should she be allowed to use one of those?" I insist. "Someone could get hurt. Eve, you didn't use it, did you?"

Eve shakes her head adamantly. "No, I just watched. It's so cool though."

That seems to be her and Stasi's favorite word of the night.

"Calm down, bro. I know what I'm doing. Tell him, Mom."

"How about we bring out dessert?" my mother says instead.

Minutes later, everyone has plates of Stasi's dish in front of us. I'll admit it's delicious. Riley compliments my sister which makes her preen.

"Here she goes," Kennedy mumbles.

I chuckle.

That's enough to set Stasi off into a twenty-minute explanation of how she made the dish, but chose to differ from the original recipe.

"You're very talented," Riley tells her.

Stasi eats the compliments up like a lap dog. But I can tell Riley's being genuine. I'm not sure how I know that but I do. I take her hand in mine, beneath the table. She stares at me, a wide-eyed expression on her face.

I squeeze her hand because I want to touch her. What I told my father earlier was right. This marriage is all about vengeance, but hell, it's not like we can't also have fun with it, too.

As I stare into Riley's brown eyes, I answer my own question. Yeah, I can have fun with my wife.

Starting with tonight.

CHAPTER 31

Riley

"Do you think she'll be all right?" I ask for the fifth time even as we enter my condo. It's just Kyle and me. I finally caved, after Eve and Stasi tag-teamed me and begged me to let her stay the night.

Kyle grunts and shuts the door behind me. "My parents raised five kids. You don't think they can keep Eve alive for one night?"

I bulge my eyes. "No, that's not what I meant at all. Your parents are wonderful. I fear that Eve might get … I don't know. Lonely or something." I stop talking because I know how silly I sound.

Kyle doesn't say anything for a long while. He looks me up and down, and I grow antsy underneath the weight of his gaze. He's my husband and he's drop dead gorgeous … yet, I hesitate to look at him for too long, let alone touch him.

Over the past few weeks, we've come to some sort of stalemate. He's less openly antagonistic, and I've grown used to having him around. But when he looks at me the way he is now, that heated passion that's always simmering beneath the surface starts to bubble up.

Or maybe it's solely on my end.

Kyle takes a step forward, our fronts brushing against one another's. "It's okay if you miss her," he says, his voice barely above a whisper.

My eyes drop to his lips. How did he know that's what I was really feeling?

I swallow before saying, "She just came back home." I still feel like a failure for missing the signs that she wasn't happy at school.

Kyle lifts a hand and tucks some of my hair behind my ear.

"Do you think she really likes it at Excelor? It's only been two weeks."

"I think she told you she likes it. We should believe her."

My shoulders slump. "The way she keeps everything in, though. How am I supposed to believe her?"

"Truth or dare, Riley?"

I jut my head backwards. His gaze remains unwavering.

"Truth," I answer without thinking.

"Did you really tell my mother I hated you?"

I nod.

"Why?"

"Because it's true."

At least, I thought it was. The way he's looking at me now, I might not be so sure.

"You probably should," I say.

"Because you lied to me."

I nod. "Because I lied to you."

"Yet, I don't."

A wrinkle in his forehead appears. It's as if his statement perplexes him as well.

"I'm not letting you out of this marriage until I get appointed permanent COO and get the retribution I'm after," he says.

I wasn't expecting him to.

"But it's not like we can't enjoy some of the benefits of marriage while we're at it."

The look in his eyes turns smoldering. A burning sensation starts low in my belly and my brain jumbles, trying to keep up.

I take a step backward, only for Kyle to take a step forward. I repeat the move, and so does he.

"What are you saying?" I know what that look in his eyes is implying. And the way he's starting to unbutton his shirt as he continues to follow me, toward the bedroom, I know. But I need to hear him say it.

"I want you, Riley. And I'm going to have you."

My breath catches, and I almost trip as I'm still slow-walking backwards.

"Have me?" The question comes out strangled.

He slowly nods and untucks his shirt to do the last few buttons. A small moan escapes from the back of my throat at the reveal of his bare chest. My fingers itch to run through the hairs that pepper his lower abdomen. Kyle wakes up early every morning for a workout. Not a day since he moved in has he missed one.

The effort shows all over his cut frame.

"I propose we call a ceasefire."

I blink as the backs of my legs hit the bed. "A what?"

"Ceasefire. For now. There's no reason for the animosity between us since you've already proven useful in helping me get back at Dean for what he's trying to do."

Useful.

I swallow down my particular hatred of that word.

I should be helpful to Kyle. It's only fitting since he hasn't called the cops on me given my lies.

"What does a ceasefire entail?" I ask.

A sly grin crosses his face. The butterflies in my stomach start flapping.

"I'm pretty sure you know."

I shake my head. "No, I don't," I lie.

"Let me show you."

With that, he wraps one hand around my head and pulls me into the hardest, deepest kiss he's ever given me. This one is demanding, all encompassing. It leaves me breathless and dizzy, yet yearning for more.

I feel the monster in his pants come to life when he braces his body against mine. My knees grow weaker by the second. The next thing I know, I'm flat on my back in the bed.

"Is this what a ceasefire looks like?" I ask, breathless.

"Almost," he says before kissing me again.

His hands are everywhere, tugging at my shirt and then my pants and finally my bra and panties. I have no idea how he's so damn adept at removing my clothing but I don't care much either. I'm too hot with him on top of me, half-naked, to care about anything other than having him inside of me.

I slide my hand inside of his jeans and briefs, cupping him. I'm still amazed that my hand can barely fit around his girth.

"You're so fucking big."

"Next time I want to watch you as you take all of me into this pretty fucking mouth of yours." He traces his thumb beneath my bottom lip.

"You're going to give me lockjaw with that thing," I tease.

He pumps his hips, and I arch my back on a moan. "And you'd love every second of it."

I bite my bottom lip to keep from blurting out that he's right.

"Let me," I say when he moves to put a condom on. I take the gold foil packet from him and remove the condom before slowly rolling it over his tip and down his shaft. Kyle lets out a low, sexy ass groan as I lightly squeeze him and then letting go.

As soon as I do, he takes my wrists in his hands and places them above my head.

"This is what a ceasefire looks like," he says, sounding as cocky and in control as ever. Meanwhile, I'm about to lose my mind.

"What is that supposed to—" The rest of the question comes out on a moan as he slides all the way inside of me. "Shit," I hiss. Every inch of my body feels stuffed.

I wrap my legs around Kyle's back to give myself more room. He takes that as a sign to take control ... not that he hadn't already.

"Fuck," he growls. "Do you know how fucking long I've wanted to be back inside of you?"

He punctuates his question with another plunge of his hips. He doesn't give me time to answer before he dips his head, taking one of my breasts into his mouth. He lightly bites my nipple. The sensation rockets through my body. I arch my back into him, wanting more but unable to ask for it because my mouth is parted on a silent scream.

Kyle shows my pussy absolutely no mercy as he pounds into me.

"Kyle!" I scream out his name because it's the only thing I can think of to yell.

"My name sounds so good coming out of your mouth like that," he says before giving me another long stroke. "Say it again," he orders.

I do. Again and again. I tighten my hands into fists and try to break free of the hold he has on my wrists. I want to touch him, to pull him closer, but his grip doesn't allow for it. When I go to demand that he let my wrists go, he surprises me by pulling all the way out.

"What—" I only get out part of the question before I find myself on all fours.

"Arch your back for me, baby," he commands low in my ear. At the same time, his large hand presses against the small of my back, arching it for him.

"Fuuuck," I hiss when he slides into me from behind.

He takes me by the hips and begins pounding again. From this angle, he's able to get much deeper. I can feel him in my damn stomach. And again, he's relentless in his quest. The entire bed shakes like crazy. I tighten my hold on the bedsheets and hold on for dear life.

"Whose pussy is this?" he demands to know.

"Oh!" I yelp when he smacks my ass.

"I can't fucking hear you, Riley. Who does this pussy belong to?"

How is he even able to form coherent sentences right now?

"Y-Yours," I manage to get out. "It's yours, Kyle." I don't even know what the hell I'm saying at the moment. Whatever I said, it must be the right thing because my husband rewards me by rubbing small circles into my clit.

"I'm going to come," I pant.

"That's the point." He has the nerve to chuckle in my ear.

Why does he sound like he's in complete control, while I'm losing my shit?

I can only ponder that question for a few beats before the orgasm rockets through me.

"That's it. Come all over my cock," he encourages.

That makes me come even harder. I'm a sucker for dirty talk. How he knows that is beyond me.

"Look at how your pussy grips me." His voice is tight, as if he's barely hanging on. When the hold of his hand tightens on my waist, I know he's about to come as well.

Another few rounds of pounding his cock deep inside of me and his entire body tightens behind me. His grip is so tight on my hips that I'm pretty sure I'll have bruising in the morning.

Yet, I don't care.

It shouldn't feel this good to feel him come inside of me, but it does. I want to feel it again and again.

"Maybe this ceasefire was a good idea," I murmur once I catch my breath.

Kyle wraps an arm around my waist and moves so that he's lying on his back and I'm flat on my back on top of him.

"Don't forget whose idea it was."

Like he would ever let me forget.

"We're just getting started," he says. "It's going to be a long night."

CHAPTER 32

Riley

"Eve, we're going to be late!" I yell down the hall for my niece to hurry up.

It's been two weeks since the ceasefire call between Kyle and I, and the three of us have grown into a comfortable rhythm.

"Coming!" my niece yells for the second time.

"Why're you rushing her? We still have fifteen minutes before we need to leave," Kyle says, coming up behind me.

I pivot around from the counter, ready to tell him off. Instead, my mouth falls open and no words come out. He's standing there with in a light blue shirt, half buttoned, tie hanging around his neck, and a light dampness from his shower reflecting in the short curls in his hair.

Staring at that beard reminds me of what we did last night. The way my juices glistened on his beard after he sat me on his face. The dull murmur of his laughter brings me back to the present moment. Kyle runs his tongue along his bottom lip.

"Got something on your mind?" His voice is husky. He knows exactly what I'm thinking about.

"Yes, that my niece is going to be late for school," I lie.

Kyle doesn't say a word as he rounds the kitchen island. In one swift move, he's around the island and cupping my ass with one of his large hands, pulling me to his body. How is he semi-hard already?

A small groan spills from my lips.

"We do have some extra time," he says in my ear, his lips brushing against the column of my neck.

I feel my insides weaken. Thank goodness, I'm saved when Eve comes bursting out of her room.

"What do you think?"

Kyle releases me with one last squeeze of my ass to face Eve. She does a little spin and then holds out her arms wide with a grin from ear to ear.

"You. Did. Not," Kyle says through clenched teeth.

Eve's smile drops. Then her eyes go wide. "I just braided it."

She turns her head to give us a better view of the side of her head. I let out a sigh of relief when I see that no, she didn't actually shave her head. She just did an intricate side braid that, from the original angle, made it appear as if there wasn't any hair there.

"Stasi taught me how to do the braid since you guys won't let me cut my hair."

"And we're not going to," Kyle says sternly. "I don't what the fuck my parents are thinking with her," he mumbles low enough so that Eve doesn't hear him.

He goes over to Eve and inspects her closely.

"Math isn't your only super power, huh? The braid looks great." Eve preens underneath his praise. He's so good with her. "It's time for breakfast. You're not going to school on an empty stomach," he tells her in that controlling nature of his.

"What took you so long getting ready?" I ask, even though it's typical for her to need constant encouragement to get going in the morning. This morning, however, she has a math exam, which often has her ready early.

"I was talking to my dad."

I pause with the coffee mug in my hand, halfway to my mouth.

TIFFANY PATTERSON

"Your father? He called?" I feel Kyle's eyes on me but don't look his way across the table.

Eve shakes her head. With a mouth full of toast, she tells us that she called him.

"Did he say where he is?"

She gives a one shoulder shrug. "No. Just that he was busy. I told him I was back in Williamsport and I like it much better than my boarding school. Especially since I get to live with you all the time again."

Her sweet smile warms my insides.

"Love you, Ladybug."

Minutes later, it's Kyle who's doing the rushing for all three of us.

"What happened to 'why're you rushing her'?" I ask once we drop Eve off at Excelor and he orders the driver to find the quickest route as possible to Townsend Industries.

"We have back-to-back meetings this morning. You have a report due to the marketing team by the end of the day. And I have that fucking business dinner at the end of this week that I need to prepare for. I still can't remember all of their names. I hate going into a meeting unprepared," he gripes.

On instinct, I reach over and squeeze his hand. "You're the most competent person I know. You'll get it done."

I don't even think about the words as I say them. But a charged silence fills the space between us. Kyle's eyes meet mine, searching for something. He flips his hand over and intertwines his fingers with mine.

After a beat, he drops his gaze to my hand and frowns. "Where your wedding rings?"

"In my bag. I don't usually wear them in the office. You know that."

"Wear them."

I blink in surprise at the hardness his tone has taken on.

"I didn't think you would want to draw attention to it. I mean, once people see me wearing a wedding ring, they'll start asking questions."

His sharp gaze meets mine again. "Put the wedding rings I bought you on your finger, Riley." His tone brokers no argument.

"Where's *your* ring?" A strange desire to possess him overcomes me. If he wants me to wear the damn rings, I want the same in return. Even if this marriage isn't real.

Kyle uses his free hand to root around his pocket. He pulls out the platinum gold band and slides it onto his left ring finger.

"Show me yours."

"You don't think I have them?" The offense is evident in my voice.

"Show me."

I suck my teeth as I search my bag for the ring box I keep the rings in when not wearing them—which is most of the time.

"They're right here," I say as I thrust the ring box in his face. I start to open the box to put the rings on, but Kyle takes it from my hand. He removes both rings and then takes my left hand.

He looks me directly in the eyes and says, "Wear these every day. Don't take them off again." At the same time, he slowly slides the rings firmly in place on my ring finger.

The all-consuming possession in his steely gaze steals my breath.

Kyle doesn't look away from me nor does he release my hand until we pull up to the underground garage. Only once he's out of the car do I feel like I can breathe again.

Kyle gets out first and then extends his hand to me.

"We're going to be late for our meeting," he says, taking my hand. "Let's go."

"Controlling bastard," I mumble as I let him lead us toward the elevator.

His only response is that cocky chuckle of his.

* * *

Kyle

Where the fuck did she get another tube of that color?

That's the excruciatingly dominant thought that pervades my mind throughout this entire ninety-minute meeting.

Riley didn't ride into work with me wearing the shade I banned her from wearing over a month ago. Yet, she showed up to this meeting with it on. And I know I'm not the only one who notices how good it looks on her.

"That's a superb idea, Riley," Barry from marketing says.

My top lip curls up at him. That's the third fucking time in this meeting he's complimented her. Yes, her recommendations regarding this project are intriguing and, in my opinion, spot on, but why the fuck is he in her face?

"I think we should—"

"Drake, what are the numbers we're talking about?" I cut Barry off to ask one of our accounting guys a question.

I barely hear the answer he gives me because I'm focused on how Barry leans into Riley to say something in her ear. I rise from my chair so fast it almost falls to the floor.

"If there's something you need to share with the group, there's no reason for you to whisper it in my wife's ear."

Gasps from all ten people in the room bounce off the walls around us. Riley's eyes bulge, and the way her mouth falls open reminds me of how badly I want my cock in her mouth.

That damn shade on her lips is driving me insane.

Yeah, this is the most unprofessional bullshit ever but the hell if I care right now.

"Did you say your wife?" a woman's voice asks.

I think it's Janet from our R&D department, but I don't care enough to turn my attention away from the fucker who's obviously hitting on my wife.

"The matching wedding rings should've been enough of a clue." I glare at Barry who looks from my left hand to Riley's. "Aren't you in marketing? You should have a keen eye for these types of things."

"Barry was asking to confirm one of the details of my report," Riley says.

My fist tightens at my side at the way she defends him.

"This meeting has gone on long enough. We've covered all of our bases, correct?"

Everyone nods.

"Fine."

I mutter something about having a follow-up meeting in a week and to leave any additional comments with my assistant. I'm around the table and taking Riley by the elbow in a flash.

"You, me, my office," I say as I practically drag her out of the room. I don't stop as I lead her to the elevator that takes us directly to my office floor. I can't stop to look at her because I might do something crazy like strip her down right in the fucking lobby and bend her over the receptionist's desk.

Come to think of it, that was one of my dreams last night.

It's bad enough that the four-inch heels she's wearing are click-clacking against the floor as she walks. That damn sound makes my heart race even more.

"What the hell was that?" Riley whisper-yells as soon as I slam the door behind her.

"Exactly my fucking question. Why the hell was he so damn close to you? And why are you wearing that color lipstick?"

"It's my favorite shade and I wear it to feel confident sometimes. Did you forget I had an earlier meeting with your father and some of the board members?"

"This isn't the first meeting you've worn that color in today?" I growl.

She rolls her eyes. "You're insane."

I narrow my eyes on her. "What the hell did Barry say to you?"

"I told you already."

She throws her hands in the air when I don't say anything. "You don't believe me?" she shrieks. "Do you think he was trying to mount me in the middle of a meeting with nine other people in the room?"

Why not? I would.

Obviously, I don't say that thought out loud.

"He was too fucking close," I growl.

"He didn't want to disturb anyone else with his question. Unbelievable," she mumbles with a shake of her head.

"Didn't you two go out for lunch yesterday?"

"Are you kidding me? What? Are you having me followed or something?"

It's my turn to suck my teeth. "Of course not. Don't be ridiculous. I had Michael call Charlotte to try to schedule a lunch with you and she told him where you were. Why did you go to lunch with him?"

She places her hand on her hip. That draws my attention to the way the skirt she's wearing hugs those damn hips of hers. The same ones I love gripping when I'm thrusting deep inside of her. The ones I know, at this very moment, are marked by my handprints from the bruising I left behind.

I can be demanding as fuck in bed, and Riley takes it—all of me—so fucking well.

Just thinking about it starts to make my cock swell in my pants. The thought of Barry or any other motherfucker getting close to her is driving me crazy.

"Stay away from him," I demand.

"I'm not a fucking dog you can order around."

"You're my damn wife."

"Which you made abundantly clear to everyone in that room. By the end of business today, everyone in this company will know we're married." She says it like it's a terrible thing.

"What the fuck is the problem with that?"

She rolls her eyes skyward. "Nothing, except the fact that this marriage isn't real, remember?"

Something in my chest twists at that reminder. "It's real on paper," I tell her through gritted teeth. "That's as real as it gets."

Her shoulders slump slightly.

"A piece of paper won't stop me from talking to whomever I want. Whenever."

"Don't test me, Riley."

"I'm simply telling you the truth." The phony smile on her face grates on my damn nerves.

I approach her, backing her up until the back of her legs are pressed against my desk. "Do you know how many times I've imagined fucking you in my office?"

The way her teeth sink into her bottom lip is telling.

I trace those lips with my thumb. "I've wanted to know what this color looks like around my dick. These fucking lips drive me crazy."

"How crazy?" Her eyes drop to my mouth.

"Crazy enough to make this entire floor hear you shouting my name."

Her breath catches. "I'm not screwing you in your office, Kyle."

I smirk. "Are you sure about that, baby?"

I trail my hand up her thigh, hating that she's wearing stockings because they deny me the easy access I'm seeking. *Oh well, looks like these are going to end up ruined.*

Riley gasps at the tearing sound of her stockings.

"Kyle, don't," she whispers, placing her hand over mine. "I have work to do."

"So?"

"You have work to do."

"And?"

I move my hand higher.

Right before my hand slips underneath her skirt, there's a knock on my office door.

"Kyle, Adam Bachleda, his assistant, Anthony Rogers, and Sam Waterson are here for your next meeting," Michael calls.

Riley immediately ducks underneath my desk.

"What the hell are you doing?" I growl at her.

"You need to take this meeting and you've ripped my stockings. I can't go out there like this."

"Get up," I insist.

"No. Send them in."

"What the fuc—"

"Kyle," Michael knocks again. Why the hell he didn't call like he usually does is pissing me off.

"Come in," I bark out in anger.

Michael enters my office with the three men trailing him. I lean over and shake their hands before all four of us take a seat.

"Kyle, thank you for meeting with us this morning," Sam starts. "As you know, I'm leaving town for the next two weeks. This is my only opportunity to speak with you before I leave."

"No—" I pause when I feel Riley's hand on my thigh.

What the fuck is she doing?

Her other hand covers my knee. She maneuvers her body in between my legs.

I clear my throat. "It's not a problem." We've had these weekly progress meetings for almost three months since I was announced as interim COO.

Sam nods. "I'd like to discuss where we are with possible redundancy and what that means for my employees."

"I've assured Sam that we'll do our best to keep as many employees as possible," Adam Bachleda says. "I've got some projections. Anthony," he tells his assistant.

"Here you go," Anthony says, putting a paper before me.

"Shit," I grunt because Riley is slowly dragging down the zipper of my pants.

All three men look at me, confused.

"Yes, that's important to discuss when it comes to the success of this merger," I tell them. "I just had a meeting with members of the marketing, accounting, and R&D teams to gauge how our strategies are going."

Sam Waterson picks up the discussion and begins talking about what he's heard from the sales team. I don't give half of a fuck about what he's talking about because my wife has just pulled my semi-hard cock out of my pants.

For the first time, I'm grateful as hell that I chose not to go with a glass desk for my office.

I inhale sharply, which none of the men notice, as they're busy discussing some inane detail the sales team mentioned. When Riley covers the tip of my cock with her mouth, I squeeze the pencil in my right hand to the point that it snaps in half.

She rolls her tongue around the tip of my dick, and I have to cover my groan with a cough.

"Are you all right?" Sam inquires. "Do you need some water?"

He's genuinely concerned.

He should be.

I'm fighting for my fucking life not to kick him, Adam, and his assistant the hell out of my office and then proceed to leave red marks all over Riley's ass for this stunt.

"What?" I ask.

I see the confusion on their faces, but Riley decides at that moment to take me all the way to the back of her throat. She's working me over with that pretty mouth of hers and the last thing on my mind is work.

"The stock price has seen a positive impact since the merger," Adam says.

Who gives a fuck about stock prices right now?

"... we hope the rumor of Townsend Industries going private is just that ..." I hear him continue saying from somewhere in the room.

I blink to refocus my gaze on him, to notice he's now standing, staring out of the window.

"Private?" I question to make it seem like I haven't completely spaced out of the conversation.

When I press my back into my chair and widen my legs, Riley takes that as an opportunity to lick the entire underside of my dick. I drop one of my hands to the top of her head, gripping her hair in a tight fist.

She always complains when I do this, saying I mess up her hair. But she loves the shit as much as I do. Sam and Adam continue to talk about whatever the hell they're discussing. I use my hand to slowly guide my wife's head up and down my length.

She feels so good. Too good.

I should stop and put my attention on my damn job.

But she has a hold over me. And it's more than just the fact that my dick is inside of her mouth right now. Even before this impromptu blowjob I couldn't focus on work because the only thing in the room I saw was her.

That reminds me of that cocksucker, Barry, and the way he whispered in her ear. He likes her. I can see it.

"Fuck," I growl out when that skilled tongue of hers does another maneuver around the tip of my dick. Thoughts of any and everyone else leave my mind.

"Is privatization on the table?" Sam Waterson asks.

What the hell are they talking about?

Oh yeah, Townsend Industries.

"That could have a major impact on my employees," he says.

"My—" I cut off and pound my fist on the desk because she's deep throating me again and I'm about ten seconds away from exploding in her damn mouth.

"What Kyle is trying to say," Adam starts.

Normally, I can't stand someone trying to explain what I'm saying to anyone else. As if I don't know how to fucking express myself. At this moment, however, I'll allow it. I'm too busy trying to think of anything except coming down my wife's throat.

"If privatization is going to happen, it'll happen," I say.

Adam shakes his head. "Kyle, let's not get ahead of ourselves—"

"As I said," I cut him off. "If it happens, you'll all be the first to know. I know you both have places to be. Sam, we'll do a call next week to go over more details about severance packages for employees."

I clear my throat and tighten every muscle in my body to keep the orgasm at bay. It's taking every ounce of my restraint. Riley is not showing any mercy.

I'm going to make sure her ass is red before the end of the day for this.

"If you all will excuse me." I only just manage to get the whole sentence out. "I have a call in ten minutes."

I pick up the phone as if dialing a number to help them get the point that this meeting is over. In seconds they're all gone, the door is closed, and I push away from my desk. I can't move too far because Riley's mouth is still wrapped around my cock.

"Fuuuck," I groan at the same time I tighten my hold in her hair. She's too fucking good at this. All of my plans to pay her back for this stunt fly out of the window as my orgasm courses through me.

Every cell in my body becomes electrified. Riley slurps down every drop I release. Watching her throat work to swallow everything I give her makes me come even harder.

When I stop coming, she finally releases me. There's a dazed look in her eyes, her lips are glistening from my come, and her grin is from ear to ear.

"Fucking minx," I growl.

"You're the one who wanted to screw at work."

"And I still want to." I rise from my chair, yank her to her feet, and spin her back to me in one fell swoop.

"What are you doing?" Now she actually sounds slightly panicked. "Kyle, we can't."

"Riley, you just fucking deep throated me in the middle of a goddamn meeting. Don't get prudent now."

"That was different. They didn't know I was in here. How are you still hard right now? I just gave you the best head of my life."

"Exactly," I say at the same time I yank her skirt up, over her hips. I suck in a sharp breath at the sight of her round ass in a pair of lacy, black panties.

"Kyle, don't you dare ri—"

Riiip!

"You were saying?" I ask at the same time I stuff the fabric of what used to be her panties into my pants' pocket. "Did you have fun sucking me off in the middle of my meeting, Riley?"

I lean over and wrap one hand around her neck, holding her to my chest. "Answer me."

She lets out a slow breath. A total body shiver courses through her. "Yes," she whispers.

"My wife thinks it's fun to have my cock in her mouth while I'm working."

She lets out a tiny moan. That sound alone sends me to full erection. I tighten my hold on her throat.

"Kyle," she pants. "The door's not locked."

"So what? Anyone who walks in my office without knocking deserves the show they're about to get." I bite her earlobe. "And then

I'll make sure they end up in the unemployment office. Do you know why, Riley?"

I pepper kisses down the column of her neck, reveling in the feel of the softness of her skin.

She shakes her head. "Why?"

"Because there's no way I'll let a motherfucker who's seen your ass continue to work at my company." I fist my dick with my free hand and line myself up at her entrance.

She whimpers at the contact. She pushes her hips back, silently begging for me to take what already belongs to me.

"They'll be lucky if I let them leave without a few broken bones for getting a glimpse of what's mine," I tell her at the same time I slowly ease into her.

"That ... that," she pants. "That's not fair."

"Fuck fair." I push all of the way inside of her. "Was it fair for you to interrupt my meeting like that?" I squeeze her neck at the same time I rock my hips into her.

This angle is good but it's not enough. I need to possess her, own her.

I lift her left leg to prop it onto my desk, opening her up for me even more, allowing me to get another inch deeper. Riley purrs, her head lolling back against my shoulder. Her hair fans out against my shirt and only two words come to mind.

She's mine.

I grip her hip with one hand and keep her locked to me by the throat with the other while I take possession of her from the inside out. She pants my name in between strokes.

"Come for me, Riley," I demand right before biting her earlobe.

She lets out a moan from the back of her throat, and I tighten my hold on her to rock her through her orgasm. Her pussy spasms around my cock. My vision blurs, and I feel slightly dizzy with the restraint of holding back my own orgasm.

Once Riley's release lets up, I pull out of her just in time. My cum splashes all over Riley's backside. Seeing it mark her flesh, my dick is like a faucet that won't turn off.

By the time I stop coming, Riley's ass and back are marked with my cum.

"I… can't… believe we just did that," she says in between gasps.

I can't stop staring at her. She looks so beautiful like this. Marked by me.

Mine. The one word that keeps coming to mind and making any sense right now.

My fucking wife.

CHAPTER 33

Riley

Kyle: I'll be home in the next thirty minutes. Picking up Eve on the way from the office.

A smile spreads across my face as I read the text. It's been almost three months since we married, a month since our ceasefire, and two weeks since that crazy office encounter. Living with Kyle like this shouldn't feel natural. He shouldn't be texting me that he'll be *home* soon, or that he's picking up Eve from school on the way.

I think about how wrong this all should feel as I break the spaghetti noodles in half and toss them in the boiling water. Eve is loving Excelor Academy and recently joined the Mathlete team, which is why she's stayed late.

This feels like a family.

At that thought, I stop like a record is scratching.

My phone buzzes again.

Kyle: Make sure the VR game is set up and ready for tonight's rematch. Eve is not beating me tonight!

I laugh at the angry face emoji he places at the end of his comment. "He's so damn competitive," I mumble.

The other week Kyle overheard Eve asking me to play the video game with her. We played a few rounds of her favorite games, but I couldn't do it for too long. Those virtual reality games tend to spark my migraines. That's when Kyle took over and played with her.

Ever since, the two have played every night after dinner. They both have their wins and losses, but Kyle always swears to get the upper hand after a loss. He's a sore loser, even to an eleven year old.

It cracks me up.

I'm still laughing, thinking about the pouting face he made the night before after his loss. I had to be the one to tell him that no Eve could not stay up past her bedtime just so he could have a rematch. I'm pretty sure he was more upset than she was.

That is until I let him take out his frustration from the loss on my pussy. A shiver runs through my body at the reminder of how many times he made me come with his hands, mouth, and dick.

"Should make him lose more often," I mutter.

Before I can return to cooking, there's a knock at the door. I'm expecting it to be another package. Probably another VR game that Kyle bought for Eve. I'm going to have to remind him that he can't buy her anything and everything he hears her mention.

It's not a delivery, however.

"Wallace," I say as I open the door to see my older brother.

"Junior," he says with a smile on his face. The expression on his face makes my stomach drop. It's like he just won the lottery. "Aren't you going to give me a hug?" He opens his arms out wide.

I awkwardly move into his arms, giving him a light squeeze before pulling back.

"Can I come in?" He doesn't wait for me to answer as he pushes through the door.

He whistles as he looks around at my open concept condo. "This is nice, sis. Not bad. It sure as hell beats that homeless shelter."

I shake my head in disbelief before closing the door. "What are you doing here?"

"I was in town," he tosses over his shoulder before heading to the kitchen. "Spaghetti?"

"Yes."

"Good. I'm hungry. I had a long flight to get here."

"I thought you said you were in town."

He pauses from rooting around in the cupboards above the counter to look at me over his shoulder. "Did I? Oh, I meant I was coming here anyway. I thought I should make my first stop to visit my sister."

"And your daughter?"

"Her too. Hey, do you mind if I get some of this?" He holds the plate out toward the pot with the simmering tomato sauce.

"It's not ready yet." I fold my arms across my chest. I don't like that he's here out of the blue. Wallace Jr. has only visited me and Eve one other time. That visit was because he was hiding out from some guys he stole money from.

"Fine, I'll wait." He places the plate down on the kitchen island like I'm the one who's inconvenienced him. He palms the island and stares at me. That glint in his eyes is never a good thing.

"I heard you got married."

Instinctively, I start twisting the wedding rings on my ring finger. I haven't taken them off for anything other than to sleep or shower since the day Kyle put them on my finger in the car.

Unfortunately, Wallace notices the move and his eyes drop to my hand. His eyebrows raise and he makes his way over to me, snatching my hand up for his inspection.

"Holy shit," he blurts out. "She was right. Look at the size of that rock."

I snatch my hand away. "Who was right?"

"Eve. She told me you married some guy named Kyle Townsend. I thought she was lying. You know how kids are. Anyway, I looked up the name and thought, nah, my sis couldn't have married into *that* Townsend family in Williamsport. So, I decided to come and check it out for myself."

His eyes search out my hand again, even though I've placed it behind my back.

"From the size of that diamond, I know it must be true. That's not a fucking cubic zirconia on your finger." He steps closer and folds his arms, leaning down slightly from his six-foot-one height. "I want in," he says.

"In on what?" I brush past him, needing to get from underneath his sneaky look. I can feel where he's leading and I want no part of it.

"Don't play with me like that, sis. You know what I mean. What game are you running on Kyle Townsend? I want to know about it and I want in."

I shake my head. Of course this is what Wallace came to Williamsport from wherever he was for this. Shiftless bastard.

"I'm not scamming him, Wallace," I say, trying to tamp down on my anger. "This isn't a con."

He lets out a laugh that rubs against every nerve ending in my body.

"Like hell it isn't." He pulls back. "You don't have to be that way with me, sis. I know the real you."

"The real me?"

He shrugs. "We were raised the same way. You can lie with the best of them—"

"That's not what's happening here," I cut him off.

He blinks and looks me over.

"I'm serious, Wallace. I'm a legitimate businesswoman with my own company now. Kyle and I met when I started doing consulting work for Townsend Industries."

No, that's not the whole truth but I can't tell my brother that. He'll twist anything I tell him around to try to make it out to his benefit. And whenever my brother benefits, the people around him end up the losers. I refuse to let him hurt Kyle or Eve.

Wallace remains silent for a long while. Then he cocks his head to the side.

"You can't be in love with him." He huffs and lets out a laugh. "Please don't tell me you married someone for *love*." He spits out the last word as if it's contaminated.

"Wait." He snaps. "You always did have … what did dad call it?" He snaps his fingers again. "A tender heart. You were soft on people," he says with a roll of his eyes. "Maybe you do believe this is a love match.

But I looked that family up. Word around town is Kyle Townsend is as ruthless in business as his father is. I know *he's* not in love."

I swallow the lump in my throat.

"Why wouldn't he be?" I ask even though I know Kyle isn't in love with me. That's not the reason for this marriage. But Wallace doesn't know the details.

He gives me a sly laugh. "Be serious, Ry-Ry. I've seen a few pictures of Kyle Townsend. He's handsome and the son of a billionaire. Word is that he's in line to be the next CEO once his dad retires."

Wallace snaps at me like he's just figured something big out.

"That's probably what it is. You said you run a consulting firm, didn't you?" He doesn't wait for my response. "Yeah, he's probably using whatever work you're doing for him to further whatever business he's got going on. Hell, I bet you even give him free consulting advice in bed and shit. No matter how we were raised, you make yourself an easy mark. All soft hearted and shit."

"Shut up."

Wallace holds up his hands. "Whatever. I'm just saying ... you have to know you're being used for whatever Kyle Townsend wants to get out of you. It's common sense." He looks around my place. "He lives here with you?"

"Yes."

He chuckles. "See? No rich man is going to live here. He won't even let you into his real home. Probably keeps his real girlfriend there. Once he gets what he wants, he'll serve you those divorce papers. He's using you. He made you sign a prenup, right?"

"That's none of your business. You haven't once asked how Eve's doing," I remind him. Even with our history, I still find it astounding how selfish my brother is.

Truly like father like son.

"Who?"

"Eve. Your daughter." I turn when the door opens behind me.

"Dad," Eve gasps as she enters ahead of Kyle.

My stomach bottoms out because this is not how I wanted my husband to meet my brother. Hell, I never wanted them to meet.

* * *

Kyle

As soon as I hear Eve blurt out that one word, my senses go on high alert. I can feel the tension in the room as we enter. I recognize Wallace Martin Jr. when my gaze lands on him. He was part of the report my Uncle Brutus and the security team provided for me.

If I didn't already dislike the son of a bitch, the tension in the room would've had me disliking him. However, it's the look in Riley's eyes when she turns to face me that tightens every muscle in my body.

"What are you doing here?" Eve asks her father with curiosity.

Riley's still looking at me as if trying to assess my reaction to this unwelcome visitor.

"I—"

"Should introduce yourself when you're in another man's home," I cut him off to say. I glare across the room.

His expression morphs from one of indifference when looking at Eve to a sly smile when he takes me in.

This motherfucker thinks I'm another one of his marks.

Idiot.

"I'm sorry. I thought Riley would've made the introductions." He looks over at my wife, expectantly. "You know, since we're family and all."

"Don't ask my wife to do shit you can do with your own mouth."

Riley inhales sharply.

"Ohh, Kyle cursed. That's another dollar in the swear jar."

I look down at Eve, whose wide, hazel eyes are on me. The smile I give her is genuine.

"You're still trying to take all of my money."

She laughs. "You made a promise." She points at the swear jar we've kept on the table next to the door for the past month. Riley set it up as a deterrent since I have a tendency to curse too much around Eve.

I pull out a twenty— the smallest bill I carry—from my wallet and stuff it into the jar.

"That's too much," Eve says.

I glare across the room at her father. "Leave it in. I have a feeling it'll be put to good use before the end of the night."

"Eve, go change out of your school uniform," Riley finally says.

"Wallace Jr.," the dickhead finally introduces. He has the nerve to extend his hand like I'm going to touch him. "Riley's older brother."

"And Eve's father," I add when he doesn't.

"Yeah, that too. You're Kyle Townsend, right? Nice to finally meet you."

His hand is still extended.

I fold my arms across my chest and look him up and down. "Do you want to explain why my wife was looking uncomfortable when I walked in?"

He briefly looks over at Riley. I move to block his view of her.

He waves a dismissive hand. "That was nothing. Family stuff. I'm sure you know how that is."

He laughs it off, and the sound makes me want to punch him.

"Wallace came for a visit," Riley says. "Dinner's almost done. We're having spaghetti tonight."

"I love spaghetti," Eve declares, reappearing in a pair of jeans and a T-shirt.

While I usually change out of my suit for dinner, I don't like the idea of leaving this scumbag alone for even a minute with Riley or Eve. Instead, I help Eve set up the table while I keep an eye on Wallace Jr. I don't miss the way he eyes everything in the apartment, including me.

"I got an A on my latest math exam," Eve says while we eat dinner.

Wallace doesn't acknowledge her accomplishment in the slightest.

"How long have you two been married?" he asks Riley.

"A while," I answer. "Why?"

He shrugs. "I'm hurt that I didn't get an invite to the wedding." He chuckles. "Hell, I need to make sure you're right for my baby sister."

"The h-word is a swear word. You have to put a dollar in the jar," Eve tells her father.

The son of a bitch doesn't even look at his daughter.

"I mean, I didn't even know she was dating anyone seriously. Then I up and hear she's married. I bet it was a nice wedding. Probably cost a lot of money," he continues.

"Why would that be?" I clasp my hands over my plate because, despite how good Riley's cooking is, I can't stomach eating in this asshole's presence.

"No reason." He shakes it off. "But seeing as we're family now, we should get to know one another better. I hear you're a businessman like me. I have this venture—"

"Does anyone want any more garlic bread?" Riley asks.

"I do," Eve says.

Wallace frowns at his sister. "Yeah, sure. How about you go make some more?"

"You know what?" I interrupt, barely suppressing my anger. "It's been a long day. How about we call it quits for the night?"

It's barely seven o'clock but I can't stomach being in this asshole's presence for much longer. However, the last thing I want to do is to knock him on his ass in front of Eve or Riley. They don't need to see that type of violence.

"Wallace, can I speak with you outside before you go?"

His eyebrows lift and his eyes shift from me to Riley, as if asking her what this is about.

"It'll be quick. I don't want to keep you too long," I say with mock friendliness. "I know you're a businessman with a busy schedule."

He puffs out his chest.

"Don't touch those dishes," I tell Riley at the same time I rise from my chair. "I'll clean those up when I return."

Wallace Jr. follows me to the door, again, not even acknowledging his daughter. Not until Eve calls, "Bye, Dad," does he toss her a half-hearted wave over his shoulder.

I crack my neck as I step into the hallway to keep from balling my fists and throwing the sorry son of a bitch a throat punch.

"Thanks for agreeing to talk with me," I tell him. "Like I said, we're both busy men so I'll cut to the chase. I think you're a smart man, Wallace."

His forehead wrinkles a bit as if he's confused. It doesn't last too long before his chest puffs out again.

"Thank you, Kyle," he says, patting my shoulder.

I glare down at his hand. He quickly removes it.

"I'm sorry we can't talk more tonight, though. The kid's got school in the morning and Riley and I have work."

"Yeah … yeah. I was just telling Riley that whatever consulting she's doing for that company of yours must be important."

"Oh, it is. But I also have business ventures of my own. Not related to my family. That's where you come in." I lower my voice in an almost conspiratorial way.

Like the sucker he is, Wallace leans in, silently seeking more information.

"I can't talk too much about it here. But I'd like to share some of the details with you to see if you'd like to partner with me."

"How much could this business of yours bring in?"

I let out a low whistle. "You could easily net somewhere in the mid-six figure range. And that's just to start."

His eyes sparkle with greed.

"Can you meet me at my office tomorrow morning at seven-thirty?" I don't wait for his response. "You know the address, correct? I assume a smart man like yourself has done his research."

He stands to his full height and nods with a proud smile on his face. "Absolutely. I knew it was a good decision to come here."

"I couldn't agree more." I shrug. "Well, let's wrap this up and we'll talk in the morning."

He makes more promises to meet me first thing in the morning before leaving. The fool is practically giddy as he saunters down the hall to the exit.

He won't have that same confidence by the time our next meeting ends.

CHAPTER 34

Riley

"I didn't know he was coming," I blurt out when Kyle re-enters our condo.

"I know," he says, sounding calm.

"Honestly. I haven't spoken to Wallace Jr. in months. That was only to get him to call Eve because she likes to talk to him every now and again."

"I know."

"He mostly stays out of our lives. In all seriousness, I would never speak to him again if it wasn't for her. But he is her father and—"

"Riley." Kyle grips me by the shoulders and squeezes. It's not painful, more comforting. "I said I know."

His facial expression is open as he looks me in the eye. I search his gaze for any hidden meaning. When I don't find any, I exhale.

"Did my dad leave?" Eve asks, catching both of our attentions.

Kyle is the first to answer. "He had to go but he said to tell you he'll miss you."

Eve's shoulders slump. "No, he didn't."

Kyle looks to me, but my surprise is as evident as his.

"He won't miss me. He barely even spoke to me." Eve's voice is forlorn. "I think he just came to meet you. When I told him Aunt Riley got married and to who he started asking me all of these questions about you."

Kyle's jaw tightens, that tell-tale muscle in his jaw ticking at his anger. He squats down low, getting on Eve's level.

"It's my fault he came," she finishes.

"No, it isn't," Kyle tells her firmly. "Your father's a grown ass man who makes his own decisions. And those decisions alone will be his downfall. Nothing he does or doesn't do is your fault. Understood?"

My heart expands at the sincerity in his voice. It grows even more when Eve's eyes fill with a lightness that Kyle seems to bring out in her.

"Can we give Aunt Riley her gummies now?"

Chuckling, Kyle nods. Eve runs over to the kitchen island and opens one of the bags they brought in with them earlier.

"Here you go." She hands me a bag of my favorite Haribo gummy bears. "Kyle picked these out for you when we stopped at the store. It's because you had one of your headaches last night."

I glance over at Kyle who's smiling at the both of us. "I told you it wasn't that bad." After playing only a few rounds of video games with Eve, my head started to hurt. I took some of my medication and went to bed early, while she and Kyle finished up the game.

"This is the right kind, correct?" is all he asks, fingering the bag of gummy bears.

"Yes. Thank you," I whisper.

He stares at me but says, "Eve, close your eyes."

"Why?"

"Just do it," he tells her.

When she does, he leans down, his lips hovering over mine. "Thank me properly."

I lift up onto my tiptoes and wrap an arm around his neck, pulling him to me. The kiss was slower than I thought it would be. Kyle's lips find mine and he pulls me under his spell. My entire body warms, making me forget all about my selfish brother showing up out of the blue.

"There's more of where that came from later," he says against my lips before pulling back.

"Can I open my eyes now?" Eve asks, making both of us laugh.

"How about we clean up since your aunt cooked dinner? Then we can go another round on your game. I owe you for last night," Kyle tells Eve. He says it with a grin, but I can hear the competitive edge in his voice.

"She's eleven," I remind him.

He shrugs. "I want my rematch."

"Um, how about a movie?" Eve snaps her fingers. "You still haven't seen *The Greatest Showman*."

Kyle's and my eyes lock. I know we're both thinking about that weekend. Kyle's eyes darken, and I have no doubt he's remembering it, too.

"Yeah, I've seen it," he says, eyes still locked on me. "But I might've missed a few things."

I try to stifle the grin that sprouts across my lips but it's a futile effort.

"We can watch it again," Eve says. "Let's hurry up and clean the kitchen. I have to do some homework and then we can watch."

I leave them to clean the kitchen, a smile still on my face as I enjoy my gummy bears.

He's using you.

My brother's accusation suddenly comes to mind when I hear Eve mention something about her father. I do my best to shake it off, but the alarm bells in my head won't allow me to.

Just like every other time in my life when he or my father were around, Wallace Jr. manages to dampen my mood.

* * *

"She's asleep," Kyle says, entering the bedroom after finishing his game with Eve.

"I should've cut him off," I tell him.

He closes the door and stands with his arms folded. He's dressed in a pair of blue pajama bottoms and a white T-shirt. The muscles in his arms bulge with every movement. I keep my eyes on those muscles when I confess, "I thought … hoped he would eventually come around. Realize what an amazing daughter he has and want to be a part of her life."

Pushing out a breath, I look away. "Stupid."

Kyle pads across the room and sits on the edge of the bed, next to me, bracing his arm across my body.

"He won't bother either one of you again," he says with such certainty that I almost believe him.

"I can handle myself. I just don't want Eve to deal with what I did." I meet Kyle's hard stare. "I was twelve when I had my first migraine. We had just moved to another city, somewhere outside of L.A. My dad had met another *nice woman*. That's what he called them. He wanted me to tell her some lie about how we had to move because I was being bullied at school and the administrators tried to cover it up.

"I remember hating the idea of telling another lie. My head started hurting as I was telling her the story. Later on, it got so much worse. I was in so much pain and he barely acknowledged me. Complained about how much it would cost him if he had to take me to the doctors."

I snort in disgust and anger.

"When I told him I didn't want to take part in his plans anymore, he called me too tender-hearted and said I need to get over it. Took years before I ever went to a doctor for my migraines. Most of them are stress-induced."

Kyle looks me over. "Is that why you had one that weekend?"

I think back to months earlier, my last significant migraine. I hadn't had one that intense in a couple of years.

"I think so," I answer. "I never liked scamming people. It was all I knew how to do for a long time. Lying to get what I want."

"And your father?" Kyle asks.

"Haven't spoken to him since the day I left his house. A few years later, I heard from my brother that he'd gotten arrested for credit card and bank fraud. I went to court during his trial and listened as he was found guilty. My last memory of my father is of him in an orange jumpsuit being led out of the courtroom in handcuffs."

He nods. "You need to talk to Eve about who her father really is."

"I'm sorry she told him about you."

He shakes his head. "I don't care about that. But she's holding on, hoping that he'll come around and care about her like a parent should. You saw how he is with her. He doesn't give a shit. He's a self-centered prick who couldn't care less about anyone but himself. After tonight, his ass won't be able to come around anyway. But Eve needs to know it's not her fault."

"You're right," I admit. "How'd you get so good with kids?"

He smirks. "I'm the oldest of five and I have a shitload of younger cousins."

I point at him. "That's another dollar for the swear jar."

"I put in twenty earlier because I knew he was going to piss me off enough to fill it up for the rest of the week."

I laugh. "He has that way about him."

"He won't be around again," Kyle promises at the same time he squeezes my thigh.

The feeling of safety that rolls through my body is sudden.

"Good." I sigh and don't even bother asking what happened with him and Wallace in the hallway.

He's using you.

Unfortunately, Wallace's words aren't as easy to shrug off. I, of all people, know that it's true. Kyle wants to get payback against Dean out of this marriage. It's not real. I just can't help that parts of this life have started to feel real.

"Kyle—" I start to ask but my phone buzzes. I glance over and inhale. "It's Dean."

It's been weeks since Dean has contacted me. Ever since that day I gave him the thumb drive at the lounge.

Kyle's jaw tightens. "Speaker."

I answer and put it on speaker. "Dean."

"You're not with him, are you?" he demands to know.

"I wouldn't have answered the phone if I were," I say while simultaneously looking into Kyle's eyes.

"God, I'm going to be so glad to get rid of you."

A spark of fear rolls down my spine from the way he says those words so cavalierly. "What did you just say?"

"Nothing." He clears his throat. "Listen, those fucking files have it all. And we're about to use it all to expose that garbage family for who and what they are."

"Why are you telling me all of this?"

"Because you're about to walk that stupid husband of yours right to his demise. In a week there's going to be a press conference. It'll be hosted by Ryan Nick."

"The alderman?" The name is familiar.

"Yeah."

"Who is he to you?" I ask.

"He's my— that's none of your business!" Dean suddenly blurts out as if he realized he was about to give me more information than intended. "Just have him there at the press conference. I don't give a fuck how you do it. That fucker is going down."

The phone clicks, and I realize Dean has hung up the phone.

Surprise catches me when I look up to see a smile on Kyle's face.

"Do you know what the press conference is about?"

He shakes his head.

"Then why are you grinning like that?"

"Because he just told us who he's been working with." His lips spread even more. "And revenge is going to be sweet."

A silence falls between us.

"That bullshit aside," he says, his voice seductively low.

Kyle runs the tip of his finger under my lip and down my chin to my neck. Goosebumps sprout up along my arms.

"I've missed being inside of you all fucking day."

My nipples harden from the way his eyes narrow.

"Show me," I whisper.

The last word barely has a chance to make it out of my mouth before he's on top of me. Kyle makes love to me slowly. Even as my phone starts to ring again, sometime later, he doesn't let me up for air.

In that silly place in the back of my mind, the space that once held out hope of having a real father or even an older brother who loved me for me, I begin to wish that Kyle and I could be like this forever.

That this marriage was about more than revenge.

CHAPTER 35

Kyle

The following morning, I'm filled with anticipation as I wait in the basement offices of Townsend Industries. This is one of the few places in this building that only a handful of people, mainly family members, knows about.

"You're lucky I love you, kid," Uncle Brutus says. "Dragging my ass out of bed early as shit for this," he mutters in the corner of the dank room.

I chuckle.

"What he said," my father adds but even more tersely.

It's six-thirty in the morning. "You both could've stayed home. I can handle these two on my own."

My father snorts. "I want to see you in action."

"Same," my uncle adds.

This morning I'm killing two birds. Wallace Jr. will be here in an hour, but first, I need to take care of another problem. I crack my knuckles as I recall Dean fucking Walsh calling my wife's phone.

"First one's here," Uncle Brutus says after getting a notification on his phone.

"Why don't you show him in?"

He grunts, exiting through the steel doors.

The wait isn't long before my uncle returns with two other men. One of them is another member of our security team. Sandwiched between the two large men is a shell shocked Jacob Hartcliff. Reporter for *The Williamsport Daily*.

Hartcliff is only about five-nine to five-ten. Considering Uncle Brutus towers over me by six inches at six-nine, he makes Hartcliff look like an adolescent.

"What's this about?" Hartcliff asks, but then jumps when the steel doors slam shut behind him.

"Our security will wait outside," I told him when he looks over his shoulder. "They can be imposing sons of bitches. And I'd like to keep this meeting as friendly as possible."

His eyes widen in fear.

I hold out my hand to the corner of the room. "You've met my father, haven't you?"

Hartcliff doesn't say anything. Neither does my father. He stands there with a scowl on his face, glaring at the reporter.

"Maybe not," I say into the silence. "He doesn't like reporters too much. I get that from him." I chuckle. "Let's make this quick since I'm short on time. You're behind the last article in *The Williamsport Daily* that came eerily close to maligning my family, correct?"

I lean in to Hartcliff, awaiting his answer.

"W-Whitney Donaldson wrote that article."

My father scoffs.

"My father doesn't like it when cowards hide behind someone else to cover their bullshit, especially when it's a woman. Another quality I get from him." My top lip curls as I glare at him. "Her name's listed as the writer, but you were the one who fed the information and all but wrote the piece for her."

"I—" He shifts attention between my father and me.

"She's already told us everything. You gave her the piece under the guise of promoting her from intern to associate reporter. Like you had authority to do that. Also, you're behind those blog posts and other articles Jayceon Carlson had published months ago, correct?"

His eyes balloon. "I'm a reporter. It's not illegal to report the news. If something comes across my desk, I have a responsibility to the public."

"I get it." I pat his shoulder. "You're like a civil servant. Doing your duty. You absolutely shouldn't be harmed for doing your job." I pause and tighten my hold on his shoulder. "But you weren't doing your job, were you? No," I answer for him, tightening my grip.

Hartcliff's face turns beet red.

"You were taking your own personal bullshit out on my family through those lies you had printed. All because back when my sister was an intern, she refused to do your bidding, right?"

Kennedy had interned briefly for *The Williamsport Daily*. Turns out, this fucker has a reputation among the female interns.

"Wh-What, no?"

"Are you calling my daughter a fucking liar?" my father roars, getting in Hartcliff's face.

"You really don't want to do that," I tell him. "Makes him angry. And me?" I pat my chest with my free hand and squeeze the side of his neck so tightly that he crumbles to one knee. "I hate it when anyone fucks with my twin. It's too bad Kennedy hadn't mentioned this years ago when it happened. Maybe some of this drama could've been avoided."

My father grunts. "Get the fuck up."

Hartcliff rises to his feet.

"Again, I need to speed this up," I say. "You're here not only because of what you did to Kennedy. This is because I also know a few weeks ago you received some information that was on a thumb drive, correct?"

A red-faced Hartcliff doesn't say anything as he looks between two pissed off Townsend men with watery, frightful eyes.

"I'll take that as a yes. Dean Walsh came to you to report that bullshit you had written up months ago, and he passed the files in the thumb drive about the supposed abandoned houses we own? Next week Ryan Nick will hold a press conference exposing my family with this information. Did I get all of that right?"

I don't wait for his answer.

"Here's what's going to happen instead. You're going to write up a series of eight articles about those houses, since they're all part of Townsend's homeless to homeowner charity program. Each article will interview the new homeowner.

"I prefer you pass it along to an all-female staff since you don't have a problem with having others do your work for you. The first article and interview will run next week on the day after the press conference. One article per week for eight weeks total.

"Once the series is complete, you'll resign from your position and never seek out a job in this arena again. Is that clear?"

"I-I ... it wasn't m-me."

"Stop talking, you're going to give me a headache. Are we clear?"

He nods.

"Good. Get out of my sight."

Seconds later, Uncle Brutus escorts Hartcliff out of the room.

My father turns to me. "You didn't even break his nose?"

"Kennedy did that when he tried something on her, remember?"

He rolls his eyes. "I'm going to call her to ream her out for not telling me about it three years ago when the fucker harassed her. Then I'm going to pay him a visit myself."

"Can't it wait until after the articles are done?"

He scoffs but agrees. "I need to get up to the office for an eight a.m. meeting."

"Good." I nod. "This next visit is more personal."

A rare expression breaks out on my father's face. "Make sure this one doesn't leave unscathed."

I crack my knuckles. "Don't worry about that."

Minutes later, my Uncle Brutus is strolling through the door with Wallace Jr. behind him. My lips spread into a devious smile because this is the real meeting I've been waiting for. Hartcliff was a warm-up.

"I thought we were meeting in your office," Wallace starts. "But this big, burly guy met me at the hotel I'm staying at to bring me here."

I wait for Uncle Brutus to exit, leaving me and Wallace alone. "Yes, consider it a special Townsend service. We are family after all."

"What's with this room?" He looks around. "Your office has to be fancier than this shit."

"It is."

Wallace, who had his back to me, spins around. That's when I punch him in the softest part of his belly. He doubles over.

"What the hell?" he strains to ask, while trying to upright himself.

I don't let him get that far when I land a right hook to his jaw. "I wouldn't let you within ten feet of my office. It's bad enough you were at my fucking home," I grit out.

He stumbles backward. "This is an attack."

"No shit," I say before throwing a jab at his face. The crunching sounds immediately followed by the waterfall of blood out of his nose speaks of the bone break. "You should've kept your conniving, lying, stupid ass wherever you were."

Anger overtakes me and all I can think about is the look in Riley's eyes last night when Eve and I entered our home. There was fear in them. That accompanied with her immediate insistence that she had no idea he was coming pissed me off. Like she assumed I suspected her of working with him or something.

I know she wouldn't.

Because I know my wife. I've come to know her almost as well as I know myself.

"You used her love of her niece to hang on to her like the vulture you are. You couldn't even look at Eve for more than a few seconds last night." I punch him again.

Wallace takes a wild swing at me, but I easily avoid it.

"She's your fucking daughter and you couldn't say more than two sentences to her. You're the worst type of man." Another punch causes him to land on his ass. "Not even a fucking man."

When he moves to get up, I hold him down with my foot on his chest.

"I would never, ever do business with someone as pathetic as you.

You're a piece of shit. Yesterday was the last time you'll ever lay eyes on Riley or Eve again."

"D-Did Riley set this up?"

"Don't fucking say my wife's name!

"In a minute, my security's going to walk back through that door and shove you in the back of the same car they picked you up in. Then they'll deliver you to the two brothers you've been running from for a few years now. We've already made the call. They graciously got on a plane to Williamsport overnight."

Last night, Riley told me about Wallace running from a gang, headed by two brothers, and how he used her to hide from them a few years ago.

"I don't suspect you'll live past your meeting with them."

As soon as those words leave my mouth, Uncle Brutus enters. "Done?"

I grin over my shoulder and nod. "Good. I want to get home before my wife wakes up."

"Please give Aunt Mia a kiss and hug for me," I say, starting to exit.

He snorts. "I'm only giving my wife kisses for me. You've got your own wife now. Go hug and kiss her. I'll tell Mia you said hi though. Stop by the coffee shop one day."

"I will. And I'll bring my wife and Eve."

He nods, and I leave that dank basement. Wallace Jr. is done for and I don't feel even a speck of guilt about it. The bastard had it long coming.

CHAPTER 36

Riley

I take note of the reporters and cameras that mill about as Kyle and I enter the lobby of city hall. Today is the day of the press conference with Ryan Nick. He's invited reporters and newspapers to attend but kept the topic quiet.

He thinks he's about to expose Townsend Industries, but what's about to happen isn't that.

"Credentials," one of the hulking security guard demands.

"Here," Kyle tersely hands him our invites. "We're on the list."

The guard's tone suddenly changes. "Right this way, Mr. Townsend."

Kyle takes my hand as we're escorted to the front row. There are numerous council members and business personnel among the crowd. Ryan Nick stands behind a podium waving at people as they enter. He pauses when he looks over and sees Kyle.

His smile widens as he waves.

My husband waves back but mutters, "Bastard."

"Kyle," Ryan actually says from where he stands, "thank you for coming. I believe you'll find today's press conference particularly interesting."

Kyle just gives him a nod as we take our seats.

"Thank you all for attending," Ryan Nick starts.

I barely pay attention as he talks about all that he intends to do as the newly appointed alderman.

"We'll work together to rid this city of corruption. I intend to hold up my promise to expose all of the big corporations and businesses that have harmed this city and its people."

He's making some big declarations. I glance over at Kyle; he grins at me and nods.

"I will first start with Townsend Industries."

Gasps go up all around the room. Cameras start flashing and reporters' hands shoot up. Eyes zero in on Kyle, who doesn't react at all.

I take that as an opportunity to raise my hand.

"Congratulations on this historic day for Walsh Technologies," I say as I rise to my feet.

"Now is not the time for questions," Ryan Nick tries to cut me off ,but I persist.

"Why don't we make time before you pull up any false evidence you supposedly have. How does it feel to know that you've invited everyone to your own burial?"

His eyes go wide.

"I-I'm sorry," Nick stutters.

"No, I should apologize. That was the wrong question. I see you've brought additional city council members in attendance today. My actual question is, you say your goal is to expose corruption, but weren't you and some of these council members paid off to pass certain housing and building permits?"

"Ex-excuse me?" Ryan blubbers.

Two of city council members sit up, looking between one another. I can feel the other reporters and cameraman shifting their attention between me and Nick.

"Or, how about this? Can you please explain why you had your nephew, Dean Walsh, blackmail me into getting hired at Townsend Industries so you can dig up dirt on the company and family that your brother was arrested for on corporate espionage charges, almost a decade ago?"

A lot of gasps and hushed whispers sound around me.

As it turns out, Ryan Nick is Dean Walsh's uncle. He's Dean's father's half-brother. A fact kept hidden until Kyle's security brought it up.

"I have the recordings between your nephew and me if you'd like to hear them."

I pull out my phone and play one of Dean's and my phone conversations. In the recording, Dean clearly has a vendetta against the Townsend family.

"Wait, maybe this one is a little more interesting." I skip to the most recent recording where I play Dean giving me instructions to show up at today's press conference.

Ryan's eyes balloon to the point they look as if they're going to pop out of his skull.

"This proves nothing! I don't even know who you are!" he says.

"Oh me?" I point to my chest before slowly sliding my sunglasses off of my face.

"She's my wife," Kyle's strong declaration ricochets through the air as he stands.

Instead of gasps and more whispers, the entire crowd goes mute as if they know that any and everything he has to say isn't to be missed.

Kyle glares at Ryan.

"Thanks for the invitation, by the way," Kyle starts with an evil smirk on his face. "I suppose from the surprise on your face, your nephew forgot to tell you that my wife would be coming with me."

According to what Kyle's security discovered, Ryan Nick had no idea how Dean Walsh was funneling information to him. He just wanted him to get evidence any way he could.

Kyle continues, "How about you use that projector you brought to open up the files you received illegally, from my company. The multiple houses in that secret file."

Ryan finds his second wind. "Yes." He clears his throat. "We know all about your shady business dealings in those homes. This ..." He presses the clicker and the screen on either side of him pops up with a detailed presentation.

"I had my assistant prepare that presentation just for you," Kyle says.

I don't even know how he was able to get the presentation to Ryan's people for them to load it up for the press conference.

"You see," Kyle turns to the crowd and cameras, "the homes Ryan believed were illegally obtained and used for whatever nonsense he dreamt up, are actually part of our charity program. For decades, Townsend Industries and my family have been involved in sheltering those who are less fortunate. We simply chose not to brag about it to the media."

He pauses.

"It's tacky." He shrugs.

"But since you and your nephew tried to use your resources to get back at my family for the pathetic excuse of a brother of yours ... well, we must expose this act of philanthropy on our part."

"That's a lie!" Ryan declares. "Those homes are where your family attacks, threatens, and even kills to get what you want!" he seethes.

Kyle doesn't even look flustered when he answers. "Ryan, I'm a little concerned about your mental well-being. As you can see, the proof is right in front of you. I've even invited a few of our past recipients to speak with the media on the new homes they received from our generous donations. Oh," Kyle snaps, "and starting tomorrow, *The Williamsport Daily* will run an eight-week series on the project. You all should check it out."

He smiles to the crowd, truly putting on a show.

"For now, though, Ryan, you will likely need to speak with an attorney regarding charges of bribery and blackmail that these friendly officers are arresting you for."

A team of agents shoves through a few reporters and their cameras to approach Ryan.

"This is absurd!" Ryan declares as the agents grab him to slap cuffs on his wrists.

"Don't worry," Kyle tells him. "The SEC, FBI, and local police have all the evidence to back up every word my wife and I have stated today."

All I can hear are reporters asking a slew of questions, and cameras clicking as they take shot after shot of Ryan's arrest.

Right as he's escorted past us, Kyle grabs Ryan's arm. "I will find out who you were working with within my company. Don't fucking worry," he says low enough for only me and Ryan to hear.

A satisfied thrill pushes through me as Ryan's carted off, along with two other city council members.

"It's time for us to go," Kyle murmurs in my ear as he slides his hand around my waist.

"I want to see all of this," I say, not looking his way.

"And I want to be alone with my wife." He says it so close to my ear that his lips lightly brush against my skin. Goosebumps spread down my neck and over my arms. His hold around my waist tightens, pulling me flush against his body.

Despite the attention now turning our way, I can only think of being alone with him.

"No questions," Kyle says, with one hand shielding me and the other wrapped around my shoulders.

Security is there to shield us the rest of the way to the car.

Once we get in, I ask, "You think there's someone else involved?"

He nods. "I suspect Ryan Nick is working with someone inside of Townsend Industries."

"It would have to be someone high up," I say, confused. "The police will also arrest Dean for his part in all of this."

Kyle nods. "They'll all get what's coming to them. Right now, I don't want to talk about them. Come here and let me convince you to work for the family business," he growls.

* * *

Kyle

"You should work for Townsend Industries," I tell Riley as I pull her onto my lap to straddle me. I'm happy as hell she opted to wear a skirt for today's press conference.

She laughs. "I already do for a few more weeks."

With a shake of my head, I tell her, "Not as a consultant. As a permanent employee. Once I'm promoted to permanent COO. We need you."

I pull out her shirt from the waistband of her skirt. Electricity zaps through me when I lay my hands on her bare skin.

"I have my own business," she murmurs. "Besides, I also have an employee that I can't let go of."

"I'll hire Charlotte, too. And double both of your salaries." I kiss her neck, making her shudder.

"No. I like working for myself."

Her words are husky. The sound pulls at my dick.

"I bet I can think of a few ways to change your mind. We'll table the discussion for now."

Right now, I only want to be between my wife's thighs.

"C'mere," I say, cupping her face for a kiss.

"We can't." She laughs. "We'll be home in a few minutes."

"I instructed our driver to drive around until I tell him to take us home." We're not going into the office today.

Riley pulls back, her arms on my shoulders. "Truth or dare?"

A smile stretches my lips. "Dare."

Her shoulders sag slightly. For a second, I think I've disappointed her somehow. *How?*

However, her expression changes so fast, I must've imagined it.

"I dare you to make me scream in the back of this car."

"Now you're making fucking sense."

She lets out a yell-laugh when I grab her by the waist and switch our positions so that she's beneath me. I tug at the buttons of her shirt and push her skirt up around her waist. I yank down the lace bra she's wearing to take one of her breasts into my greedy mouth.

She tastes so fucking sweet. My cock instantly goes hard. I have to fight the urge to strip out of my pants and jam my dick so deep inside of her that she loses her voice from screaming. As much as I want that, I want to taste every inch of her body before I do.

"Kyle," Riley mumbles my name, causing warm, fuzzy feelings and shit to flow through my body.

I want to hear her say my name just like this for the rest of my life.

I've had that thought so much lately that it no longer surprises me. Instead of saying it aloud, however, I move down her body. I force her legs over my shoulder so I can enjoy my meal.

Riley's pussy is unlike anything I've ever tasted before. It's sweet and reminds me of the taste of honey. If I could bottle this shit up and season all of my food with it, I would.

Since I can't, I settle for eating her out like she's my favorite meal. Because she is. Her moans and groans only make me want more. I want her writhing beneath me, calling my name, unable to control herself. Riley's a screamer. She can't let it out all the time at home or work.

Today, though, I want to hear every fucking syllable.

I run my tongue around her clit while also inserting two fingers deep inside of her. I scissor my fingers, hitting her walls but also readying her for my cock. Riley raises her hips, openly begging for more. Within minutes her legs tighten around my head, and she's coming.

The guttural moan that she lets out boosts my fucking ego. I lap up all of her juices happily. Not until her body stops trembling do I pull my cock out.

Riley springs up from her position and quickly straddles me. I yank her skirt up even higher to watch as my dick enters her.

"You're going to rip my skirt," she says breathlessly.

"I'll buy you a hundred more," I say. I don't want anything in the way of the view of me taking her.

"That's ridiculous—"

I cut her off with a kiss. "Stop talking, and sit on my dick, wife," I growl.

A shudder runs through her body when I run the tip along her pussy lips. Riley wraps her hands around my neck and positions herself over me. I brace my hands on her hips.

"Watch me make you mine, wife," I demand.

I slowly slide her down onto me, and the jolt of electricity that rockets through me gets me every fucking time. I haven't worn a condom with her ever since the first time I took her raw in my office. While I manage to pull out every time, a piece of me wants to drench her pussy with my cum.

"Keep your eyes open," I order when her eyelids begin to slip shut. Her eyes spring open and she gives her full attention to my cock as it makes her mine.

"Good girl," I murmur. "Ride me, Riley."

She begins a slow, steady movement of her hips. She rises and falls on me over and over. My eyes are glued to the way she moves, taking me like a fucking champ. I cup the back of her neck and pull her to me for a kiss. I want to consume every part of her. Not just for today, either.

Our bodies are merely conduits for the ways in which we're compatible.

"I'm coming," she pants against my lips, her hips moving wildly.

"Come all over my dick," I tell her. As if my statement was exactly what she needed to let go, her inner walls begin trembling. They squeeze me, milking me for my orgasm. Yet, I fight like hell to hold off until her orgasm passes.

When it does, I lift Riley until she's completely off of me and place her onto her back. Riley immediately cups her breasts, pushing them together around my cock. I can't hold off any longer as the orgasm tears through me.

Jets of my cum fall onto her chest, lower chin, and lip. I swear a secondary orgasm sparks off at the sight of Riley licking my cum off of her lip. She finishes off by sitting up and taking my cock into her mouth to squeeze out the last droplets.

While watching her throat move from the work of swallowing my semen, the only thing I can think is, *I'm going to fucking keep her.*

CHAPTER 37

Riley

I inhale a deep breath when I see the number on my screen.

It's Dean Walsh. The bastard has been on the run the past few weeks since that press conference. He's got balls calling me.

"Riley, are you all right?" Patience, Kyle's mother, asks as we exit the Good Society Community Center. His mother, aunts, and grandmother founded the community center years ago, but changed the name so that it wouldn't be too closely linked with Townsend Industries.

For the past two months since meeting Kyle's parents, I've volunteered at the community center in partnership with the Girls on the Move program.

"Yes, I'm fine," I lie to my mother-in-law. "Just a call from work." She knows about the nonsense with Dean, as does everyone in the family. But I don't want to worry her.

Patience frowns. "Kyle is not making you work on weekends, is he?"

"No, nothing like that."

Her smile is wide. "Good. Since you came into his life, his father and I have noticed how much less time he spends at work."

"I'm sorry. Eve insists that we all have dinner together in the evenings, and for some reason, he can't say no to her."

Patience raises an eyebrow. "I wasn't saying that his working less is a bad thing. The amount of time he spent at the office used to concern me. He got his workaholic tendencies from his father."

"Well, it's paid off seeing as how he's worked his way up to such an important role in such a short period of time."

She nods thoughtfully. "But business isn't everything. I think he's finally figured that out." She waves as she heads to the car waiting for her.

I turn to head toward my car.

"Oh, Riley?"

I pause to look back at my mother-in-law.

"I don't think Eve is the only person my son can't say no to."

I wrinkle my forehead, wondering what she's trying to say, but the ringing phone in my hand distracts me. I smile and wave at her before getting into the car.

I let Dean's call go to voicemail again.

When I arrive, I'm surprised to find Kyle and Eve playing another round of their video games. They're so into the competition between them that they don't hear me enter. I stand there watching them. Kyle lightly shoves Eve, making her giggle.

When she shoves him back, he lets out a grunt and promises that he's going to kick her butt in this round. These are the moments that I store away for later. For when Kyle gets his official title as COO and he'll want this marriage annulled.

That's the way this is going to go. I know it. I just wish it wouldn't end that way. I also hope that Eve doesn't hate me too much when Kyle is no longer a part of our daily lives.

Thinking about it causes a pain to shoot through my chest.

"Aunt Riley's home," Eve says. "We can finally bake the cookies we bought."

I shake off my previous thoughts and fully enter the apartment. "Did someone say cookies?"

Eve nods excitedly. "We bought ingredients to make chocolate chip. Stasi told me her secret recipe. And she gave me notecards with all of the instructions."

My phone starts ringing again, and I look at Kyle.

"Hey, Eve, why don't you put our game away and set out the ingredients for the cookies while I talk to your aunt?" Kyle suggests.

Eve happily agrees while Kyle takes me by the arm and guides us down the hall.

"What's wrong?" he asks before the door is even fully closed. He searches my eyes, the pinched skin between his eyebrows signaling his concern.

"Dean."

That one word causes a scowl to make its way across my husband's handsome face.

"I should've taken care of his stupid ass already."

Without another word, Kyle takes my phone from my hand and answers. "What the hell do you want?" he demands.

There's a pause and I can't hear Dean's response.

"Yeah, I thought you would like that." He chuckles, and it sounds as if it's mocking whatever Dean has just said.

"Let me listen," I whisper.

Kyle turns away from me. I hate the rejected feeling that grips me. *Does he think I'm no longer useful to him? Is that it? He got what he wanted out of me and now he no longer wants me included?*

"You won't be speaking with my wife now or ever again," I hear Kyle say. "By now you should've figured out that your plan was dumb as shit from the beginning. Did you really believe *you* of all people would be the downfall of my fucking family? Do you know who we are?"

"What's he saying?" I whisper, desperate to hear more.

Kyle finally obliges and presses the button to put Dean on speaker.

"Fuck you!" he shouts, sounding even more disturbed than usual.

"You dumb fuck," Kyle berates.

"Yeah?" Dean counters. "You think you're so fucking smart and in control. It wasn't like that when you were sixteen." He lets out a cackle. "You actually thought I was your fucking friend. You let me into your house and everything. Just like that bitch. Then you fucking married her. You probably believe she really loves you."

I flinch from Dean's words.

A stormy expression clouds Kyle's face. I can almost see the steam coming off of him.

"Listen here, you stupid son of a bitch." His voice is so deep and full of malice that I wrap my arms around my body, shielding myself from the impact of his words.

"You're dumber and less equipped than your pathetic ass father. You had almost a decade to do better and your whole fucking end goal fell down around your face. You're a bigger loser than he was, and for calling my wife a bitch, your fate is going to be uglier than his ever was. I'll see you soon, motherfucker."

With that Kyle hangs up the phone and tosses it onto the bed. "Don't answer his calls ever again."

I have no intention of speaking to Dean Walsh again, but I don't like the way he thinks he can order me around.

"What if I do?" I say with my hands on my hips.

He gives me a hard glare. "Then I will be forced to put your stubborn ass over my knee."

I hate the way the shiver automatically rolls through my body. The smirk that lights up Kyle's face tells me he notices it, too.

My body always betrays me when it comes to him.

"You would like that, wouldn't you?" His voice deepens and he trails a finger beneath my lower lip. He has some sort of weird fascination with my lips.

"Maybe," I say on a whisper.

"Aunt Riley and Kyle, I'm ready!" Eve says from outside of our door.

Kyle pecks me on the mouth. "Save that thought for later. Coming," he calls to Riley.

"Wait." I stop him by grabbing his arm.

For a few beats I just stand there, my heart hammering in my chest. The words I want to say are on the tip of my tongue. But so is my fear. What I have to say will likely change everything between us. However, I can't keep it in any longer.

"I love you," I blurt out in a rush. "I-I know that's not what you wanted from this marriage. Or its intention. But …" I clear my throat. "I love you." The words feel right coming out of my mouth even if his reaction terrifies me.

"Come on!" Eve shouts through the door. She starts knocking. "What are you guys doing in there?"

My grip slips from Kyle's arm as he moves to the door to answer it. "We're coming. Show me where you've put the ingredients," he tells her. He gives me one last look over his shoulder before my niece leads him to the kitchen.

My heart feels as if someone just stomped on it.

CHAPTER 38

Kyle

"This motherfucker," I gripe as I see Brendan Chastain's name on my phone.

Like I don't have enough to think about with Dean's dumb ass still missing three weeks after the press conference. More important, Riley told me her true feelings. For the first time ever, words stuck in my throat when she told me those three words.

Not today, though. It's a Saturday morning and Eve spent the night over my parents' house because she and Stasi made plans for early this morning.

Today, I'm going to tell Riley I'm in love with her, too.

"What?" I answer, regretting that I gave him my cell number months ago.

"Kyle, we should meet for coffee while I'm in town." He actually sounds like he thinks we're friends.

"No," I say while I lean against the doorframe and watch my wife sleeping in our bed.

When she rolls over, one of her legs sticks out from underneath the blanket. My dick instantly grows hard.

"How about sometime next week? I can extend my stay," Brendan continues.

"What the hell about no don't you understand?" I growl under my breath to keep from waking Riley.

"Kyle, man. I know you're probably pissed that I exposed the real Riley to you."

My entire body stiffens.

"But you should be thanking me. You would never have found out about her if it weren't for me. I mean, hell, if she slept with me to get my money, I know that's what she did for you. Good for you for using her to take down Walsh's family. I never would've thought—"

"What the fuck did you just say?" My tone is cold enough to freeze hell.

Brendan hesitates. "You married her to get what you wanted, right? Fuck, I should've thought of something like that. All she did for me was—"

I hang up on the dumb fuck because I'm blinded by rage.

"Hey," Riley's groggy voice reaches me.

When I can finally focus enough through my anger haze, it's to see a small smile playing at her lips.

"Was that Eve? Did she have fun with Stasi last night?"

I tighten the hold of the phone in my hand. It's ringing again. Chastain.

"Yeah, they're having a great time," I tell her. Then I press the button to answer the phone.

I make sure the phone is on and then turn the volume all of the way down as I stroll to the bed.

Riley gasps when I strip her of the blanket and sheets. She's wearing only a thin T-shirt and the cotton panties she likes to sleep in. I place my phone on the nightstand next to her side of the bed.

I know I'm an asshole for what I'm about to do but Chastain needs to get the message.

"What are you doing?" Riley moans, somewhat sleepily, as I begin pulling her panties down her long legs.

"Do you know one of my favorite things about you?" I ask her.

She shakes her head. "What?" There's a hitch in her voice as I spread her legs.

"What you taste like first thing in the morning." I lean in and inhale the scent of her pussy. "It's like your pussy has been marinating just for me overnight."

She lets out a laugh. My dick pushes against the zipper of my jeans, straining to get free. I don't listen to it. Instead, I lower myself between her legs.

I love you.

I recall the words she told me days ago. The most perfect gift she could've ever given me. Her heart.

"Let me show you," I mumble against her lips before I circle her clit with my tongue.

Riley rolls her hips and lets out a low moan.

I slowly run my tongue against her lips and then around and around her swollen button.

"Fuck, Kyle," she says, her lower back bowing off of the bed.

I don't let up as I inch my shoulders underneath her knees, keeping her legs spread for my mouth. She tastes so fucking good that I start to lose my shit. I become greedy, seeking more of her taste on my tongue. Even Riley's first orgasm doesn't stop me. If anything, the opposite happens. I continue lapping her up, seeking out another orgasm.

Riley's hands pull at my hair. The tiny prickles of pain make me harder, and I push her thighs farther apart. It's not until the second orgasm rockets through her body that the possessive haze hovering around me starts to recede slightly.

I move up Riley's body to see her eyelids half closed and a crooked smile on her beautiful mouth. I kiss the hell out of her, letting her taste herself on me. I pull away from her and kiss the tip of her nose.

My fucking wife.

The only three words that ring through my head as I stare down at her.

"We're going to be late," she murmurs, reminding me that we have a prior engagement this morning. Another one of her Girls on the Move volunteer events.

I nod and move away from her, grabbing my phone from the nightstand. "You should go shower. We'll finish where we left off later."

I don't look back as I stride toward the living room. I turn the volume up on my phone, noticing that the bastard hasn't hung up. I knew he wouldn't. That pisses me off even more.

"Did you hear that?" I ask through gritted teeth.

"K-Kyle? Is that …"

"That's exactly what you think it is. The one and only time you've ever heard my wife make those sounds. Or ever will."

"I-I—"

"Shut the fuck up. You've lied on my wife, thinking you could use her past to fucking bond with me? You're a selfish, spoiled, lacking talent son of a bitch who only gets by on the name of his parents. Riley saw you for the chump you are a mile away. Live with it. The only reason I'm letting you continue to breathe is because you didn't have something to do with Dean's blackmail. He used you, too.

"You're not angry at Riley for stealing from you. You're pissed and embarrassed that she did it without ever letting you touch her. I know my wife never fucked you. This is your final warning. If you ever mention my wife's name out of your pathetic mouth again, let alone imply that you had anything physical with her, I'll demolish you. Trust me when I say I will take pleasure in ending you. Don't ever fucking call me again."

I end the call and tighten my hands into fists with the desire to punch Brendan fucking Chastain in his face. But undoubtedly that'll be the last time I hear anything from him.

I turn around to head back to the bedroom, but the sight of Riley stops me. She's standing there, frozen, dressed in one of my white, button-down shirts. Usually, the sight of her in my clothes makes me rock hard.

But it's the tears in her eyes that steal my breath.

"D-Did you … have him on the phone?" Her voice is clogged with unshed tears.

"Riley..."

I take a step in her direction, but she holds up her hands.

"Don't come near me."

That's when the first rip in my heart starts.

"Why would you do something like that?"

I shake my head. "It's no big deal," I say, but it sounds like bullshit even as it comes out of my mouth.

She scoffs. The laugh she lets free is brittle. "Not a big deal. Just like I'm not a big deal to you either, right?"

"What? Of course you are. You're my fucking wife," I say, my voice growing louder.

"Right. For as long as you need to secure your role as the COO. To get whatever you need." She juts her hand at the phone in my hand. "And to make Brendan look like a ... what did you call him? Right. A *chump.*"

The first tear falls from her eye.

"Don't come near me!" she screams when I attempt to approach.

I hate the look on her face. As if I'm the last person in this world that she wants anywhere near her.

"You used me. Just like ..." She trails off with a shake of her head. "That's all I ever was to you."

"What are you saying? You're my damn wife."

"You keep saying that like it means any damn thing!" she yells.

"It means everything. I wouldn't give anyone else my last fucking name."

"Right," she scoffs. "No, you needed someone to use as your pawn. I'm just the best person for the job." She shrugs. "It's my own fault anyway. I did start off trying to deceive you. I was such a fucking fool to believe maybe we were building something real."

"This is real," I insist.

"Is it? Or is it just for whatever you can get? Until you get promoted to COO. Now that Dean and his family's scheming are out of the way, that's all that's left between us, right? Your fucking promotion."

"Chastain was fucking lying on you!" I yell.

"So what? I don't give a damn what he says about me."

"I do," I growl. "He needs to keep your name out of his mouth."

"Why? Because you don't want it to ruin your reputation, right?"

I shake my head in disbelief. She's got everything all wrong. I don't give a damn about anyone else. This is about her … my wife. Mine.

"I mean, then what good am I to you?" She scoffs again and folds her arms.

"Stop fucking saying that!"

"Why?" she screams. "It's the truth. Hell, you must think I'm a damn fool. I've gone and fallen in love with you when you've never even shown me the inside of your house."

"My house? What does that have to do with anything?"

"It means that time and time again, I've given you my truth, but you've never given me yours!" Riley shouts.

By now, tears are streaming down her face. Each one rips another hole in my heart.

"Get off of me," she growls and squirms when I encircle her in my arms.

"Riley," I say, still trying to hold onto her.

"No!" she yells, now pounding my chest and arms with her fists. "Let go of me. I don't want you to touch me. You used my heart like every other fucking man I trusted. Get off of me."

"Riley, I lo—"

"Don't!" she screams while landing a loud smack across my face.

I don't feel the pain from her hit because the pain in my heart consumes my entire body. Seeing her standing in front of me with tears in her eyes, knowing it's all my fault, is an all-encompassing pain that no physical wound could ever match.

I let her go, even though everything in me screams for me not to.

She takes a step away from me, her chest heaving up and down. "You got what you wanted. In two weeks, you'll be crowned Townsend's permanent COO." Her bottom lip quivers. "And we'll annul this marriage. Our relationship is done."

She spins on her heels and storms into the bathroom, slamming the door behind her.

There's no way I'm letting it end there. I can barely breathe as I pound on the door.

"Riley, open this fucking door!" I demand. I try the doorknob over and over again, knowing it's useless. She's locked me out. Out of the door and out of her heart. But I don't give up because that would break me.

"Open the goddamn door, Riley!" My knuckles bruise as I pound on the door but I don't give a shit. I know if I keep it up, I'm going to break the door down, but that doesn't matter. My wife is on the other side. And she's hurting. Because of me.

"Riley!"

She doesn't answer.

"What's wrong?"

A small voice jolts me out of my panic. I turn to see Eve and Stasi standing at the front door, staring at me with wide-eyed expressions.

"Is Aunt Riley okay? Is she hurt?" Eve runs to the door.

"N-No—" I stop to clear my throat because my voice is hoarse from yelling. "She's fine. I just had to yell over the shower so she could hear me."

Eve's shoulders slump in relief. My sister continues to look at me suspiciously.

"Mom's downstairs. Eve forgot her favorite T-shirt she wanted to wear today."

"We're going to the mall and then to a picnic," Eve declares.

I nod and don't say anything as they head to her room.

I stand there like a fucking fool because I can hear the shower going. Riley won't even acknowledge me standing here.

"Bye, Aunt Riley," Eve yells.

"See you later, Ladybug," Riley calls through the door. On the surface it sounds cheery, but I can hear the tears still in her voice.

My sister's final look of suspicion haunts me as they both exit.

I've just destroyed my marriage.

CHAPTER 39

Riley

"You look like crap," Charlotte tells me when she enters my office.

I hang up from the phone call with Aaron Townsend and his assistant. I finished giving him one of my end-of-job reports regarding the Waterson merger.

"Thanks," I murmur, turning toward my computer screen. It's been five days since my blow up with Kyle. Every day is a struggle to breathe, let alone get through it.

"These should help you feel better."

When I finally turn to her it's to see yet another vase of flowers in her arms. Another bouquet. This one is huge and composed of pink roses and purple hyacinths.

"You know," Charlotte says as she heaves the oversized bouquet onto my desk, "that's the third bouquet that's come this week."

I glance over at the other two that sit on my windowsill but I don't say anything.

"Considering that today is only Wednesday, I'm wondering if I should expect to have to lug these things into your office every day this week."

I snort. "I told you to tell the delivery guy to take those flowers wherever the hell they came from."

"And I told *you* he said that the sender said he'd lose his job if he didn't make sure those flowers were delivered to you."

"He was bluffing," I mumble.

"I don't think so." Charlotte plops down in the chair across from me. "For one, that husband of yours is scary." She shivers. "Even though he did call me to apologize about that first time he met me in that meeting."

"He did what?"

Charlotte nods. "Yeah, a few months ago. I thought you made him do it."

"No." I shake my head. "I didn't even know he was rude to you."

Charlotte waves it off. "No big deal. He gifted me with like six months' worth of free lunches at any restaurant in the city to make up for it. That's why today's lunch is that French restaurant I love but is way too pricy for my budget."

I don't know what to say because I had no idea. However, I tamp down on the way my heart gets all soft from what Charlotte's said. Kyle's probably just using her, too.

He did ask me to work for him and said he'd hire her as well. He probably thinks she'll put in a good word for him or something.

"I would bet the twenty bucks I keep in my wallet for emergencies that he'd be out of a job before the close of business if those flowers didn't get delivered. And the shop would be shut down," my assistant continues.

"Did you need something?" I ask.

She shrugs. "It's my lunch break so I thought I'd come in and disturb you. Hey," she snaps her fingers, "you know I looked up what pink roses and purple hyacinths mean."

"And?"

"They mean forgiveness or regret. Basically, 'I'm sorry' with flowers."

I glance over at the other bouquets. Both of them are a mix of pink roses, blue and purple hyacinths. At the center of every one of the bouquets is a singular red rose. I hate the way my heart speeds up slightly just by looking at them. Yet, I can't throw them out.

"Don't you need to go pick up whatever you ordered for lunch?"

"It's not ready yet. Anyway, how long are you going to take to forgive him for whatever he did?"

"That's what I'd like to know."

We both look up toward the door to find Kyle standing there looking like some sort of Adonis—his body taking up most of the space of the doorway, dressed in a perfectly tailored suit.

Despite how well he's put together, I see the bags under his eyes and the redness within them. He hasn't slept well in days since he's back on the couch.

Good.

"You can't keep showing up to my office, Mr. Townsend." This is the third time this week.

You can hear a pin drop.

I dare to steal a look his way to find his jaw rigid, facial expression a storm cloud.

"Kyle, or better yet, your husband." He moves closer and slams his hands on my desk, leaning over me. "Never, *Mr. Townsend*, Riley," he says through gritted teeth.

"Would you look at the time? I think my food's ready." Charlotte all but bolts out of the door, leaving me alone with my husband.

"How long are you going to keep this shit up?" he asks.

"How dare you come in here asking me that like I did something wrong!"

"You have done something wrong. You're still contractually obligated to Townsend Industries for the next week and a half," he declares.

"Unbelievable," I murmur. "Are you here to threaten to sue me for not fulfilling my contractual obligations, simply because I'm not at your beck and call?" I stand from my chair and glare across my desk at him.

"Any and all reports that I have been requested of me from Townsend have been delivered on time."

"Dropped off by Charlotte. Not you."

"I've delivered my major reports, had my end of contract meetings with all of the department heads, and am ready to turn in my final files by the end of next week when this contract ends. I've done my job."

A muscle in his jaw ticks. He knows I'm telling the truth. There's no real reason for me to continue showing up at Townsend Industries.

"Now, if you'll excuse me, I have to prepare for a business meeting later on today with a potential client."

"No," he growls with a shake of his head. "You're still obligated to Townsend Industries for another week and a half. I won't allow you to meet with another potential client. That could be considered a breach of your contract."

"You are seriously disturbed. Do you know that?"

"Yes. Because my wife won't fucking talk to me." His voice starts to rise. "Even at home you barely say two words to me."

I hate that he still calls it home. I told him that he should go back to his real home, the place I've never been to. But every night after work he keeps showing up, eating family dinners with us and playing video games with Eve. Like nothing's changed between us.

"I've apologized. It was a fucked-up thing I did with Brendan. I should've never let him hear—"

"This isn't about Brendan," I declare not for the first time. "Yes, that was unacceptable." I point at him. "But this is about you. Your damn drive to always win, to be the best, to control. You don't want me to forgive you because you know what you did was wrong. You want forgiveness just to say you won."

"That's not true."

"Isn't it?" I don't wait for his answer. "How could it not be? Our marriage isn't real, remember? You're probably scared that the board will find out this marriage is a sham before your promotion becomes permanent. Don't worry, they won't hear it from me. Now you can leave."

"I told you to stop saying that shit. This marriage is real!" he insists.

"How? How is it real, Kyle? Our whole relationship started out on a lie, remember? That's my fault. But I was stupid enough to fall in love with you. However, you never felt the same for me, and no matter how many bouquets of flowers you send that won't change anything. Now get out!"

"I'm not going anywhere," he declares before taking the seat Charlotte vacated.

"We're having lunch together. I've had my assistant order our meals. They should be here any minute."

"I don't want to eat with you."

"Whether you do or you don't, you're going to."

I'm so mad I could scream. Just looking at him makes me want to slap him ... again. Once wasn't enough.

I let out a howl of frustration. "I can call the police on you for trespassing or harassment or whatever."

"Call them. Here." He hands me his cell phone. "They'll arrest me, and I'll come right back here once I'm released."

"Not if I get a restraining order." It's a bit farfetched but I'm not above making the threat.

"I don't mind breaking the law just to be near you. You're my fucking wife."

I don't know what's worse ... the way he says it with such conviction or the way my heartbeat quickens every time he says it.

But does he love you?

Not once has he said those three words. He has yet to let me fully inside of his heart. *I can't— won't give myself to him again.*

"Not for much longer," I say, folding my arms.

CHAPTER 40

Kyle

My entire body feels hollow as I watch Riley get up from the dining table as soon as I sit down. It's been over a week since our fight. No matter how many bouquets of flowers I send, or the number of times I apologize, she refuses to budge. According to her this whole marriage will end the day I become permanent COO.

That's where she's wrong. I fully intend to have both. Riley is my fucking wife.

"You screwed up, huh?" Eve's voice catches my attention. She's finishing up her bowl of oatmeal before Riley has to take her to one of her mathlete practices.

"Yeah, I did."

"Big time," she says, sounding wiser than her eleven years.

"How do you know?"

She shrugs. "One time before we moved to this place, I was jumping up and down on our couch with cranberry juice in my hand and spilled it all over. It was a white couch," she tells me. "Aunt Riley was mad. Real mad. And then, I lied and told her it wasn't me. She got even more mad about me lying to her."

Eve raises and drops her shoulders. "But, after I told her the truth, it only took a day for her to forgive me. She's never gone a whole week without speaking to me. That's how I know she's really mad at you."

I thought we'd done an adequate job of shielding all of this from Eve. Every night after our video games, Riley goes down the hall to read. I've acted like Riley and I are still sleeping in the same room, but after Eve goes to bed, I'm forced out here on the damn couch. I do it because I don't want to wake up with my eyes scratched out.

But I also can't *not* be in the same home as my wife.

"Ladybug, are you almost done? We need to leave soon," Riley comes up the hall to ask, not even throwing a look my way.

People say *I'm* cold. They obviously haven't met my wife when she's pissed. Riley's downright frigid.

"Yup. I have to wash the dish."

"Leave it," I tell her. "I'll put them all in the wash."

Again, Riley doesn't acknowledge me as she and Eve head out of the door.

"Bye." Eve waves.

"C'mon," Riley tells her before she can finish saying good-bye to me.

"Dammit!" I growl, feeling stuck and not knowing what to fucking do. The flowers aren't working. Neither is showing up at her office every day, or the many apologies.

I need something else.

Visit your parents. The dream I had months ago suddenly comes back to me. The one from Emma.

So, once I finish putting the dishes in the dishwasher, I grab my keys and head over to the people I trust the most in this world.

* * *

"A friend told me to come visit you guys," I tell my parents as they sit on the couch in the living room.

My eyes meet my father's. A knowing look comes over him. He nods and then knocks me on my ass with three words.

"You fucked up."

"Aaron," my mother admonishes.

"Thanks, Mom," I say.

"Don't thank me. You did fuck up," she counters. "I wanted to be the one to say it first. Your father's right."

A rare smile creases my father's face. "Thanks, sweetness." He leans in and kisses her cheek.

I grumble, "Can you two cut the PDA out for two minutes to focus on me?"

My father grunts. "I thought you said once they're out of the house, we'll have more time alone?" he says to my mother.

"Later." She swats his arm.

I roll my eyes. "Back to me. Look, I've already admitted what I did with Brendan was messed up—"

"So much," my mother interrupts. "You're lucky all she did was smack you. Why on earth would you do something ridiculous like that?" She tsks and shakes her head.

My father nods in agreement. He leans forward, looking me in the eye. "I thought I told you to be better than me."

Pain squeezes my chest.

The last thing I ever want is for either of my parents to be disappointed in me. But it's their disappointment coupled with the haunted look I keep seeing in Riley's eyes that causes the real agony. She thinks I don't love her. That I only want her for what I can gain from her. To use her.

Like her piece of shit father.

And her good for nothing brother.

I've tried to show her with actions that she's my entire world.

"You haven't shown her enough," my mother says.

I didn't even realize I said that out loud.

"How? I'm with her every day. I've slashed the hours I spend at work to I spend more time with her and Eve."

"You say that like it's a sacrifice," my mother says.

"It wasn't," I declare. "It isn't. Hell, I didn't even realize how many fewer hours I've been clocking in."

I stand and start pacing because there are too many emotions moving inside of me to sit still. I feel like my wife is slipping from between my fingers, and with her my entire reason for being.

"Work used to be my main priority. Making sure Townsend Industries was the best. But it's taken a backseat." I speak without thinking. "She wasn't supposed to become so important to me. That was never the goal. I couldn't help it. It's like I woke up one day and she and Eve were the only things that mattered to me. I can't live without her, or without her knowing it."

"Do you trust her?" My father asks.

"With my entire soul," I answer without a second thought.

I continue pacing, my mind whirling with what the hell I will do if Riley really calls it quits on our marriage.

"I know I said once I became permanent COO that I'd annul our marriage, but I can't. I fucking can't do that."

I stop pacing and turn to face my parents when there's nothing but silence coming from their direction. To my surprise, and anger, they're both staring at me with smiles on their faces.

Well, my mother's smiling. My father's only half scowling.

"I told you she was the one when I saw her last year." My mother looks over at my father.

He nods. "You're always right."

My entire body stiffens. "Last year," I repeat.

My mother's smile widens. "You didn't think when you brought your wife home for dinner that was the first time I've seen her, did you?"

"Riley knew you before then?"

She's shaking her head before I finish the question. "We never formally met. I attended part of an event for Girls on the Move, and she was there. We didn't get a chance to speak but Angie, the director, spoke highly of her. There was something about her. So …" My mother shrugs.

"I did some research on her background to figure out who she was. I had hoped to arrange something like a blind date between you two. I certainly didn't intend for her to become blackmailed into your life, but I guess fate had other plans. Oh well, it worked out.

"You're in love," she finishes.

My shoulders slump at hearing my mother's words. They cause my head to spin even more. It really means Riley and me are meant to be.

"I can't lose her," I tell my parents.

"Success means jack shit if you don't have your priorities straight." My father stands and comes over to me. He cups the back of my neck, pulling our foreheads together.

"I could've made you COO on a permanent basis if I wanted," he reveals. "The board could've tried to stop me, but I would've done it. You weren't ready. Not because you can't handle the business side." He looks over at my mother.

"You needed balance. I let my career and drive to success eat up too much of my life when I was your age. It almost cost me everything."

He looks back at me. "You need to make this right with your wife."

"That's what I came to you both for. And that's all you have to tell me?" I hold up my hands. "How?"

"Tell her how you feel." My mom says it as if it's that easy.

"I've tried. She won't listen."

"Then make her listen. And show her. Not with bullshit flowers," my father continues. "Show her by giving her what she really wants."

"I've given you my truth but you've never given me yours."

Her words come spiraling back to me like a ninety-mile-an-hour fastball to the forehead.

I'll show my wife my truth.

CHAPTER 41

Riley

Today's the day. The day Kyle meets with the board and the CEO to become declared the permanent COO at Townsend Industries.

And the last day of our marriage.

I've tried to prepare my heart for this. I've known all along that our marriage wouldn't go past this date. It's too bad that I can't make myself stop loving him automatically.

It's bad enough I haven't seen Kyle in days. He left a voicemail for me days ago when I wouldn't answer his call, saying he would be gone on business for a few days. I didn't bother asking what it's about.

Yet, each night he sends me a voice message. Each message starts off with a declaration of love for me and Eve. Then he goes into some story about this or that. The first message he told me about how he felt as a kid being bullied by an older boy because he had trouble reading. He mentioned that though his father taught him not to be ashamed, it took years for him to fully get past the embarrassment.

"It still sticks with me sometimes." Those were the words that finished his story.

That night I received another flower delivery accompanied by a massive box of Haribo gummy bears.

I hate to admit that I ate them while relistening to his message.

The second night, his story started off silly as he talked about hating that his birthday falls on April Fools' Day. Then it turned serious when he mentioned the attack on his mother that led to his and his sister's premature birth.

Another delivery.

Last night's message wasn't a story about his past. In it he confessed to how nervous he is to accept the role as COO. How he fears not living up to his family's expectations.

That was the one that made me cry while I ate the grilled cheese and tomato soup he had delivered for dinner.

I don't know what he thinks he's doing with these messages. I want to tell him to stop but I also look forward to receiving them each day.

"Riley?" A knock on the door from Adam Bachleda startles me. His expression is drawn as if something heavy weighs on him.

This is my last day here at the Townsend Industries offices and I expect to walk out with a heaviness in my heart but at least partially relieved. Despite our crumbling relationship, Kyle deserves to be made COO on a permanent basis. I want that for him.

But something on Adam's face gives me pause.

"There's a problem," he says.

I stand as he enters the office I've been using since I started consulting with the company.

"Due to all that's come to light from the press conference a few weeks ago, it's also come with the realization that you may have breached the terms of the nondisclosure agreement you signed when you became a consultant at Townsend Industries."

I blink in surprise. That is the last thing I expected to hear come out of his mouth. I try to think of how to respond, but he beats me to the punch when he adds...

"Moreover, since Kyle didn't immediately report you to the board or the proper authorities, it's not looking good for his promotion."

I take a deep breath as I try to process all that he's saying. Not much of my role in what happened with Ryan Nick via Dean Walsh made it to the public. I have a feeling Kyle has something to do with that. However, what Adam's saying is that he and the board are willing to use what I did against Kyle.

Slimy son of a bitches.

"I wanted to make you aware of this situation before our meeting. Seeing as how it looks like we cannot, in good conscious, make Kyle our COO. And we, the board, have the votes to overturn any action his father might take. I'm certain his father will understand."

His words are regretful, yet his tone suggests he's anything but.

That's when something hits me. I inhale. "It's you," I blurt out. "You're behind this. I knew that voice in the bathroom the night of our dinner sounded familiar. Anthony Rogers, your assistant, was there," I say.

That day I was under Kyle's desk, I heard his assistant's voice then, too.

"He was working for you."

"I have no idea what you're talking about," Adam says, the sympathetic expression slipping from his face.

"Is the board all here?" I demand to know. I don't wait for his answer. I brush past him and rush out of my office to take the elevator. Bachleda follows, but I have the doors close before he can reach them.

I charge through the lobby, down to the boardroom where Kyle's permanent promotion is supposed to take place. All heads turn to me. I quickly scan the room, noting that Kyle and his father aren't present.

Good.

It'll be easier for me to get this out without him in the room.

"You can't do this," I declare.

"Ms. Martin, you're early for our meeting," one of the board members states.

"I told her what we found out," Adam says, entering the room.

"Yes," the other guy says. "It's unfortunate we had to find out the way we did. We do have a list of other Townsend employees who will make for great candidates as COO."

"He's behind all of this," I tell them, pointing at Adam.

"This is absurd," Adam says.

"Riley, this is highly unprofessional. I understand you're upset," another man from the board adds.

I feel at a loss knowing I won't be able to prove to these men my suspicions about Adam.

"Look, whatever information you were told about me is true," I decide to confess. "I did come into Townsend Industries with intentions to deceive the company. I was blackmailed. You heard it at the press conference."

"But you could've gone to the police or to us," Adam says. "That you didn't is still a violation of your contract. Kyle also knew about it."

"Kyle knew nothing about it," I lie. "Not until the morning of the press conference."

They all look between one another.

"It's true," I say, garnering their attention again. "He didn't know. I deceived him as well. Any information that was leaked about Townsend Industries is my fault and my fault alone. He has no idea of what happened, and you shouldn't take anything out on him."

"What about the files that were leaked?" another board member asks. "How did Ryan Nick's people get that?"

"Me," Kyle says as he enters the boardroom.

Everyone goes quiet.

I blink and stare at my husband.

Kyle comes to stands beside me. "Whatever my wife just told you is all bullshit."

Gasps fill the room. My mouth drops open in surprise.

"Kyle—" I say but he cuts me off.

"If you want to punish anyone it'll be me. You will not come after my wife. She's the sole reason that Dean Walsh wasn't able to become more of a problem for this company. Without Riley's help, I never would've figured out who was behind all of this.

"Not to mention the ways in which Riley's hands-on consulting work aided in improving our company's employee-turnover rate in such a short amount of time. And how smoothly the merger with Sam Waterson's company is going, all thanks to her."

He looks at me with such softness that my knees weaken. I glance down to see he's taken my hand into his. I should pull free of his grasp, but he tightens his hold. Hope swells in my chest that he's silently telling me he won't let me go.

"More than any of that," he continues, "she's the love of my fucking life. So," he turns to face the room again, "if you even think of hurting her in any way, you'll have to go through me first. As all of you know, I'm a formidable opponent."

There's stunned expressions from just about everyone in the room.

"Be that as it may," Adam Bachleda speaks first, "Kyle, we cannot let someone who knew this deception was taking place right under our noses, and didn't say anything, become the next COO of this company. As the board, we have the ability to overrule any decision your father makes should he not comply with our determination."

"Consider this my resignation," Kyle declares.

"What are you doing?" I whisper-yell at him. I need to tell him about my suspicions about Adam Bachleda.

His only acknowledgement of my question is to squeeze my hand. Yet, he continues to glare down at the rest of the people in the room.

"I'll make it easy for all of you. You want to hold someone accountable, then it'll be me. And *only* me. I quit Townsend Industries. I'll fucking start my own company and use every bit of my knowledge and savvy to pay every single one of you back for this."

A few grumbles around the room sound.

"Kyle," one of the men says, "it's not about you. It's about the stockholders. We have an obligation, and if someone doesn't take responsibility for this—"

"That's enough," Aaron Townsend's booming voice slices the air. "I've just filed the paperwork with the SEC to privatize Townsend Industries."

There's a slew of murmurs from the board.

"If you all were paying attention," Aaron Townsend continues, "you should've seen this coming." He turns stormy hazel eyes, that remind me so much of Kyle's, to me. "One of you in particular."

He turns and glares at Adam Bachleda.

"Thanks to my daughter-in-law, who told me she recognized your assistant's voice while out to dinner with my son and while he was in a meeting with you and Sam Waterson, I was able to put two and two together," he tells the room.

"Oh shit," I murmur.

I remember last week's call when I told him about the familiar voice I heard in the bathroom while out to that business dinner with Kyle. And again, only weeks ago, in Kyle's office.

I couldn't pinpoint the voice but knew I had heard it before. Kyle's father must've figured it out.

"Because your good-for-nothing son couldn't hack it here, you wanted to ruin this company," Aaron says through gritted teeth.

"You've ruled this company with an iron fist for too long," Adam Bachleda declares, rising to his feet.

A few officers and federal agents enter the room a beat later. It's clear what their intentions are by the shiny handcuffs in one of the lead agent's hands.

"Now, you can take that money that Ryan Nick used to bribe you to pay for a fucking criminal attorney. Oh wait, the feds will freeze that money along with most of your other assets."

Aaron turns to me and nods. His face is set in a scowl, but I somehow think that's him giving me his approval.

"Come with me," Kyle says, taking me by the hand, not waiting for me to reply.

"Where are we going?" I demand as we make our way down the hall.

"Someplace where I can put you over my knee for what you just did."

We come to a stop at the entrance for the private elevator where Kyle punches in the code.

"What?"

Instead of answering, he whirls around on me, cupping my face. At the same time the elevator doors slide closed, locking us in.

"Don't you ever do that shit again. It's not your job to fall on the sword for me. Ever. That's my job as your husband. Do you understand me?" He shakes my head a little. There's a slightly unhinged look in his eyes. However, I can't help but mess with him even more.

"I don't need your permission to do or not do any damn thing." I push him away from me and fold my arms across my chest. "Besides, you're not my husband for much longer, right?"

A low growl starts from the base of his throat.

"You're determined to have a red ass before this fucking day ends."

He takes my hand as the elevator doors open to the underground elevator.

"You still haven't told me where we're going. There's a shitshow happening upstairs. Shouldn't we be there for it?"

"What's happening between you and me is more important," he says with such earnestness that it hits me right in the chest.

But I can't fold. "Kyle, nothing has changed between us."

"Let's play a game, Riley," he says just as a car pulls up next to us.

The driver gets out and holds open the back door.

"This isn't the time for games."

"It's the perfect time. Truth or dare. Ask me," he tells me.

I raise an eyebrow and look between him and the car.

"Ask me, Riley."

"Truth or dare, Kyle?"

His eyes gleam as he says, "Truth."

My shoulders sag as the air leaves my body. The one thing I've always wanted from him.

"Let me show you my truth, Riley." He holds out his hand to me.

* * *

It doesn't take long to get to where Kyle's taking me.

"We could've walked," I tell him as we enter another underground garage of one of the tallest condominium buildings in the city. It's only about a ten-minute walk from Townsend Industries. Making the drive barely five minutes.

"Come with me," Kyle says as he waves the driver off and takes my hand to get out of the car.

"Where are we?" I ask.

He presses the button for the elevator before turning to me. "My home."

I silently take that information in as we ride up to the fifteenth floor of the building. Kyle tells me which floor Kennedy and Diego live on. By the time we come to his door, I hold my breath as he places his thumb on the lock to scan his fingerprint.

"I'll have to add your and Eve's prints to unlock the door and for the main entrance." He says the words so casually, as if we're going to be spending a lot of time in this place.

As we enter, I take in the massive size of his condo. It's a loft-style apartment with concrete floors, and massive floor-to-ceiling windows that let in tons of sunlight.

"This is my home, Riley." He moves to stand by my side.

My hand slips from his hold as I take a step forward to look around. I scan the living room with the low sitting sectional couch, glass coffee table, and massive big-screen TV mounted above a mock fireplace. The color scheme is black and gray with a few pops of white.

Even the kitchen counters and cupboards are black.

Glancing around, I run my hands up and down my arms. There isn't anything particularly wrong with the space, but it feels off for some reason. I can't quite put my finger on it.

"After what happened with Dean when I was sixteen, I swore never to let myself trust anyone outside of my family enough to get that close to me. I've never had anyone outside of my family over here." I keep my back to him. "But that isn't why I've never brought you here.

"This week is the first time I've been back here in months," Kyle says, coming up behind me. "I've lived here for four years and never realized how much it never felt like home. Not until moving in with you."

He turns me to face him.

"That's why I never brought you here. After that first weekend at your place, this space never felt like it fit anymore. I wanted to be around color, sleep in a bed with so many pillows that it's almost inhabitable for human bodies."

"Shut up." I shove his shoulder, making him laugh. He's always teasing me about the number of pillows on my bed.

"Most importantly, this place didn't have you. Wherever you are is my home, Riley." His eyes circle his condo as if taking it in for the first time. "I knew you wouldn't love it here."

I turn and look over his space again. He's right. As beautiful as this condo is, it isn't me. It feels cold.

"This is where you've been this week?"

"A few nights. I also went to L.A."

"For business."

He nods. "I paid Chastain back for the money you took from him."

I gasp. "I wanted to do that." I'd told him that months ago that I had been saving money to pay Chastain back.

"I know, but I don't ever want you to be in the same room as him. I made him sign a nondisclosure contract that's rock solid. He's not allowed to ever mention your name again."

"He's still breathing, right?" I squint at Kyle.

"For the most part."

"Kyle..."

"He's alive and he'll never bother us again. Aside from that, I was never far from you."

"Is that all you had to tell me?" I ask.

"Partially." He takes my hand and walks us over to the living room. On the coffee table there's a folder. Kyle picks it up and hands it to me.

"What's this?"

He dips his head at the folder. "Open it."

I scan the first page of the documents. "Brightside Community Shelter," I whisper the words. My vision blurs. "Did you..."

"You said you wanted to honor Edith Warnock, the woman who helped you so much when you were living at the shelter. It's in partnership with Girls on the Move. I've donated the funds to have the shelter built and to get it started and running for the first two years. It's strictly for homeless teens and young adults with juvenile records.

"It'll have education courses, computer skills, technical training, and even grants for those wanting to start a business. I thought Brightside would be a fitting name. Both for Edith and because that's how you make everyone around you feel. Without noticing, you are the bright side people are looking for."

I look him in the eye. "Even you?"

"Especially me."

Another flood of tears.

"If you don't like the name, though, we can change it."

"The name's perfect," I whisper.

Kyle moves in front of me and cups my face to wipe away the tears that have fallen.

"Thank you."

With a shake of his head, he announces, "There's nothing to thank me for. I should've done this and so much more for you."

"More? Like what?"

"Like tell you how deeply in love with you I am."

I suck my bottom lip in between my teeth. His confession wraps itself around my heart and releases all of the doubts that have accumulated in my mind. It was one thing to see those words via a text message, but to hear them out loud is something else entirely.

"And I can't give you that annulment, Riley. Not without telling you the truth."

"Which is?"

"You own me. Mind, body, and soul. I'm yours. My entire world would shut down without you in it. Don't ask me to annul our marriage. You are my life now."

When I drop my head, Kyle's hand is there, lifting my chin to meet his gaze. He's so steadfast and sure that it's on the tip of my tongue to tell him that I'll give him everything he wants.

"When you got hired as a consultant at Townsend you told me that I would just have to trust you. Do you remember that?"

I nod, recalling telling him that in that boardroom.

"I do. I trust you with my entire being. Now I'm asking you to do the same. Trust me with your heart, Riley. I promise to keep it safe."

Kyle leans in to kiss me, and that's when I gather my emotions and take a step back, moving out of his hold. I can't have his lips on mine. It'll make me forget everything I need to say.

"Stay there." I point at the spot where he's standing, between the coffee table and sectional, while I move behind the sectional. I need the space between us. Yet, the way Kyle narrows his eyes tells me I only have a few seconds before he does something crazy like leap over the couch.

"I'm serious, don't move."

His hands tighten into fists at his side from the restraint he's exhibiting. I stifle the grin that wants to break free.

"I won't ask you to sign the annulment."

His shoulders sag from relief.

"I love you, too. It feels good to say that."

"And you should tell me every day for the rest of our lives," he says with so much authority that it makes me laugh.

"I need to hear it, too. After all, words of affirmation are my love language."

He nods firmly. "Done. I love you."

"Well ..." I draw the word out as my eyes circle the room. "If I'm bargaining, I also want you to continue the flower deliveries. They're really pretty and make my office smell good."

"I already have deliveries scheduled for the next six months."

I laugh.

"And I'm not coming to work for Townsend Industries on a permanent basis."

Kyle's expression falls. He frowns deeply, then shrugs. "I have the rest of our lives to convince you."

I have no doubt that he'll try. I glance up the spiral staircase. "That's the bedroom, right?"

He nods slowly, his eyes darkening ever so slightly with lust. My body warms from the inside out from that look. I lift my hand to the top button of my shirt. Kyle traces every movement I make with his eyes.

"Truth or dare?" I ask.

"Truth," he says without hesitation.

"Thank you for telling me your truth, but I'm in the mood for a dare." I reach the second button of my shirt.

Kyle's eyes glint with mischievousness, and in a heartbeat he's up and over the sectional, stomping toward me like a caged animal that's been set free.

"You're playing a dangerous game, Mrs. Townsend," he says as I reach the third button of my shirt, exposing the black lace bra underneath.

"You think so?" I back up until the back of my foot hits the first stair. "I like dangerous games." I slowly make my way up the stairs while being stalked by my husband.

I inspect the spacious bedroom with high, slanted ceilings, and a bed large enough to fit four full-grown adults.

I reach the final button and remove my shirt altogether, tossing it at Kyle. He swiftly catches it.

"What's this?" I ask as I inspect the contents on the top of his vanity. I find my favorite perfume, moisturizer, and multiple tubes of my favorite red lipstick.

Kyle comes up behind me. He strokes his hands up and down my arms. "I knew you would end up here eventually. I bought all of your favorites."

I turn to face him with the lipstick in my hand.

"Perfect." I coat my lips. "I dare you to let me see what this color looks like on your dick ... again."

CHAPTER 42

Kyle

Perfect.

That's the only word I can think of to describe my wife when she drops to her knees. The red color on her lips is already enough to make my dick as hard as a brick wall in my pants.

Riley undoes the belt and button of my pantsuit and pulls me free. I'm already hard for her. I stay semi-hard whenever she's around. Seeing her on her knees in front of me will do me in every single time.

When she wraps those perfect, red lips around my cock, I have to brace my hand against my dresser or I'll fall over from the way my knees weaken. Riley takes me all the way to the back of her throat. All I can see is the way those plump, red lips are devouring me.

I guide her head up and down the length of my cock with my hand. But Riley doesn't need my direction. She knows me too well. Within minutes, I'm trembling from the weight of my impending orgasm.

I don't want to come in her mouth. As perfect as it is. I need to be inside of her. It's been almost two weeks since I've fucked my wife.

With all of the strength I can summon, I pull myself free from her greedy mouth. A loud *pop* sounds around the room. Riley's lips are glistening from my precum. I run my thumb along her bottom lip before forcing it inside of her mouth. She hungrily licks it clean.

After pulling her to her feet, I quickly dispose of her bra, skirt, and panties. She does the same with the remainder of my clothing.

"Do you know how much I've missed you?" I pin her body beneath mine on the bed.

She shakes her head, fanning her hair out on the silk pillowcase I bought specifically for this moment.

"Let me show you," I say against her lips. I kiss her deep before moving down the length of her body. I give her the same treatment she just gave me, and when she comes on my face, I dive in for more. Not until she's on the verge of her third orgasm do I pull away and position my body between her legs.

I grab Riley's hands in mine, kissing each before I lay them flat against the bed above her head.

"I love you so fucking much," I tell her.

The expression that lights up her face is the only thing I need to survive. When I ease inside of her, I genuinely feel as if I'm home. That locked out of heaven feeling that's been with me for two weeks melts away. I make love to my wife slowly, deliberately, and tell her in word and deed that I'm never going to let her go.

Nothing in this world matters more to me than her.

"Fucking love you!" I curse and yell out when I can't hold off the orgasm any longer. Riley pulls me into her as I come inside of her for the first time.

But far from the last.

CHAPTER 43

Kyle

"You know we could've made a baby this weekend," I tell Riley as I wrap her in my arms from behind.

It's Monday morning and I've spent the past two and a half days not letting my wife up for air. Eve spent the weekend with my parents and Stasi. We're on our way back to their house to pick Eve up and take her to school since she complained about missing the both of us the night before when Riley called her.

My wife turns to me. Her eyes search mine. "How do you feel about that?"

I bend down to kiss the tip of her nose, then her forehead, and finally her lips. "We have Eve. She wants a younger brother or sister."

Riley's face scrunches. "She told you that?"

I nod. "A few weeks ago. Said she doesn't mind being the only kid, but she wishes she had some brothers or sisters like I had growing up."

"Do you think we're ready for that?"

"Ready or not, it'll probably happen sooner rather than later because after this weekend there's no fucking way I'm pulling out from now on."

She pulls back and folds her arms. "Don't I get a say in the matter?"

"You had a whole lot to say last night from what I remember. *Oh, Kyle, right there! Don't stop, baby ... come inside of me,*" I mock.

She punches my shoulder. "First of all, I don't sound like that. Second, a pregnancy won't happen," she says with confidence. "Not for a while."

I look at her with narrowed eyes.

"Ever since that first time we didn't use a condom, I went to the doctor to get on birth control. I hated the idea of taking a pill every day, so I opted for the injection. It lasts for twelve weeks. So, until we're ready to have a baby, we don't have to worry about that."

"What if I'm ready now."

Shaking her head, she laughs. "You're ridiculous. How about we try being married for at least a year or two before we go adding babies to the mix?"

I shrug. "Suit yourself. I'm not going anywhere. I'll be ready when you are."

"We have enough on our plate already," she continues. "We still don't know where Dean Walsh is. We're starting a whole new community shelter. Everything at Townsend is still up in the air."

I plant a kiss on her lips again. "Don't worry about my job. The board has enough to be concerned about with Adam's arrest and my father and uncles finally making the move to privatize. I'm still the COO. We'll get that cocksucker Dean soon. And the shelter will be a massive success."

I spin her toward the door even though I don't want to leave what feels like the safety of this cocoon we've been in for the past three days.

While I have no regrets about keeping my wife locked away from the world and basically in bed and naked for the past three days, I do know she's right. There is one main issue that remains unresolved, that's irritating the fuck out of me.

Dean Walsh.

The bastard has no more cards left to play. Everyone he leaned on for his revenge is either in jail or mired in public scandal.

That should satisfy me. It doesn't.

He's still out there. He hasn't tried to contact Riley again, but I know that doesn't mean he's gone completely away.

I push thoughts about Dean to the back of my mind as we pick up Eve from school. On the way home, I have the driver drop us off in front of the building.

"Can we stop at the store to pick up the ingredients for cupcakes?" Eve asks since we're making them for dessert and for her to take to school tomorrow.

"We can get it delivered," I offer.

"But there's that store right across the street," Eve whines.

"She's right. It'll save time," Riley adds. "I'll go with her. You can go up, and we'll be there in a few minutes."

My lips purse. It's right across the damn street but unease courses through me at the thought of letting either one out of my sight. I might be taking this possessive husband thing too far but whatever.

"Not a chance," I tell them both as I wrap my arms around Riley and Eve and walk us across the street to the small grocer.

Eve is floating on cloud nine for some reason. I think she's feeling the ease of the tension between Riley and me. I can't help but laugh as she twirls around with a can of icing in one hand and a box of cake mix in the other as we exit the grocer.

"She's so happy," Riley says to me, smiling at Eve. "What's gotten into you, Ladybug?" Riley calls as we all stop at the crosswalk.

"We're a real family," Eve says as the light changes for us to cross.

But her words almost keep me in place. A family.

"We are," I say, making Eve's smile grow even wider.

"Sir!"

I turn to find the store clerk. "Your wallet."

I pat my pocket. "Shit." I was so caught up watching the women in my life, I forgot my damn wallet right on the counter.

"Thank you," I tell the clerk. By the time I get back to the crosswalk, both Eve and Riley have started to cross.

A smile comes to my face as I recall Eve's last comment. I get so caught up in the moment that I barely notice the screeching of tires. It's Riley's yelling that snaps me out of my trance, though.

"Eve!" Riley yells in a tone of voice that I'll never forget as long as I live.

Riley runs right in the direction of the oncoming car. "Eve! Look out!"

"Riley!" I shout in a voice unfamiliar to my ears. I see my entire life flash before my eyes the moment when Riley pushes her niece out of the way of the oncoming vehicle. The car misses Eve by inches but it doesn't miss Riley.

In that moment the entire world, right along with my heart, stops.

CHAPTER 44

Riley

"Why hasn't she woken up yet?" I hear a deep voice say even though my eyes are still closed.

It's Kyle's voice. My husband.

The strain and fear in his words make me want to open my eyes. But it feels like there are bricks sitting on top of them.

"Mr. Townsend, we need you to calm down," a female voice says.

I don't recognize the woman. *Where am I? What's going on? Why is my husband afraid?*

He's not scared of anything.

"What's wrong with her?" Kyle demands to know.

Wake up! I tell myself. I don't know what's going on, but I have to tell him that I can hear him. We can find out what's wrong together.

I struggle to open my eyes barely halfway. I can't make anything out. It's all blurry. I try another tactic by turning my head. I realize I'm in a bed. I move my head against the pillow, straining to face the direction where the voices are coming from.

"K—" I try to say his name but can only make out the first syllable. My throat burns from the attempt, but I force myself to try again.

"Ky—" I make out more this time, but I don't think he hears me. He's still asking the woman why I'm not awake.

"Kyle," I croak out.

"Kyle, look," another voice rings out. *Patience?* Is she in our bedroom?

"Riley, baby?"

I fight like hell to push my eyelids all the way up. A groan escapes my lips from the effort, but I somehow manage. Everything in front of me is blurred. I manage a few slow blinks before the images in front of me focus.

"Kyle." His name comes out with a little more ease this time around. "Wh-What h-happened?"

"You're awake." He sounds relieved but the tears streaming down his face spark renewed worry in me.

"I'll get Eve," someone says.

His mother.

I follow her movements. That's when I conclude that we are not in our bedroom. We're in a hospital room. I'm in the hospital. My body takes this moment to come back online. A wave of pain, emanating from my right leg, courses through me.

"She's in pain," Kyle says to the doctor who's now moved to the other side of the bed. "Give her something," he insists.

"I have to check her out first. If you could—"

"I'm not going any fucking where," he insists, taking my hand and holding on for dear life.

I don't say anything while the doctor and nurse check me over. Kyle never leaves my side. I'm able to answer all of the questions the doctors ask me with relative ease, considering how slow my mind feels like it's going.

"We'll get you something for the pain," the doctor assures me.

"Aunt Riley!" Eve says as she rushes past the medical staff. The redness in her eyes tears at my heart. "Are you okay?" She approaches but looks as if she's scared to touch me.

The memory of what happened resurfaces.

TIFFANY PATTERSON

Walking out of the store.

Me watching my Ladybug look so happy as she crossed the street singing a song she made up.

Kyle trailing a few feet behind because he'd left his wallet.

And then the sound of rubber tires and a loud engine as it barreled toward my niece.

"Come here, Ladybug."

She falls into my arms and starts sobbing. "I was so scared. Kyle said you would be okay, but it's been almost a whole day since your surgery." Her tears soak the thin fabric of my hospital gown.

When my eyes meet Kyle's, he also has the same redness in his eyes. I extend my hand to his.

"I'm fine. Nothing's going to happen to me." I say it for the both of them. "Just a few broken bones."

Mainly in my right leg. A sprained wrist and a slight concussion. All in all, it could've been a hell of a lot worse.

"Are you sure?" Eve asks as she stands again.

"Positive. Come cuddle with me," I tell her.

She does, and before I know it, light snores are coming from her. She must've been up all night.

Kyle flanks my other side.

"I never knew there were hospital beds this big or comfy," I joke. We're clearly in one of the private sections of the hospital.

Kyle doesn't grin. He keeps stroking the side of my face, checking me over. When his gaze finally drops to mine, he murmurs, "I'm so fucking sorry."

"For what? It was an accident," I whisper.

He shakes his head. "That motherfucker did it on purpose."

"Who?"

"Dean Walsh. He was the driver."

"Did they catch him?"

He nods.

"Then it's over," I say, feeling comforted that Dean didn't injure Eve at all and that he's behind bars.

Yet, Kyle says, "It's not over. But it will be soon."

The dark meaning behind his words isn't missed on me. A part of me wants to tell him to forget it, to let the police and authorities handle it.

But I know my husband better than that.

He'll never let Dean get away with what he did.

CHAPTER 45

Kyle

"This isn't a place I ever wanted you to visit," my father says as he comes up behind me.

We're in the basement of one of the abandoned buildings my family owns. Very few people on earth know about these properties because it's not a place anyone ever wants to enter.

I look into my father's eyes, and then past his shoulder into the eyes of my three uncles and my grandfather. Finally, I lock eyes with Diego. The look in his eyes is as hard as the one I'm certain is displayed in my gaze.

"You've all known we'd end up here one day."

My father looks back at the rest of the eldest men in our family. They nod in agreement.

I don't say anything as I go over to grab the wooden baseball bat that's leaning against the wall. Bat in hand, I make my way over to the center of the room. At the center, Dean Walsh sits strapped in a wooden chair, duct tape on his mouth.

I rip off the tape.

"You wanted so bad to prove these properties exist." I circle the room with my eyes before landing back on Dean. "You did your best to end up here, didn't you?"

"Fuck you. This is illegal!" he yells, as if that will change his fate.

"That didn't stop you from blackmailing my wife, did it?" I hold the bat in the perfect swinging position. "I'll let you know something, Dean. These houses," I circle the room with my gaze, Dean's eyes trailing mine, "… aren't for business. No. We don't need to kill for business. This space is only for motherfuckers who commit the most egregious acts against our family. Hurting our women."

Dean's eyes widen in terror.

I swing the bat and narrowly miss Dean's head.

He ducks but can't go far as he's tied to the chair. He starts hyperventilating, making me laugh.

"Don't act frightened now. You were tough as shit when you were behind that wheel, right?" I swing again. And again, I intentionally miss Dean's head.

Then I move in closer and flip the bat upside down, poking it underneath his chin so his eyes meet mine.

"You know, it was always going to end like this for you and me." I thrust the end of the bat higher, straining his neck. "Ever since I heard the way you spoke to my wife."

I step back and take his right hand, placing it on the wooden stool beside him. Without a second's hesitation, I drop the business end of the bat right onto his hand.

I don't know which is louder; the crunching of the bones in his hand, the cracking of the wooden stool beneath it, or Dean's howls of pain.

"You should've stayed underneath the rock you crawled from out of. And you damn sure should've never, ever toyed with my fucking family." I swing the bat again, cracking his knee.

More shrieks of pain.

"You know what?" I say, placing the bat against my neck and then turning to face my father, uncles, and grandfather. "This doesn't seem fair. He's all helpless and shit."

They all grin at me.

"You get your craziness from me," my Uncle Tyler says with a laugh.

"Have you forgotten who his father is?" my Uncle Carter asks with folded arms.

I ignore their comments, knowing my crazy is all my own. Turning to Dean, I smile down at him.

"I'm going to let you go."

He jumps when I approach again. I begin unraveling the ropes that have him bound to the chair.

"You're free," I say, stepping back.

"R-Really?"

I nod. "Yup." I turn my back to him and wink at my family before I turn and say, "Under one condition."

"Wh-What's that?"

"You're completely free to go ... *if* you can make it up the stairs and out of the door in the next thirty seconds."

He blinks, looks past me to my family, and then back at me again.

"It's not a trick." I pull out the burner phone I brought with me. "I'll start the clock." I set the timer for thirty seconds and hold it up for him to see. "Go."

He pauses, but when I wave the phone with the timer going, he limps past the chair. He curls over, almost falling. I fold my arms and watch him try to get halfway across the room to the staircase.

An evil grin creases my lips when I hear the first screams of agony as his bare feet make contact with the broken glass spread all over the floor.

"What is this?" he screeches.

"Oh, we did a little redecorating in anticipation of your visit. Hope you've got thick skin." If he makes it past the glass, there are the upturned thumbtacks on the stairs he'll have to deal with next.

"Fifteen seconds left," I call out right as Dean screams when another piece of glass inserts itself into his foot.

He crumbles to one knee. When he lands on his injured hand, another yelp of pain comes from him. I should say that I feel bad, and the guilt is tearing at my soul.

It's not.

The only thing I can think of is seeing my wife lying in the street after he hit her. Hearing Eve cry for Riley to wake up and holding my teary-eyed eleven-year-old as she asks me over and over if her aunt will be okay.

By the time the buzzer sounds on the phone, all I can see is red. Dean has only made it to the third stair. Without another thought, I make my way through the glass, crunching the shards beneath my steel-toe boots.

"You wanted so fucking badly to find out about these houses. Why're you in such a rush to leave, motherfucker?" I demand as I grab Dean by the back of his shirt and yank him back down the stairs.

As soon as he lands on his back, I land a blow to his midsection with the bat. That's when I completely black out. I don't know how many times I hit him or where. All I know is that I take my anger and guilt for not getting in between Riley and that car out on him.

When I return to reality, my uncles and father are restraining me. Someone takes the bat out of my hand. It's my grandfather.

"It's done, son," my father says.

"It's time we show this bastard our family's pig farm," my grandfather states.

"His death is already listed as death by fire from the police accident," my Uncle Joshua reassures. "You need to go take a shower."

My father nods. "Never return to your wife dirty from this type of shit."

All of my family nods.

I do as they say, knowing that once I'm cleaned off, I'll go home to Riley and Eve, knowing they're safe.

EPILOGUE

Three Months Later
Riley

"How're you feeling?" my husband asks as he comes up from behind me. We're in the middle of our wedding reception at Townsend Manor—his grandparents' sprawling estate on the city's edge.

The hand he places against the skin of my back causes electric tingles to course throughout my body.

I'm glad I'm wearing silicone pasties underneath the plunging neckline of my wedding dress.

"Like I'm walking on a cloud." I smile up at him.

His eyes scan my face for a beat, a pinch in his eyebrows as if he's gauging whether or not I'm putting on a show. Over the past three months, we've planned this extravagant wedding, reserved our itinerary for our month-long honeymoon in Europe—two weeks of which Eve will join us—and started receiving recipients at the newly renovated Brightside Community Shelter.

That's all on top of continuing to run my business while Kyle has firmly taken on the role of Chief Operating Officer at his family's company.

To say it's been slightly stressful would be an understatement.

Hence Kyle's concerned expression. I had another one of my migraines last week due to the stress. But it didn't last long.

"Are you sure?" His hand cups the back of my neck.

I lean into his body, not because I'm tired, even though we're at the end of a long day, but because he always has that pull over me.

Moving away from him, I hold my arms as I twirl around. "Do you like my dress?"

I've switched to my second gown for the reception. It's a backless, mermaid-style dress with a plunging neckline and trumpeted skirt. At first, I hesitated in choosing it because it's a lot more revealing than the princess style dress I wore for the wedding ceremony.

Kyle grins down at me with that mischievous glint in his eyes. "That goes without saying."

"Well, say it. Words of affirmation, remember?"

He chuckles before saying, "I love this dress on you, baby. You look fucking amazing, and I will love it even more when it's lying on the floor of our hotel room."

I gasp in mock horror. "Bite your freaking tongue. This dress will never see the bedroom floor." The price tag alone for this thing ensures I will handle it with care. Even with my greedy husband trying to get it off of me.

"If you say so." He chuffs as if I'm the crazy one. "It looks like I lost my dance partner for the night." He nods over to the far side of the spacious dance floor that's been created for our reception.

Eve's laughing as Kyle's younger brother, Andreas, spins her around.

"You know, you could take some tips from your younger brother. He's a lot more charming than you," I tease at the same time Kyle wraps me in his arms, and we begin swaying to the slow song that starts to play.

He quirks an eyebrow. "Do I have to mess up my brother's movie star good looks to get you to stop looking at him?"

"Please don't. What if Townsend Industries goes belly up, and you need him to keep acting to support your entire family?"

He huffs. "My stubborn wife owns her own company and refuses to come and work for the family business. We'll get by on her income."

Laughing, I lay my head against his shoulder. I let Kyle move our bodies to the rhythm of the music while I watch the dozens of family members, friends, and business associates around the room.

I wave at Sharonda, who's DJing the second half of our reception. She blows us a kiss.

Family.

That's the only word I can think of when I look around the room. My eyes land on my mother-in-law. Her smile is a mile wide. I suspect she's even happier than Kyle and me. Wherever my mother-in-law is, my father-in-law is never too far behind. He wraps her up from behind and looks on at his son and me.

He's a hard man to read, but I suspect he approves of our union. Kyle's siblings, cousins, uncles, and grandparents all join in on the dancing.

"Your parents aren't going to dance?" I ask, lifting my head.

Kyle snorts. "My mother wants to spare her toes for a little while longer. My father dances like shit. Thiers inherited that lack of talent from him."

I glance over to find Kyle's youngest brother, and twin to Andreas, holding up against the wall in his tuxedo. He's on leave from the military to attend our wedding. Even from this distance, I can make out the sadness in Thiers' eyes. While they're the same shade as Andreas', who has a natural sparkle, his twin's is different.

It could also be the scar that runs down the center of Thiers' face, starting just above his right eyebrow and ends beneath his left eye.

"An accident," Kyle told me when talking about how his brother got the scar. The heaviness in his voice when he said it lets me know there's a story there. One I won't ask because I know it'll come to light eventually.

I make eye contact with Kennedy. She gives me a thumbs-up as she's the one who helped me pick out my reception dress.

She recently took on a new job as an investigative reporter at a major publication in Williamsport. Kyle says it's part of his plan to have the family take the next step in building an even larger conglomerate. Kennedy tells him almost every time he brings that word up to go fuck himself.

I wave back at my sister-in-law when she blows a kiss our way.

"I don't know if I like how much you two get along," my husband says.

"Why?"

He frowns. "She'll try to convince you to take off with her on one of her ventures, and I can't go more than a night or two without you in my bed."

"You can come with us."

He snorts. "You can keep your ass at home."

I roll my eyes. "I'm not going anywhere. Well, we are going to Europe for four weeks, but that's for our honeymoon." Just thinking about it brings a smile to my face. We're doing two weeks in France and then another two weeks in Italy with Eve joining us for the second half of our trip.

She's on summer break so the timing is perfect.

"I wondered where the hell he'd gone off to."

I look over my shoulder to see Diego, Kyle's best man, entering the ballroom.

A smile tips my lips. Kyle's cousin dutifully holds out an elbow for his date to wrap her arm around. The woman at his side is beautiful. The pair exchange a look but quickly shutter their expressions as if they have something to hide.

"What's up with that?" I wonder out loud.

"I'm not the only one who thinks those two look like they're hiding something, huh?" Kyle asks.

"No." Whether they admit it or not, there's more than friendship between Diego Townsend and his best friend, Monique Richmond.

I hope they figure it out soon.

An easy silence falls between us as we look into one another's eyes. His gaze is penetrating and all I see is loving shining back at me.

The spell is broken by the shrill sounds of clanking glass. I glance around the room to find our family smiling at us as they tap their champagne flutes with the silverware.

Kyle cups my face and leans lower. "I love you," he says against my lips.

"And I love you, my husband."

He captures my lips in a kiss that curls my toes.

When he pulls back, he rests his forehead against mine. The both of us are slightly breathless.

"It'll always be like this between the two of us," he promises. Then he glances around the room, his face falls. "Do you think she'll be okay with it?"

I look past my shoulder to see Eve giggling as she dances with a group of her new cousins and Stasi.

"She will," I say.

"What if—" I press a kiss to his lips.

"She loves you," I tell him, though, to be honest, I'm a little nervous about what we plan to talk to Eve about during our trip.

But the mood is too good to dwell on that.

All I want right now is to revel in the love between me and Kyle and our family. In this moment.

* * *

ABOUT THE AUTHOR

Looking for updates on future releases? I can be found around the web at the following locations:
    Newsletter: Tiffany Patterson Writes Newsletter
    Patreon: https://www.patreon.com/tiffanypattersonwrites
    Website: TiffanyPattersonWrites.com
    FaceBook Page: Author Tiffany Patterson
    Email: TiffanyPattersonWrites@gmail.com

More books by Tiffany Patterson
    The Black Burles Series
    Black Pearl
    Black Dahlia
    Black Butterfly
    Forever Series
    7 Degrees of Alpha (Collection)
    Forever
    Safe Space Series
    Safe Space (Book 1)
    Safe Space (Book 2)
    Rescue Four Series
    Eric's Inferno
    Carter's Flame
    Emanuel's Heat
    Don's Blaze
    Non-Series Titles
    This is Where I Sleep

My Storm
Miles & Mistletoe (Holiday Novella)
Just Say the Word
Jacob's Song
No Coincidence
Personal Protection
The Townsend Brothers Series
Aaron's Patience
Meant to Be
For Keeps
Until My Last Breath
Aaron's Gift

Tiffany Patterson Website Exclusives
Locked Doors
Bella
Remember Me
Breaking the Rules
Broken Pieces
The Townsends of Texas Series
For You
All of Me
My Forever
The Nightwolf Series
Chosen
The Ahole Club Series (Collaboration)**
Luke

Made in United States
Cleveland, OH
05 September 2025